I'M YOUR GUY

I'M YOUR GUY

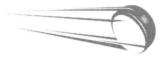

SARINA BOWEN

Tuxbury Publishing LLC

ONE

Tommaso

I'VE GOT A HALF HOUR, and an empty house that needs furniture, so I walk into the Upholstery Emporium with my platinum card and a sense of purpose.

I pull up short when I see what I'm up against. There must be an acre of furniture in front of me. Why does the world need three hundred different couches? I just need *one*, preferably large enough for a guy who's six-two. And I need it delivered before Christmas.

Not so much to ask, right?

Except I'm standing in an ocean of sofas. And chairs. I probably need a couple of those, too. But they're on the other side of this vast space. Does that make any sense?

And does anybody work here?

I glance around, but nobody fits the part. There's a couple holding hands. Shoppers, obviously. I spot another guy, but he's leaning against a wall next to a door marked *Office*, a jacket over his arm. Probably waiting for a salesperson, just like me.

Something makes me look twice at him, though. And when I do, I forget all about furniture. He has reddish-blond hair that looks soft to the touch. His toned body is sharply dressed in tight trousers and a deep-blue, button-down shirt.

There's really no other way to put it—he's smoking hot. Hollywood hot. With piercing blue eyes and a pouty mouth. Not that I should notice that.

A glance at my watch tells me that I've already wasted five minutes, and I'm no closer to having a furnished house.

My eyes do another sweep of the store, still looking for a salesperson. When I don't find one, my gaze makes an involuntary trip back to Mr. Hottie against the wall. I've spent my whole life trying not to notice attractive men, but sometimes a face comes along that stops me in my tracks.

Shut it down, DiCosta.

Mr. Hottie's spine suddenly straightens, and I don't want to be caught staring, so I look away. That's when I catch sight of another man striding purposefully across the room. A salesperson. *Bingo.*

I flag him down. "Excuse me, sir, do you work here?"

"Of course." His tone is about as friendly as the bark of a rabid coyote.

But I have money and an empty house, so I persevere. "I need to find some furniture, and I'm in a hurry."

"Do you have an appointment?"

Shit, *really?* I shake my head.

He gives me a condescending look that confirms what I'd already expected—he's a dickwad. "Do you at least know what you want?"

"Not a chance. But I have an empty three-bedroom townhouse." *And a big fat bank account, you arrogant little prick.*

As my mother would say, he's working my very last nerve. I've grown accustomed to getting good service in Denver. The city loves me. But this guy? He sighs like I'm ruining his day.

"What style is your townhome, sir?"

"Style. Um..." I tug at the collar of my shirt, because I don't know a damn thing about home design, and that's why I came here in the first place. "It has... Well, there's a fireplace in the living room."

"Stone? Brick? Contemporary? Early American?"

I close my eyes briefly and try to picture the fireplace. "Stones, I think."

He snorts. "Where is it, and when was it built?"

"It's in Boulder. Not new, but newish? The kitchen has white countertops." The kitchen was a selling point for me. My mother likes nice kitchens. When she visits next month, she can cook if she's feeling up to it.

"You should look around, then." He waves a hand toward the acre of furniture. "The floor is laid out by style. You've got your midcentury modern." He points at some sofas. "Your tuxedo. English roll arm. Lawson style—those are kind of sloppy, but some people are into that. Chesterfield style, which are stuffy, but again— some people are into that."

I'm so fucking lost already. They just look like couches to me.

"As a baseline, what do you think of this style?" He stops in front of a lime-green sofa.

It's a horrible color. One time we got a rookie player drunk on vodka and Gatorade, and he barfed that exact shade.

"That's not the one for me."

"Why? Is it the button tufting? Is it the camel back?"

"It's *bright* green."

The salesman actually rolls his eyes. "The color doesn't matter at this point. Every piece of furniture in this store is available in three hundred different fabrics."

"Three hundred?" That is not a selling point.

"How do you feel about the shelter shape?" He points at a brown one.

"It's okay."

"Or the Chesterfield?"

I shrug, because I can't remember which one that was.

"How do you feel about welting?"

Again, I have no idea what that means, but I'm saved from answering. "Look what the cat dragged in," he says with a growl. I follow his gaze to Mr. Hottie, who's still waiting by the door marked *Office*. "Excuse me a moment. I have to take the trash out."

As he stalks toward the office, Mr. Hottie begins to look nervous.

Not my problem, I remind myself. It's actually easier to browse without that man's help. I walk among the sofas for a moment, trying to picture them in my living room. They're all kind of bright, with lots of bold colors and showy fabrics, and I'm in too big of a hurry to special order something.

When I spot a gray one, I cross the room to check it out. There's a tag attached to the arm, but when I flip it over, there's only a baffling list of serial numbers that means nothing to me. The only words that make sense are *Made in North Carolina*.

"You've got *some* nerve!"

The anger in the rude salesman's voice makes me flinch. But it's not directed at me. It's coming from behind the office door, only a few feet away.

"This isn't a consignment shop," he snaps. "It's not my problem that your boyfriend split, or that you took a job with assholes. And if you don't set your delivery date by next week, I will not be responsible for my actions."

Yikes. I can't imagine what Mr. Hottie did to deserve all that venom.

But again—not my problem. My phone rings, and I yank it out of my pocket, because my family is having a rough time, and I need to be available for them.

Nope. It's my agent. Maybe she knows something about couches. "Hey, Bess? I'm in a furniture store. Do you happen to know what a Chesterfield is?"

"Not a clue," she says. "Sounds like a British soap-opera character."

"Huh. What about an English roll arm?"

"Sounds like a judo move."

I smile for the first time today. "How about a tight back? Or welting?"

"Oh—I know this one. A 'tight back' is a compliment for a really nice ass. And 'welting' is what happens to my husband's body after a really rough game."

I burst out laughing, because Bess always makes me feel better. Hiring her was the best decision I ever made. "So I guess you can't help me pick out a couch?"

"Lord, no," she says. "I don't go into stores unless Tank makes me. Even then, I expect a bribe."

"I knew I liked you." Giving up on the search, I sit down on the nearest sofa. "So what's on your mind?"

"Just had to let you know—the brand decided to go with someone else." She sighs. "I'm sorry."

"Don't be," I say immediately. "Nailing down sponsorships is the least of my problems right now."

"I know," she says gently. "But I won't give up. Someone is going to come along and offer us a deal."

"It really doesn't matter," I insist. "I don't need the money."

"Speak for yourself," she says, and I can hear the humor in her voice. "But it's more than money, DiCosta. If we get one brand to shine their love on you, then others will follow. We want the world to see you as more approachable. It will make everything easier."

Bess is smart, and she knows what she's doing. But I just don't have the bandwidth to worry about my reputation right now. "We'll get there," I say mildly.

"I know it," she agrees. "Now go buy a couch. I'm no help with that, but I could find you a decorator if you need one."

"Wait." This had not occurred to me. "Can I *hire* someone to shop for my couch? That's a thing?"

"DiCosta, trust me, you can hire out *anything*. Call me after practice if you need a decorator."

"Will do." We hang up, and I rise as the office door bursts open.

The asshole salesman comes striding out, with Mr. Hottie following him.

"Don't come back here until you've solved this," the salesman says.

"Got it," Mr. Hottie replies in a tight voice. He saunters past me. Even his gait is sexy. Under his breath, he says, "Worst store in Denver, anyway. It's not like I'm dying to shop here again."

Later I'll wonder what made me do it, but I follow him outside like a puppy. "Excuse me, sir?"

Hottie turns around. "Who, me?"

It takes me a moment to answer, because he's really spectacular up close. I didn't know eyes came in that deep, stormy shade of blue. And I can't decide what color his hair is exactly. More like ginger than chili powder...

His eyes narrow, and I suddenly remember that I was saying something. "Yeah, I had a question for you." I jam my hands in my pockets and try to focus. "If this is the worst store in Denver, what's a better one? I need to buy a lot of furniture on a tight timeline. And that guy just wants to spit a lot of jargon at me." I jerk my thumb toward the store. "Not helpful."

"Yeah. Big yikes." Mr. Hottie frowns. "That guy wouldn't help his own mother out of a ditch. You're not a designer, right? You're shopping for yourself?"

"Trying to."

He flashes me a quick smile. "Then go somewhere that actually likes its customers. Crate and Barrel. Macy's. Room and Board." He shrugs. "Or if you want to hire somebody to handle it for you, I'm your guy."

"Wait, you're a decorator?"

Eyebrows lift over those intense blue eyes. "Interior designer."

"Oh. What's the difference?"

"The pay scale. Theoretically." He sighs. "And level of training. Designers have..." His gaze abruptly swings toward the street. "Oh *fuck*." Then he dashes away from me, midsentence.

I see why. There's a traffic cop standing at the bumper of a battered Subaru, writing out a parking ticket. I hurry to follow, because I'm pretty sure this man can solve all my problems.

"Officer, it *just* expired," Mr. Hottie sputters.

"Too late," the cop says.

"I'll leave *right* now," Mr. Hottie tries.

"*Wait*," I argue, because this is unacceptable. "We were having an important conversation."

The officer doesn't even spare me a glance. "The meter is expired. And this ain't your first offense. Car's got a rap sheet. I gotta call a tow truck to impound."

"*No*," Mr. Hottie whispers. "No, no, *no*..."

"Hey, officer?" I try. "You a Cougars fan?"

His chin snaps upward. "Sure. Why?" His gaze zeroes in on my face. "*Oh, shiiit*," he says as he recognizes me.

"Yeah, I'm running kind of late. I asked my assistant to park here and wait for me, but I didn't give him enough change for the meter. The fault is mine." I pull an envelope out of my pocket. Inside are a pair of comp tickets to an upcoming game. I was going to hand them over to the PR department for charity, but they can have the next pair instead. "Take this, just as a friendly gesture. And then do whatever you need to make this right."

For a long second, I don't think he'll take the bait. But then he slowly reaches for the envelope, nudges it open, and exhales. "Row C. *Whoa.*"

"Enjoy 'em," I say. "Now what else do we have to do to get right with the City of Denver?"

He looks down at the beat-up car as if he's never seen it before. "Move the vehicle, gentlemen," he says briskly. "Be on your way." He turns and walks off down the street, shoving the envelope in his pocket as he goes.

That settled, I turn toward the designer again. "Do you have a business card?"

TWO

Carter

WHAT JUST HAPPENED? This thirst trap in an Italian suit just saved my ass. But how?

"Did you just *bribe a cop*?" I ask in a strangled voice.

"I incentivized him," the man says with a cocky tilt of his chin.

"Um..." *Isn't that illegal?*

I keep my mouth shut, because this man could break me in half. He's tall and broad, with so many muscles that even the finest imported wool can't hide them. He has dark hair, a Mediterranean skin tone, and the kind of perma-scruff that only some men can pull off.

The kind of scruff that would give me beard burn in fun and interesting places.

He points at my car with a broad hand, and I can't help but notice its roughness. He has hands like a construction worker's, and yet he's wearing shoes that probably cost more than my past-due rent.

"You've really got to move your car now," he barks. "And I have somewhere to be. But first give me a business card. I need furniture, and I need it soon."

I blink. This has been a disastrous day, and I can barely function right now. But I have business cards in the cup holder, and I snap to attention. "Right. One sec." I open my car door and grab a card. "Here. Call me if you're serious about furnishing your house."

"Serious as cancer," he growls. "Thanks." He strides away, all dark-blue suit and attitude.

I watch him go, and the view from the back is just as fine as the front. In my line of work, I've gotten used to dealing with the rich and the beautiful. His entitled attitude is pretty familiar, with one big exception—he just did me a huge favor.

My bank account contains exactly twenty-seven dollars. I literally cannot afford to pay for a parking ticket, let alone the whopping fine you get when your car is impounded. The wolves are howling at my door.

Yet Mr. Italian Suit just chased one of them off with his dark brown eyes and a cash bribe. No, wait. It wasn't cash. Tickets to a game, maybe? I don't follow sportsball, so I didn't catch which one.

It doesn't matter, anyway. I just hope the guy calls me. The holidays are approaching, which means the design business goes into a lull. I'm going to be eating a lot of ramen until after New Year's. If I can afford to eat at all.

I climb into my car and start the engine. It's a short drive back to my apartment building near the University of Denver. When I turn onto my street, I slow to a crawl and check for the landlord's presence.

Yikes—he's right out front, organizing the recycling bins. I quickly pull into an on-street parking space and cut the engine.

I'm late on the rent. Really late, and it's the second time this has happened. Mr. Jones is on my case, and he has a quick trigger finger for those Ten-Day Demand forms that landlords use to threaten eviction. If I don't catch a break soon, I know he'll come for me.

Sitting here hiding from my landlord in my car, it's hard to feel optimistic. A year ago, I had a boyfriend who loved me, and we were co-owners of a growing design business. I thought all my dreams were coming true—that our business would expand and my student loans would continue to shrink.

But I let my guard down, and I made bad choices. I trusted the wrong people. And when our design business hit the skids, our relationship collapsed like a paper lantern in a rainstorm. Six weeks ago, I came home to find Macklin packing his clothes into a suitcase.

"Where are you *going*?" I'd demanded. But in my gut, I already knew he was bailing out.

"Phoenix," he'd said, giving me an apologetic look. "I got a buddy there who works in real estate. They need a home stager."

I was so startled—and so enraged—I hadn't even known what to say. "That's it? You're just leaving me with this mess we're in? Where is the love?"

At least he'd had the decency to flinch. "You don't love me. Admit it."

"I do too!" I'd yelped, because I didn't want to cede any points to him at all.

"You don't," he'd insisted. "You're pissed off at me all the time."

"Because we're in debt! And you're the one who put us there."

Another flinch. "Yeah, but are you really surprised? We don't have a storefront. We don't have enough contacts in the industry, and nobody will ever give us capital."

"That's not what you used to say!" I'd argued. "You were sure this would work."

"Was I?" He drops his head for a moment before he zips up another duffel bag. "We were so cocky. We made fun of those guys wearing orange aprons at the Home Warehouse, selling cheap kitchen cabinets. Like we were so much better than that." He rolls his eyes. "We're clearly not cut out for running a business. We shouldn't have even tried."

That last blow had landed hard. Ten minutes later, as the door clicked shut behind him for the last time, I realized that the loss of my dreams hurt a lot worse than the loss of my boyfriend.

Clearly not cut out for running a business. Shouldn't have even tried.

The only saving grace is that he was already out the door before I dissolved into tears of rage.

Once again, I'd trusted the wrong man, and once again he'd

betrayed me. I'd been left with credit card debts from a horrible client. And a lease, of course.

Without Macklin around to help out, I'd quickly fallen behind on the rent. A friend found me a night job as a model for a life drawing class at the art school. Four nights in a row, I'd posed in my underwear while a room full of retirees wielded charcoal pencils.

But that had been a one-time gig, and now my rent is late again.

Still hiding in the car, I pull out my phone and bide my time by checking my email. I'm desperate for a new client. Or—even better —a payment from the one who's the root of all my problems.

The evil Mrs. Clotterfeld.

Six months ago, she hired us to redesign a three-million-dollar mansion in southeast Denver. Macklin and I had celebrated with a sushi dinner. The Clotterfelds are notable Denver socialites. When she chose us as her designers, we were sure we'd finally hit the big time.

Sure, she was arrogant and shaky with the details. So many clients are. But she signed our contract and paid the first part of our fee.

My bank account had never been so happy with me. At first, things had gone smoothly enough, notwithstanding her atrocious taste. She was a fan of gold piping and paisley. I'd been willing to smile my way through all the tassels, even if the place ended up looking like a cross between Downton Abbey and a high-priced bordello.

Macklin took on most of the work with her, while I'd serviced our other clients. But I hadn't realized she'd begun to slide on paying for her purchases. And—like a fool—Macklin let her get away with it. He hadn't told me right away, either. He'd known I would panic.

And, yup, I'd panicked, even if I'd understood the bind Macklin was in. She was our golden goose, and he'd been afraid to offend her. A guy couldn't accuse one of the richest women in Denver of being a deadbeat and still ask her for referrals.

Except she *was* a deadbeat, and Macklin, making a really

horrible decision, had put fifteen thousand dollars of custom upholstery on my personal credit card.

The order had come in weeks ago, and it's still sitting on the loading dock at Upholstery Emporium, where I'd gone today to beg for more time to pay.

More time won't even help, though. Mrs. Clotterfeld has clearly dumped me, just like Macklin did. And since my idiot partner paid the deposit instead of getting the money upfront, she feels free to walk away.

Mr. Jones is *still* out in front of the building, so I start a new email on my phone. My sternest one yet.

Dear Mrs. Clotterfeld,

The furniture you ordered from the upholsterer is past due, and the store has insisted that we arrange for immediate payment and delivery. If you do not make immediate payment, they will send it to an outlet shop, while I send your debt to collections.

Please forward the payment by end of business today, or there will be no way left for me to help you.

I reread the sentence and then replace "today" with "tomorrow." That's the problem with ultimatums. Once the deadline is past, you weaken yourself by extending it.

God, if only there was someone to tell me how to handle this. A lawyer could help me, but I can't afford one. Not only am I broke, but I'm demoralized.

I thought Macklin and I were in love. We weren't.

I thought I was a savvy businessperson. I wasn't.

I thought I was on the rise—that after all my hard work, I'd finally launched my little business. Nope and nope.

And now the guy at Upholstery Emporium is threatening to tell every design shop in Denver that I'm bad news.

Nobody is coming to save me. And the worst part? I got played by a man who doesn't pick up his own socks, and by an old woman who thinks that purple paisley is fashionable.

When the landlord finally retreats, I shove my phone into my messenger bag and climb out of the car. I walk quickly up the block and make it to my door without seeing his narrow, little ferret face.

But when I spot the notice taped to my door, I quail inside. I yank it down and read it.

To my horror, it isn't the same Ten-Day Demand as I got last time. This one is different. It says *Notice to Quit*.

Mr. Flynn:

This serves as your official Notice to Quit the premises. As a repeat violator, the property owner is within his rights to begin a nonnegotiable eviction process. Payment of back rent is due by November 30th, but will not halt the eviction.

You are ordered to quit the unit by month end, or the sheriff will remove you and your property from the premises.

Oh. Shit.

I read the letter three times, but it gets worse on every pass. So I close my eyes and lean my head against the wooden door to my apartment.

My former apartment.

Housing is hard to find. And nearly *impossible* to find if you can't scrape together a security deposit, plus first month's and last month's rent.

This is it. My breaking point. I'm going to end up combing Craigslist for whatever roommate-wanted situation sounds the least creepy.

If I can even afford that.

And November thirtieth? That's two weeks away.

Just as I'm processing this thought, the old bastard sneaks up behind me. "Carter Flynn. You read the notice? Take note of the date."

I whirl around, furious. "November thirtieth? Who could move that fast? I need until New Year's at least."

His wrinkled mouth twists. "No can do. I do not run a charity, Mr. Flynn. I have two buildings, sixteen units. If even two of them are stiffing me, I come up short of cash."

"I'm not *stiffing* you," I growl. "I'm being stiffed by a client. And it means that—"

He holds up a hand, cutting me off. "Are you even hearing me? I know *exactly* what that means. You can't meet your obligations, plain and simple. Whatever bad decisions you made are not my fault. Get your fancy-ass furniture out of my apartment, or law enforcement will do it for you on the morning of November thirtieth. I'll call ahead to make sure they're right on time."

I can only gulp, because I feel so stricken.

He's absolutely right. As Taylor Swift would say, *I'm the problem. It's me.*

"Got it?" he snarls. "This isn't a warning. This isn't something you can talk your way around. Someone else will live here on December first—someone who can pay the damn rent."

Sheepish now, I nod. Then I go inside and close the door while I still can.

THREE

Tommaso

I ARRIVE at the stadium six minutes later than usual, and the disruption of my routine makes me unhappy.

Call me disciplined. Call me superstitious. Call me whatever you want, just don't call me late for game night.

I bleep the locks, straighten my suit jacket, and head inside.

"Tommaso! Tommy boy!" My teammate David Stoneman shouts as I hang up my coat in the outer locker room. "How's the new pad? Did you christen it yet?" He wiggles his eyebrows in a ridiculous way.

Stoney, the team clown, is not even expecting an answer to this question. But someone else gives him one anyway. "He can't. First you gotta sage the place. *Then* you can break it in."

"Sage it?" Stoney asks. "Wut?"

"It's a purification ritual," explains Ted Kapski, our team captain. "You roll a big blunt—but not with pot. With sage. Then you trail the smoke through every room. Keeps the ghosts away."

"You're shitting me." Stoney's eyes narrow. "Is this like that time you told me that kiwi fruit were actually testicles?"

Kapski's eyes brighten. "You don't believe me? Put a hundred bucks on it." He reaches for his wallet.

"Noooo." Stoney holds up both hands. "Keep it in your pants,

Kap. I'm not losing any more money to you this week. I just assumed that if rolling a blunt for your house was a thing, I'd'a heard about it already."

Everyone laughs, and I move past these clowns and into the dressing room. I need to get into some workout clothes and start activating my body. We're playing Carolina, and we're favored to win. But every game matters, and I take nothing for granted.

I'm almost ready when I'm buttonholed by Tate, our team publicist. He's the kind of guy with a spray tan and a million-dollar smile. Always looks like he's just come back from having his teeth whitened. "Got a second?" he asks.

"Make it quick."

"Uh-huh." He grins, and I'm practically blinded. "Wouldn't have to grab you on game night if you answered my emails."

I play dumb. "Email?"

"Yeah. I sent you a message about our trip to Trenton. It's not until after the holidays, but they're asking for a group photo of all the DiCostas in hockey. For a puff piece about family legacies."

My stomach literally churns. I'd seen *Trenton* in the subject line of his email. And then I'd deleted it. "I hate photo shoots. And puff pieces."

"Are you kidding me?" Tate frowns, his expression darkening. "Given the circumstances, I thought you'd jump at the chance to be shown in a positive light."

"Then you'd be wrong. And it's a bad idea, anyway. Why would I remind the whole world that my..." I almost can't get the next word out. "...family and I had a disagreement in the past?"

"It wasn't a 'disagreement.'" He uses air quotes. "It was a brutal, bloody fight on ice. Which isn't so unusual in hockey, except you and your cousin were *on the same team* at the time."

"Like I don't remember," I say through clenched teeth. The fight was the absolute low point in my life. And if Mr. Smiley PR Man had grown up with my asshole cousin? He would have bloodied him, too.

"The fact is, you threw the first punch."

Not if the rest of my life counts. "Again, I was there. But do you really want to put me in this mindset before a game? I might blow my stack again."

He isn't so easily manipulated. "Look, Tommaso—you have no social media. No endorsements. Nothing to rehab your image except that one video we made of you petting puppies at the shelter."

"So I'll pet some more dogs. Or kittens. Or saber-toothed tigers. Or even a motherfucking shark. It's all a better use of my time than posing with my asshole cousin and his dickhead father."

Tate shakes a finger at me like I'm a misbehaving child. "Pretty sure saber-tooth tigers are dead and gone. Just like your reputation."

"Sir, my stat sheet is my reputation. Don't you wonder why two other DiCostas suddenly want a photo shoot with me? Spoiler alert —it ain't out of love."

"Not born yesterday," he says curtly. "Your star has been rising since your move to Colorado, and now they want some of your juju to shine down on them. But this is still an opportunity, don't you think?"

"Nope. This is just karma."

He laughs, but I'm not joking. My toxic family members have been a powerful force in my life. And until I moved away from them two years ago, I never really understood how deep the poison ran.

After our ugly fight, Trenton traded me to Colorado. It was supposed to be a punishment for making the team look bad. Practically the whole world wanted to tell me how badly I'd fucked up.

Except the Colorado Cougars. Coach Powers had a different take, telling me, "You're a talented player, DiCosta. You can do great things if you keep your head on straight. I'm happy we got you on the cheap, but you need to do me one special favor—no fighting on my ice."

"Uh, no fighting *anyone?*" I'd had to clarify. This is hockey after all.

"Nope. Leave it to your teammates, unless it's absolutely necessary. And under no circumstances will you throw the first punch," he'd said. "I didn't trade for you to gain a new enforcer. I want you focused as a skills player. Can you do that?"

"Yessir." It had been an easy promise to make.

And I've kept it. It's been two years since I took a fight. And I've been playing the best hockey of my life.

Meanwhile, my uncle got demoted. When I left Trenton, he'd been an assistant coach for the big-league team. But the franchise recently sent him down to the minors.

And my cousin? His stats are sliding, too.

"Look," I tell Tate. "I know these guys better than you. There's no way they have any interest in helping me repair my so-called reputation. You can't trust them. The fact that I'm outperforming Marco means he'd rather sabotage me than help."

Tate shrugs. "You're the better player, and I believe you when you say you're the better man. But when I google your name, the very first thing that comes up is an image of you punching your cousin in the face. Did you hear about the youth-sized jerseys?"

"What jerseys?"

"*Exactly*," he says with a smug little smile. "Your jersey sells okay in adult sizes. But nobody buys one for their kid, because the fans think you're a violent man who'd just as soon slug his cousin and his uncle."

"Only when they deserve it."

He rolls his eyes. "You've said that before, but you haven't said *why*. Care to explain?"

"*Fuck* no."

His expression goes dark. "Fine. But if you don't do the puff piece, people will keep drawing their own conclusions about you. The internet is really good at making up shit that's worse than the truth."

"I don't care what the internet thinks," I lie.

He looks heavenward. "But your *team* does. It's literally my job to worry about your reputation. Who cares if Vin and Marco are just being greedy? This photo is still a smart move for you. It's called taking the high road."

I groan.

"Think about it—you're going to be in Trenton anyway. A photo takes ten minutes. Twenty, tops. Show the world a smiling hockey family. Change your image. Make your mom happy. That's her family, too, right?"

Hell. Now he's really hitting below the belt. My mom is the only reason I haven't turned him down cold. "Yeah." I clear my throat. "I'll think about it."

"You do that. Now go warm up." He slaps me on the back, and that blinding smile comes back. "Have a great game, DiCosta."

Yeah, thanks for nothing. Now I'm stressed out, and I'm ten minutes behind on my pre-game regimen.

Leaving him, I jog down the corridor and through the bowels of the stadium. There's a row of exercise bikes set up outside the training room, and I'm relieved to see that my favorite one—second from the end—is still available.

Only I've made a crucial error. I left my earbuds in my car.

Fuck. Now I'm open to conversation, which is a thing I don't enjoy before a game.

Sure enough, my teammate Hudson Newgate takes the bike next to mine, sets up his ride, and then asks me a damn question. "Settling into the new place yet? Like the neighborhood so far?"

"The neighborhood is great." This is the only polite answer, because we're neighbors now. The townhouse I just bought is directly across the street from Hudson's.

It *is* a nice place, and Red Rock Circle is a desirable neighborhood. I got lucky. The seller was impatient to move, and I was in a hurry to close. Good deal for both of us.

"And the house?" he asks.

"It's, uh, empty," I say, resigned to talking to him. "No furniture."

"Damn, really? Moving truck is late?"

"Nah, I don't own anything. When I moved out here, I rented a furnished unit in a new complex. You know—the model unit that they show people. And there I stayed."

Newgate nods with understanding. "So you need to do some shopping. Furniture takes a while to show up, too."

"Does it?" *Fuck.*

"As the guy who used to get traded every year, this is actually my area of expertise. What you need to do is choose the items they stock, not the custom finishes. You gotta call and ask, though. On furniture websites, they'll show you three colors of a couch, or whatever, but only one of them has a short lead time."

Hell. "So this is a time suck, is what you're saying?"

"Sad but true. And then there's delivery—that's another nightmare. They give you a window of, like, six hours. And they expect you to sit at home and wait for it."

"No way," I grumble. "No can do."

"Yeah, with our schedule, you'll have to hire someone for that. Unless the stars line up just right. Maybe Gavin could help let delivery guys in."

When he mentions his boyfriend, I turn my head to study him. As I sometimes do.

Hudson used to be just another teammate. He's a solid guy and a hell of a player, like a lot of our crew.

But a year ago, he did something that absolutely blew my mind. On a road trip, he gathered us together and came out to the whole team, including management. He just stood there in a crowded room and referred to himself as "the only bisexual man I can name in pro hockey."

I don't think I slept for three days after that.

Ever since, I find myself watching him. Not in a sexual way—I'm not attracted to him. It's more like I'm *fascinated.* Here's a living, breathing defenseman who had fourteen goals last season, and he goes home at night to a *boyfriend.*

It's like Stoney with the burning sage—I never knew that was a thing. Newgate blew up my brain, and then blew it up a second time when he brought Gavin and their little girl to the coach's preseason barbecue three months ago.

"This is my boyfriend, Gavin," he'd said, laying a hand casually on the other man's arm. As if it was the easiest thing in the world.

I'd stared. Sometimes I still do it. Like right now. Hudson is still talking to me, and I haven't been listening.

"Gavin works most days until two o'clock. But usually, he's home after that. Or he can be."

"That's a really nice offer," I manage. "Let me see what I can find to buy, and then I'll ask the store how delivery works."

"Cool," he says. "Moving is the worst. I'd bring you a casserole, or whatever it is neighbors do. But cooking isn't really my thing."

"Think you can let that slide."

"Maybe Gavin and I should bring over some beers one night when we're not on the road."

"Sweet," I say. "Better wait until I get a sofa, though."

"Deal."

Then we both increase the resistance on our bikes and pedal like hellions.

When gametime comes, it's a slog. Whatever advantage we were supposed to carry into the matchup looks shaky by the end of the first period. Carolina is up 1-0, and Coach Powers is pissed.

"This is *your* ice. A mediocre team is running you all over it. Turn the dial up and bring out the heat. They got one fucking goal, and now you need to show up and answer for it. Stoney, where's the chaos? They aren't afraid enough. And DiCosta—"

Fuck.

"—you look distracted. Don't make Hessler do all the work."

"Yessir," I grunt, and he moves on to yell at someone else.

He isn't wrong. I am distracted. And I'm unsettled. This month has been one of the worst of my life. So much family stress. So much guilt. And now I'm letting it fuck up my game.

My mother is probably sitting home in New Jersey, watching me on ESPN, too.

That's a sobering thought. I rub my temples and try to regain my focus, which has been missing all night. Every great athlete knows how to shut off the noise in his life.

Tonight, though, the noise is sinking me.

We go out there and fight like hell for the second period. Things go a little better, and Stoney ties it up with some help from Newgate.

I'm having another shaky period. Coach doesn't even bother ripping me a new one over it, and somehow, his silence feels worse. Like I'm not even worthy of coaching.

We skate onto the ice for the third period, and my head is throbbing. "We've got some momentum now," Hessler says.

"No thanks to me," I grunt.

He thumps me on the shoulder. "It's not over yet, man."

But the tie holds deep into the third period. I just have a dark feeling about this game. Like it's already beaten me.

You're playing like a pussy. Stupid bastard.

Even though he's two thousand miles away, Uncle Vin's voice still rattles around in my head at moments like this. It started when I was a kid, and he'd come to our bantam games. He'd stand behind the bench, red-faced, spittle flying.

I'd wanted to please that man more than I'd wanted to breathe. He'd been a professional hockey player, so clearly, he'd known what it took to succeed.

He'd repaid my attention by addressing me as "you little bastard," which he meant literally. "Can't call you DiCosta," he'd jeered, "because you don't really qualify."

It was true, I guess. If unnecessarily harsh. DiCosta is my mother's name. My parents never got married, and I haven't seen my father since I was a toddler.

None of that should've mattered, though. And Uncle Vin's bullshit had the unintended effect of galvanizing me. I'd been determined to win hockey games if only to spite him.

It had worked, too. I'd been a high-draft pick for Trenton right out of high school and started on a DI college team my freshman year.

Eventually, Uncle Vin retired from the pros and finagled a position on the coaching staff for Trenton, his old team. It had meant more of his verbal abuse at the training camps, but I was used to it.

Or so I thought. *"You still got the same bad habits as when you were a kid. And I'm gonna break you of every one of them. I'm gonna break you, period."*

He liked to humiliate me in front of the team. Every mistake I made, he made sure everyone knew.

I haven't seen Uncle Vin in two years, but every time I have a bad game, I still hear him screaming at me.

The volume is lower now, though. I can almost tune it out.

We set up for another faceoff. The sweat streams down my face, but I find that quiet place inside myself where there is only hockey. The ref drops the puck, and the fans roar. But that's just background noise. Kapski wins the faceoff. He flips it to Hessler, who flips it to me.

Head down, I skate the puck forward. Stoney is open, but my gut says not for long. So I fake the pass and drive onward.

It only takes them a couple seconds to figure out what I've done, but the delay is enough. I slide past Carolina's winger and evade a poke check from their D-man. Running out of new ideas, I fake the pass to Stoney, and then I shoot it to Kapski.

Who scores.

The lamp lights, and I feel myself sag with relief. *There you go, Uncle Vin, you asshole. Cheers.*

Four minutes later, we've clinched the game. I drag myself back to the dressing room, feeling lucky to have survived with my dignity intact.

But now I'm wiped. If it were possible to fall asleep in the shower amid twenty other hockey players and a blaring stereo speaker, I probably would.

Coach says a few rousing words while we're getting dressed, but

I'm too tired to process it. I can't wait to drive back to my empty townhouse and crash on my only furniture—a king-sized mattress.

As I shove my phone in the pocket of my suit jacket, I find a business card and pull it out.

Carter & Macklin Interior Designs.

It takes me a second to remember where it came from. But then Mr. Hottie's face swims into view in my mind.

Carter. Or maybe he's Macklin? Either way, he knows about furniture. *I'm your guy*, he'd said. Maybe I could hire him to shop for me and to wait for delivery, too.

"Night, fellas!" I call out.

"Nice recovery, DiCosta!" my coach calls out.

Gotta hand it to Powers—he's nothing like my uncle. Powers tells you when you're fucking up, but he tells you like you matter.

I walk through the bowels of the stadium, my gym bag over my shoulder. When I reach the underground parking lot, I stop for a moment beside my car.

And I tap Mr. Hottie's number into my phone.

FOUR

Carter

IT'S A CHILLY DAY. On the drive out to Boulder, I turn on the radio. The first thing I hear is Madonna belting out "Santa Baby." It's a cute song, but I'm not in the mood. She wants a diamond ring and a luxury car and a yacht.

Don't we all, honey.

When I change the channel, the next station is playing a Christmas tune, too, so I shut off the radio entirely.

I can't even think about the holidays without getting anxious. For one thing, business will be slow. Rich people tend not to start any big home renovations during the holidays. They're busy spending money on other things, like luxury gifts and beach vacations.

If I get any work at all in December, it will be only holiday decor —trees, garlands, and throw pillows. Those jobs are paltry. And often tacky. Home design is my life, but even I don't want a chic Christmas tree—they have no soul. I prefer a cacophony of family keepsakes. Like the trees we used to decorate at home with the wreath I made out of tinfoil when I was seven, and the felted bird my father gave my mother the year she rescued a baby owl who'd survived a raccoon attack on its nest.

Home is Briarton, Montana. I have conflicted feelings about the place. But not so conflicted that I don't feel an ache when I think about how expensive a flight home would be.

I don't have the money for a ticket, so this will be the first time ever I won't be going home for Christmas. I haven't even broken the news to my mother yet.

I'm dreading that, too.

My car is almost out of gas, and I can't afford to refill the tank. I shouldn't be driving thirty miles to meet with Mr. Italian Suit. His real name is Tom DiCosta, and he sounded pretty desperate on the phone a few days ago.

"There's a lot to do," he'd said. "And I'm in a hurry. I need to play host during the holidays, and it has to be impressive."

My first impulse had been to celebrate. A rich dude needs to make himself look even richer? *Let's go! My body is ready.*

Lately, though, my natural optimism has taken some hits. So my next reaction had been caution. I'm deeply in debt, and even a big job like this might not be enough to save me.

Besides, a hundred things could still go wrong. The client might get sticker shock when we discuss the cost. He might expect me to work for almost nothing. He might just be an asshole.

"Use the left-hand lane to turn left," says Google. "You have arrived at Red Rock Circle."

So I have. When I make the turn, I find myself in a development of recently built semi-detached townhomes. Sometimes a housing development is where good design goes to die. I've seen some horror shows with boxy little rooms and low ceilings.

This place is more interesting than I'd expected. For one thing, the houses aren't all identical. They're attractive, with peaked rooflines, and a mix of wood finishes and trendy industrial metal cladding.

I've definitely seen worse.

After locating Mr. DiCosta's unit, I swing my car into the visitor's parking spot nearby. Normally, I would try to hide my heap of a car from the client's view. Nothing says failure like driving a fifteen-year-old Subaru with rusted wheel rims. But this client has seen my car already, so the damage is done.

I hurry up the short walkway to his front door and knock. He makes me wait, and while I stand there on his doorstep, a doom loop cycles through my brain.

I worry that he changed his mind and didn't even have the courtesy to cancel our meeting.

I worry that I won't get the job.

I worry that I *will* get the job, but it will turn out to be a disaster. He'll be a raging narcissist like Mrs. Clotterfeld, and he'll find some new and terrible way to take advantage of me.

This isn't like me. I used to feel a surge of excitement every time I met a new client. But that's gone now, and it's depressing. I liked my life better when I trusted people.

It's cold out, too, so I rub my hands together impatiently. Where is he? I step back for a glimpse through the picture window. Is he even home?

That's when I spot my potential client striding toward the door while hastily pulling a T-shirt over his head. Wowzers, the man is *ripped*. Muscles bulging everywhere. It's the kind of body you only see on TV.

Or—fine—in porn. His abs line up in a neat egg-carton pattern, and his V-cut is so sharp a man could cut his tongue on that thing.

Those abs of glory quickly disappear behind the T-shirt, which is for the best. If I drool all over this man, I'll never get this job.

Clients want us to kiss their asses, but not literally.

The door finally swings open, and he greets me with a scowl.

My confidence withers by another degree, and I brace myself to hear him say that he won't be needing me after all. "Morning," I say with false cheer. "You did say eleven o'clock."

"Right. Sorry," he says gruffly. "Running a little behind this morning. Got back to town late last night."

"It's no problem," I say through a pasted-on smile. Because I really do need this job. Even if he's the kind of jerk who values his own time above everyone else's. Even if he's a nightmare to work with.

I promised myself I wouldn't design for any more assholes, but I don't have a choice. Without this job, I might be sleeping on the streets next month.

Another long beat goes by, and he's still scowling. Finally, he opens the door a little wider. "Come on in. You can see what we're dealing with. I wasn't joking when I said I needed everything."

Indeed he does. The door opens into a small vestibule, which leads into a spacious, open floor plan. There's a generous seating area and a fireplace. To the rear, at the left, a wide, arched doorway draws the eye into a gourmet kitchen with a dining alcove. To the right, a staircase to the second floor is tucked into the corner.

I walk slowly into the center of the living space and lift my eyes to the high ceilings with their rough-hewn beams. The airiness of the space is appealing. It's large, yet still scaled to the human form. The front window faces northeast for good afternoon light.

And that's when I feel it—the frisson of excitement I always experience when faced with a new job. Maybe this guy is a dick. Maybe my business is still doomed.

But I could make this place *amazing*.

He clears his throat. "What do you think?"

"Good vibes. So much potential. And it's roomy without being cavernous. What's on the second floor?"

"Two bedrooms, two bathrooms. But I'll only use one. I'm putting my guestroom back there—in the room behind the kitchen." He points toward the rear.

I'm already nodding. "That's a nice separation of public and private space. I like it."

"There's a partial basement, too. But we can ignore that for now. There's enough to worry about already, and not a lot of time to do it."

He's not wrong. The only furniture in this room is a beanbag chair plopped right in front of a TV. And the TV sits directly on the wood flooring.

Wow. This guy needs *everything*.

"You weren't kidding when you said it's a big job." And repainting the living room will have to come first. The walls are an unfortunate shade of ochre.

"Yeah," he grunts, retreating toward the kitchen. "Will this even work? Can you get this place livable by the holidays?"

Livable? I could make this place into the snuggest, hippest, most inviting home in Colorado, as long as the budget is generous.

I follow him into the kitchen, and I don't let myself sound too excited. "What's the exact deadline? The holidays can mean different things to different people."

He pulls a loaf of sourdough bread out of a bag on the counter. "Let's say noon on December twenty-third. That's when she arrives."

"Okay," I say, pulling out my clipboard out of my messenger bag, and scribbling down that date. And now it's time for my pitch. I take a deep breath. "Mr. DiCosta, this space has a lot of potential. It's great. But right now, it's an empty shell. It's a house, not a home."

He raises one dark eyebrow in a skeptical expression.

I press on. "My job is to gather a full picture of your home life, and then interpret your preferences, values, and tastes into my design. By the time I'm done, you won't want to leave."

Usually, the client smiles right about now, but DiCosta is rubbing his forehead, like I've just given him a migraine. I watch the muscles in his forearm work and wonder if he does body-building as a hobby.

"Dude, look," he says.

My heart drops. Nobody ever got a job with a sentence that starts *Dude, look...*

"I don't mean to burst your bubble. That's a pretty speech, but we need to be on the same page. If I hire you, it's because I don't have time to even *think* about any of this. I hate shopping, but I also hate sitting on a damn beanbag chair to watch the game."

Fearful that I'm losing this gig, I start nodding like a puppet. "Must be murder on your back. We can fix that."

He shrugs. "I don't need a therapist or a Zen master. I just need a solid guy who can magic this place together in a damn hurry. And not bug me too often with the details."

Oh hell. This man has no idea what he's asking. No decent designer would agree to those terms. "Listen, I understand the time constraints. And we'll get to that in a second. But unless mind-reading is a real thing, this job isn't possible without some buy-in from you. Everyone has preferences, even if they don't realize it. Even if they'd rather have a colonoscopy than go to the mall."

He snorts. "Yeah, busted."

"I've heard every word you've said. I'd really like to work with you, and I'm willing to do all the leg work. But I'm not clairvoyant, Mr. DiCosta. You'll have to make yourself available to approve the things I pick out for you. That's the only way this works."

"Oh," he says, his expression falling.

I hope I didn't just talk myself out of this job. "Please believe me when I say that you don't want to turn a stranger loose with a big budget and no direction." I point at my chest. "Even this stranger, who has impeccable taste. So, if I take this job, we'd still have to communicate. Frequently."

His jaw works as he thinks this over. "But you'd handle all the shopkeepers, right? I'm not going back to that sofa store."

"I solemnly swear on this slab of quartz composite—" I place my hand on the countertop. "—that you will not have to speak to a single salesperson. I'll do all the actual shopping, and bring you ideas for approval."

"And no jargon?"

"No jargon," I agree. "If anyone tries to talk to you about welting or button tufting, I'll fight 'em off with a wingback chair."

In spite of his beard, the corners of his mouth twitch. "Fair enough. So how would this work?"

I rub my hands together. "You mentioned there's a visitor you're trying to impress? Let's start with that as a goal. What kind of statement are we making?"

He pulls a bread knife out of a well-furnished knife block. His kitchen is stocked, I notice. "The visitor is my mom."

"Your *mom*," I repeat. That isn't at all what I was expecting.

"Yeah," he grunts. "We don't see much of each other, and I bought this place so we could have a nice Christmas together. So that guestroom—" He points toward the rear of the house again. "—should be furnished really nicely for her. The bathroom, too."

"Right," I say, recovering from my surprise.

I don't point out that for less money he could have booked a luxury vacation for the two of them. Somewhere that already has furniture. "Let me take a look," I say instead.

After passing through the kitchen area, I inspect the back room, which is probably meant to be a den. It's a nice size, but utterly empty. It lacks a closet, but otherwise it would make a fine guestroom. Bonus—the walls are white and not that piss yellow from the living room.

The three-quarter bathroom is also cheery, with white subway tile and a pedestal sink.

"Just curious," I say, returning to the kitchen. "No furniture at all?"

He shakes his head as he puts two slices of bread in the toaster. "Long story. My wife got the house in our divorce. Since then, I've been living in a model unit at an apartment complex."

"Ah, I see."

"Yeah. I was the last new tenant in the building, so I negotiated to rent the furniture, too." He shrugs. "Never had to buy a thing. Not the couch, not even the art on the walls."

I suppress a shiver just imagining the cheap, soulless furniture the real estate developer had put in that unit. "Okay, then it's time for an upgrade. Assuming I could furnish this place in time for you to host your mom, I'm going to need a lot of information from you. I'd need to know your taste, your budget..."

He looks up from his work. "Avocado toast?"

"Sorry?"

He points at the avocado he's slicing. "I'm making avocado toast. Want a piece?"

"No thank you," I say automatically. "You go ahead, though." Eating on the job isn't very professional. I couldn't do that.

"My budget is flexible," he says. "I don't tend to buy expensive things, because I'm not home enough to enjoy them. But I'm in a big hurry, so I realize I can't be a tight-ass about prices right now."

That's well put, but still not helpful. "Okay, but my idea of expensive and yours might vary wildly. For example, couches start at around two thousand dollars and can go as high as fifteen thousand. A dining table might cost about the same. You'll also need rugs, dining chairs, end tables, lamps..."

"Yeah, yeah. I know," he says. "Doing it all at once is gonna cost a mint. Maybe you could make a list, with estimates. Just so I won't have too much sticker shock." His toast pops, and the scent of bread fills the room. I watch, mesmerized, as he begins to drizzle the bread with olive oil.

Specifically, I'm watching his forearms flex as he works. They're musclebound and covered with fine black hair the same color as the happy trail I happen to have glimpsed on his abs...

Stop it.

To distract myself, I pull my laptop out of my messenger bag, open it on his countertop, and fire up a spreadsheet.

It doesn't help matters that Tom DiCosta is totally my type. He's scruffy enough to appeal to my lifetime cowboy fetish, but I also like that little wrinkle of concentration on his forehead as he works. I like men who can think, as well as throw me around in the bedroom.

But I won't even *have* a bedroom unless I land this job.

I start typing a list of furniture items. "Your TV needs a table?"

"Yep." He mashes avocado slices onto the toast.

My stomach gurgles audibly, because I haven't eaten today, and I'm out of groceries, because I can't afford to buy more. "A sofa and two chairs... or, alternatively, a sectional and one chair. An area rug, at least ten feet long, but twelve would be better..."

"I've got a measuring tape in the garage," he says.

"We'll get to that in a minute. TV console. End tables. Lamps. We could easily fit a dining table for four in that alcove." I point to the space. "Would you need it to be expandable to seat six or eight on holidays?"

He shakes his head. "Not a chance."

"Four it is." I make a note.

"Don't forget the bedrooms," he says. "I have a mattress on the floor right now. King-sized. I should have a frame. And a dresser. Downstairs, my mom will need a bed—double or queen-sized. Not too high off the ground. And a dresser and a table or whatever."

"Okay. Two bed frames, one mattress. Bedside tables. A dresser in each room?"

"Yeah, that makes sense. And...sheets and stuff."

Sheets and stuff? What are we, fourteen? "So...bed linens. Are you a fan of quilts, or duvets and covers?"

"Whatever you'd normally choose. I don't think about decorating." He picks up a salt grinder and seasons the masterpiece he's made. Then he moves to the refrigerator and pulls out a bottle of fresh-squeezed orange juice—the kind you get from a gourmet store.

It's the color of sunshine, and I gaze at it longingly. It's been a while since I had enough cash to go out for brunch with friends.

Those were the days.

Tom opens a cabinet and produces two juice glasses. He pours, and then slides one of them over to me, without asking.

Okay. Well. I guess it's just good manners to share a drink with the man. "Thank you." I lift the glass. "Cheers." When I take a sip, it tastes like heaven. "What's your taste in furniture?"

"Just normal stuff." He shrugs.

"Normal stuff," I echo slowly. "That could mean so many things. Where did you grow up?"

"Tom's River, New Jersey."

Interesting. He doesn't speak with a Jersey accent, although he does give off a kind of urban vibe. "Okay, listen. I grew up in

Montana, and my aunt Betsy thinks it's *normal* to put a wagon-wheel chandelier in every room, have salt and pepper shakers in the shape of cowboy boots, and hang lots of dead animals on the walls. You see what I'm getting at?"

He scowls again, and it's much more attractive than it ought to be. "Okay, no dead animals. Just keep it simple, and we'll be fine." He puts the avocado toast onto two plates, and then slides one of them over to me. Parking his hip against the counter, he takes a bite.

I eye the plate he's passed me with some confusion. Did he not hear me when I said no? That's another red flag. Clients who don't listen are frustrating. And I can already tell that getting stylistic opinions out of him will be like pulling teeth.

But, fuck it. My mouth is watering already. I pick up a piece of toast and bite into its crusty edge. Then I groan, because I didn't know bread could taste so good. It's yeasty and salty, with just the right olive oil tang. The avocado is perfectly ripe and creamy.

Even if this whole job evaporates before cocktail hour, it might be worth it just for a taste of this glorious toast.

FIVE

Tommaso

I HAVE A PROBLEM.

No, I have several of them. But the newest one is the outrageously attractive man standing in my kitchen. The one who just let out a groan of pleasure.

It's not that I'd forgotten that he was attractive. It's just that I'm pretty good at ignoring hot men in my life. I work with men all the time, so I have to keep a certain remove. It's a skill I've developed.

Or so I thought. But I wasn't prepared for Carter to walk in here and throw me off my game with his flashing blue eyes and big opinions.

Having him here in my personal space makes it worse somehow. The more we talk, the livelier he gets. His cheekbones are splashed with color, and he waves his hands around when he talks.

Today he's wearing an oxford-cloth shirt in an eggplant shade that would look silly on me. But the color makes his blue eyes pop.

Focus, DiCosta. "You're from Montana, huh? You don't look like a cowboy."

"No kidding," he says through a bite of toast. "That's why I left. Not a lot of appetite for fabulous, gay designers in the little town where I grew up."

That shuts me up—the way he just flung it out there. With a

casual shrug, too. Like calling himself *gay* and *fabulous* is no big thing.

"Design is meant to be personal," he says.

I nod, but then I don't hear much of the next few sentences, because my brain is like a busy squirrel, distracted by all the little details. The chiseled planes of his Hollywood face. And the color of his hair. Like gingered straw.

This part of me—the greedy part—mostly stays in its cage. I keep the door locked tightly at all times. Once in a while, though, I meet somebody who rattles the bars.

And maybe my defenses are down. It's been a rough couple of months. It kills me to admit it, but I'm coming a little unglued.

Now here's this dangerously appealing man in my house, with his excitable gestures and bright eyes. My brain is like, *Look! A shiny new thing! What would it feel like to run our fingers through his hair?*

Yeah, no. And now Carter wants to hear all about my "tastes and preferences"? That is a dangerous conversation. And every time he looks over at me, my brain makes up a brand-new "taste" or "preference" in regards to him.

It's distracting. I don't like it.

Meanwhile, he seems to want this job, but he's full of contradictions. He gets excited when he talks about furniture, and he seems to care a lot about design. Yet he drives a car-shaped pile of rust.

He also turned me down when I offered him breakfast. But then he eyed the food like a junkyard dog. Now he's eating it like it's a race, and he's trying for a podium finish.

He's confusing. Yet I really need his help, and the clock is ticking. I'll probably have to take a chance on this guy, even if it's risky. Even if he makes my heart pound.

That's not a plus.

"So how would this work?" I ask, pulling my head back into the game. "You'd be doing a lot of shopping for me. How are you compensated?"

In other words, let's cut the bullshit and discuss the things that really matter.

He drains his juice. "There are two ways to pay a designer's fee. Sometimes we charge a percentage of the bill. But in your case, I think a flat weekly rate makes more sense. If we work together, this is a big job that would dominate my working hours during the holidays."

Huh. "What kind of flat rate?"

He takes a moment, pacing around the kitchen, hands on his trim hips. "The tight timeframe makes this job weird. I'll spend a lot of time calling around, bargaining for fast delivery."

"Can you, uh, take delivery, too? I'm not home very much."

He stops pacing and stares at me. "That's not usually how it's done."

"Yeah, I bet." I heave a sigh. "But I travel a lot for work. A *lot.* And I need more than your usual clients. I need Christmas decorations, too. Hell, I even need Christmas presents."

He blinks.

"So tell me this—how much would five or six weeks of your time cost? If you could spare every minute. So that would be, like, a tenth of your annual salary." I brace myself to hear a crazy number.

My visitor rubs his handsome chin. "I'll have to drop everything else. But the holidays are usually slow, to be fair. Still, I'd have to charge you four thousand a week, for five weeks. And that's *before* you get to the cost of the furniture."

Oh, phew. That's not too bad, seeing as I don't want to do the work myself. "So that's twenty grand total for the design fee." I rarely spend twenty thousand dollars on anything—but it shows. My nicest possessions are the Lexus SUV in the carport and the high-end exercise equipment in the basement.

But I make two million a year, so this is probably the right moment to part with some cash. I just wish I knew if Carter was a good guy, and reliable, or not. "I could pay you week to week, right?"

"Of course," he says, pacing again. "I'm sure it sounds like a lot of money. But I could make this place look great. On one condition

—we paint the living room. I'm good at my job, but even I can't work around that yellow."

I step into the living area and look at the paint, possibly for the first time. And I see what he means. "It's like urine, am I right?"

"I wasn't going to say it, but yeah." And then something new happens. Carter *smiles*. It's like the sun coming out. I get stuck staring at him again, because he looks like a whole new person. There's a dimple in one of his cheeks, and I have the strangest urge to measure it with my thumb.

"Painting takes time," he says. "But I know a guy we could hire. That would be my first call."

Oof. "That sounds complicated."

"A little. But do you really want to buy furniture to match a paint color you hate?"

"They're just walls," I say. "I can live with them."

Those blue eyes widen. I'm good at reading people, and I can sense a wave of disbelief with a side order of frustration. He tries not to let it show, though. "But this is your *home*. You're going to *live* here, right?"

The way I travel? It kind of doesn't matter. But I don't mention that. He doesn't seem to know what I do for a living, and I don't feel like explaining it. "What color should walls be? Plain white?"

Again, a look of disbelief. "That's one way to go. But the thing about walls is that you don't have to paint them all the same color. To save time, we could paint most everything a warm shade of white, except for the accent wall..." He indicates the fireplace wall. "That's where I'd put a color that picks up the chimney stones. A slate shade, maybe."

I don't know what color "slate" is. But I just nod, because he seems to know what he's talking about.

His eyes narrow again. "Slate is a greenish gray. It's not the only choice, though. I'll bring you some samples."

Maybe I'm not the only one who's good at reading people. "Sounds better than this pee shade."

He grins. "Right. Now let's talk about your personal style. What kind of furniture do you like? And don't say 'normal.' One guy's normal might be a La-Z-Boy recliner and a foam beer cozy. And one guy's normal stuff might be marble statues and lava lamps."

"Uh, I see your point." Recliners are for guys who shout at the hockey game on TV but can't do a single push-up. "Just, you know, comfortable. Not fancy."

"Sure, but there's different—"

"—types of comfortable," I finish gruffly. "I get it. But I just don't know what you *call* the stuff that I like. And reeling off a bunch of descriptions is probably not gonna be a lot of help."

His expression softens. "Of course. I'll grab some pictures. One sec." He opens his laptop again.

My phone rings. It's right on the counter in front of me, and my new house is so empty that the sound echoes. My blood pressure jumps. And then it jumps again when I see my sister's name on the screen. *Shit.*

"Sorry, I have to take this." I grab the phone.

"Go ahead," he says cheerfully. "I'll use the time wisely."

I swipe to answer. "Gia? Everything okay?"

"Hi, Tommaso!" she shouts over a lot of ambient noise. "This is not an emergency call."

My heart rate eases, but only a little. "I'm glad to hear that."

"I know, baby bro." I can barely hear her, because it sounds like she's standing in the middle of a rave. But it's just her children's voices. Three rowdy boys make a lot of noise. "One sec. HEY! TRY TO GO FIVE MINUTES WITHOUT TOUCHING YOUR BROTHER. JUST FIVE!"

"Bad day?"

"Nah, they had too much sugar. Now I'm paying the price. Wait, let me step into the laundry room." The background noise suddenly dampens. "That's better. I just called to ask how you're liking the new place?"

"It's a work in progress. How's everyone on your end?" I wander away from the counter and into my new guestroom for a little privacy.

"When you say *everyone*, you really mean Mom, right? I can hear your stress from here."

"I mean both of you," I argue. "You're doing a lot, and I'm frustrated that I can't help out more."

"I know you are. But no one blames you for getting traded. And we all knew it would be good for you to get away from New Jersey for a while."

Even after two years, this comment gives me heartburn. The implosion of my marriage was the most shameful moment in my life. Thinking about it still makes me want to howl.

"Even so," my sister continues, "you're still helping us from afar. Mom is pumped up about visiting you at Christmas. She really wants to see you. And I'm pretty excited to finally go on my cruise."

"Yeah, awesome." My sister's husband bought the family a cruise, but they had to postpone when my mother got sick. "Have a strawberry daiquiri for me."

"Oh, I plan to. Separate bedroom for the kiddies, too! Sexy times for me and Brian."

"Gia! I don't want to hear that."

She cackles. "You are the biggest prude."

I change the subject. "So how is Mom feeling?"

"She's hanging in there. You realize that's the best possible status now, right?"

"Yeah," I sigh.

"Chemo is hard, Tommy. I'm not going to pick up the phone one day and announce that everything is magically wonderful and that she's joined a kickline in Atlantic City."

"I know," I grumble. But part of me secretly believes that these last few months were all a horrible mistake, and that the doctor will tell us that Mom is actually fine. "Is there anything in particular I should have in the house for her? I found a guy who'll help me furnish the place in a hurry."

"I wondered how you were going to pull that off. But honestly, Mom would sleep on an air mattress to spend time with you."

"*That's* not happening. I'll take better care of her than that."

"I know you will. But comfort is not what Mom cares about. If you want to make that woman happy, take better care of *yourself*."

"Me? I'm fine."

"Fine is not the same as great," my sister says quietly. "Mom worries about you."

"That's just her default setting."

"No, it's bigger than that. She thinks you're lonely. And this year has been a big wakeup call. Her new motto is 'never wait to be happy.' You want Mom to relax? Show her that you're settling into your life out there."

"I'm buying a truckload of furniture."

"That's just window dressing, though. Even the nicest sofa can't love you back."

"So? What else do you want from me?"

My sister is quiet for a second. And then she asks, "Are you dating anyone?"

We never talk about this, and I can't tell if the vague wording is intentional. Maybe I'm just paranoid. "Nope. Too busy."

"Well, that's a shame," she says. "It's been two years, Tommy. The world is full of nice people. Go find one."

Again with the lack of pronouns. This conversation is making me uncomfortable. "I'll get right on that."

"You do that. Mom would be over the moon if you were dating someone nice. It would give her a real lift."

"Gia, you're laying it on a little thick, here."

"Fine." She sighs. "She also has a new thing for soup dumplings. And don't forget how much she likes those chocolate-covered cherries at Christmas."

"Right. I won't forget."

"Okay, it sounds like I gotta go break up another fight. Love you, Tommy! Bye!"

My sister hangs up on me, and I finally exhale.

SIX

Carter

WHILE MR. DICOSTA takes his call, I pull up a bunch of photographs on a handful of browser tabs. I'm trying to predict what "normal" might look like to my new client.

Even though I hate that word. *Normal.* Such a loaded idea in a complicated world.

I choose four different living rooms. The first is very cheugy with a family-style overstuffed sectional. My second pick is a midcentury version, just in case DiCosta has powerfully good taste to match his powerful glutes. The final two images show rooms that fall somewhere in the middle.

When he returns, I'm ready. "Join me over here?" I beckon toward my side of the counter.

He does. Sort of. But he's still three feet away from the screen.

"Can you even see from way over there? Okay, first takes—which one of these gets your engine going? If any?"

He moves closer, grunting an acknowledgement of the question. Big grunter, my potential client. After another scowl, he points at a photo before returning to his side of the counter.

"Ah! Nice," I say. "That one has a kind of mountain-chalet vibe. Cozy and a little rustic."

"Uh-huh. Nice stuff, but not... stiff? Doesn't look like a hotel room."

"Great! I agree." Now we're cooking with gas. "What else do you like about it?"

He shrugs those broad shoulders. "There's a lotta wood. Wood is nice."

Oh honey. I bite back about a dozen dirty jokes. "The wood makes everything warmer, doesn't it? And the fabrics are also a little rustic. Wool. Mohair. That plaid throw..."

"Sure. Do something like that," he says. As if it's all settled.

"Okay, good start. Now let's think about how that would play in your space." I beckon him into the living room and stand in the corner by the front windows. "You picked out the TV wall already by placing the set there." I point.

"It doesn't have to stay there," he mutters. "That was just for quick."

"No, you chose that spot for a reason," I try to explain. "Because it felt natural to you to face the front windows. The other focal point in this room is the fireplace wall. So, you'll want seating that faces both. That means an L-shape sectional, or a sofa and chairs."

"All right. Sure."

"Since you like the mountain look, we can do a coffee table and end tables made from oak or even a rustic pine. And I think we'd pick a color from the fireplace's stones to paint an accent wall. Right there." I point again.

"What about a rug?" he says. "It echoes in here."

"For sure. Let's talk about colors."

"Nothing bright," he says. "That's another thing I liked from the picture. It's subtle."

"Uh-huh. But even if we do the furniture in earth tones, you'll still need an accent color." I squint at the fireplace. "How do you feel about purple?"

He's already shaking his head. "No way. Too much like Brooklyn."

Brooklyn? I spin this association through my brain and come up blank. Does he mean *gay?* I mean—I'm wearing a purple shirt right now. Nothing else makes sense.

Hell. I promised myself I wouldn't work for assholes. I *promised.* Yet here I am, ready to brush that comment under the proverbial rug, because I need twenty grand the way that Harry Styles needs spandex jumpsuits.

Besides, I want to see what this room looks like when it's done right. "How do we feel about red?"

"Nah." He shakes his head. "Reminds me of Trenton."

Again, I'm stumped. He'd better not mean that in a racist way. "Fine. Tell me what colors you *do* like."

He frowns. Like he's never considered this question in his entire life. "Blue is okay. If I had to pick one."

"Blue," I say, nodding in an exaggerated way. "I'll keep that in mind."

"Cool." He claps his hands together. "I'm sold. So how do we get this done?"

I blink at him. Did he just give me the job? "Uh, first I'll have to draw up a quick contract. I can't do any work until we've agreed to the terms."

He nods. "Sure. I get it. How long will that take?"

"I can give you a contract within twenty-four hours. And I have references you can call, too. You haven't worked with a designer before, but there's a lot of trust involved. After all, I'll be in your private space."

"Yeah, I know." He flinches. "But I'm also in a hurry."

"Right. Well." I spin around. "Can I take some photos and measurements, then? Normally I'd do a whole floor plan and draw some elevations."

He gives me a look. "That's jargon for...?"

Oops. "Um, vertical drawings of the space when it's finished. But those are time consuming."

"I don't need drawings, I need furniture."

"Got it. You want this done on the unholy-rush plan. Shop first, ask questions later."

"Yeah, that's the truth." He actually grins, and it catches me off guard.

The man's smile is dangerous. I've personally done many stupid things for men whose smiles aren't even half as potent.

But then the smile drops. "You'll also need cash. After I sign your contract, I'll cut you a check for the first week's work, and I'll ask my credit-card company for a card in your name. To make your shopping easier."

Something inside my chest loosens when he says that. Because that *exact* arrangement would have saved me from the trouble I'm in with Macklin and Mrs. Clotterfeld.

If only I hadn't been so stupid to trust them both.

"Sounds good," I say with a sigh. "We'll shape up this place in no time."

"Cool." He paces closer to me, and I hold out my hand, ready to shake. This is a big moment for me. This client could save my whole business.

But at the last second, he pivots. "The tree goes right here."

"Sorry?" I shove my hand in my pocket to salvage my dignity.

"The Christmas tree." He plants himself in front of the picture window. "Mom will see it when we drive up. She'll be thrilled."

"Of course," I agree softly. That's the whole point of this job, anyway—creating homes that make people happy. "She'll love it."

SEVEN

Tommaso

AFTER CARTER LEAVES, I pace around the house like a caged tiger. The meeting went well, but I feel unsettled.

He was right when he said that inviting someone into your home feels like a big deal. I'm a private person. I'm not used to sharing my space—or my thoughts—with anyone.

Carter seems to know what he's doing. I only wish he were more chill. Like, I don't see why he needs me to approve everything. I spend half my life in hotel rooms. I'm used to having no control over my surroundings. I'm a low-maintenance human.

Or I was, before he made me notice the hideous paint color in my living room.

Damn it.

And it wouldn't even matter if the paint color were the only thing I'd noticed while he was here. But I also noticed the way his arms flexed when he leaned against the breakfast bar, and the way his face flushed when he got excited about something.

What I need is a very boring decorator. I should have posted an ad. *Wanted: one self-sufficient designer with immediate availability to go into dreadful shops and talk to salespeople about welting. Whatever that is.*

Will ask me questions only when absolutely necessary.

Ideal candidate does not have big blue eyes, a flashy purple shirt, or a hot smile.

I let out a groan and do another lap of the lower floor. My footsteps echo in the empty rooms.

Pausing in front of the kitchen counter, I grab my phone and dial the first number on Carter's reference sheet.

"Good morning, this is Kathy of Kathy's Kitchens. Can I help you?"

"Uh, hi. I just interviewed a designer named Carter Flynn. He listed your name as a ref—"

There's a squeal and then Kathy launches into a verbal avalanche of praise for Carter. I don't understand half of what she's saying. But apparently Carter's "colorways" are inspirational, and his "visual organization" is top notch. Whatever that means.

Bottom line, this woman loves Carter. Although her closing statement is a little odd. "That boy deserves a break. He's capable of anything. If you hire him, I hope you're one of the good ones."

"Uh, thanks," is all I can manage. "You have a pleasant day."

I hang up and take another lap. As I'm passing the picture window, I see my teammate Hudson outside on a ladder in front of his window. His boyfriend—Gavin—stands beside the ladder, holding a string of lights.

My feet stop on their own accord. I watch as Hudson sticks a couple of hooks onto the house and then positions the lights across them. Gavin makes some kind of comment, and then Hudson reaches down and casually strokes his hair.

Then he hops down, moves the ladder a few feet, and starts over. I'm frozen in front of my window, still as a statue, watching them. As if I'm witnessing something far more unusual than a couple of guys doing a little work outdoors.

Because to me, it is.

EIGHT

Carter

ON MY WAY home from DiCosta's place, I say a little prayer.

"Dear Lord in heaven, did you send me Tom DiCosta? Or are you sending me back to Montana? Because I think it's one or the other.

"If you send me back home to Briarton, I will get a job at Home Warehouse. I will wear that tacky orange apron, and I will sell cheap paint and beige carpet tiles with a smile. I will accept my fall from grace as honorably as I can.

"But if you send me a twenty-thousand-dollar lifeline, I swear I'll learn my lesson. I won't trust another man for the rest of my life. And I won't have masturbatory fantasies about my new client. That would be rude. I guess maybe you showed me those abs of glory to lead me into temptation. And those big, rough hands..."

I sigh. "I can be a good boy. And financially savvy. I just need one more chance."

The Lord says nothing. But maybe he's thinking it over.

When I get home, I sit right down and work up a contract for Tom DiCosta. His email address is HotShotDiCosta at gmail, which makes me roll my eyes. Only a man child would call himself a hotshot. He's probably a finance guy. Or a surgeon. Someone with a god complex. I should probably know more about him before I decide to work with him.

I type *Tom DiCosta* into the Google search bar. But then my fingers hesitate over the Return key. The truth is that I can't afford to ask too many questions. If I talk myself out of this job, I might as well pack my bags and drive back to Montana.

If he works for big pharma, and his company is busy mowing down the rainforest, do I really need to know?

No, I do not. I close the tab, hit Send on my email and hope for the best.

With that done, I double down on adulting. First, I send Macklin a one-line email, asking him for his half of the rent money. *You really left me in the lurch*, I explain. As if he doesn't know.

He'll probably ignore me, but I have to try.

Then I call my friend from art school and brace myself to ask for another favor.

"Yo! Carterliscious!" Rigo shrieks into the phone. "We missed you at brunch this week. And last week. And..." I can practically hear his wheels turning. "And I haven't seen you at the gym! Where the hell have you been? Didn't anyone tell you that it's important to party with your friends after a breakup?"

If my friends didn't have pricey taste in brunch, I probably would be partying with them. "It's been, um, a little rocky on this end of town. In fact—" I swallow hard. "I called to ask if you know anyone who's looking for a roommate. I need to find a new place to live. Uh, quickly."

"Oh, *honey*. The rent is too much?"

"It's way too much without Macklin here. And I'm in kind of a hurry. I've only got until the end of the month."

There's a beat of silence while Rigo does the math. "Holy shitballs! You got evicted?"

"Yup." Redheads blush easily, so I'm probably the color of one of Andy Warhol's soup-can paintings right now. Luckily, Rigo can't see me. "Like I said, it's been a rough patch."

"Oh Carter. You can crash here for a little while if you need to."

"Really?" I didn't want to ask. But if he's offering...

"You totally can, at least before the holidays. We just found out that Buck is coming back from deployment at Christmas."

"Oh wow! You must be so excited."

"Honey, you have no idea. It's been four months, and I'm out of my mind. We are going to have *all* the sex when he gets home. On every surface of this apartment."

I laugh. "Yes, you are. And that is why I will make sure to find a roommate before his plane touches down in Colorado."

"*Evicted*, though," Rigo says sadly. "What are you going to do with your furniture?"

"I don't know," I say, glancing at the midcentury furniture that Macklin and I had picked out together. It's nice stuff. But I don't need all these reminders of my ex, and I can't afford a storage unit. "Craigslist, maybe."

He groans. "After all that work you put into it?"

"It's fine," I say quickly. "Designing interiors is my jam. I can just start over. I've done it before."

Rigo makes a frustrated sound. "Do you need me to see if the fine arts department at school is looking for models again? The term will be ending any day now, but I could check."

"Great idea," I say quietly. "Thank you." It's not like I have a lot of dignity to defend. Stripping down to my underwear in order to buy some groceries? Sure. Why not. "Thanks, Rigo. You're a good friend."

"Not good enough," he grumbles. "I should have noticed you weren't coming around."

"It's okay," I say quickly. "I'm fine. I just have a lot on my plate. But this morning I had a meeting with a potential client. If I get the job, I might need to hire some painters in a hurry."

"Yeah?" His voice perks up. "Don't lose my number. I want to buy Buck something outrageous for Christmas, so I could use the cash."

Now I'm sorry I brought it up, because DiCosta is probably not going to pull the trigger. He's probably interviewing another designer right now. One who drives a nicer car and who isn't quite so desperate.

And one who isn't quite so gay. I got a strange vibe off him. Like he was uncomfortable and didn't quite know how to talk to me. If that's his issue, then I guess I'm better off without him, right?

Right.

My bank account, however, is not. Nor is my empty stomach.

I hang up with Rigo, and then drop my head into my hands. I've got to stay positive. A guy who's about to sell his furniture on Craigslist can't afford the luxury of a doom spiral.

Ping. Ping. My laptop chimes twice in quick succession.

Warily, I raise my head. I can't afford any more bad news today.

But when I check, I discover an email with a signed, scanned copy of the contract I sent to Tommaso DiCosta. The only message is: *Okay, Montana. Let's do this.*

The other message is from PayPal, and the subject line says, *Hot Shot DiCosta just sent you $4,000.*

NINE

Tommaso

WE'RE SITTING in the video room watching tape for our upcoming game against Philadelphia. I'm having trouble concentrating. It's partly because I already know Philly's best tricks.

But that's not the whole problem.

This morning, on my way to practice, I'd let Carter Flynn into my home. Right this moment he's in my living room, painting the walls a shade called *Damask*.

Otherwise known as white.

There are, apparently, a million shades of white paint. Carter chose this one because "it has a very clean undertone. It's warm without being too yellow, which you need in a north-facing room. And it doesn't take on green or pink hues."

That's a lot of overthinking if you ask me. But I'm well aware that people can overthink anything. Like me, for example, sitting here in the video room replaying my first look at Carter this morning when I opened the door. He'd stood there with a ladder and a box filled with paint cans. Wearing spattered old camo-print pants and a threadbare T-shirt in spite of the cold temperatures.

He'd smiled at me like I was his favorite person in the world. "Morning! Hope you're ready to have your home transformed!"

I'm always a little sluggish in the morning. That must be why I couldn't say anything intelligible. Instead, I'd stood there for a long beat, staring at the spray of faded freckles across the bridge of his nose. They made me want to put my mouth right there...

God, I'm a mess. Hours later, I can't stop thinking about the tune he'd whistled as he'd laid drop-cloths on my living room floor.

Or the shape of his ass in those pants.

"Don't worry," he'd said. "We're using odorless primer and paint, and I'll have a fan going. You won't have any trouble with the air quality."

"Thanks," I'd muttered before peeling my eyes off his backside as he bent over to straighten the cloth. "I'm from New Jersey, remember? We don't worry too much about air quality."

"Naturally."

God, I'd been *flirting*. So that's when I'd made myself walk toward the door. "Thanks for this."

"No problem, Jersey."

The nickname had made me smirk.

"I'm expecting a helper at any minute," he'd said. "We should make a lot of headway by the time you're back from work. But it's still a two-day job."

"No problem."

I'd gotten into my car and driven away. But my mind didn't make the trip with me. So when the lights finally come on in the video room, I can't even remember which clips we've just watched.

"Don't get up just yet, boys," Coach says. "Your teammate needs a moment of your time before you head home."

Hudson Newgate stands up and faces the room.

"Wait," Stoney asks. "Is this about Girl Scout cookies? My nutritionist is asking me to cut back on sugar. She says I need to develop some willpower. So if Jordyn is selling thin mints again, imma have to step out of the room."

Newgate snorts. "You're safe until February, Stoney. But her Brooklyn troop is still singing your praises from last year."

"Hang on." Ted Kapski, our team captain, raises his hand. "Stoney—you're cutting out sugar. But didn't I *just* see you drink a

Frappuccino?" He points at the big cup on the table in front of my teammate.

"That's *coffee*," my teammate sputters. "Don't mess with a man's caffeine supply."

Kapski rolls his eyes. "Right. What was I even thinking? Go ahead, Newgate."

Newgate crosses his arms and smiles at us. "I just want to say up front that you guys have been incredible these last few months, since Gavin and Jordyn moved to Colorado to be with me. I'd been really worried about coming out, but you've made us feel welcome."

"Damn straight!" Stoney calls out.

"Nice choice of words, dingus," someone hoots.

"Dingus is a slur," Stoney says testily. "I don't feel safe right now."

Someone throws a napkin at him.

Newgate ignores them. "This is just a head's up. Today I let management know that I intend to come out publicly during the holidays."

If my brain had a soundtrack, there would be a loud record scratch right about now. Newgate is going to do *what?*

"The publicity department has been ready with their statement for months. But I liked the idea of letting some time go by before I made any kind of public acknowledgment. And I don't want to hold a press conference, because that implies that my personal life is newsworthy, when it shouldn't be."

Our coach claps from the first row of seats. "Hear, hear."

"Someday, a queer dude in sports won't be the kind of thing people hold press conferences about." Hudson shrugs. "So I've chosen a talented hockey journalist, and I'll give her an exclusive interview. She'll write her story, and that will be that. Any questions?"

Volkov—our big Russian goalie—raises his hand, and then asks a question in heavily accented English. "How bad do I fuck up first guy who is dick about this?"

"That's my question, too," someone else calls out.

Hudson is already shaking his head. "Don't overthink this, guys. Anyone who trolls me isn't worth our attention. Besides—this isn't going to be a big deal. I bet nobody cares."

My stomach drops, because he's wrong. People care. A lot.

I know because I'm related to some of them.

TEN

Carter

RIGO IS up on the ladder cutting in the crease between the wall and the ceiling, while I'm squatting on the floor to paint baseboards. If I'm lucky, this will be a two-day job. That's all the time that Rigo could give me. His painting business is fully booked, and he reserves a third of his time for serious painting in the studio.

Worst-case scenario, I'll finish it up myself on the third day.

Rigo brought his Bluetooth speaker with him, and he's blasting ABBA tunes while we paint. I'm a little sick of "Dancing Queen," but he says up-tempo music makes him paint faster.

Unfortunately, I don't hear the key in the lock, and so I don't notice that my client has arrived home until I feel cold air on my skin. I whirl around awkwardly and let some paint drip onto the drop cloth, like a dope.

Shit. I hastily set the brush down on the pan and stand up. Rigo cuts the music, thank God. "Hello!" I sort of squeak. "Didn't know you'd be home so soon!"

He'd said I could paint while he was "at work." I'd assumed that meant all day, until at least five o'clock. It's only two, but here's my snack of a client, with a gym bag over one shoulder, two large pizza boxes in his hands, and his usual scowl on his face.

I hang my head, because a more professional designer would

have asked and not assumed. "We can be out of your hair in half an hour."

"It's okay," he says gruffly. His eyes dart from me to Rigo, who's still on the ladder.

Rigo's giving Tom a weird, wide-eyed look and hasn't said hello at all.

That's odd. He's my chattiest friend.

"I got a double order of pizza, so I could share," DiCosta rumbles. "Let me just put this on the counter and get out some plates." He walks out of the room.

Rigo's eyes follow him, and then he hastily climbs down the ladder. "Holy shit," he hisses. "You never said you were working for Tommaso freaking DiCosta!"

"Um... What?"

Rigo's eyes are like saucers. "He's a D-man for the Colorado Cougars. Can you get tickets?"

Tickets? My eyes track Tom in the kitchen. Come to think of it, he's awfully tall. "That's, uh, a basketball team?" I whisper.

I hear a snort from the kitchen, so I know I've been overheard. My ears begin to heat. This is mortifying.

"*Hockey*, you dope," Rigo whispers back. "God, Buck is going to lose his mind over this. Don't you google your clients?"

"Um..."

Tom steps back into the room. He's removed his jacket, revealing, yup, a tight-fitting blue shirt with *COLORADO COUGARS* emblazoned on the front. Their logo designer had obviously just been phoning it in. There's a pair of crossed hockey sticks below a snarling cougar's face. It's not subtle.

Neither are the muscles popping out all over the place under that shirt.

"Pizza's still hot," he says. "I've had a long day already, and I'm diving in. Got one with meat and one without, because I didn't know what you like."

"I love pizza!" Rigo says. Then he practically gallops after my client into the kitchen.

57

Reluctantly, I follow. I'd rather we let the hot grump eat his food in peace, but Rigo doesn't know the definition of restraint, so I join them just to keep a leash on my friend.

That's what I'm telling myself, anyway. The pizza smells amazing.

"It's a shame Carter hasn't found you a dining table yet," Rigo says, helping himself to a slice of the vegetarian pie. "Or a set of stools for this counter. That would come in handy right about now."

"Working as fast as I can," I say stiffly. And then I select a piece of veggie pizza, too, because Tom seems to favor the meaty one. I bet he could eat an entire pizza all by himself. After all, he's a professional athlete.

I'd had no idea. When I'd met him at the furniture store, he'd been wearing a very sharp suit. But the abs of glory make sense now.

"Honestly, Carter," Rigo says through a bite of pizza. "I would have thought you'd learned to google your clients. Especially after that disaster with—"

"*Rigo.* Shut it," I say, exasperated.

Tom doesn't pay us any mind, though. He's already demolished his first slice of pizza, and he's reaching for his second.

"Listen," Rigo says to him. "I gotta ask a favor. My husband gets back from deployment in a few weeks. It would make his whole year if I could get your signature on a jersey. I'll save up for one, buy it in the shop, and maybe pass it to Carter?"

"Sure," my client grunts. "I'll sign whatever you need. Newgate lives across the street. You want him to sign, too?"

"Newgate?" Rigo says this word with startled awe. "No way! That man is a *snack*. Which house?" He turns toward the living room, as if on his way to gawk out the front windows.

I grab him by the back of his shorts and haul him back. "Stop drooling on the hockey players. We're here to *work*."

Rigo sighs. "Yeah, sorry. But this is very exciting to me. This will make a *great* Christmas gift for Buck. I know how much he'd love a signed jersey, because we bid on some of the Pride jerseys last year. But the prices went sky high."

"Yeah, right?" Tom says. "I've always wondered who buys those."

"Wait, why?" Rigo demands. "You think there aren't any queer hockey fans?"

"I didn't say that." Maybe it's a trick of the light, but my client's ears seem to be turning pink. "But those jerseys raised a hundred grand. So that's, what, four grand for a shirt I wore for thirty minutes? That's a lot of coin."

"It's for charity." Rigo shrugs. "Good excuse to blow the budget. And there's plenty of queer hockey fans right here in Colorado. What do you think was playing on the TVs over at Sportsballs during the playoffs?"

"Sports..." Tommaso coughs. "...balls?"

"Best name for a gay bar ever, right?" Rigo asks cheerfully. "Plenty of hockey fans also fly the rainbow flag."

This whole line of conversation is surely *not* what DiCosta bargained for when he hired me. "Hey, Rigo? We really need to get back to painting, so we can get out of Mr. DiCosta's way."

"Call me Tommaso," he says. "Got an extra brush? I'll join you."

"Sweet!" Rigo says. But then he frowns. "Hold on, isn't it game night? Aren't you supposed to be resting?"

My client grabs another slice. "Not a napper," he says through a bite of pizza. "And there's no way I'm gonna sit around while two other guys paint my house. Who does that?"

"Literally *every* other client," Rigo says. "That's kind of the point of hiring painters."

Tommaso pulls a grouchy face that I'm starting to know very well. "Nah. This project is on a tight deadline. I got two hands. I can paint."

Ten minutes later, I find myself on my knees in front of the baseboard, showing Tom how to paint the trim. "We don't have to prime this part, because the trim is already white. Tomorrow, Rigo and I will paint over the primer he's putting on the walls right now."

"Got it," he says.

"Hey man, you might want to change," Rigo says. "Don't get paint on the team shirt."

"Eh. I got dozens of these." But then he carefully rests the brush on the rim of the paint can and strips off his shirt.

I nearly swallow my tongue. Those abs of glory make another appearance at point-blank range. I can see every chiseled curve. Every thread of neatly trimmed dark hair that dusts his happy trail...

The glory is gone a moment later, though, when he puts the shirt back on inside out.

When I remember to breathe again, I see Rigo on the other side of the room, fanning himself dramatically. I'm just lucky he didn't whip out his phone to take a video.

I motion him back up the ladder. "Come on, man. We're on paid time here."

"You are a slave driver," Rigo says, but he picks up his brush and gets back to painting.

Since Tommaso is here, it's the perfect time to think about the accent wall. I open two quarts of paint that I've purchased, and I use two fresh rollers to paint big swatches on cardboard. Two coats each.

"What's that for?" Tom asks, watching me.

"These are samples for the fireplace wall. The paint chips you get at the store are too small to show you what a color really feels like. I wanted you to be able to see it at scale, before you choose."

He squints at the cardboard. One shade is a gray-green slate and the other one is a grayed-out plum. "I dunno. It's just a wall."

Rigo laughs. But I'm more annoyed than amused. "This is your *home*," I sputter. "Let's not forget you'll have to stare at it every day for a decade."

"So which color looks best? You're the expert."

I take a deep, cleansing breath. "Both of these shades are complementary to the stones in the fireplace surround. See?" I pick up the green one and hold it up beside the fireplace. Then I do the same for the plum. "They both look good. Personally, I think the plum brings more to the party. It's a little warmer. I know you said that purple isn't your favorite color. Too, uh, Brooklyn, I think?"

"Nah!" Rigo says from up on the ladder. "Brooklyn's purple is more eggplant."

"Agreed," Tom says. As if either one of them is making any sense at all.

"So that shade of purple isn't a dealbreaker for Cougars," Rigo says. "And that green is fine, too. It's not at all a Dallas green. Minnesota, though?"

"Mmm," Tom says. "I hadn't thought of that. But it's not really the same."

"Same as *what*?" I demand. It's like I'm the only one in this room making sense.

"You can't choose an accent shade in your competitor's team colors," Rigo says haughtily. "That's just bad juju."

"*Exactly*," Tom agrees.

"Oh," I say slowly. That comment about purple had something to do with a competitor's *team* colors?

"Who you playing tonight?" Rigo asks. "Philly?"

"Yeah," Tom grunts, his brow furrowed as he paints a stripe of paint on the baseboard.

"You're not wearing anything orange, right? Wouldn't wanna jinx yourself."

"*Fuck* no," Tom says. "Wasn't born yesterday."

"Uh-huh," Rigo agrees. "What color car you drive?"

"Nebula gray pearl," Tom answers immediately.

"Oooh, savvy," Rigo says. "Nobody has gray in their logo. L.A. kinda ruined black and silver, yeah?"

"Yeah. Can't be too careful."

I've totally lost control of this conversation. "Guys, remember me? Can someone confirm that none of Tom's enemies have either of these colors?" I hold up both cardboard samples.

Two men turn to stare at me with thoughtful frowns. "I think you're all clear with both of those," Rigo says.

"Yup." Tom nods.

I summon the last shred of my patience. "Okay. Thank you. Now which one of these colors do you like better? Which one do you want to look at while you're sitting in this room having a cup of... whatever warrior gods drink to wake up in the morning."

His mouth quirks up on one side. "Gun to my head? I kinda like the slate green better."

"Slate green it is," I announce. "Was that really so hard?"

He returns to his baseboard. "What's it called, anyway? The color."

I check the can. "Secret Garden."

"Uh-oh," he grumbles. "That's Vancouver's motto."

My blood pressure doubles. And then I realize he's grinning. "Are you fucking with me right now? Seriously?"

"Sorry." He chuckles. "Couldn't resist."

Rigo laughs, and I feel like pushing over his ladder. "Hey, DiCosta," he says. "What do you think of Vancouver's new goalie?"

The two of them start nattering on about hockey. But with all three of us painting, we're getting the work done ahead of schedule.

My belly is full of pizza, I'm gainfully employed, and Secret Garden is a kickass accent color.

Honestly, things could really be worse.

ELEVEN

Tommaso

"HOW BAD ARE WE TALKING ABOUT?" Bess asks as I pull into a parking garage in Cherry Creek. "Bad enough to get taken off the roster in Nashville?"

"No, no," I say quickly. "In retrospect, it was just a bad day. Coach wasn't pleased with my performance. But it isn't the end of the world. I didn't need to call you. I just, uh, panicked. Sorry."

"You can always call me," she says smoothly. "And everybody has a bad practice once in a while. But why did this one feel like a catastrophe?"

"I dunno," I mumble, looking for an empty parking spot. "After the third time I blew a drill, Coach looked pissed. I thought you might hear from him."

"Well, I didn't."

"That's a relief." I honestly don't know why I called my agent. But my anxiety has roared back to life this week, and it makes everything seem like a disaster. "I'd better go and let you get on with your day."

"Where did you say you were headed?" Bess asks as I pull into a space.

"I'm shopping for furniture again."

"God, I'm sorry," she says. "You have my thoughts and prayers."

"Thanks. I did what you said, though. I hired a guy to help me with it."

"Oh! See? I knew you were smart."

"You're the only one who thinks so."

"I doubt that. But, Tommaso, before I let you go, you should know that the publicist—Tate—is on my case."

"Oh shit."

"Yeah. He wants me to convince you to do this photo shoot. Apparently, you told him you'd think about it, and the poor man doesn't seem to realize you're blowing him off."

I snort. "If I say no, he'll just argue."

"Hearing you. The problem is that his argument has merit. We *all* want to see your reputation improve. There's a reason I can't find you any lucrative endorsements. And that reason is..."

"Photographs of me punching a family member. I already know this."

"As I said, you're a smart man, and I'm sure you had your reasons. But if you never tell anybody what they are, then the Tates of the world won't leave this alone."

"Loud and clear, Bess." But my stomach gives an uncomfortable twist, because I'm *never* sharing my story.

Everybody says they want to hear it, but they really don't. Everyone has always let my uncle get away with his racist, homophobic bullshit, because he knows how to win hockey games. And it's the same with his son's blatant bullying.

It's literally the story of my life. Me at twelve, trying to get in and out of the locker room before my cousin can make rude, sexualized comments about my skinny body. I was playing up a league, which meant I was always the smallest.

Me at thirteen, as Marco grabs me by the neck and pushes my face into his crotch, while the other boys jeer. *That's what you're really after, isn't it? Tell the truth, little homo.*

And hearing my uncle's echoing laughter afterwards.

By fifteen, I'm working out like crazy. Drinking protein shakes like water to bulk up and fight back. And trying not to react whenever he invents a new nickname for me, each one worse than the last.

Teenage nights lying in bed, sleepless as their abuse echoes through my head. And knowing, deep down in my soul, that Marco sees something true about me when he squints at me through those soulless eyes.

The shame of wondering how he spotted it before I did.

"I can live without endorsements," I tell Bess now. "What I can't live with is smiling for a picture with two of the worst assholes in hockey."

"Okay," she says quietly. "If this is important to you, I won't question your convictions."

"Thank you. I mean it." Bess is widely known to be a fantastic agent. She's smart, and she listens to her clients. That's why I hired her after my old agent (a former teammate of my uncle's) fired me.

"Still, I wouldn't be doing my job if I didn't explain all the angles to you. Tate is trying to do right by you, even if you can't get on board."

"Uh-huh. I do realize that."

"So how about this—I'll be the bad guy. I'll tell him you're not doing the shoot."

I cut the engine to my car and drum my fingers on the steering wheel. The only reason I haven't given Tate a firm *no* is that my mother would appreciate the gesture of me doing the shoot. It's got to be stressful to have her brother and her son at odds.

"Let me think about it some more," I tell Bess.

"Sure, boss. Just say the word. And good luck shopping. You're gonna need it."

"Truer words. Later!"

We hang up, and I walk out of the garage and straight into retail mayhem. Carter says that the Cherry Creek part of Denver is thick with furniture stores. "If we can't find your couch in one, we'll just walk to another."

Like that's a selling point.

I locate the correct store and push through the double doors. "Can I help you, sir?" A young woman asks immediately.

That's a good sign, I guess. "Thanks, but I'm meeting a designer. Oh. Found him..."

A flash of ginger has drawn my eye toward the top of the escalator, where I see Carter waving to me. When I catch his eye, he *smiles*.

Now I'm like a fish swimming toward a shiny lure. My stupid feet point themselves right to that escalator, and thirty seconds after that, I join him in a vast sea of sofas, chairs, and tables.

Christ.

"Don't panic," he says firmly.

I notice he's wearing a plum-colored shirt again. And it's hard not to stare at the tantalizing V of bare skin above the first button. So I avert my gaze.

"You look like a feral cat who's about to bolt."

"It's that obvious?"

"Yup. That wild look in your eye. Which I do not understand, because shopping for furniture is my favorite thing ever."

"Huh. As my mama says—there's no accounting for taste."

He rolls his stormy blue eyes and then pats a clipboard in his hand. "Calm down. I've already spent two hours looking at everything in the store. I've taken notes, and now I'm going to show you a few things that I think you'll like. It won't hurt a bit."

I exhale. "Let's do this."

"First, we're going to pick out a couch. I know you'd rather just see photos, and some of the things you need will be chosen that way. But you can't experience fabrics in a photo. And besides—your ass needs to try out a couch before you buy it."

There is a certain logic to this, I guess. But when he said "ass," my eyes went directly to his.

Shopping is torture on so many levels.

"Here we go. What do we think of this?"

He's led me to a generously sized navy-blue sofa. There's nothing special about it, but that's totally okay with me. I sit down and run my hand across the fabric. "It's fine. And it won't show stains."

"Very true," Carter says. "This one is in stock, and ready for delivery. The cost is three thousand dollars."

"What do you think?" I ask him.

"The roll arm is a little cheugy. And—more to the point—I find the bench to be a little shallow for you. This is not a tall man's couch."

Now that he mentions it, the seat isn't as deep as I am. "It's in stock, though? My mother would fit on this couch just fine."

"Are you sending it home with her after New Year's?" he asks.

"Of course not."

"Then this ain't it, chief. I won't let you sit on this for years just because you're impatient."

I sigh. "Is there another option?"

"Uh-huh. And it's just across the room."

I follow him to a second sofa, but this one is white. "Dude. I'm almost afraid to sit on that," I complain. "I can't do white."

"Don't drag my picks until you have all the info. They have one in stock with this fabric in charcoal gray." He pulls a square of fabric out of his pocket.

I take the square and run my hand over the soft surface. "All right. That's kinda nice. What do you call this? Velvet?"

"It's called chenille, which is French for caterpillar."

"*What?*"

He grins. "Don't panic. This is made out of cotton. It's soft, it's rugged, and I kind of love it. Now sit down."

Dutifully, I take a seat. And there's plenty of room for my big, tired body. "This rocks."

"Go ahead," he says. "Put your feet up on the coffee table. Let's give it an honest try."

"You sure? My mama would spank me for putting my shoes on a coffee table."

"There will be no spanking," Carter says, his eyes flashing.

My body heats. I look away from him and prop my feet on the

coffee table. It turns out I'm too tired to think up any more inappropriate thoughts right now. I lean back, and the sofa catches me in its pillowy embrace. "Okay. This is living."

Carter sits down right beside me and kicks his feet onto the coffee table next to mine. He leans back and sighs, too.

We're just two dudes kicking back in the middle of a furniture store. It ought to feel weird, but it doesn't. I only feel relaxed.

"Now we're talking," he says dreamily. "Think of coming home to this after a long trip. You're in your living room. Are we facing the TV or the fireplace?"

"The TV." I feel my heart rate slow down. "Say what you will, but after a long day on the road, I'm a zombie in front of the screen."

"Everybody needs some Netflix therapy after a long day. Even super-stud athletes."

I snort. "What's your favorite show? Wait—I bet you watch HGTV."

"Not often. Some of those designers are hacks. You probably don't go home and watch hockey after work, either."

"You'd be surprised."

He turns his handsome face toward mine. "Seriously?"

"Well, yeah. I have to play most of those teams twice a season. Watching them is good preparation. It's, like, homework. I'm checking to see what mistakes they make. Where they're vulnerable. How they fight when they're angry."

He gives me a sideways glance. "Of course."

Oops. The mention of fighting has made him go quiet. "Let me guess—you finally googled me?"

"I might have."

"And the first thing you saw was me whaling on my cousin. And then my uncle, when he decided to try to break it up?"

He clears his throat. "That might have come up."

I'm so tired all of a sudden. "And now you're sorry you took this job?"

"No way," he says softly. "You're not that scary. So far, since I've met you, you've fed me twice, you've dug me out of a financial hole, and you've been super nice to my pesty friend. So I figure whatever happened in Trenton, they had it coming."

My throat is very scratchy all of a sudden. "I like to think so. Not my finest hour, though."

"What happened?"

That question again. "I kinda snapped."

"That happen a lot?"

"Not to me," I assure him. I don't know why I'm still talking, but I don't want Carter to think badly of me. "That was, like, twenty years of payback delivered in two minutes. Unfortunately, I'll be living it down for the rest of my career."

"What did they do? Just so I know not to do the same thing."

I let out a bark of bitter laughter, and then I surprise myself by telling him a tiny sliver of the truth. "My personal life had just imploded. My cousin, who is the biggest turd you'll ever meet, spent several weeks taunting me about it. And then I lost my mind."

Carter gulps. "That's pretty ugly. I'm sorry."

"It was ugly," I admit. "Broke Marco's jaw. Landed a couple punches on Vin, too, before it was over. He wanted to press charges, but the franchise bribed him not to."

"So you're saying that I'm sitting beside a troublemaker?"

"Pretty much."

"Hmm," he says. "Google says you got traded after that fight."

"Yup. No man was ever as happy about a trade. Worked out great."

"Except for your lack of furniture," he points out.

"I told you—I had rental furniture. And my ass never knew the difference until I sat on this sofa. What is this thing stuffed with? Clouds?"

"Memory foam and down feathers."

"You're ruining me for all other sofas."

"Good," he says. "Because you look beat, Jersey. Like, tired to the bone. And I hate thinking of you going home to that empty house and having nowhere to relax."

That nickname again. It makes me smile. "I'm not going home," I say. "I'm going to the airport for a flight to Tennessee."

"Right." He shakes his head. "Crazy story you just told me, though. Have you seen your cousin since the fight?"

"Only twice, on the ice," I admit. "I dread every game against Trenton. He wants a rematch, but if I fight him again, my coach will be pissed."

"Big yikes. So what do you do?"

"Grind my teeth instead." And now I'm sick of talking about myself. "We were never close, anyway. You have a big family?"

"No way," he says. "Since my father died, it's just my mom and me."

His father died. My stomach lurches. "Oh shit. When did he pass?"

"When I was nineteen. Heart attack."

"I'm really sorry to hear that." And suddenly the couch's magic is lost on me. I sit upright and take a deep breath.

"It's okay," he says. "I've had a few years to get used to the idea."

An electrical burst of anxiety pulses through me. I stand up from the cloud couch and inhale. "Buy the couch, okay?"

"I will," he says. "And I'll arrange for delivery as soon as I can. Right after the living room paint is dry."

"Oh, right. Hold on." I dig a hand into my suit pocket and extract a keychain. "My extra key. I'll be out of town."

Then I do something that's surprisingly difficult for me, considering what I'm paying this guy to furnish my house.

I hand it to him.

TWELVE

Carter

TOMMASO CAN'T MEET my eyes as he hands me the key. He thinks I don't understand how difficult it is to let someone else into your life, even if it's just for a paint job.

But I know more about this than he thinks. Nobody becomes an interior designer by accident. In order to do this job, you have to have an understanding of what a client's home means to him.

Even when the client doesn't quite understand it himself.

"Thanks for this," I say quietly. "I won't abuse your trust."

"Not much to steal," he says gruffly.

I scramble to my feet and tuck away the key. "It's not just about valuables, big man. It's about privacy. And I would never violate yours."

His dark eyes flash with something unreadable. "Thanks. I appreciate it. Now what else are you going to make me look at? Time's a-wasting."

That guy who spilled his guts to me on the sofa? He's gone. The big, gruff hockey player is back in the driver's seat.

I steer him toward the dining section, where I point out two different tables. "They've both got a rustic vibe to them," I point out. "This first one is all wood, nice joinery. More traditional. But I also like that one—with the iron base. It has a more industrial feel."

The corners of his mouth quirk up, and I watch him scrutinize my two choices. "Huh. Okay. I like them both."

"Try the chairs," I suggest. "Maybe they'll sway you."

Frowning, he takes a seat at the first one, looking lordly in his business suit. Like a warrior knight at the Round Table. He runs a rough palm over the wood. Then he gets up and crosses to the other one. "What's the story about the girl in the bears' house? Trying all the furniture?"

"You mean Goldilocks?" I take the seat next to his.

"That's the one. I'm not her."

"Not a fan of porridge?"

He flashes me a grin so quick I almost miss it. "Sure am. But I don't have a strong feeling about these chairs. They're both comfortable enough. The tables are both great, too. You think either one would fit into the dining area?"

I let out a gasp of mock indignation. "You think I'd show you a table that didn't?"

"Calm down. I'm just asking. Which one do you like best?"

"This one." I pat the top of the table where we're sitting. "The iron base is hip. Very single guy. Very butch. If I went home with a guy and he had this table? I'd think—this dude is *lit*."

He lets out a bark of surprised laughter. "Then it's an easy choice. Get this one."

"Excuse me, sir?"

We both look up, and I'm briefly confused, because the woman who's interrupting us isn't wearing a name tag. She's just a stranger in sweatpants.

Wait—the sweatpants are blue. Cougar blue. I don't know which marketing dude chose that color, but there are better shades in the Pantone deck. It's too loud.

But I digress.

"I'm just...wow," the woman says breathlessly. "I never expected to see you in Crate and Barrel!"

"That makes two of us," Tommaso says under his breath.

"Would you mind signing for me?" She presses her hands together and bats her eyes. "It would make my whole year."

"Uh, sure." Tom rises from his dining chair and pats his pockets, coming up with a Sharpie. Which can only mean that this happens to him a lot. He looks oddly embarrassed, though. "You have, um, a piece of paper?"

I'm just about to offer him my clipboard when the woman pops one of her feet onto a dining chair and angles her leg toward DiCosta. "Oh no. Sign right here. These are my special game night sweats."

Tommaso's ears turn pink, and I don't know why I'm so tickled by this. He uncaps the pen, leans down, and quickly scrawls something near her ankle.

"Omigod, thank you so much! Selfie?"

My favorite hockey player proceeds to take the most awkward photograph in the history of photographs, while I struggle not to laugh.

The woman thanks him profusely and then gallops away.

"That was amusing," I say after she's out of earshot. "I guess your reputation isn't that tattered."

He runs a sheepish hand through his hair. "Depends. I do well with certain demographics."

I double over laughing.

After I can breathe again, I make Tom look at some rugs in a carpet store down the street. But he keeps checking his watch, and I can tell I'm losing him.

"Go on, then," I finally say. "Go do whatever it is that you do to a bunch of other hockey players in Nashville. Good luck tonight."

"Game is actually tomorrow," he says, pinching the bridge of his nose. "We fly in the night before."

Considering how tired he looks, I think that's probably for the best. I send him off, and then spend another hour wrangling the furniture store's delivery department into giving us special treatment.

Which they do, because I am awesome at my job. Sometimes. When I remember to behave like a professional.

The next day is Friday, and I spend the morning selling furniture to people who found me on Craigslist. At nine, ten, and eleven o'clock, various people show up at my door to purchase my belongings at rock-bottom prices.

There's one piece I didn't price low enough, because I couldn't bear to. It's a Drexel bookcase in walnut. It's wide and short, which isn't the current fashion in bookcases. I'd been asking three thousand dollars, which is about half what it's worth in a retail shop.

No takers, though. And now I'm stuck with it, and I have no idea what to do about that.

By one o'clock, my apartment is empty and forlorn. I load up my boxes of books and kitchenware into my car. That only leaves some duffel bags with clothes and one pristine vintage piece of furniture made of walnut.

It takes me an hour to carefully drag it out of the building, inch by inch.

Mr. Jones, that coward, watches me from his window upstairs. As if I can't see him. Finally, I look up at him and make a beckoning motion.

Then I wait, wondering if he's too chicken to face me. But no—he comes shuffling out a few minutes later, zipping his coat.

"Help me lift this onto the roof of the car," I demand. "Then I'm out of your hair."

"Your car's not big enough for that thing," he grumbles.

"You want to be rid of me? Just help me lift it."

He must really want me gone. Because the jerk helps me.

"Why is there a bookshelf on top of your car?" is the first thing Rigo asks when he arrives at Tommaso's place at three o'clock.

"Because I wasn't going to leave something worth five grand in my apartment."

"Five *grand?*" He whistles. "Okay, but where are we going to put it? You've seen my place."

"I don't know," I say, returning to my paint roller. "I was thinking I might put it here in Tommaso's living room for a few days. He'd have somewhere to put his TV until I find him a media console."

"Excellent plan!" Rigo tosses his coat onto the bean bag chair. "Hey, let's move it now. The hockey game comes on in a couple hours. We can watch him play Nashville."

My pulse leaps at this idea. That photo of Tom fighting his cousin wasn't the only picture I saw when I googled him. There was also this photo of him lifting his hockey jersey, the abs of glory on full display...

A wave of guilt crashes through me. I can't be having thirsty thoughts about my client. That's not what he signed up for.

"We shouldn't use his TV," I say. "He deserves his privacy."

"Dude, you are an excellent human being. But it's just watching a hockey game. It's not like rifling through his underwear drawer. Not that I wouldn't like to." He cackles. "Come on, I worked a full day already. I'm painting with you for fun."

"I'll think about it," I say primly, and my friend rolls his eyes.

Then I pull out my phone and shoot off a text.

> Hello from your living room. Vibe check—is it cool with you if I put a piece of my furniture under your TV until I find you a TV console? Either way, Rigo is threatening to turn on the hockey game while we paint.

A half hour later I get a reply. It's typical Tommaso.

> Sure, go ahead.

I can't tell if he's annoyed or truly indifferent. Oh well. This is my month for imposing on everyone. Tonight, and every night for the next couple of weeks, I'll be sleeping on Rigo's sofa.

Fun times.

Rigo and I paint as fast as we can while the light fades outside. And then we carry some box lights in from Rigo's truck and set them up so we can paint after dark.

We've almost finished the first coat when Rigo says, "Let's order some dinner and set up the TV. We can watch a little hockey while the first coat dries."

"Okay, sure. But don't order anything for me. I brought a sandwich."

"Ooh. Anything good?"

I shrug. "Just a PB&J. I'll be eating a lot of that this month."

Rigo sets down his brush. "Why? I thought you were flush with cash from Mr. Hockey Hottie."

"Uh, no. I still owe fifteen thousand dollars on my credit card, and I'm behind on my student loans. There's no way I can rent an apartment until I pay that down. I wouldn't pass the credit check."

"Jesus," Rigo whispers. "I didn't know it was that bad."

"Yeah, but I promise I'll be out of your hair the minute Buck comes home."

Rigo shakes his head. "Why aren't you suing Macklin, as well as your client? It doesn't make sense for you to pay off furniture you don't own and never meant to buy."

"Oh, I've fantasized about it for sure. But suing people takes months and thousands of dollars. It would cost more to make them pay than I can afford."

My best friend sags. "God, I'm sorry."

"I just need to spend another couple weeks eating peanut butter and treading water. That's the price I pay for making stupid decisions."

And starting a business with a terrible human who only cares about himself.

"My God, you have shitty taste in men. And clients."

"Thanks. I noticed."

He grins. "We have to find you a nice soldier like mine. Or—wait—a rich hockey player."

I laugh, but my heart skitters. Every hour I spend with surly, buttoned-up Tommaso DiCosta makes him even more fascinating to me.

And the weird thing? Sometimes when I make him laugh, I feel like he might like me, too. Just as a friend, of course.

But maybe he needs more of those.

Maybe we all do.

—————

Rigo orders way too much fried chicken and potato salad for one guy. It's a very thinly veiled mistake meant to include me, and I am grateful.

But I almost can't enjoy it, because I know he's going to tire of that pretty fast. It's hard to be the needy friend. I'm so tired of being broke and worried.

I'm seated on the drop cloth, finishing up my chicken, when the hockey game comes on. And there he is, in high definition—Tommaso in his gear, hockey stick clutched in one hand while the national anthem blares.

"Lookin' good!" Rigo calls, clapping his hands. "Let's do this, boys!"

It's startling to see Tommaso's familiar frown on the TV screen. My heart shouts *I know him!*

But now I feel like that woman in the furniture store, demanding his autograph on her leg. Eager to claim a piece of him.

I won't be that guy. I'm not even interested in hockey, right?

After climbing to my feet, I throw my paper plate away, climb the ladder, and get back into action with my paint roller. There's work to be done.

—————

I last all of ten minutes before Rigo's shouts and curses draw me right back down the ladder.

"That was a great deke!" Rigo's gaze is glued to the TV. "I think we can win this one. And your man DiCosta looks fierce tonight."

I gulp when the camera shows me his face. It's sweaty now, and his murderous expression is strangely hot. It's all that intensity. Like a leopard stalking a tasty gazelle.

And then he pounces! He chases after a competitor, boxing him in and then skating *backwards* at top speed, all while antagonizing his opponent with lightning-fast jabs of his stick.

He snags the puck, and before I can blink, he's off in a new direction, passing to a teammate, and then boxing a new opponent out of the action.

A whimper of longing escapes my chest.

"What?" Rigo says. "I missed that."

"Nothing." *Keep it together, Flynn.*

"Did you just whimper when DiCosta made that play?" Rigo laughs. "I thought you weren't a hockey fan?"

That's what I thought, too.

THIRTEEN

Tommaso

WE FLY HOME after the game, and I don't make the turn into Red Rock Circle until one in the morning. Newgate's place across the street is lit up like a literal Christmas tree.

My house is dark as a tomb, of course.

I make my way inside, flip on the overhead light, and get a shock. In my absence, the whole room has been transformed. It's hard to know where to look first.

For starters, the new white paint is clean and crisp. I wouldn't have guessed painting over that yellow color would make the room look bigger, but somehow it does.

Next, my gaze lands on the fireplace wall. It looks smashing in slate green. Like it was always meant to be that color.

When I step a little farther inside, I notice the TV is sitting on top of some kind of long, low shelf made of dark wood. Carter said this particular piece of furniture would be only temporary, but it looks really good anyway, confirming my original impulse to choose wooden furniture for this room.

Most surprising of all, the drop cloths and painters' gear have disappeared from the floor. In their place is a spacious rug, centered on the shining floorboards. It's patterned in subtle hues and thick underfoot.

The rug looks vaguely familiar. I'm sure Carter showed it to me in the rug shop, right about the time my anxiety was kicking in. I'd gotten twitchy about making it to the airport on time.

He'd noticed. He'd cut our time short, gave my elbow a squeeze, and told me he'd choose something to show me later.

I guess he meant right now, because there's a note in the center of the rug, and I pace over and pick it up.

Dear Tommaso,

You're not the only one who doesn't know jargon. So I'll just say this: good job sportsing tonight. I can tell you were sportsing harder than the other team, because the scoreboard said Colorado 4, Nashville 2 when you were done.

Also, Rigo got very excited and did some jumping up and down on the ladder.

We're insured, I swear.

Anywho, I hope you like the rug. Unlike furniture, rugs can go out on approval. You have fourteen days to decide if you like this one. Bear in mind that your couch arrives on Monday, and I want to see them together.

Maybe I'm just high on paint fumes, but doesn't this place look great?

Toodles,
Carter

Toodles?
It's the middle of the night, but I'm laughing out loud. The place

does, in fact, look great. The rug is soft under my shoes, and it's tempting to lie down on it.

But I march upstairs like a good boy and hang up my suit. The house is so quiet that I can hear the sound of my zipper when I remove my trousers.

Carter's note comes back to me, and I snort into the silence. *Sportsing.*

The weird thing is that I could hear his voice when I read the note. Like he's already under my skin. So now I'm standing here, grinning like a crazy person.

I am a man with a lot of secrets, and tonight, my biggest one is that coming home to that note was even more exciting than coming home to a very stylish living room.

After a visit with my toothbrush, I get into bed and set my alarm on my phone.

That's when I notice the text from Carter.

> Rigo and I are done painting. Wait. Actually I'm just going to write you a note and leave it in the LR. Later!

I quickly reply.

> Got it, thanks.

It's late. But instead of closing my phone, I reread his brief message, like a weirdo.

Stop it, DiCosta.

Gathering my wits, I press the button that puts my phone to sleep.

Or at least, I try to. But in the messaging app, there's a little icon in the upper righthand corner of the screen, shaped like a movie camera. And if you happen to brush your thumb over it at 1:16 in the morning, in your exhaustion, you might accidentally initiate a video call.

Which I do.

To make matters worse, I don't notice right away, because I've tossed the phone on the bed. The ringing sound confuses me, but then I realize what I've done.

Now I'm lying in bed, mostly naked, staring at the screen in horror as Carter's face blinks into view.

"Well, hi," he says, looking amused. "You hate the rug this much? Need me to haul it away before morning?"

I'd answer him, except he's shirtless, too, and all my brain cells are busy taking in his lean chest. There's some muscle definition, but he's not bulky. All that *skin*. He's draped his arm casually over his head, pale skin against rumpled red hair...

Hell. He'd asked me a question. I try to dredge it from the depths of my mind. The rug? "N-no," I stammer, scrambling to sit up. "Sorry. The rug is fine. I, uh, didn't actually mean to call you."

His eyes grow amused. "Yeah? Hit that little video button by mistake? That happened to my ex-boyfriend all the time. He was kind of a klutz, though."

Ex-boyfriend. My brain files that away for some reason. As if I really need to know whether or not Carter is single.

"Sorry," I say again. I don't know if I'm apologizing for the call or for the way I'm blatantly staring at his chest. He doesn't have a lot of chest hair, but it's reddish and finely textured. I want to pass my hand over his pecs and feel it against my palm.

My cock thickens in my underwear.

I'm a complete mess.

Carter doesn't seem to notice my distress. "You didn't wake me up or anything. I was just sitting here scrolling through shower curtains. Do you have any deep thoughts about shower curtains?"

"Uh, no? But why are you still working on this at one in the morning?"

Carter's smile fades. "Well, I've had a stressful few months. My brain is basically a doom loop, and it's more fun to brainstorm a theme for your bathroom than to think about my future."

Oh.

I open my mouth to say that I'm pretty sure my bathroom does not require a theme, but something else comes out instead. "Why the doom loop? Are you okay?"

Carter's blue eyes widen. Then he relaxes against the sofa and lets out a sigh.

My entire body tightens.

"This is embarrassing to admit, but I'm a better designer than I am a businessman. Recently, I let a client get the better of me. And when stuff went wrong, my business partner bailed. He was also my boyfriend."

"Oh shit."

His smile is fleeting. "Like I said, it's been a rough patch. Your job came along at exactly the right moment, and it's probably going to save me. But when I close my eyes at night, I'm still prone to disaster scenarios." He gives his head a quick shake. "You know what? Let's not discuss this."

"I'm sorry. That was a personal question, and it was out of line." *Seriously, pull it together DiCosta.*

"But I didn't have to answer it." He shrugs, and all the muscles in his upper body jump appealingly. "I don't even know why I did. I *never* tell my clients anything negative about my life. It's unprofessional, for starters. And most of them expect me to project a certain *joie de vivre*."

"What did I say about jargon?"

He laughs suddenly. "Sorry. That literally means *the joy of life*. That's the kind of performance some clients expect from me. They've cast me in the role of their fabulous gay designer." His blue eyes twinkle. "They have a certain vision—gossip and brunch and me pouring the perfect Cosmo. That's a pink cocktail..."

"That one I know," I tell him. "My sister likes a nice Cosmo now and then, on girls' night."

"Exactly." His expression grows thoughtful. "Tell me this—have you ever ordered a Cosmo?"

"Fuck no. I'm more of a beer guy."

"You don't say." He smiles softly. "But have you tasted one? Because maybe we're *both* typecast. You're starring in the role of the broody, potentially violent hockey player, and I have to maintain my fabulous visage." He waves a hand in front of his smiling face. "I shouldn't complain, I guess. I like my job, and Cosmos are tasty. But nobody expects me to be grumpy or anxious."

"I'm not allowed to be anxious, either," I point out. "Whatever goes wrong, I'm just supposed to bulldoze my way through it."

"Yeah, I bet you are." He nods wisely. "The fierce warrior king, mowing problems down with his sharp skates and his big stick."

I snort. But he isn't wrong. And I don't think I've ever had a more truthful conversation in my life. "That's exactly right."

His smile slowly returns. "You are a very refreshing client, Tommaso DiCosta. You don't want me to entertain you. You just want me to do what I do best, so you can concentrate on what you do best."

"That's true. But..." I take a deep breath, and inch closer to the truth. "I also grew up with the message that I'm not supposed to care about rugs and towels. Like it wasn't even an option. And until I met you, that didn't even seem weird."

His eyes widen. "Oh wow. Yeah. That's why almost all my clients are women. Gender expectations are pretty limiting."

Tell me about it.

"So now that your eyes have opened, does this mean you've suddenly developed deep opinions about the color scheme for the downstairs bathroom?"

"No sir." I shake my head.

"And you still might burst into flames if you're asked to think about it?"

"Quite possibly."

He smiles. "All right. I'll handle it and send you a couple of choices. The shower curtain has to *match* the bathmat and the towels. Just so you're prepared."

"I'll brace myself."

His smile widens. "Good. I noticed you're on a trip next week. Rigo showed me how to see your game schedule. You're going to Buffalo and Boston and Winnipeg."

"Am I? Shit. That's a lot."

He laughs. "I don't make the rules. But we'll have to change strategies. I'll email you some pics, and then maybe we'll catch up on a call? You'll need to weigh in on a few things."

"Okay, yeah." *Another call with Carter.* "Let's do that."

"Fab!"

"Now I should let you go, though," I force myself to say. "Sorry to interrupt your late-night web scroll."

His smile disarms me, like it always does. "It was honestly a pleasure. Get some sleep so you can do good sportsing tomorrow."

My chuckle is low and soft, which isn't like me. "I'll do that."

The screen goes dark when we end the call, and I lock the phone for real this time and set it onto the floor.

I wonder what Carter would think if he knew how attractive I find him.

Nothing, probably. He probably has his pick of guys, all of them less messy than me.

FOURTEEN

Carter

CARTER

Vibe check! What did you think of the living room chairs? I need to make a decision and schedule delivery.

TOMMASO

I liked the blue one.

Wut???

The TOWELS were blue. I asked about the chairs.

Oops. Sorry. Chairs? I liked the brown one.

head desk They were ALL brown. They're leather. Some were darker brown. Like cognac. Some were more of a caramel. But their shapes were different. And the scale.

But I can't see the scale in these photos. And they were all fine. Pick one. My ass is going to be on the cloud couch anyway. The chair is for guests, and I almost never have those.

First let me reframe the question. Do you want your infrequent guests to sit on a chair that cost $1800 or one that cost $3600?

> Pick the cheaper one. We are not snobs here.

>> Speak for yourself. I am very bougie. But I like the $1800 chair just fine, so that's the one you're getting.

> Wait, was it cognac or caramel?

>> Is this a serious question?

> No.

>> Then you can see it when it shows up.

> Fine. We done? I gotta go do some sportsing now.

>> Done FOR NOW but I am shopping for beds today and I'm going to need you to look at them after you're done sportsing.

> I don't care what the bed looks like. My eyes will be closed when I'm in it.

>> I get that. (Sort of?) But you might own this furniture for fifty years. If I pick one you don't like, you'll be cursing my name until I'm 75. So humor me and look at the beds.

> I'll look. But don't be mad if I can't tell them apart.

>> I'll make it memorable. I like a challenge.

"CHECK IT OUT," Rigo says, and I look up from my phone.

We're both seated at the little dining table in his kitchen. I helped him find this table, and every other stick of furniture in this place. It wasn't easy, because the apartment is tiny.

Luckily, I'm a shopping genius. This table seats two but expands to seat six for dinner parties. I even found him some stackable chairs that are hiding in the closet somewhere.

He offers me his phone, and I take it. "What am I looking at?"

"There's a picture of DiCosta on Instagram at a furniture store. And I think you're in it. Isn't this your arm?"

I squint at the photo. And, yup, I recognize that sofa we're sitting on.

Seems like the woman in the sweatpants—the one who'd asked for DiCosta's autograph—snapped a pic before she approached us. Or maybe it had been another shopper entirely.

Whoever it was, she cropped me out of the shot, of course. And gave it a caption:

Omigod, my future husband is shopping for a sofa! I'll pick one for you, baby! We'll break it in together! #hottommaso #cougarshockey #gocolorado

"People are weird," I say slowly. "It's like they take ownership of him, you know? *My future husband.*"

"Yeah," Rigo agrees. "I've heard people say that before, and it always sounded cute. But it's less cute when you remember that's a real person. It's just creepy."

"Yeah." I shake my head. "Hey, Rigo? Can you come to a store with me after work today?"

"Sure. Why?"

"I need to take some video of beds, and it would help to have an extra set of hands."

"Beds, huh?" He laughs. "I'd love to help *hashtag hot tommaso* find a bed. In a totally non-creepy way."

I spend the morning working on Tommaso's house. I repaint the cabinet in the downstairs bathroom. It had been black, which I'd found too harsh. But when I'm done, it's a soothing slate-green color, a couple shades darker than the one on the fireplace wall.

Then I paint the mirror frame the same color.

This room is also getting a fluffy rug and a canvas shower curtain with a subtle botanical print on it. His mother will be very comfortable in here. But it's not too girly for a single-man athlete's house, either.

After lunch, I call my *own* mother and break the news that I won't be coming home for Christmas. "Mom, I'm so sorry. But my bank account hates me right now, and I just can't swing it."

"Oh, baby," she says with a sigh. "I'm sorry you're struggling. What if I bought the ticket?"

"You can't!" I squawk. "You're saving for that cruise with your girls."

She sighs. "But I love you more than the girls."

"And I love you. But tickets for the holidays are seriously pricey. I already checked. If I come and see you during January, when my life is a little more stable, we'll save a pile."

She's quiet for a moment. "Okay, there's a lot to unpack there. In the first place, I was going to suggest that we skip the church service this year, anyway."

"Oh." It takes me a second to realize why she'd say that.

Last year we'd run into Cal at the Christmas service. He was my high school ex. The one who disavowed me entirely after someone saw us making out in the back of his truck.

That was years ago, and I'm totally over him, if not the trauma of trusting a cowboy.

But there he'd been—with his wife and their two little girls—at last year's Christmas Eve service. It had been awkward for me, and probably for him.

At least I hope it was.

"That's a nice idea, Mom, but I promise this isn't about the church service, or avoiding Cal. I legit can't swing a trip home right now."

"Is it bad, honey?" she whispers. "Will you be okay?"

I hesitate before answering, because my mother will know if I'm lying. "It *was* bad, Mom. Macklin left me with a huge mess, and I really should have known better."

"Oh, sweetheart. Someday you'll find a good man. I just know it."

I'm not sure she's right. "In better news, I got a big design job for this month, and it's going to help me get my head above water.

Meanwhile, don't, uh, send Christmas cards to the old address. I've moved out of my apartment."

"Carter! Really? Was the rent too much?"

"It was. But I'm working on alternatives and staying with Rigo. I'll be okay, Mom. I promise."

But I'm not sure she believes me.

FIFTEEN

Tommaso

WE HAVE a pregame meeting over lunch in Buffalo. I'm picking at my fries and trying to find my focus.

"We gave up our last game in this arena, so we're here to change the tune," Coach says. "You play a better technical game than these guys, and I expect to see that technique shine through this evening."

Yessir, I privately confirm. I need to play well tonight. I've been inconsistent, and it's driving me a little batty. My anxiety is through the roof.

Coach finishes his remarks, and gives the floor to Tate, my least favorite of the staff. "I'll be quick," he says.

I snort, because everybody knows that people who say, "I'll be quick," are the kind of people who are incapable of being quick. It's just a fact.

"First up, it's time to send me the names of your dates for this year's black-tie events. The first one is a benefit for the Denver Children's Hospital. All are expected to attend, so shoot me the names of the WAGs you're bringing, so I can do the seating chart."

"'Scuse me!" Kapski says from the table next to mine. "It's not just wives and girlfriends anymore."

My gaze darts instinctively toward Newgate, who's calmly stirring some milk into his coffee.

"Hey, my bad," Tate says. "I'm just used to saying 'WAGs' without remembering that it's an acronym. I'll do better. For Newgate."

Newgate looks up and catches me staring at him. "No offense taken," he says. "Happy to list Gavin as my date for the benefit. Although by February, a lot of Denver will already know his name."

Tate smirks. "I'm glad you're braced for that. And speaking of which—we have a date for Newgate's news article. It's going to publish the week of Christmas. We locked in that timing because we're hosting Brooklyn—Mr. Newgate's former team, and a friendly crew—for our first game after the holiday."

"A game I expect to *win*," Newgate says. "I love those guys. But I also love to watch them lose."

The whole room laughs.

"Brooklyn will get a heads-up about the event," Tate continues. "We're going to make the night special. The national anthem will be sung by the Rocky Mountains Gay Men's Chorus. And we'll offer Pride jerseys in the spirit shop. Profits will be donated to You Can Play and other equality charities."

My first thought is: I wonder if I can snag one of those Pride jerseys for Carter's friend Rigo.

My second thought is more like a slow-motion car crash. Which teams are we playing right *after* that Brooklyn game?

I dig out my phone and pull up the schedule. My stomach twists when I see the result.

Trenton is our first game on the road after Newgate's announcement. That's the same game where I'm supposed to pose for photographs with the worst two men in hockey.

And *then* I'm supposed to take the ice and behave like a gentleman while Marco and his teammates throw homophobic chirps at my teammate?

It's going to be a disaster. And nobody else seems to have any idea.

I push my plate away.

When the lunch meeting is over, I flag down Tate in the lobby.

"DiCosta!" he says with a jocular slap to my back. "Let's talk about your PR stuff, shall we?"

"Not so fast. I'm actually worried about the timing of Newgate's announcement."

Because the universe hates me, Newgate appears beside me. And he looks *pissed*. "Yo, DiCosta. Do you have a *problem* with my announcement? Or with me?"

Oh my fucking God. "I do *not* have a problem with you."

"Sounds like you got a problem with something," Tate says darkly. "How about you leave the PR to me?"

"Guys," I try again. They need to understand what's at stake. "Trenton is a rough crowd. That organization is a bunch of angry assholes."

Tate glowers. "I understand that you have some history with that team. But Newgate is going to be Newgate whether they like it or not. If they're badly behaved, it just makes *them* look bad."

I throw up my hands. "Fine. You have it all figured out. I'm just a guy who's trying to make your life difficult. But then don't count on me doing that fucking photo shoot in Trenton."

His frown deepens. "Why? That makes *you* look like an asshole."

"Then maybe I am one," I snap.

Their jaws drop as I turn and walk away.

I'm in a dark place when game time rolls around.

Luckily, Newgate and I aren't paired together, which is good, because I can barely look him in the eye. I didn't mean to go off on him, but I don't plan on explaining myself, either.

I'm rattled, and my game goes to shit. And just to make things worse, there's a guy I know from summer hockey on the opponent's team. A friend of Marco's from our high school years.

This isn't unusual. When you've been playing a while, there's always a familiar face or two on the other team. This guy—Dutka—has recently clawed his way up from the minor leagues, I guess.

Unfortunately, he decides to take a little trip down memory lane. "You still a pussy?" he chirps as we fight for the puck in the corner.

I don't bother to reply, but I don't win the puck either, and the sound of his grating laugh as he skates away makes me want to choke him.

The next time we're face to face, he tries again. "Heard you don't fight anymore. Too shy? That's fucking lame."

"Bite me, dumbass." That's the best I can do as we tussle over the puck.

I win it this time. But he gives me a stick to the kidneys for my trouble. The ref doesn't notice.

The game is tied up by the third period, and my teammates look tired and demoralized. Dutka decides to make a blatant hit on Stoneman, who doesn't even have the puck.

Maddeningly, the refs don't call it, and Dutka gives me a smirk meant to rile me up.

Unfortunately, it works. My patience is hanging by a thread when we meet again before the next faceoff.

"Marco said to say hi," he jeers. "'Give the little cocksucker a kiss,' he said."

It's not a very original taunt. I've heard worse. But hearing my cousin's name come from Dutka's ugly mouth gets my nerves jangling. Like there's nothing I can do to ever get him out of my life.

Then the asshole opens his mouth one more time. "They told the press you got traded for fighting your teammates. But the guys in Trenton say that's not why."

My eyes are supposed to be on the ref, who's setting up to drop the puck. But this jab works, and I flick my eyes toward Dutka.

He grins. "Marco said it's because you like to eye-fuck guys in the shower." Then he drops his gloves.

Suddenly my gloves are down on the ice, too, and I'm grabbing Dutka by the jersey.

It happens so fast. He barely has time to lift his hands in a fighting stance before I punch him. Hard. My hand blooms with pain, and he reels back.

He tries to recover and return the favor. I take a hit to my face, before dodging the next punch. Then I unleash a whole lot of pent-up fury on him, and seconds later he goes down.

The refs pounce. Hands drag me back, and the whistle is deafening. The penalty box opens, and I skate toward it in a daze.

They say you like to eye-fuck guys in the shower. It's a fucking lie. But I'm choking on it anyway. It's hard to breathe when you're this angry.

Across the rink, Coach Powers stares at me, his furious expression as easy to read as a fist to the face.

Colorado gets the win, but just barely. And no thanks to me.

"We had a deal," Coach snarls at me in the training room, where I'm icing my hand. "You don't fight unless it's unavoidable."

"It *was*," I bark. "He hit Stoney. And then he provoked me."

"For fuck's sake! That's just Wednesday in hockey," Coach growls.

I don't point out that it's Tuesday. "Sorry, Coach."

"We had *one* rule. You're not the guy who settles the score, no matter who mouths off to you. Got that?" he snaps. "You could seriously fuck up your hand, not to mention your sketchy reputation. And for what? Jumping on a middling player who looked at you funny?"

My hand throbs. So does my lip. "Yessir." I have the horrible thought that Coach Powers will decide I'm not worth the trouble and trade me. Right before Christmas. Right after I bought a house.

Hello, doom loop. Nice to hear from you again.

"What's going on in that big head of yours?" he asks. "Tate says you might have some kind of issue with a teammate?"

I taste bile in my throat. "Absolutely not, Coach. That's not true. But I've got some stuff going on at home."

"Your mother is ill?"

"Uh, yeah," I say, startled. It's not a state secret, but I don't talk about it, and I haven't got a clue how he would know that. "But I won't let it continue to affect my attitude."

His grumpy chin lifts. "See that it doesn't. And see the trainer about that hand."

That night, we fly to Boston, touching down in the wee hours. My ice pack has melted, and my hand still throbs. There's a bus waiting to take us to a hotel, and I'm the first to board. I turn on my phone and take a seat. Then I plaster on my don't-talk-to-me face and put in my earbuds.

My mind is static, but I open up my phone, trying to look busy and unapproachable.

I've got several texts that I'm afraid to answer. One from my mother, asking if I'm okay. Another from Gia that's probably the same.

But there's also one from Carter. And I'm not a very strong man tonight, so that's the one I click.

> Hey, Jersey. The sportsing looked hard tonight. I'm sorry.

Oof. It hadn't occurred to me that Carter might have seen that fight. Somehow that just makes it worse.

> Luckily, my job is easier than yours. I found a bed for the guestroom. (See pic below.) And I found four potential beds for you. I made a video about them. And you said it's hard to keep furniture straight, so I'm giving you LOTS of background info.

> Not to be a pest but can you pick one fairly
> quickly?

I look at the picture and see a nice white bed frame that Mom will certainly like.

> I like the guestroom pick. Go for it. Watching the
> video now.

I click Play. I was not expecting to see Carter's face in the video, but he winks into view, freckles and all.

"Hi, Jersey! This is your fun and fabulous designer reporting for duty." He makes jazz hands toward the camera. "This genius has found four different king-sized beds that fit our aesthetic, and all are available for quick delivery. I need your top two picks in case the salesperson lied, okay?"

The camera cuts to a view of Carter lying sideways across the bed in a furniture store. He makes a sweeping motion with his hand, like a gameshow host. "This is choice number one, the sleigh bed. It's called that because the headboard is curved, like a naughty Santa's sleigh."

I shock myself by barking out a laugh. My teammate in the seat in front of me cranes his neck to see what I'm laughing at.

But I don't share.

"It's very big and heavy. Makes a statement." Carter thumps a fist against his chest. "It's made in North Carolina of cherry wood. And please notice that it's higher off the floor than some choices, so if you have a habit of falling out of bed, this might not be the right one for you."

I snort, and the scene cuts to another location. This time, Carter is standing beside a stocky bed in a blond wood. He leans a knee against the mattress and makes another gameshow gesture.

"Choice number two is a captain's bed." He uses air quotes. "That's what you call this design with drawers underneath. See?" He steps aside and the camera moves to show big, deep drawers underneath the mattress. He opens a drawer and tosses his coat inside. "Great storage. Big enough to fit extra blankets, all your sportsing gear, or the dead bodies of your enemies."

I shake my head, but there's a smile practically splitting my face in half.

When the scene shifts again, Carter is holding an empty martini glass and standing in front of a grandfather clock. "Intermission! Time for a joke. Did you hear the one about the furniture store that won't stop calling me? All I wanted was *one nightstand*."

"Oh God," I whisper. "Terrible joke." But you couldn't have paid me to stop watching.

The scene switches to a closeup of Carter's face. "Okay, choice number three is a four-poster bed. The jargon is self-explanatory. See?" The camera draws back to show Carter sitting cross-legged on a different bed, this one surrounded by—wait for it—four bed posts.

He pauses to make prayer hands, like a yogi. "I don't know where this one was made, because the salesperson is more interested in taking selfies than talking to customers. But this is a classic design. Very phallic. And if you're into bondage, or you've ever had pole-dancing fantasies, this could be the bed for you." On screen, Carter hops off the bed, grabs a bed post in one hand, rolls his head back and does an absolutely filthy grind of his hips.

I laugh so suddenly that the guy across the aisle gives me a strange look.

The scene resolves again. He's lying across a handsome bed with a thick wood frame, his chin propped up in one hand.

And there's a fake rose between his teeth.

He plucks it from his mouth and then twirls it in the air. "Okay, I saved my favorite for last. This platform bed is quarter-sawn oak and made in Vermont by lumberjacks in red flannel. It has very solid joinery. You don't use a box spring with this one, so it has a firmer feel than some beds. And it's big and hunky." He shrugs. "Kind of reminds me of you." He salutes the camera. "And that's it, Jersey. Hope that was memorable enough that you'll pick one. Don't be a stranger!" He waves, and the screen goes dark.

I look up from the screen and realize I feel calm for the first time all day.

And I also realize that he called me a hunk.

Sort of.

I'll take it.

SIXTEEN

Carter

TOM GETS my video message at eleven p.m. my time.

I wait for a response.

And I wait.

I should put my phone down and close my eyes. Rigo is already asleep. But nope. I just hang out here on the sofa and wait to see if he'll respond.

It's pathetic. I don't know why I'm so invested in this client. It's not just the project, although I'm enjoying the work.

Maybe it's the hockey. I've watched more sportsing this week than ever before in my life. I don't always understand the game. But the sight of all those male bodies colliding is damn sexy. The speed. The action. The friendly butt pats. Who knew?

The fights are *not* a selling point. I don't really get it. And when Tommaso lost it at that guy tonight, I couldn't quite believe my eyes.

He looked *angry*. Like there was more at stake than a tie game. And by the time he'd finished his penalty minutes, I'd decided that he must have had a reason. Not that I'm going to ask what it was.

The truth is that I'm crazy about Tommaso. Every time we interact, I appreciate him a little more, even if I don't always understand him. There's a lot of depth to him that he's reluctant for others to see. And I can tell that he saves up his smiles for special occasions.

Which means that every time he smiles at *me*, it's like winning a prize.

I let out a sigh, and luckily there's nobody around to overhear it. Crushing on clients is dumb. And crushing on *straight* clients is twice as dumb. I know this. But I can't seem to stop checking my phone anyway.

Finally, at midnight, he replies.

> Dude, you're killing me. I needed that laugh so bad. But people on the bus were staring, so I had to wait to check into my hotel room to watch it again.

And, yup, I feel like I've won the lottery. This time it's me who hits that little video call button.

For business reasons, of course. I need to know which bed he likes best.

He answers immediately. And there's my client, shirtless, like last time.

In bed, like last time.

My foolish heart goes thumpity-thump. "Hey, Jersey. So I guess I got your attention?"

"You could say that." He slowly grins, and I've won the lottery again.

Except for one problem. "Is your lip okay? That looks painful."

He touches a knuckle to his split lip and then shrugs. "I'm just lucky it's not worse."

"So..." Oh hell. I guess I'll just go for it. "What happened there?"

He leans back against the pillow and sighs. "That guy is a dick, and his chirps got personal. He was spoiling for a fight, so I gave him one. Now my face hurts, my hand hurts, and Coach is pissed off. At least we got the win."

"Yeah." I clear my throat. "Did you, um, care for any of these beds?"

"Wait. There was furniture in that video?"

"*Dude.*"

We both laugh, and then I realize something crucial. Sure, he might just be joking, but he basically just said that he was paying too much attention to me to notice the beds.

I feel warm all over.

"Seriously, you made that fun." He tips his head back, and I can't help but notice all the muscle definition in his neck and shoulders. "It's been a *day*. And I guess I like that last one—the platform. That looked good."

"Excellent! I like that one for you. What's your second choice?"

He smirks, but it looks tired. "I can't pick the four-poster, or you'll wonder about my hobbies."

"No, I won't. I swear."

"Joking." The smirk gets bigger. "The captain one, I guess. The other two make too much of a statement, if that makes sense."

"Sure. Now what about bedding? We're replacing your quilt? No offense, but it looks like you've had it since high school."

"So what if I have? Don't judge."

I cackle. "Your frugality is commendable. And so was your taste in high school. When I was a teenager, I designed a pillow with Harry Styles's face on it."

A grin splits his beard. "I might need to see that."

"No, you don't," I say firmly. "I've grown as a designer since then. And don't ask me what I used it for."

He throws his head back and howls, and I admire his strong jaw.

Is there any embarrassing thing I won't say just to make this man laugh? Probably not. "Talk to me about colors in your bedroom."

He shakes his head. "You're the color guy."

"Yeah, but your fixation with team colors is a minefield I can't cross alone. Although the bedroom is the most private room in your house. So if you have a fetish for the wrong team's colors, nobody has to know." I wink.

He rolls his eyes. "Let's keep it simple. I've always liked navy blue. Dark green is okay, too. Not into bright patterns."

"Fair, fair. You want me to just pick stuff that I think you'll like?"

"Of course, I do. You're the one who insists on discussing this stuff." He shrugs. "And feel free to do the guestroom however you think it should be done. You can send me links if you want, but you could also surprise me."

"Good, because I found that bed at the mattress store, of all places. Don't tell *anyone* that I chose a piece of furniture from Bob's Denver Bedrooms. They'll take away my bougie card. But Bob gave us a package deal and free delivery at the end of this week."

"Hooray for Bob," my client says.

"Bob for President," I add cheerfully. "Do you have more sportsing to do tomorrow? Should I let you go?"

His smile drops again. It often does that when I mention hockey. "We'll have practice, but the game is the following day. That means downtime."

"You say 'downtime' the way other people say 'oral surgery.'"

"I know." He rubs his forehead again. "More time for the doom loop."

"Hmm. If tomorrow were my day off, I'd be googling *the best gay bars in Boston*. Then I'd get my drink on."

I expect a laugh, but his stare turns unexpectedly intense. "Getting shitfaced the night before a game is probably not a great strategy. Although it is tempting."

"Uh, good point." Way to sound like a professional. "Follow me for more wellness tips. I'm here all week."

I get another smile from him. "Your wellness tips are some of my favorites. Honest."

And now I'm all gooey inside. "I'm doing my best with what I've got. Can't make your job easier, but I can make your backside more comfortable when you come home."

He swallows roughly. "I'm starting to appreciate that."

"We all need a refuge, Tommaso. Even tough guys like you."

He nods, and now we're having a staring contest of startling intensity. His gaze is almost *heated*.

Then he *licks his lips*, and maybe I'm having a fever dream.

"I'd better go," he says quietly. "Thank you for all that you do for me."

That's not all I could do for you...

I mentally slap myself. "Take care," I say, my voice like gravel. Horny gravel.

"Good night."

We sign off, and I set my phone down and click off the designer lamp I made Rigo buy.

I lie there in the dark, heart thumping. Is there some kind of spark between us? Am I crazy?

Probably.

Nonetheless, I fall asleep wondering what it would feel like to kiss a big, strong hockey player with a carefully trimmed beard.

A guy can dream.

SEVENTEEN

Tommaso

OUR PRACTICE STARTS at noon the next day, and judging from my coach's pinched expression, I can tell he's still angry at me.

I guess I deserve that. If I were a better player, I wouldn't have let that punk rattle me.

So I pour everything into our workout, and then I scrimmage as if there will be a quiz later. But when practice ends, it's only four o'clock, and I'm faced with more free time than a guy can really use in a strange city. I play a little poker with the boys in the lobby bar, but I keep winning, and by the time I'm up four hundred bucks, the other guys get bored.

"You have the best poker face in hockey," Kapski grumbles. "How 'bout you take us out for Italian food with your winnings?"

"Sure thing."

Dinner eats up another couple of hours. Stoney tells jokes, and Newgate gets razzed for ordering the chicken at a restaurant that's famous for its pasta, because he avoids carbs.

Inevitably, Kapski asks me about the fight. "Why'd you go nuclear on that guy?"

I'm prepared for this. "Illegal hit on Stoney. Then he had the balls to brag about it. I thought he needed a proper welcome to the big leagues."

Kapski shrugs it off. After all, it is hockey.

Eventually we're back in the hotel bar, nursing beers, and guys start to turn in for the night.

Newgate takes a call from his boyfriend. "Hey, babe." He gets a soft smile on his face and drifts away from the bar.

"I might hit another bar," Stoney says to everyone and no one. "You in?"

A couple guys take him up on it, but I return to my room. It's only ten o'clock, which means ten more hours of solitude.

I sit down on the bed and check my messages.

Nothing. Not even a missive from Carter asking me to look at dish towels, or whatever.

But now I'm thinking about him. *I'd be Googling the best gay bars in Boston.* His statement had stirred me up inside, for a variety of reasons.

I can't help but picture Carter in a crowded bar, surrounded by men who find him as attractive as I do. Hell, he might be at his favorite Denver pickup spot right now. Jealousy zings through me.

Carter's life is so different from mine. I've *never* googled "best gay bars in Boston." Or St. Louis. Or Buffalo. Or any of the other places I visit in a year. Because I feel like I can't.

Hell, I *know* I can't.

Still, I open the browser on my phone, and I type the words into the search bar. Just to see how the other half lives. *Best gay bars in Boston.*

And wow. The first link is to the top *ten* gay bars in Boston. As if some of them didn't make the cut. *Ten.* Isn't that a lot? It sounds like a lot. And when I scroll, I notice that one of them is in the same neighborhood as my hotel.

I delete the tab. Then I push my phone away and do a face plant into the pillow.

There's no way I'm going to one of those bars. There's no point, because I don't want to meet a stranger, and I don't even know how to flirt.

Besides, my current obsession is a red-haired designer, and he's miles away in Colorado.

But it's weird to think that I *could* do it. There's literally nothing stopping me.

Except everything.

Three days later, the team jet touches down at the Rocky Mountain International Airport. From there, it's only fifteen miles home to Boulder. After a three-game road trip, I'm feeling every single one of them.

Can't wait to get out of this suit, but I was so eager to leave the airport that I forgot to remove my tie before I started the drive home.

I finally pull onto my street at about six p.m. A *Bob's Denver Bedrooms* truck is leaving my driveway, and my house isn't dark, like usual. It's all lit up inside. And there's a lit Christmas wreath on the front door, too.

Wow. It looks like a home now. Not an empty shell.

I ditch the car in the carport, grab my suitcase, and hasten toward the front door, which is unlocked. When I step inside, I almost don't recognize the place. The sofa has arrived, along with a leather chair. And there's a sturdy coffee table that looks vaguely familiar, too. I have a distant memory of Carter showing me a photo and saying it was made from "reclaimed hardwood," whatever that means.

At the time, I'd thought it sounded dirty.

But now—like everything else he's chosen—it looks like it belongs here in front of the fire that's crackling away behind a new iron fire screen. Ditto the tidy woodpile stacked in a metal holder beside the fireplace. And the set of fireplace tools on the opposite side.

A fire in the fireplace? My mother will love it.

I love it, too. As a matter of fact, the room looks so comfortable that I want to hurl myself at the couch and never get up again.

"Is that you, Jersey?" Carter appears in the doorway to the kitchen. He stops there, and I watch his gaze sweep me from head to toe.

His lips part softly and, in real time, I watch his cheekbones flush with color. Then his gaze goes heavy-lidded and lazy.

Oh Jesus. That *look*. It makes my body tighten. "Hi," I say stupidly.

Carter blinks and seems to snap back into his senses. "Hi," he says briskly, clapping his hands together. His words tumble out at top speed. "Nice suit. Wow. Long day, right? Sorry to be, uh, in your space, but they just delivered your mom's bed. Want to see?"

I try to take that in. "Um, yeah. Let me just get out of this suit."

Carter swallows, and his color deepens. "You go ahead and do that."

Damn, my fireplace must be good at its job, because it's suddenly about a million degrees in here. "I'll just be a minute. Would you mind if I order some dinner? Kind of starving. You want something?"

His mouth opens and closes a couple of times. "Okay, yeah. I have some things to show you anyway."

Like what? My dumb brain offers up a few very improper suggestions. "Great."

"Tell you what, I'll order something for us both," he says. "What do you want?"

You. I literally shake myself. "Um... Burgers? Chicken? I eat everything, so long as it's not too spicy. Use my credit card."

"Cool. I'll handle it." He gives me a strangely sheepish look and heads back into the kitchen.

I take a deep breath and then carry my suitcase upstairs to change.

There are more surprises up here, too. The platform bed—my favorite choice from Carter's video—stands proudly in my room. It's freshly made up with crisp sheets in a blue-and-white striped pattern. There's also a new comforter in navy-blue corduroy.

To top it off, a throw pillow is propped in the center of the bed. The color is Cougar blue, and the decorative stitching reads: EITHER YOU LIKE HOCKEY OR YOU'RE WRONG.

My shout of laughter probably shakes the house.

Still chuckling, I strip off my tie, my dress shirt, and my suit. I grab a pair of joggers out of my suitcase and pull them on. I'm just yanking a T-shirt over my head when my phone rings.

Mom Calling.

I answer immediately, of course. "Hey, Mom. Everything okay?" I squint at her image on the screen. Her hair still looks shiny, but her face is a little too thin.

"Everything is absolutely fine," she says with a smile. "Just calling to see if you'd made it home from your road trip. Your lip looks better."

"Doesn't it? I just got home. But look!" I turn the phone around. "See my new furniture? This place is really coming together."

"Wow, baby. That is nice."

"Wait until you see the living room. Hang on." I trot down the stairs and stand in the center of the room. "See? It's beautiful."

"Look at you! Furnishing that place like a grown up." My mother cackles. "I never knew you had such nice taste."

"Oh, I don't," I assure her. "But I had some help..."

"Tommaso? You want fries or mashed potatoes?"

I turn instinctively toward Carter, who's hovering in the entranceway to the kitchen. And since I'm holding my phone away from my body, my mom immediately asks, "And who is *that?*"

Fuck. I turn the phone around to face me so fast that I almost drop it.

"Who's your new friend?" my mother presses. "He's so *cute.*"

"*Mom,*" I say, startled. "Don't jump to conclusions. That's Carter, who's helping me furnish this place. It's his *job.*"

This conversation is weird. I don't like it. And I hurry upstairs again, so we can talk privately.

"Oh, honey. For a second there, I thought..."

Whoa. My blood stops circulating.

But she clears her throat and doesn't finish the sentence. That's what we do. We don't finish difficult sentences.

Even so, my heart has resumed pounding madly inside my chest. "I hired him to help me furnish this house in time for your visit. He worked late tonight."

"Oh," she says again. "That's nice."

"It is," I agree.

"You know what would be nicer?" she says with a shrug. "If you had someone waiting for you when you came home from a road trip. Someone who wasn't just a friend or a helper."

"Mom."

"What? I've learned this year that you should never wait to be happy."

"Got it," I say tightly. But I'm replaying what she's just said. The recent lack of gender-specific pronouns. First my sister, and now her? Maybe they've been discussing me. The idea makes my skin prickle.

I don't talk about my sexuality. Not to anyone. And I'm not starting now. My only move is to change the subject. "Besides nice furniture and chocolate-covered cherries, what should I be sure to have in the house for you when you visit?"

"Not a thing, baby boy." She smiles. "Groceries can be ordered. I'll bring my own tea, because I have a new favorite. I just want to see you. And meet any new friends that might be around."

I don't take the bait. "Sounds fun, Mom. I'd better go. I'm supposed to look at... I don't even know what. Lamps or fabric or something."

"Enjoy!" she says with a cheery wave. "Sounds fun!"

I disconnect. And not a moment too soon.

EIGHTEEN

Carter

I HADN'T KNOWN he'd been on a video call. I'd just been working on the dinner order.

But his mom's voice is still echoing in my head. *Who's your new friend? He is so cute.*

Something in her tone made my skin prickle with awareness. Like there was more to the question than I would have expected.

And in Tommaso's answer, too. *Don't jump to conclusions.*

I'd been listening so hard that I forgot to breathe. But then he'd run upstairs fast enough to leave a contrail.

So what did I just overhear? Why did she ask it like that?

God, it is none of my business. I don't have any right to be curious.

I place our dinner order, and then open his refrigerator to retrieve the drink ingredients I'd brought with me today. I feel a little foolish. Like I'm trying too hard, and it shows.

But it's too late now. I retrieve some ice from the freezer and make two cocktails. If he's not amused, he doesn't have to drink, right?

Plus, it gives me something to do with my hands.

I'm almost calm again by the time he enters the kitchen. He

leans against the countertop, muscles flexing beneath his form-fitting tee, his face revealing nothing.

My stomach jumps with nerves, because this guy always overwhelms me. I can't explain my reaction to him, and I can't seem to control it, either.

His dark eyes land on my cocktail shaker. "Hey, what's that?"

"Well..." I laugh awkwardly, and then bang the ice cubes around in the shaker one more time. "I had this whole plan when I realized you were going to turn up before I made it out of here tonight. I thought if I made you a cocktail, you might look at some fabric samples with me."

Those broody eyes widen. "You made me a cocktail? What kind?"

"It's, uh, a Cosmo. I meant it as a joke. You said you'd never tasted one, so..."

His beard quirks as he smiles. "Really? You're hilarious. Okay, let's do this. I feel like I'm on vacation right now. My house looks amazing, and somebody made me a pink drink."

The tight band inside my chest relaxes by a few degrees. "That was the idea. To get you good and relaxed so that I could make you think about curtains."

"Curtains?" He gives me a look of genuine horror. "What do I know from curtains?"

"Nothing, and that's fine," I say quickly. I open a cabinet and pull down two wine glasses, because he doesn't own martini glasses. Nobody's perfect. "I just need to show you some fabrics and get your opinion about window treatments."

"Window *treatments*." He pronounces it the way some people say *rat poison*. "Okay, fine. And what are we eating?" He absently pats the abs of glory, which are poorly hidden beneath a threadbare T-shirt.

"Fried chicken, mashed potatoes, and sweet-potato fries." I pour two drinks out of the shaker, and Tommaso reaches for one of them. "Hold up, Jersey. This needs a garnish."

I reach over and swat his arm away. Or at least I try to, but my fingers land on his forearm, and it's like pushing on heated steel. Awareness of him zings through my body.

Our eyes meet, and his are smoldering. But then he withdraws his hand. "A garnish, huh?"

"A *garnish*," I repeat, but it comes out with the same tone that I might use to say, *lick me all over*.

Do I need a cold drink, or what?

I hastily cut a couple of lime wedges—not my tidiest work—and then affix them to the glasses. "Cheers," I say, lifting a glass and handing it over. "Drink up, Jersey. We're talking about curtains whether it kills you or not."

"It might." But he smiles, and those dark eyes are warmer than I've ever seen them. He touches his glass to mine and then takes a sip. "Hmm."

"Tasty, right? And I promise—it won't turn you gay."

Unfortunately, I say this as he takes his second sip, and he almost chokes.

Oops. *Way to make everything more awkward*. It's my superpower.

While he recovers, I pull a stack of fabric swatches from my bag on the floor. "All right—curtains." I plop the swatches onto the counter. "They aren't very exciting. But they are useful. Your bedroom windows offer no privacy right now, so I figure you want to fix that as soon as possible."

He shrugs. "I just change in the bathroom. Problem solved."

"You are practical to a fault, and I admire that. But hear me out."

He takes another sip of his pink drink and cocks his head. "I'm listening."

"There are people who *approach you in shops*. That's cool and all, but they also post your picture on Instagram. It's dark out right now—" I point toward the windows. "—and with the lights on, anyone with eyes or a camera can see inside. I mean, there must be *something* you do outside the bathroom that you'd rather not advertise?"

And, yup, I somehow steered the conversation back to sex. Oops.

Tommaso doesn't miss it. His eyes go hot. Like, *molten*. But he doesn't say anything.

I'm so confused. Do we have chemistry? For real? Or am I just a sad, horny boy with a crush on the hot athlete?

"So..." I take a gulp of my cocktail. "I just thought you might want to put up some curtains in the living room and the bedrooms. I can pop shades into the bathroom windows, too. That's easy."

"All right," he says, clearing his throat. "Let's have some curtains. I'll choose a fabric, if I must."

"Excellent." Setting my drink down, I turn to the pile of swatches. For starters, there are eight white ones, so I lay them down in a row in preparation for explaining their differences.

But he doesn't let me. He puts a finger down on the first one—the Belgian Linen—and says, "That one."

"You barely looked!" I yelp. "And we have to consider whether you want light *filtering* or blackout..."

He puts both hands on the counter and flexes his arms. His eyes are glittering with humor, plus something dark and wild. "You *asked* me to choose a fabric. I chose a fabric. What is the problem, exactly?"

He's teasing me, and I like it way too much. "*What the fuck.*" I swipe my hand along the counter and gather the swatches into a lump. "Fine. Sure. How about this? If you can choose the same one again, I'll accept your choice without further discussion."

"Hallelujah," he mutters, reaching for the cocktail shaker. "Go ahead. Lay 'em out. I got this."

All the swatches are white, so I doubt he'll be able to pick out the same one again. But I don't like to lose, so while he's topping up my glass, I jam the Belgian Linen into the pocket of my khakis.

Then I line up the remaining seven squares of fabric. "All right, now which one did you like again?" I take a confident swig of my drink and wait.

His broad brow furrows as he examines the squares. I have to admit, this many choices is overkill. But I'd planned to show him that they all filter light a little differently...

"You dirty rat," he says suddenly. He sets his drink on the counter and squares his body toward mine. "Where is it?"

Uh-oh. I've underestimated him. And my poker face is probably terrible. "Where is what?"

"Carter." His expression turns as playful as I've ever seen it. He takes a step closer to me. "Look, I was just being a dumbass. I'll let you explain curtains to me, I swear. Just as soon as you admit that you're cheating at your own game."

I take a step backwards and struggle mightily not to glance down at my pocket. "I can't imagine what you're talking about."

"Uh-huh." He smirks. "Where is it?"

There's a big, muscular hockey player advancing on me. If I didn't know him so well, I might even be afraid. But I'm not, even though his shoulders are broad enough to blot out the sun. There's a smile playing at the corners of his mouth. It's a smile that promises vengeance...

He comes at me like a boxer, feinting as though he's about to grab me. Since he's a skilled athlete, I totally believe it.

I am not, however, a skilled athlete. So I take an immediate step backward, pressing a hand on the pocket where the illicit fabric square is hiding.

A split second later, as Tommaso lets out a victorious laugh, I realize I've been had. He lunges toward my pocket.

It's all over but the crying, but I'm having too much fun to give up so easily. I slide to the side, pressing my back against his stainless-steel refrigerator, and grab his thick wrist in a last-ditch effort to avoid capture.

"Oh no, you don't." He smirks. Then he performs the kind of ninja maneuver they probably teach at athlete school. He gathers both my hands in one smooth motion and pins them over my head.

I stop breathing, because all my favorite sexual fantasies start off just like this.

Then? He plunges his hand into my pocket to grab the linen square. Which means his thick fingers are fishing around at my inner thigh. So naturally I take a stuttering breath, as all my blood rushes south.

Lord forgive me, but all the inappropriate thoughts I've ever had about him come rushing back at once, and my hips move of their own volition to press against him.

His hand goes instantly still, his eyes flying to mine.

I expect him to recoil. But that's not what happens. Instead, he stares at me for a long beat, while his chest saws in and out with ragged breathing. His eyes go darker than I've ever seen them, and his gaze drops to my mouth.

I'm still pressed against the refrigerator, basically losing my mind. I have a bit of a kink for being manhandled, so my misbehaving dick is liking this way too much. He can almost certainly tell.

"Fuck," he whispers.

"Okay," I volunteer, because I'm not in control of my faculties.

Somehow, we're caught up in one of those tractor beams from a sci-fi movie, moving closer without knowing how or why.

Then his mouth is on mine. Or maybe mine is on his. I don't even know who moves first. But I finally know how soft his beard is, and how great his hard body feels against mine.

The first kiss is just a taste. Like dipping your toe in the water and finding it warmer and more welcoming than you'd expect.

But then he kisses me again, more urgently. My hands are still trapped overhead, so all I can do to show my approval is to part my lips against his firm ones. Our teeth click, and he grunts. The abs of glory pin me against the fridge, and his tongue sweeps into my mouth.

My body goes slack and pliant, because I can be very obedient in the right hands. And his are the right hands. One of them is holding me in place, while the other one clamps onto my hip.

I suck on his tongue, and he makes the sexiest noise I've ever heard in my life—it's a cross between a groan and a growl. I drink that noise down, and then I tilt my head again, tasting him from another delicious angle, wondering if I have enough wiggle room to grind against him. His thick shaft presses against my hip, and if I could just get a hand free I could—

His phone rings on the kitchen counter. Loudly.

Tommaso yanks himself back as if he's just received an electric shock. Before I can even blink, he's released my wrists and moved halfway across the room.

All I can do for a moment is stand there and gape at him. What just happened? And why did it have to stop?

"Fuck," he says, raising both hands to his eyes. "I'm sorry. Fuck."

"Um..." I look down at my khakis, clearly tented by my erection, as my sludgy mind wonders exactly what he's apologizing for.

That was just about the most exciting minute of the year.

I open my mouth to say so, but his expression stops me cold. His gaze is laser-beamed on my wrists, and I realize I'm rubbing them absently. There's a bit of redness where he'd gripped me. It's no big deal, but his face is such a thunderstorm that I can't speak.

His phone is howling like a banshee. He finally grabs it and checks the screen.

"I've got to take this," he says icily. "We'll talk tomorrow."

Tomorrow.

He wants me to *leave?*

My face burns as I numbly collect my wits—and my fabric samples. Tommaso is already on the phone in the living room as I shove the samples into my bag with shaking hands.

It's just dawning on me that I kissed my best client and the only person who's keeping me out of bankruptcy. And he's upset about it now.

God, I really am the worst businessman ever born.

Truly the worst.

NINETEEN

Tommaso
_____

WHAT DID I JUST DO?

What the *hell* did I just do?

This is the soundtrack in my head as I take a seat on my new sofa. My heart is pounding. My blood runs hot.

"Tommy, are you listening to me?" my sister demands.

"No," I practically growl, and she laughs as if I've said something funny.

But there is nothing funny about the sound of the backdoor closing on Carter or the shame that's coursing through me.

"Hey! You *begged* me for an idea for what to get Mom for Christmas, and I finally have one. So pay attention or I'll give it to somebody else."

I take a ragged breath. If I'd been focused on the right things—like Christmas with Mom—none of this would have happened. "All right, what is this idea?"

"She wants a weighted blanket."

"A what?"

"A weighted blanket," my sister says slowly. "It's a special kind. They're heavy and help you sleep solidly."

"She having trouble sleeping?" My blood pressure goes up another degree.

"Doesn't everybody sometimes?" my sister asks softly.

Why yes, they do. I'm probably never sleeping again. I can't believe I *kissed* him. It was tremendously inappropriate. The man is *working* for me. But it was just so fucking stupid.

I've completely come unglued.

"I can send you some links. Just don't get sticker shock," my sister says. "They're expensive, and you're cheap."

That's okay, Carter can pick one out, my brain says.

Then I want to slap myself. Carter is probably not even speaking to me right now. I didn't just kiss him. I *pinned him to a sheet of stainless steel* and *restrained* him.

I left marks on his wrists.

God, I want to die of embarrassment.

"Tommy?"

"Weighted blanket," I croak. "Got it."

"Are you okay?"

No way. "Just, uh, tired. Got home an hour ago from a road trip."

"Ah," she says. "Can I bend your brain about one more thing, though?"

"I guess."

"Look—my hairdresser says that Cousin Lisa says that Uncle Vin and Marco are trying to set up a reconciliation with you. But that you're, um, too afraid to meet up with them."

"*Afraid?*" I sputter. "What the fuck?"

"I know," she says with a sigh. "It's just smack talk. But I thought you'd want to know what they said."

I groan. "Those fuckers. I know just what to get them for Christmas—a dictionary. So they can look up the word *reconciliation.*"

Gia snorts.

"The only thing I'm *afraid of* is putting my fist through their faces again."

"What is this meeting supposed to be about?" Gia asks.

"They want to do some kind of photo shoot for an article about families in sport. A puff piece."

"And you said no?"

"My publicist thinks it would be good for my image. But I disagree. They just want to use me."

"Hmm," Gia says. "Would it help your career, though?"

"I doubt it." But the truth is I don't really know. "Did Mom hear about this?"

"She hasn't said anything. But we use the same hairdresser."

What a fucking mess this is. "Gia—be honest. Has Mom said anything to you about Marco or Vin lately? Am I making her life harder by not doing the whole kiss-and-make-up thing?"

My sister thinks before she speaks. "Mom doesn't complain."

"But is that because it doesn't matter? Or because she doesn't know what to say?"

"I honestly don't know. She probably sees Vin and Aunt Mimi at church."

"True. That's gotta be awkward."

"But Tommy? The truth is that your spat with those guys makes *my* life harder."

"Wait. Why?"

She sighs again. "Aunt Mimi and Cousin Lisa used to see Mom for lunch sometimes. They used to go to the same book group. Little things. And if you hadn't blown up with Vinny and Marco, they'd still be around. They'd be helping out, probably."

"With Mom's treatment?"

"Yeah," my sister says quietly. "Trips to the chemo unit. That kind of thing. Mom's circle is smaller than it used to be. People took sides."

I close my eyes in despair. My mother never told me she'd lost friends because of me. But I can see how that might happen.

"Look," Gia says. "I don't want to put pressure on you. But you never told us what that fight was really about. We're on your side. It's just that we don't even know what we're protesting."

I rub my forehead where a headache is already forming. "Is Mom, like, sad about it? Or worried?"

"Not that I can tell. I'm sure she wishes our family was more like a TV comedy than a bar brawl. But she doesn't blame you. She trusts you. To me, all she said was that whatever Marco did, it must have been bad."

"Shit." I sigh. "Thanks for telling me. I'll give it some more thought. I'm sorry this is your problem, too."

"You could just tell me what happened," she says.

"Yeah, I'm not doing that."

Bang bang bang. Someone pounds on my door all of a sudden. And my heart leaps.

Maybe it's Carter? Maybe he wants to yell at me, which I richly deserve. "Hey, Gia? I have to go. Thanks for the gift idea." I'm already walking toward the door. "Don't forget to send me an idea of what you want for Christmas."

"I want nothing. Bye, little brother! Be good."

If only.

She hangs up, and I fling the door open.

It's just a delivery guy, holding a big bag of food that Carter had ordered.

He didn't even get to eat it. I made that impossible for him. How am I going to look that man in the eye again?

I dig a twenty out of my pocket and tip the delivery guy.

Then I put the entire bag in the refrigerator. Because I'm no longer hungry.

Instead of eating, I go downstairs to my home gym and work out like I'm prepping for the zombie apocalypse.

Then I take a shower and dry myself off with brand-new towels that Carter chose. They're navy blue, and there's a note propped on the vanity.

Jersey—
I washed these towels for you already, so hopefully they won't bleed navy dye onto your clothes. But you might want to keep them separate for a couple more washings.

And I hope you like that decorative pillow on the bed. If you don't, just say so.

Stores don't really sell snarky hockey pillows in Cougar blue, so I made it myself.

Toodles—

Carter

Naked, I walk back into my room and grab the pillow off the bed. I run a thumb over the stitches. There's a blue-and-white patterned border, and then blue text on a white rectangle. *Either you like hockey or you're wrong.*

He *made* this? With his *hands*?

I fling myself face down onto the bed that he made up for me, feeling like the worst human in the world.

No, the third worst. But still, it's a podium finish.

TWENTY

Carter

I DRIVE to Rigo's apartment, but he's not there.

If I don't talk to someone right now, I'll die. So I open the FindMy app and locate him at the gym where we both have memberships.

My head is such a mess that I change into workout clothes and drive right over there, eventually locating my temporary roommate at a squat rack. "Can I work in?"

He blinks up at me, surprised. Then he slides out from under the bar. "Sure, pal. I'm having a shitty day. But I swear you look worse."

"Oof. Is it that obvious?" I put a modest amount of weight on it and take his place. "So what's wrong?"

"Now Buck isn't sure he'll be home for Christmas." He lets his face hang.

"Oh shit," I strain under the weight. "God, I'm sorry."

It occurs to me, though, that Buck's absence means I can probably stay a little longer with Rigo. Which might be very important, given the night I just had.

"It is what it is," Rigo says listlessly. "I knew what I was getting into by marrying a soldier. It's just that..."

"It's just what?"

"It isn't logical." He swallows hard. "But I worry more at the end of a deployment. Like maybe he'll let down his guard."

"Oh, honey. He won't. But love is kind of a damned-if-you-do, damned-if-you-don't kind of thing, isn't it?"

"Definitely," he growls as we switch places again. "Okay. Now tell me your thing."

I'm still unsettled and very confused. "You and Buck follow hockey pretty closely, right?"

"Of course." He lifts the weight.

"Has there ever been a queer player on the Cougars?"

His eyes widen. "Publicly? No way. But statistically, sure. There must have been."

As I watch him lift, I try to figure out how much I'm willing to say.

"What's up with that question?" he finally asks. "You're being weird. You rarely go to the gym, for starters."

"You either," I grumble.

"I need to believe that my husband is coming home. He's going to be ripped from all that time on an army base, so I gotta put in some effort."

I picture Tommaso's hot body pressing against mine, and I close my eyes. I did *not* imagine how hungry his kisses were, or how deeply he was into it.

But the second his phone rang, he *freaked* out.

"You're not going to pass out, are you?" Rigo asks.

"No," I insist.

"Then you're up. Lunges." He takes some weight off the bar and points at me.

We lunge and lunge until my legs are about to fall off. Rigo pulls me toward the row of treadmills and tells me to do a cooldown.

He waits until we've been trotting side by side for a couple minutes before asking, "So what the hell happened? Did your boss make a move on you?"

I gulp.

He whistles under his breath. "Jesus, really? And you didn't hit that?"

"Oh, I would have. But it was just a kiss." Although it wasn't. We practically devoured each other. "I don't think he meant to do it, because he kind of lost his mind afterward. And, God, don't mention this to *anybody*."

"I would never. Maybe he surprised himself," he suggests. "You are pretty cute. Who kissed who?"

I try to think. "It's blurry. We were tussling over some fabric samples."

"Sounds *hawt*." Rigo fans himself. "Listening to you talk about thread counts could make a man lose his mind."

"You shut up."

He snickers. "I'm only sort of joking. It sounds like you've made a real effort for this client. Going out of your way to accommodate him. Making it fun."

"I make a real effort for *all* my clients," I insist. "You have to meet them where they are. And Jersey doesn't like to talk about fabrics, so sometimes I have to make a game out of it."

"Hmm," Rigo says. "Do you have cute little nicknames for all your clients, too?"

I sigh.

"Before tonight, did you ever get that vibe off him?" Rigo asks.

That's the twenty-thousand-dollar question. "I *thought* I did, once or twice. But I also thought it might be wishful thinking."

Be careful what you wish for. I'd thrown myself at that man, and I might have cost myself the best job I've had all year.

"Look," Rigo says, punching the stop button on his treadmill. "I like him, too. But if he panicked, that's not a good sign."

"I know," I groan. "I hope he doesn't fire me."

Rigo cringes. "Don't let it fester. Let him calm down overnight, then tomorrow you could clear the air."

"That's good advice," I say, stepping off the treadmill. "I can own my part in this." After all, an hour ago I was grinding against him. It's not the first time in my life I chose sex over caution. But it ought to be the last. "I can save our working relationship. I can be calm and professional."

"I know you can," Rigo says soothingly. "It might be okay."

"It will," I insist. "I'll be the most professional designer in the metro area."

"Starting tomorrow, though. I'm going to get you drunk first."

"Oh good," I say quickly. "I accept."

Things are looking better already.

My improved mood lasts about twelve hours, but in the morning, two things happen to test my new cool, professional demeanor.

The first is that I wake up so sore that I can barely hobble around Rigo's tiny apartment.

The second is that Tommaso DiCosta deposits twelve thousand dollars into my bank account. That's the entire payout for the rest of my work for him, per our contract. And I nearly lose my mind.

There's nobody around to listen to my rant except Walter, Rigo's cat. "Oh no he doesn't!" I hiss at Walter. "The man is trying to *fire* me over a kiss that he initiated?"

The cat looks at me disdainfully.

"Fine, that part is still blurry. But isn't he even going to give me a chance to explain myself? Or apologize? That's ridiculous. It's cruel, is what it is."

The cat doesn't seem to care, so I do the only reasonable thing. I get dressed in my tightest jeans and my best gingham dress shirt—the blue one—and then I drive over to Tommaso's house and bang on the door.

I wait. It's a lot like my first visit here. I'm wondering whether he'll answer the door, and I'm also wondering if he'll be a dick if or when he does answer it.

This time, I don't peer through the window. I don't want to see the abs of glory. I'm going to stay in my lane. I'll be a professional even if it kills me.

Just when I think he's going to blow me off, the door opens, and there he is, filling the doorway with his sexy, broad shoulders and his glowering face. Although today his expression is more of a sheepish glower.

I match it with my own grumpy face. "Are you going to invite me in?"

After a brief hesitation, he opens the door wider and steps back.

I stride into the room and start right in. "Are you firing me?" I demand. "Did you pay me out so you didn't have to see me again?"

"No," he says with a deep frown. "I paid you out so that you wouldn't have to come back and work for the guy who—" He snaps his jaws shut.

"—kissed the hell out of me?" I fling my arms wide. "Can't you even say it?"

"That's only one way to put it," he growls. "I *restrained* you. It was practically a hostage situation."

Ah. I think about that for a second. And, sure, it had been a very aggressive kiss. The best kind. "Sure, fine. You have some very toppy energy. But I happen to like it that way."

His eyes flare. And then he closes them and exhales. "Still, it's not in our contract, right?"

Then let's renegotiate, my evil brain suggests. "It was the best sixty seconds of my month until you practically flung yourself out the window afterwards."

The glower returns. "You can't possibly take this personally. I'm obviously attracted to you. Which is a huge problem for me. I can't, uh, handle that right now."

"Handle what? Kissing?" I press, because I'm in a mood.

"*You*," he says firmly. "Or anyone."

"Oh." My anger deflates. "You are so confusing."

"I'm sure that's true," he says, looking everywhere but at me. "Look, I didn't pay you as some kind of brushoff. I did it because you told me your last client took advantage of you. And I didn't want to be that kind of client."

"*Oh.*" My face begins its telltale burn. Who's the asshole now? Yup, it's me. "Well, I appreciate that."

He blows out a breath. "I'm sorry to be such a mess of a human. I'll do better."

There's something about the way he says this that makes me sad. Because it sounds like something I'd say. "It's fine. Really. I'm a pretty messy human right now, too."

He hits me with his chocolate-brown gaze. "You're not messy at all. You know *exactly* who you're supposed to be, and you don't care who sees it."

"Oh, Jersey." My heart sags. "I'll take that compliment. But my professional demeanor needs a little work."

He crosses strong arms across his wide chest. "We can agree to disagree. I think it looks pretty good on you. Just putting that out there. And then we'll never speak of this again."

I smile, because this bit of praise lights me up inside. I *like* him, damn it. All two hundred grumpy pounds of him. And it's a problem. "Look, I want to finish this job. I'm not a quitter. But if you need me to dial back our interaction a little, I can live with that."

He rubs the back of his neck like he's uncomfortable. "I don't want to tell you how to do your job. But I find you very distracting."

Tommaso DiCosta finds *me* distracting? I file that away to think about later. "Tell you what. I'll make most of my visits when you're out. I have a lot of shopping to do, anyway. We'll be fine."

"Okay." He clears his throat. "And I'll try to act a little less like the crazy person that I am."

Well, shit.

He picks up a gym bag and shoulders the strap. "And now I have to get to practice. Sorry to cut this meeting short."

"Okay. Well." I make myself turn toward the door and step outside. He follows and locks the door. "You have a nice day. I guess I'm going to shop for lamps. Bedding for your mother. Towels for the downstairs bathroom. And, uh, curtain fabric."

He goes still at the mention of the curtains. When I glance at him, he's blushing furiously. "Just pick any fabric," he says tightly.

"Maybe that light-filtering kind you mentioned. I haven't lived here in the summertime yet. It's probably pretty bright."

"*Yessir.*" The soft word slips out in a bedroom voice, because my professionalism is a work in progress.

"Carter," he growls.

"Sorry, sorry." I take a breath. "I'll handle the window treatments. We'll never discuss curtains again."

"Thank you. 'Cause I clearly can't handle it."

I snort out an awkward laugh.

"But Carter?"

"Yeah?"

He looks over his shoulder and once again those dark brown eyes destroy me. "That pillow? Incredible. Can't believe you *made* it. I love it. And when I show it to my mom, she'll flip."

Warmth blooms inside my chest. "Thank you. Something to do with my hands when Rigo puts on the hockey game."

"Well, it's really cool. So, uh, thanks."

We stare at each other again. *Oops.* I know I should stop. It's just that I really like his face.

Luckily, this heady moment is interrupted by a shout. "Hey, DiCosta."

We both turn to see a guy in a Cougars jacket trotting across the street. Thanks to Rigo's hockey habit, I recognize Hudson Newgate.

"Sorry to ask," Newgate says as he approaches. "But is there any chance I could catch a lift to the rink? My battery is dead."

"Sure," Tommaso says. "You want a jump, though?"

Newgate shakes his head. "Already tried."

"Okay, let's go."

We head off the porch, and when we reach the street, Newgate greets me. "Hi there," he says. "I'm Hudson Newgate." He thrusts out a hand.

"Hi," I say stiffly. But then I offer my hand, because you never know when you're going to meet a client. "I'm Carter, the interior designer."

His eyes widen. "*Really.* DiCosta is going upscale?"

Tommaso rolls his eyes. "I don't know shit about furniture. Carter does. Now my place looks amazing."

"You gonna have us over to see it?" Newgate asks. "That would be fun."

"After the holidays, sure." Tommaso turns to me with a two-finger salute. "I'll catch up with you later?"

"Of course. Have a nice day at the office."

A little smile forms at the corners of his mouth, and then he turns away. I watch them go, conflicted.

I came here spoiling for a fight. I wanted to hash it out.

Obviously, he wants to smooth it over and pretend it never happened.

So I guess that's what we're going to do.

TWENTY-ONE

Tommaso

ON THE WAY to the practice facility, I'm lost inside my head.

It's a blessing that Carter turned up on my doorstep this morning, because I hadn't known what to say to him, and I'd been doomed to brood about it all day long.

Still, I almost didn't survive the encounter. Finding an indignant Carter on my doorstep—his hair shining in the morning sunlight, face flushed and animated, eyes flashing—made me want to kiss the hell out of him all over again.

I like it that way, he'd said. *The best sixty seconds of my month.*

Yeah? Well, it had been the best sixty seconds of my *life*. But he can never know that.

"You okay?" Newgate asks me from the passenger's seat, and I realize I haven't said a word for five minutes.

"God, sorry. I'm such an asshole," I say immediately.

He laughs. "Not really, but I can tell you've got a lot on your mind."

"It's really loud inside my head. And I can't say I'm dealing with it very well."

"Huh. You know what? I used to be like you."

The hair stands up on my arms. "What? What do you mean?"

"I used to churn on the shit that bothered me. Kept myself up at night."

"Oh." I relax a few degrees. "So what did you do about it?"

"Nothing." He snickers. "I wore a groove around the same bull-shit for years. But then I met Gavin. He more or less told me that we couldn't be together until I figured out how to process some of my own crap. So I did that, and life got better."

"Oh," I say again. I'm a brilliant conversationalist today.

"You got a lot going on," he says. "Coach is pissed off at you. And moving is hard, right?"

"Yeah. Very hard," I lie.

Last night the only *very hard* thing in my life had been in my shorts.

Luckily, it's a short drive to our rink, and we get there without any further issues. It's game night, so we have a brief skate and a video meeting. Coach Powers spends most of the meeting picking apart Vancouver's offense in preparation for tonight. But then he touches briefly upon our next few opponents.

When I see Trenton's red jerseys appear, I get heartburn imme-diately.

I'm not the only one, either. Robbie Hessler, another defense-man, lets out a groan. Then he elbows me. "You'd better not be injured this time. I need your sharp elbows against those goons."

"Not a problem," I mumble.

Except it is. Every time we have to play that team, I have a week's worth of high anxiety beforehand. For good reason. Marco will spend the game trying to get me to fight him. And I'll spend the game avoiding it.

Last year, we avoided the typical showdown, because Marco had some kind of injury that kept him off the ice for our first matchup. Then, later in the season, I had a shoulder injury that kept me off for two games, and when Coach Powers somehow extended it to three, I was a scratch for the second Trenton game.

When I'd asked Coach about it, he'd said, "I want you rested."

Although he might have meant, "I want to keep you out of the gossip blogs."

I guess I'll never know.

But our first Trenton game is coming up fast. And seeing Marco's ugly face on the screen at the front of the room isn't doing anything for my attitude right now.

The video session finally ends, and I push back my chair.

"Five more minutes, guys," Coach says. "Tate needs a word."

The PR guy comes strutting up to the podium and sets a shopping bag on it. "Hey, kids. Three things."

I hold back a sigh.

"First, let's have those RSVPs for the black-tie events. Second, we're doing a gift-wrapping party on the eighteenth. This year we broke our own record and purchased four hundred gifts for homeless children in Colorado. But those gifts need wrapping. Five o'clock right here in the building, okay? Wives, girlfriends, *and* boyfriends are encouraged to help out."

"What about kids?" someone asks.

"If they can wrap, I want 'em." Tate reaches into the shopping bag. "Last thing—a quick vote. We've got two possible designs for the new Pride jerseys. These will be available to fans beginning immediately after Newgate's announcement. Here's the first one." He shakes out a blue jersey with a printed logo on the front.

And I stare.

It's... Wow. There's no getting around it. The jersey is *hideous*. The cougar has been redone in an anime style that ought to look cool, but Tate must have hired a discount illustrator. Because it's awful. The cat looks like a baby bunny with a rainbow between its claws.

"What's, um, the other one?" Newgate asks.

With a white-toothed grin, Tate pulls another jersey out of the bag. Unfortunately, it's the same bad styling but in a different pose, and this time they've splashed the whole logo in pastel rainbows.

The room is silent. Nobody wants to say it. Least of all me. This has nothing to do with me. And I don't care about things like jersey designs. I never have.

But Jesus Christ. Does Tate have eyes?

I raise my hand. Then I lower it again. Because this isn't my circus. These aren't my monkeys.

Fuck it. I can almost hear Carter's groan in my head when I look at that logo. I raise my hand again. "Tate, I don't know, man. Those designs are kind of an insult to my eyes."

The whole room snickers.

"DiCosta?" Tate snaps. "Why is it always *you* who has a problem with this particular event I'm planning?"

Every player in the room turns to look at me, and so does Coach.

Fuck. "Look, I'll wear whatever jersey you hang in my stall. But those logos are ridiculous. I don't think that's what queer hockey fans see when they close their eyes at night."

Tate drops the jersey on the podium and stalks in my direction. "Have you even *met* a queer hockey fan?"

"Yeah," I say quickly. "I have." *And you're looking at one, buddy.*

Tate looks like he wants to kick me in the nuts. But then Newgate speaks up. "I'm with DiCosta on this. Some people might see that logo as too different. Maybe even insulting. Can't we have the regular cougar on, say, a tie-dye jersey?"

"Yeah, *that*," I agree. "Just make that."

"Anybody else agree?" Newgate asks.

A room full of hockey players raises their hands.

Tate gives me a look that's meant to incinerate me. "Fine. Okay." He shoves both jerseys back in the bag. "Your opinions are noted."

He stomps out of the room.

I could have just kept my mouth shut, I guess. But lately I'm no good at that anymore.

We win that night, and I don't disgrace myself.

When I get home, though, my house is pitch dark, and it makes me feel a little depressed.

Worse, there's a set of papers on the new coffee table for me. Carter's made a carefully annotated print-out of every penny he's charged to my credit card, and the letter that accompanies it says, *Dear Mr. DiCosta*.

Not *Hey Jersey*. Not even *Tommaso*.

There's no video. No jokes. Just a stilted note asking me to approve another list of upcoming purchases, including guest-bath towels and a shower curtain. The guest quarters also need throw rugs, bedding, and a chair. Both bedrooms need dressers and bedside tables. He's planning lamps for every room of the house.

There are questions at the bottom.

What about wall decor? It should be something meaningful to you.

I glance up and realize that my walls are bare. I don't have cute family photos the way some other guys do. I don't even have a potted plant.

The last question he's asked me is about the screened-in back porch.

Do you want deck furniture? I mentioned it once, and you said we'd talk about it later. But I haven't pressed you. It's not that useful in December, but I could order it for you at any point. Just let me know.
Sincerely,
C. Flynn

The formal sign-off makes me feel salty. But he makes a good point. When the warm weather comes, I'll want to go outside, and a normal guy would use the deck to have a couple of friends over.

Normal. Carter said he hated that word. And I've never been a very normal guy. Or a very social one. I've always felt like I had to keep my guard up. There are people in my life who made sure I felt that way, and I really never questioned it.

Okay, this is a lot of overthinking about deck chairs.

I grab the pen Carter left and get to work on my reply.

Dear Carter,

I'm sure you're right about all this stuff. Honestly, I don't know why you'd put wallpaper up in the guestroom, but if you say it needs it, then do what you have to do.

Don't forget about Christmas decorations, though. Mom loves Christmas. I'm really looking forward to getting a tree.

Deck chairs—yes. Why not. Come summer I'm sure I'll appreciate it.

As always, thank you for your help,
Tommaso
P.S. Do you know where I should look to buy my mom a weighted blanket for Christmas? All suggestions appreciated.

I leave our sad little communications on the table and take myself up to bed.

TWENTY-TWO

Carter

LISTEN, *bitches. I am a very good designer.*

These are my thoughts as I step back to admire Tommaso's guestroom.

It's been seven days since I've set eyes on my client, but his guestroom looks *smashing*. I've papered one wall in a stormy, desaturated blue, printed with a life-size lattice of birch branches which "grow" toward the ceiling. It's very organic and soothing.

I've pushed the new bed—with its white headboard—up against the birch wall. And I've ordered bedding in whites and faded blues.

When I'm done, it will be striking, yet cozy. Interesting, but not weird. And it fits the rustic, masculine vibe of the house.

I can't wait for Tommaso to see it. Not that I'll be here when he does.

After a glance at the time, I gather my wallpaper supplies and clean up. Tommaso usually comes home from practice around two, and it's already noon.

Time to hustle. The new, professional me is *never* here when my client returns from a hard day of sportsing. Tommaso didn't ask me to stay out of his sight, but that's what I've done. It's for my sake more than his.

I haven't sent any cute texts or called him by a nickname. There haven't been any silly videos. Or pink cocktails or late-night video calls.

Hitting the reset button on our relationship has been good for me. A lack of professionalism always gets me into trouble. I needed to remember that I'm capable of behaving like a grownup.

It's boring, though. Every time I see something funny in a store or a catalog, I'm so tempted to tell him about it or take a silly photo and send it to him.

I miss him. It's a problem.

On the bright side, I've used my big paycheck to pay down my credit-card bill and catch up on my student loans. I also set aside a few thousand dollars to secure a lease on a new apartment, and I've begun calling landlords.

Except they keep saying the same thing. *There's nothing coming open until after the New Year. But we'll call you if that changes.*

Something will come up, though. It only takes one. And Rigo knows I'm trying to get off his sofa.

"Don't stress," he told me last night. "Honestly, I shouldn't be alone right now. Another holiday without Buck is depressing."

Just to make sure that I'm not wearing out my welcome, I made him my famous chili with Fritos for dinner last night. We ate it in front of the hockey game, of course. I was very professional about that, too. I only moaned *one* time. It was when Tommaso licked a drop of Gatorade off his lip as the camera did a closeup on his sweaty face.

And then last night I woke up from a *really* sexy dream. A toppy, bearded man had been sucking me off on a charcoal-gray sofa with slate-and-plum-colored boucle throw pillows.

My sex fantasies have highly specific settings. It's an occupational hazard.

When I woke up this morning, I ordered Tommaso some plum-colored boucle throw pillows.

But that's neither here nor there.

I know I shouldn't be dreaming about my client, but as long as I keep those thoughts to myself it's fine, right?

Right.

I spend the afternoon dropping by two different apartment complexes and putting in applications. Because you never know. I apply for a part-time job in the design department of one of my favorite furniture stores, even though I'm overqualified. It doesn't pay that well, but a regular paycheck would reduce my stress.

"We won't have anything until after the New Year," the manager says. "But I'll hang onto your resumé."

"Got it," I say with a patient smile. "If something comes up, think of me!"

I'm on the right track. I just have to have faith.

When I return to Rigo's place, he's not home yet. I sit at the little kitchen table and send off some emails to former clients, letting them know that I have availability in January.

I don't look up until a key rattles in the lock. I snap my laptop shut and prepare to tell Rigo all about the major-league adulting I've done today.

But when the door swings open, it's not Rigo standing there.

It's Buck, in head-to-toe camouflage, with a rucksack on his shoulder and a broad grin on his face. "Guess who found a flight home, baby!"

Our eyes meet, and we both freeze. "Buck!" I say after I find my voice. "Wow, Rigo is going to be over the moon!"

He swings the bag onto the floor and grins. "Hey, Carter! Rigo mentioned you were staying here for a while. How's life?"

"It's great!" I say, popping off the kitchen chair as if it were on fire. "Actually, I was just leaving. Rigo is going to be so happy that you made it home before Christmas."

"I got so lucky! But you don't have to run off just yet."

"Actually, I do." So you can get *so lucky* again. "I have somewhere to be."

He doesn't question it. "Where's my guy, anyway?"

"A painting job in Centennial. He's probably stuck in traffic on 25. Want me to check? You could surprise him."

His face lights up. "Yeah! Ask him what he wants from the burrito shop. I've been dreaming about Mexican food for months."

"On it." I pull out my phone and text Rigo, telling him I'm going to treat for dinner and asking how far away he is.

RIGO

Ooh! I'm fifteen minutes out. Get me the chicken enchiladas but you don't have to buy.

"Fifteen minutes," Buck says with a huge smile. "I can't *believe* it. I'm gonna hit the shower."

My heart trembles for both of them. As soon as Buck disappears, I start ferrying my belongings out of the living room and into my car. It's just dawning on me that I'll have to go to a hotel tonight.

There are a couple weeks left of December, and if I can't find a new place to live before New Year's, even a cheap hotel will eat up my savings.

Nevertheless, I smile at Buck when he reappears in fresh jeans and a Cougars hoodie. "Got a minute to carry my sewing machine downstairs?"

"Sure." He frowns. "But why are we moving your sewing machine? I don't want to chase you off."

"You're not. I'm going to a client's house first thing tomorrow to hem his curtains." I don't add that I won't be back. There's no need to make Buck feel bad about this. "Rigo is due any minute, too. Wouldn't it be cool if you were standing in his parking spot when he pulled in?"

"Hell yes." He grabs my sewing machine by the handle. "Let's do this."

It's snowing lightly as Buck loads the machine into my car. "Anything else you need?"

"Nope. I'm all set. And look!"

He turns his head to see Rigo's pickup pull into the lot. "Aw yeah!" His smile is so wide that it's probably visible from space. "I've been dreaming about this for weeks."

The lump in my throat makes it difficult to speak. "Go get your man."

"I'm going to make a proper entrance," he says, stepping behind a neighboring Jeep to conceal himself.

After getting in my car, I start the engine and carefully back out of my spot.

But I can't make myself pull away yet. I roll down the window and watch, because it's not every day I get to see a love story play out in front of my eyes.

Rigo takes a moment to get out of his truck and retrieve his bag from the backseat.

"Excuse me, sir." Buck steps out from behind the parked Jeep. "You look familiar."

Rigo freezes at the sound of his husband's voice. Then his work bag falls to the asphalt, and he covers his mouth with both hands.

I stop breathing as he slowly turns around.

His face when he spots Buck—I've never seen so much love and relief in one place before in my life. He *runs* toward his husband. They both run. Buck catches Rigo, and my friend throws his arms around the bigger man's body. Buck lifts him off the ground.

In the history of hugs, there has never been one quite so exuberant. As if those two could extinguish the time and space between them by perfecting their embrace. Rigo's back heaves, and Buck clamps a hand to the back of his neck. Snow falls gently into their hair, and they don't notice.

My eyes are burning, and I finally remember to breathe.

Someday I want a hug like that.

Just one.

I drive away and leave them to it.

Several hours later, I'm sitting in bed, counting down the hours until daybreak.

Well, I'm sitting *on* a bed. Not in it. I'm too skeeved out by the Happy Hours hotel to pull the musty bedspread over my body. I'm lying on the top sheet, fully clothed, including my shoes.

One of the occupational hazards of interior design is mentally redecorating every room I enter. I'm a talented guy, but I could never make this place beautiful. Not with these low ceilings. And not with the cloud of despair that permeates the place like mildew.

I've left the ugly gray drapes open, so I can see my ancient car. My whole life is inside it, and if someone decides to break in, I'll...

Actually, I don't know what I'd do, except call 911 and panic. This place costs less than a hundred dollars a night, but it's terrifying. I witnessed a drug deal while I was unlocking the room's flimsy door.

Tomorrow I'll have to find something a little less squalid. But after you include hotel taxes, a reasonable room costs at least a hundred fifty dollars, and a few weeks at that rate will empty my savings. If that happens, Montana is my only option.

Bye bye, Colorado. Bye bye, entrepreneurship.

If I think too hard about it, I'll cry. Instead, I sit up late reading reviews of weighted blankets, so Tommaso's mother can get the very best one for Christmas.

I compose an email with my top three picks. The hotel Wi-Fi barely functions, so I end up ditching my laptop and sending a text instead.

I lean back against the headboard and try to drowse. Someone is yelling drunkenly in the parking lot. Loudly. I can't make out the words, but there's violence in them.

Dear Lord in heaven, I pray. *If this is a test, I hope to pass. But maybe this is a hint that I need to go home to Montana and regroup.*

Is that it?

Hmm.

I know you're under no obligation to give me what I want. Or to make it easy. But I am a little confused. I'm listening. I will accept what's coming to me. But if you want me to buckle down and try a little harder, just send me a sign.

I open my eyes, and my phone rings.

TWENTY-THREE

Tommaso

OH, for fuck's sake. I can't believe I did it *again*. I was trying to click through the link Carter sent me. But I guess my big finger hit that little video button.

I hear the chiming sound of a video call connecting, and suddenly Carter and I are blinking at each other in the dark, each of us illuminated only by the light of our phones.

But it's enough. For the first time in a week, I see those calm blue eyes and drink him in.

"Hi," he says. "What are you doing up?"

"Uh, sorry." I put a hand over my face. "I was trying to click on one of the blankets you sent me, and I..."

"Called me instead?" His eyes twinkle.

"Seems so. Yup."

A tentative smile blooms on his irresistible face, and somehow it fills all the empty spaces inside my chest. "Doesn't matter. I was up, too."

"I appreciate the blanket research. I'd never heard of this thing before now. But my sister insists it's the right gift."

He shrugs. "People swear by them. I haven't tried one. Never had any trouble sleeping until lately."

"You too, huh?"

He frowns. "Look, I know I'm not supposed to ask. But are you okay? Last time we saw each other, you seemed a little strung out."

I scrub a hand over my face again. "I'll survive. Did you ever have a time when you just can't seem to get right with the world? Like everything you try is wrong?"

"Yup. That sounds pretty familiar." Carter starts to say more, but then he startles like he's heard a loud noise, and he focuses on something beyond his phone.

"Everything okay? Where are you?" He's leaning against an unfamiliar headboard. "Did you find a new place?"

"I'm, um, staying with friends," he says. "But this isn't a great neighborhood. The street noise keeps me on edge."

Oh hell. He's up late, because he's *scared*. "Is the door locked nice and tight?"

"Sure is!" he says quickly. "No problems there."

"Well, good. We should both put our phones down and try to sleep. But let me just say one thing."

"What?" he asks, tipping his head to look right at me. "I'm listening. Sleep is overrated."

"I gave two different teammates your contact information this week. They'll probably just hand it over to their wives, but you might get a call."

His blue eyes widen. "Oh, wow. Thank you."

"It's the least I could do. Thanks for being so good to me even when I've been..." I have to take a breath just to get the rest of the sentence out. "...a damn mess, and the worst client ever."

"*Jersey*." He shakes his head. "I don't know what you're going through, exactly. But if you want to be the worst client, you've got to try a little harder to be an asshole. You're not even top five at this point."

I snort. "That's good to hear."

His eyes dip. "I know I'm not supposed to say this, but I really like you. A lot. And if circumstances were different, I'd show you just how much."

145

For a moment, I forget to breathe. Nobody says things like that to me.

"Anyway." He rolls his shoulders, as if he's suddenly self-conscious. "Just thought I'd say that, since we don't see much of each other anymore. You're going to Arizona tomorrow, right?"

"That's right," I manage.

"Cool. I'll get some work done at your place while you're gone. You have a good game, okay? I haven't forgotten about your Christmas tree, by the way. I just need to get the curtains up first."

The damn curtains. I don't even want them. Every time I look at that white fabric, I'll be tasting his kiss.

"Good night, Jersey," he says softly.

"'Night, Montana," I say quietly.

Then I make myself hang up.

TWENTY-FOUR

Carter

AT DAWN, after a very uncomfortable night, I take a shower in the ugly little bathroom, and then I get the hell out of that hotel.

In my car, I pass Starbucks with a longing glance, opting for a fast-food breakfast sandwich and low-budget coffee. I take a seat at a table and open up my laptop. The stores don't open for another few hours, but there's always internet shopping.

Today I'm focused on lighting. Asking for Tommaso's opinion still yields mixed results, but I try, nonetheless.

CARTER

Which of these lamps do you prefer?

TOMMASO

Lamps? I thought I had enough lights?

You have almost none, unless you're counting the ceiling fixtures. And I'm not. Life is more beautiful with good lighting. So please click and pick.

How about you choose instead? I'm getting ready for a day of sportsing.

His quick answer makes me smile. I picture him sitting on the end of the bed I found him, drinking a cup of coffee. And it makes me happy to imagine him in a comfortable space that I designed.

> Okay. Cool. But when we're sitting on the couch after sportsing, reading our sportsing magazines, do we care if the lamp beside us has a dimmer switch?

We don't care as long as the beer is cold.

> Noted. Good news—there's going to be a side table to rest that beer on. It has a wood finish. So I'd better find you a coaster for under that beer, unless you have coasters?

I do not. My rental apartment furniture was made of something plasticky and indestructible.

> Sounds tragic.

It held my beer up off the floor tho. [Shrugging emoji]

This is as chatty as he's been since our strange adventure against the refrigerator. So of course, I can't resist teasing him.

> We learn. We grow. One of these days you'll walk into a friend's house and think—OMG that paint color looks like piss. Don't these people have eyes? And the moment you form this thought, somewhere a little gay unicorn will get its wings.

LOL! Don't make me laugh, my ribs are bruised.

> Wow. Does that happen a lot?

Of course. But the trainer will tape me up before the game tonight.

> And you think my job is weird?

Dude, I'd take bruised ribs over a trip to the mall any day of the week.

After sending the emoji with a hand in front of its eyes, I stop texting, even though it's fun.

Because I'm a professional, damn it. Even if I'm technically homeless. Even if my office is at a table at McDonald's.

After breakfast, I make some more calls to landlords, but the only units for immediate occupancy are the ones that I could never afford.

I turn to Craigslist, which I've already combed for reasonable situations, and for one heart-stopping moment I think I've spotted a prime new listing for a studio apartment in my price range.

Until I notice the phrase, *In a 55+ community*.

After briefly contemplating a gray-haired disguise, I realize that they'd probably check my ID. So that's a no-go.

Luckily, my afternoon is more productive. With Tommaso safely on his way to Arizona, I let myself into his house and set up my sewing machine on his dining table. It's time to hem the curtains.

I'm so sleepy, that a couple of times I put my head down on the table and doze.

Meanwhile, snow falls in fat flakes outside the window. I keep the thermostat low, because I don't want to run up Tommaso's heating bill. As the evening fades into night, I eat the sandwich I'd bought on my way over here and contemplate my options.

Rigo has texted to ask where I am and to offer his sofa.

I politely decline. He and Buck need their privacy. Rigo once told me that after a deployment, it takes work to get back into the swing of being a couple. Togetherness is important to them, and I'd never want to get in their way.

I have other friends in the area, but none so close that I feel comfortable asking to crash on their sofa.

More curtains, then. I can just keep going. In fact, I could take a catnap and then hem the curtains until dawn! I can pull an all-nighter and then drive to the gym at dawn for a shower.

It's not the same thing as crashing in an unwitting client's home, right? I'd be working. That's what he's paid me for.

Problem solved.

I switch off the overhead light to give my eyes a break. And then I stretch out on the floor, taking care to set an alarm for thirty minutes of shuteye.

All I need is a power nap, and then I can hem curtains all night. Like a professional does.

TWENTY-FIVE

Tommaso

THE SNOW IS FALLING fast by the time I make it back to Boulder. Even with the plows out on the roads, the drive is slow. When I finally reach Red Rock Circle, it's two thirty in the morning.

I slide my key in the lock and step inside. After shutting the door and dropping my bag, I take a breath of semi-chilly air. My house feels cold, because I always turn down the thermostat when I leave.

When I flip on the overhead light, I think of Carter. *Life is more beautiful with good lighting*, he insists. So it must be true.

Smiling, I take another step inside.

And there's Carter, sprawled out *on the floor*, face down on the rug.

He's *collapsed? Oh, Jesus.*

I'm on my knees a second later. "Carter?" I shake him gently. "*Carter.*"

His eyes fly open, and he sits up with a gasp. "Huh? What?"

"Are you okay?" I demand, sitting back on my heels. "Did you pass out? Are you sick?" My heart is still pounding from the sight of him lifeless on the floor. As if I'd stepped into an episode of *Law & Order*.

He scrubs his face. "No! I'm fine. I was just...exhausted. I meant to take a catnap and then finish the curtains. And I thought you were in Arizona?" He squints at me.

"I was. The flight is only an hour and a half, so we do it as an out-and-back."

"Shit." Carter buries his face in his hands. "So unprofessional. Again." He staggers to his feet. "Sorry. I'm going."

"Where?" I demand. He looks half asleep and dead tired. The rug has made a pattern on his face. But it doesn't stop me from cataloguing all the things I've missed about him. The pouty lips are looking extra pouty tonight. And the freckles on his nose stand out against his pale skin.

He's here in my living room, and I'm so happy to see him.

"Uh...I'll go to a hotel. Or something," he mumbles, lurching toward the dining table and grabbing his phone. Then he curses and picks up an empty paper coffee cup and a sandwich wrapper. "Sorry about the mess. That should be my tagline," he mutters.

"Carter." I rise to argue, but he scurries into the kitchen, and I hear the sound of the trash drawer opening. "*Carter*," I repeat as he reappears. "Take a breath. Why would you go to a hotel?"

His eyes narrow at me. "It's a thing people do when they need to sleep."

"Sit down a second," I order.

Miraculously, he does. He lands heavily in a dining chair and blinks up at me with tired eyes.

I can't help myself. I put my hand on his messy head and smooth his hair back. It's just as soft as I've always imagined. Then I give his shoulder a squeeze. "You look wrecked, Montana. When's the last time you had a really good night's sleep?"

He shrugs. "I'm getting by."

"That's not what I asked. Why aren't you staying at Rigo's?"

"Buck came home." He sighs. "Just showed up, with his fatigues and his rucksack, like a returning hero. Rigo *cried*. I've never seen two happier people in my life. So I got the hell out of there. Spent last night in a really sleazy hotel. But I could go to a better one..."

For some reason, the words of that woman from Kathy's

Kitchens jump into my head. *That boy could use a break.* I hadn't really understood how close to the brink Carter was. He hadn't wanted me to know, and I totally understand why.

But now I'm onto him. And I care too much to let him piss away his salary on a pricey hotel where he won't be afraid to go to sleep. "Look, it's almost three in the morning. I think you should tuck yourself into the guestroom and regroup tomorrow."

His eyes take a longing glance toward the back of the house. "I couldn't do that. I'm not a charity case."

"Nobody said you were." I cross to the thermostat and crank it up. "But I also know you've been avoiding this place when I'm not on the road, and that's an inconvenience. What if you just stayed here for a little while? It would make your job easier. Just a week or two."

He looks up at me with an expression so raw that I can see all the way into his overwhelmed soul. "Tommaso, I'm pretty sure I'm the *last* person you want lurking around your house. I make you uncomfortable. And what would your mother think?"

I take a slow breath. Honestly, that question makes my heart race. It always has. "We'll deal with that question later."

He gapes at me. "Tommaso, I can't—"

"Look," I interrupt. "I know you're hellbent on bringing your business back from the ashes. And it's none of my business how you get there. But I consider you a friend, and friends don't let friends drive off in a blizzard and blow their savings at the Best Western. That's how it is."

He stares at me for a long beat. "I really appreciate that. And I'll stay here tonight. But if you change your mind tomorrow, I'll figure something out. Seriously. I'll be fine. I always am."

"I won't change my mind," I insist. "I want to do this for you. Because..." How do I put this without sounding creepy? "Getting to know you has made a difference to me. It's made me question some decisions I've made. And the people I surround myself with."

He leans back in the chair. "You mean—because you never met a queer guy until last month?"

"It's not quite that bad," I say immediately. Then I think about it for a moment. "It's almost that bad."

His smile is tired.

I lock the front door and find my bag where I'd dropped it on the floor. "Look, I'm going to bed. Practice tomorrow is optional, and I'm leaning toward skipping it. See you after we both get some sleep."

Several hours later I open my eyes, and then immediately close them when I get nailed with bright sunlight.

My first thought is: Carter was right that I need curtains.

My second thought is: Carter is singing "Dancing Queen" in my living room.

I tuck my hands behind my head and smile up at the ceiling. He's *here*. Right downstairs. And it makes me so much happier than I have a right to feel.

But I don't rush downstairs, because I'm vain like that. I take a minute to wash my face and brush my teeth. Then I head down the stairs to greet my favorite designer.

The music has shifted to "Take a Chance on Me." Carter doesn't seem to know the lyrics, because he's humming, "Ba-da-*ba-ba*-BAHHHH, ba-da-*ba-da*-BAH. Take a chance on meeee."

I pause on the stairs. He isn't just singing on that ladder. He's *dancing*. My jaw drops, and my eyes track the circle of his hips and the perfect shake of his ass.

I thought I was coordinated, but I've never seen anyone use a level and a pencil and a tape measure at the same time, all while shaking his tush to the music.

"Take a chance on me..."

I wave, to get his attention and prove I'm not just staring at him like a creeper.

Carter turns and spots me. Unfortunately, his reaction is a little more violent than I'd hoped. He flails, and for a moment, I'm sure he and everything he's holding will land on the floor. But only the tape measure drops with a clatter.

"Sorry." I descend to the living room. "Didn't mean to sneak up on you."

He climbs off the ladder and turns off the music, his face reddening. "It's so late that I thought you'd gone to practice after all."

"Nope. Slept in for the first time in months."

"Same." He rakes his hair with one hand. "Sorry about the music."

"I'm not. Coffee?" I head for the kitchen.

"Oh, I'd *die* for coffee." He follows me.

"Hey, you should make yourself at home. There's basically a lifetime's supply of coffee pods in here. And I have a grocery delivery service, where I order the minimum. But I'm gone so often that I end up throwing food away." I open the refrigerator. "You eat eggs and bacon? I'm starving."

He regards me warily. "Go put on a shirt first. The abs of glory are distracting me."

"The...what now?"

He waves a hand in my direction. "It's challenging enough for me to be a professional. But you have me falling off ladders with this sleepy, half-naked, sex-hair look, and it's not okay."

"Huh. All right." Self-conscious now, I run a hand through my hair, and he groans, his face flushed.

My groin tightens, but I back away, then head up the stairs to dress more appropriately.

Keep it together, I remind myself. He's here to work. And I didn't invite him to stay so I could climb into the guest bed with him. Though the thought holds a lot of appeal...

Stop it, DiCosta. Be cool.

As if I even knew how.

When I return to the kitchen, Carter has made two mugs of coffee. I accept one and then shoo him back to the living room while I cook. Half an hour later, I carry two heaping plates to the dining table. There's thick-cut bacon, cheese omelets, and strawberry waffles.

"Oh God," Carter moans when I set a plate in front of him. He tosses a curtain onto the floor and picks up his fork. "Strawberries are my favorite thing in the world. And where did you learn to cook?"

"My mother taught both of us. Me and my sister. She said everybody should know how to cook."

"Your mom sounds great," he says, digging right in.

"She is." And feeding him makes me ridiculously happy.

I haven't fed anyone since I was married. That was the best part of my marriage—cooking and eating together. We made a lot of sense in the kitchen, but not so much in the bedroom.

"What?" Carter asks.

I can't admit that eating breakfast with him makes me think of being married. "Just thinking I hadn't used the waffle iron in a long time. Waffles for one is kind of pointless. I usually just have the omelet."

"Well, I'm here for this," he says and takes another bite.

My heart swells. "Sleep okay in the guestroom?"

"You have no idea." He sighs. "Then again, I chose the mattress myself."

"That room turned out so cool. My brain just doesn't work like that. I've never looked at a room and thought—that wall should look like a birch forest. I look at a wall, and I see a wall."

Carter takes a bite of bacon and makes a hum of appreciation. "Making things look nice is my only marketable skill. When I was nine years old, I pulled up a corner of the wall-to-wall carpeting in my bedroom and discovered oak floors underneath. By the next weekend, I'd sanded and refinished that floor, and made a papier-mâché shade to cover the ugly ceiling-mounted fixture. When I announced ten years later that I wanted to go to school for interior design, nobody was surprised."

I gaze at him with the kind of wonder that's getting harder and harder to hide. "So that's just how you're wired. To look at a blank spot and fill it with something better."

He smiles. "I guess. But sometimes it feels like an affliction. I mentally renovate every room I'm in. High school was torture. Lots of cinder block and fluorescent lighting."

"Tragic."

He picks up his fork and starts eating again. "I can put up with a lot of teasing from a man who makes strawberry waffles. But enough about me. How did you get your job?" He swirls a bite of waffle in syrup.

"My mother's family is thick with hockey players. I never had a dad around, so she signed me up to play sports with my cousins and my uncle."

His eyebrows lift. "The same uncle and the cousin you punched?"

"Those are the ones. My cousin Marco and I are almost exactly the same age, so we've been head-to-head competitors our whole lives."

"At hockey?"

"At everything. But, yeah, mostly hockey. It made me a better player."

He gives me a strange look. "Because you needed to prove yourself?"

"Pretty much. My uncle Vin is my mother's brother. He had a good run in the pros, but no championship ring. So now Marco is supposed to get him one. My cousin has heard every day of his life that he's destined for greatness."

"Uh-oh," Carter says.

"Yup. Lots of pressure on that asshole. The fucked-up thing is that I used to be jealous of it. All that praise." I shake my head. "Uncle Vin spent a lot of time telling me I was a useless little shit who'd never amount to anything."

Carter's eyes widen. "He said that to a *child?*"

"Oh, for sure. He called me a bastard, and he meant it literally.

See also, 'useless fuck' and 'waste of space.' I heard it all. And when I got older, it only got worse." *Pussy* and *faggot* were particular favorites of his. But Carter doesn't need to hear that.

"And does your mother know this?"

"Well…" I try to think how to explain it. "She doesn't know the details. She knows that Vin can be a dick, because he's not that good an actor. And she knows Marco is prone to occasional violence."

Confusion stirs in Carter's eyes. "And that's okay with her?"

"It's complicated. When I was three years old, my father kicked me down a staircase…"

"*Jesus.* Were you hurt?"

"Not badly." I shrug. "Gia says I blacked out. She was four at the time. But I didn't break any bones. Little kids bounce back pretty easily. And I don't remember the incident. My mother came home to that—and Gia wailing her head off—and packed us up and left him that day."

"God, I'd *hope* so."

"Well, yeah. Some women have no place to go, though, right? But when all this went down, Vin was getting paid seven figures. So he bought a little house in their old neighborhood and moved my mother in."

"And you," Carter says slowly. "And your sister."

"Right. It's where I grew up. My mother still lives there, and Uncle Vin still owns the house."

"I see. So you're supposed to be the grateful nephew for the rest of your life?"

"Pretty much," I agree. "I grew up knowing that it was my job to take all the crap that Vin and Marco dished out. That it was my cross to bear, if I wanted to keep the peace. And especially if I wanted to play hockey."

"While he verbally abused you for funzies?" Carter asks.

I shrug. "That's just the way it was. And then I started outperforming Marco at the rink, and that made him even nastier. But at least on the ice, I understood why he hated me. It made sense."

Carter stabs angrily at his last bite of waffle. "I guess? It's still awful."

"We were both picked by Trenton in the draft. I was picked in the first round, but Marco didn't go till later. Vin almost lost his mind." The memory actually makes me smile. "The hockey draft doesn't mean you go right to the majors. Marco went to the minors first, and I tried college. It got me out of their orbit for a little while."

"And then you got married," Carter says casually. But I can tell he's curious.

"That's right. To a woman."

He keeps his eyes on his plate. "And how'd that go?"

"Not great," I say quietly. "Whatever you're imagining, it's probably correct."

He glances up quickly, but there's no vindication in his sad eyes. "I'm sorry to hear that."

"So was she," I say, trying for a joke.

"And since then, you...?" He leaves the question open.

"I've been single."

"I see. Because...?"

"Because my life is complicated. That's, uh, more than I've ever told anyone else, by the way."

He goes still on his side of the table. "Thank you for telling me."

"Figure I owe you at least a partial explanation."

He shakes his head. "You don't, though. It's nobody's business but yours."

Sounds nice when he says it, but I'm not sure it works that way.

"So after all this time..." He sips his coffee. "Who's winning?"

"Hmm?"

"The contest," he says. "You? Or Cousin Marco?"

I answer without a thought. "Me. Definitely me. The stat sheet doesn't lie."

"But he's still a problem for you," Carter says. "Still a thorn in your side."

"At least I don't have to look at his ugly face every day like I used to." I take another bite of bacon. "And it doesn't count if I still need an antacid every time I hear his name, right?"

Carter's eyes widen. "Um..."

I laugh, because even Marco doesn't bother me much when I'm eating bacon and eggs at a table with Carter. That's got to mean something.

If only I knew what.

TWENTY-SIX

Carter

AFTER BRUNCH, I load the dishwasher and wash the griddle. I know how to be a good guest in someone's home. I have lots of practice by now.

It kills me to admit that I need to accept Tommaso's offer to stay here for a few days. It's not what a professional would do, and I hate the idea of mooching off a client even more than I hate glass coffee tables and millennial pink.

On the other hand, I hate bankruptcy more. So I'm just going to suck it up and be as gracious as I can while avoiding homelessness.

Tommaso heads outside with a shovel for a while to deal with the snow on the front walk and the back deck. After that, he disappears into the basement. I hear music and the distinct clank of metal plates as they're stacked onto a barbell.

I don't picture his big, strong body straining to push that barbell over his head. Nope. Not even for a minute do I imagine the taut, sweaty abs of glory or his rippling biceps.

There's grunting, too. But I'm strong. I ignore it. And anyway, I'm busy with the curtains. I've finally got them all hemmed, and now I need to hang them.

I'm adjusting the ladder when Tommaso emerges from the

basement, red-faced and sweaty in a tight T-shirt. "You need any help?"

"It's under control," I say quickly.

"Cool. Just say the word." He trots up the stairs, and eventually I hear the shower running.

After climbing the ladder, I use the pencil to make a mark on the wall where the curtain bracket belongs. And I absolutely do not think about water sluicing over the abs of glory. Because I am a professional.

Unfortunately, professionals only have two hands, and by the time I get to the longest curtain rod—the one for the living-room picture window—I'm unable to hold the rod level, measure, and make pencil marks all at the same time.

Tommaso comes back downstairs just as the curtain rod threatens to topple from my hands. I cut off my string of curses and ask for help. "Could you, uh, hold one end for a sec?"

"Of course." He carries a chair over from the dining table and stations it at the other side of the window. "Ready?"

"Thanks." I lift the hardware into place and pull a level out of my back pocket to check our positioning. "Can you raise your rod another quarter inch?"

"Uh, yup." He chuckles. "My rod is raised."

"*Tommaso DiCosta.*" I mark the spot where the bracket should go. "Did you just make a dirty architecture joke? I love those."

A grin splits his beard. "All right. Let's hear some."

"Okay—you know how your glass shower stall upstairs is shaped like a box?"

"Yeah."

"When they join glass into a corner like that, it's called a *butt glaze.*"

His laugh is so loud that it echoes off the window. "You're kidding me."

"God's honest truth."

His abs shake as he laughs. "Pass me the pencil? And tell me another one."

I hand over the pencil so he can mark his end. "For starters, the place where a new building goes up is called the *erection site*."

He snickers.

"First they raise the *studs*." I wiggle my eyebrows. "And then windows can be *double hung*, or *triple hung*..."

He snorts.

"Then there are *pipe penetrations*. And houses always get either *rigid* insulation or *blown* insulation."

"Wow, Carter. I had no idea that interior design was so interesting." He gives me a hot smile.

"Just doing my job, sir. Now pardon me while I employ my *drill* to *screw in* these brackets."

He just shakes his head.

No, seriously, I'm ready to drill. It takes me about half an hour to screw all the brackets onto the walls. And then I start stringing curtains onto the poles and hanging them up all over the house.

Except, of course, for the upstairs bedroom. I've been avoiding it because Tommaso is upstairs packing for another trip out of town.

"Hey, Jersey?" I call from the bottom of the stairs. "Do you mind if I hang two curtains upstairs before it gets dark? It'll just take a couple minutes."

"Come on up," he calls. "I'll help you."

I ascend the stairs. I only venture to the second floor when he's not home, and I never linger. I respect his personal space. But the moment I enter the room today, it seems to shrink, and we're both doing our best to ignore the king-sized bed beside us.

The ladder isn't necessary for this room. I choose a window and we stand side by side while I make my marks and screw the brackets into the wall. He's close enough that I catch the clean, sandalwood scent of his shaving soap.

"Looks good," he says, his voice gruff. "Thanks for this."

We turn to face each other, and we're standing too close

together for it to feel casual. Or maybe it's just never casual between us. An electric hum crackles through the air whenever I look at him. It's real, and we're trapped inside it.

Tom's gaze is practically burning me up inside. My fingers itch to reach for him, but I don't. He made a point to say that he considered me a *friend*. And I'm starting to realize this man might not have enough of those.

He blows out a breath. Then he sits down on the rug I chose and rests his back against the wall under the window. "Can I tell you a secret?"

Confused, I sink down and lean against the side of his bed. We're still close—closer than two men usually sit. Unless they're us. "Of course."

He doesn't quite meet my eyes. "It's obvious that I'm attracted to men in general, and to you in particular. But I'd never acted on it before I met you."

"*Oh.*"

Oh wow.

"That's not actually the secret. That's just the background information. And I wasn't lying when I told you that meeting you..." His dark eyes search my face. "...sort of shook me up a little. But there's a couple of other things going on in my life right now that have me coming unglued."

"Like what?" I whisper.

Smiling, he shakes his head. Like he can't quite believe whatever he's about to say. "One of my teammates is planning to come out as bisexual in the next couple weeks. He's in a relationship with a man. And he's going public."

My heart leaps. "Really? Rigo and Buck will lose their *minds*."

"You think? This is in the vault, by the way. It's not my secret to tell."

"Oh, hell yes. It will mean so much to gay sports fans if there's a living, breathing queer athlete in professional hockey."

"You mean one who's *out*," he says pointedly.

I flinch. "Yeah, sorry. There have to be other queer hockey players."

"What do you think will happen?" he asks quietly. "When people hear his announcement? Tell me the good stuff."

"Because you're worried about the bad stuff," I realize.

"I am," he admits. "Players can get thrown out of a game for a racist or homophobic slur. But there's a lot the refs don't hear. A *lot*."

"Okay. Yeah." I swallow. "And that sucks. But this player probably knows that. He knows how to handle himself, right? And he's looking forward to being honest about his life and finding out who his real friends are."

Tommaso nods slowly. "Yeah, okay."

"And the fans..." I can't help but grin. "This guy will be a *legend* down at Sportsballs, for starters. Every queer hockey fan will be walking on air, okay? They better order a *truckload* of jerseys with this guy's name on the back."

He tips his head back against the wall, looking thoughtful. "It will mean a lot to some people."

"You have no idea. New hockey fans will crop up *everywhere*, because one guy had the balls to let the world know that a queer hockey player looks and plays just like the rest of his team. He'll never pay for another drink again."

Tommaso barks out a laugh. "That definitely didn't occur to me."

"You've been stewing about this?" I ask.

"I might have been," he says, crossing massive arms over his chest. "People can be ugly. And hockey is so insular. We listen to the same music. Have the same days off. Drive the same three car models."

"And you literally wear matching outfits all the time."

He laughs. "There's that."

"But I'm guessing—maybe this is out of line—a guy in that situation might spend years unable to picture what it would be like to be the only gay guy on the team."

Tommaso drops his head. "Yeah, he might."

"And maybe his cousin uses a lot of gay slurs?"

He blows out a breath, staring at the carpet as if there's something written there. "Yeah. And maybe his uncle spent a decade calling him a faggot and a homo."

I gasp.

"And," he continues, "maybe a guy still hears those words in his head whenever he makes a mistake. Like they belong in there."

"Oh God." My chest hurts. "Jesus."

He shrugs his big shoulders. "I don't even know how they knew. Maybe it was just a lucky guess."

"Oh, it *was*," I assure him. "Guys like that find your sore spot and then jab it. I bet you reacted one time, and that's all it took."

"Maybe," he says slowly. "It shouldn't matter now."

I make a noise of dismay. "You say that. But we carry some of that shit around for years. I still have dreams about being bullied in high school."

"You do?" He stares at me.

"Occasionally. Most of my dreams are, like, Ryan Reynolds is blowing me in his Deadpool costume. Or I'm hired to design a sex lair for Prince Harry."

Tommaso laughs suddenly. "Of course you dream that."

"But everybody has their shadows. They show up from time to time."

His smile fades, replaced by the intense frown that I've grown to love. "I'm surprised. You just seem so *you* all the time. Like the bullshit doesn't get you down."

I reach out and cover his hand with mine. But he does it one better—he flips his hand over and clasps my fingers. And now I know how it feels to have Tommaso DiCosta hold my hand.

It feels amazing. But I can't let myself get distracted, because this is the most important thing I know. "Look, being me is the only way I know how to be. For better or for worse. Sometimes it's easy, and everything just clicks. And sometimes it means lying awake at night, remembering that time my secret high school boyfriend called me a fairy in front of his cowboy friends."

His grip on my hand tightens. "Seriously?"

"*Seriously*. But fuck him. Not literally, because he was the top. But still—*fuck him*. I finally gave up and moved away. And now I hear he cheats on his wife. Miserable people are not our responsibility."

Still gripping my hand, he leans back against the wall and sighs. "I shouldn't care what other people think. I just don't know how to stop."

"You'll stop when you choose your own freedom over theirs. When the scale finally tips, and you would rather be on the other side. That's how it worked for me, anyway."

He blows out a breath. This is a man with a *lot* on his mind.

A man I'm crushing on. But he's also a friend, and so I do the difficult thing. I slip my hand out of his, and I get to my feet and put a little physical distance between us. It's either that, or I'm going to climb in his lap and kiss the hell out of him.

He told me he's not in a place where he can act on our attraction.

The least I can do is listen.

TWENTY-SEVEN

Tommaso

I'M glad I convinced Carter to stay at my place, because I have to jet off for another road trip, and I like the idea that he's holding down the fort while I'm away. I couldn't guess why, but knowing my house isn't empty makes me feel less lonely.

And I really like knowing that he's not worried about where he'll sleep.

On the road, we're back to communicating by text, and I find myself coming up with reasons to chat with him.

TOMMASO

Christmas is coming soon. We need a tree, and I want to pick it out.

CARTER

OMG! We found something you want to pick out. Alert the media. Do you have a Christmas tree stand?

Fuck no. All I have is a single stocking my mother sent me last year. But, hey, at least I have a mantle now.

Okay, I'll take care of the stand and the decor. I was going to do the tree tomorrow. But I could wait for you.

It has to be fresh! And it has to be a Fraser fir.

Who's the snob now? Okay, how about the night you come back from your game in New York? We can buy it and put it up together.

Yes. Done.

Wait! CRUCIAL QUESTION. Colored lights or white?

JFC, I can't believe you have to ask. I'm shook. There is only one right kind of lights for a tree.

OMG a test! Okay. I can do this. I'm closing my eyes. I'm picturing you as a child, in front of a New Jersey Christmas tree. You're eight, and probably already a broody guy. You want a new pair of skates. And you're staring up at...

...

Colored lights!

Phew! For a second there I thought maybe we couldn't be friends. Colored lights are the real ones. White ones are for posers.

I happen to agree with you. But on the other hand, I didn't want to be accused of buying you a string of Dallas / New Jersey / Boston / Portland lights. I'm not a traitor.

Christmas lights are an exception to the rule because if they're all on one string, they cancel each other out.

Also there's no major league team in Portland.

Good to know.

I'm playing great hockey. Finally. I feel loose and not all up in my head. Coach is happy with me.

On the jet home, Tate the publicist stands in the aisle and shows us the revised version of the Pride jerseys that he's ordered. "These are nothing special, but they get the job done," he says with a grudge in his voice.

He holds one up, just briefly, but I can tell at a glance that it's much more attractive. The rainbow tie-die effect is rendered in broad horizontal stripes, from red at the shoulders down to purple at the bottom. And the logo is stitched in white on the front.

"I'll pass these around so you can get a good look," he says, tossing the shopping bag to Newgate. "Any last-minute notes I'll need to hear sooner rather than later." Then he sits down.

When the bag comes to me, I dump it out in my lap. All three jerseys look the same, but they're in different sizes. And they all look better than that horror show he'd shown us originally. They look great. Carter's friend Rigo would kill for one of these, right?

That gives me an idea. An evil one.

Sometimes those are the best kind.

In the airport, I grab my bag off the luggage carousel, hurrying to get home. It's not that I'm eager to see Carter, I'm just happy to be home.

That's what I'm telling myself, anyway.

As I'm turning toward the exit, Hudson Newgate calls my name, and I'm forced to turn around again.

"Sorry," he says, looking sheepish. "There's something wrong with the starter in my car, and it's in the shop for another day. Could I get a ride home?"

"Yeah, sure. Actually, there's something I need you to autograph."

"Aw, buddy. I'm touched, because I thought you weren't really a fan of mine."

I snort. "It's not for me."

"Figures."

After we climb into my SUV, I dig through my carryon. "Could you sign this? And also keep it on the down-low?"

He eyes my bag with an amused glance. "I'm kind of afraid to find out what's in there."

I pull a jersey out of the bag. It's the prototype of the tie-dyed Pride jersey. "Kind of stole this," I admit.

"From the PR guy?" Hudson barks out a laugh. "Why?"

"He had three of them, and I figure he didn't need them all. And I know a fan who wants to give his husband a signed jersey for Christmas. But these won't be available till after." I hand him a Sharpie. "Do you mind signing?"

"You are a sneaky fuck." He bites the cap off the pen and signs the jersey. "If you get busted for this, I'm gonna say you forged my signature."

"Yeah. Fine."

He chuckles and hands back the pen and the jersey. I tuck them back into the bag and then toss it into the backseat.

When we're finally on the road, I ask my phone to send a message. "Siri, text to Carter Flynn."

"What do you want to say?"

"Tell Rigo I got him a special jersey for his man. But there's a catch. It's an embargoed design. He can't share it on social media until after Christmas. It's signed by me and Hudson Newgate. No charge by the way."

"Message sent."

We ride in silence for several miles. But then Newgate says, "Hey, I think I owe you an apology."

"For what?"

"For getting in your face that time and asking you if you had a problem with me coming out."

"Eh. I was being weird that day."

"Hmm." He's quiet for a moment. "DiCosta—you're not actually homophobic, are you?"

"*Fuck* no."

He laughs. "See? I'm sorry. I got defensive, which is awful, because you were really just trying to caution me."

"Nah. Just forget it."

"But maybe I shouldn't." He takes a breath. "I'm going to do this —the decision is already made. But when you voiced a valid concern about the game against Trenton, I refused to hear it. It's like I'd decided that it would all go fine, because that's how I *need* it to go. Even though I've put this off for years, for a reason."

This hits way too close to home for me, so I say nothing.

"Like, I need to keep telling myself there won't be any real ugliness. That it will be a lifetime highlight reel clip."

"A what?"

"You know—a clip for the highlight reel of your life. We can't *just* play hockey, you know?"

"I don't know anything," I tell him. "You shouldn't listen to me about this stuff."

"You say that now. But I think you know *exactly* who's going to be a dick to me, yeah?"

My neck prickles. "I might have witnessed some really bad behavior in the past."

"Right. Okay." He sighs. "Part of me doesn't really care. Sticks and stones, etcetera. I don't give two shits what other people think. But here's my nightmare scenario—a bunch of our games turn into bench-clearing fights. And it's all because of *me*." He swallows. "Could be a *very* long season."

"It won't be like that," I insist.

Except I'm exactly the wrong man to reassure him. He must know it, too, because he gets quiet again. Then he asks, "You know who's not too worried, though?"

"Who? Coach?"

"No—Gavin. My boyfriend. He's been an out gay athlete his whole life. He says people suck, but most of them don't, and you just get on with it."

"He ought to know." And I want to believe him. Now more than ever.

We're almost home when my phone announces a new message. I take my chances and let Siri read it aloud.

Jersey, you rock! Rigo is so pumped! He says to say thank you. And he also says that he and Buck think Newgate is the hottest Cougar.

Beside me, Newgate bursts out laughing. "So at least I'll still have two fans when this is all over."

"Aw, buddy," I tease. "You'll have three. I'll still be your fan."

He punches me in the arm. "Hey, do you think those guys would want a ticket to our game against Brooklyn? I'm not using my comp seats that night."

"Of course they would." I pull into the carport. "But why aren't Gavin and your daughter sitting in your seats?"

"Gavin doesn't want her face televised, so they're sitting up in the owner's box for privacy."

"Oh shit."

"Yeah." Newgate does some neck rolls, as if in pain. "It's been fun thinking about all these little details. Like—will some batshit homophobe post our nine-year-old's picture on Twitter?"

"Jesus." The idea makes my stomach cramp. "I'd like a few minutes alone with anyone who'd do that to you."

"Let's hope you won't need them." He gets out of the car and grabs his bag. "Thanks for the lift."

"Anytime!" And I actually mean it.

Then I grab my own gear and hurry inside. But I'm sad to find that Carter isn't there. There's a note on the coffee table.

> Out looking at apartments. I made a whole lot of chili. And there's toppings. Dive right in.
>
> And while you're eating, please look at the pages I marked in this catalog. It's deck furniture.
>
> It won't hurt a bit.
>
> —C

. . .

He's right, it doesn't hurt a bit, since I'm also enjoying a kickass bowl of chili with diced onions, cheese, and sour cream. It's harder to hate furniture when someone has fed me a hot meal.

Honestly, though, all the deck furniture looks the same. I end up scribbling on one of the sticky notes he's left inside the catalog to mark the pages. *Pick whichever kind will last forever without any help from me.*

That night it's Volkov's birthday party, so I have to go out with the team, even if I'm not in the mood. The house is quiet when I get home.

The new curtains in my room shield me from the sunlight at dawn. But at seven thirty, I roll over, and just the thought of Carter here, under my roof, makes me wake fully.

That's all it takes. I'm up and showering and dressing for the day.

When I make it down to the kitchen, the guestroom door is closed. I make myself a cup of coffee, and by the time I'm contemplating breakfast, he stumbles in wearing boxers and an old T-shirt, his hair standing on end. He blinks sleepily. "Morning."

"Morning." I'm cataloguing all the little details, like the muscles in his calves, and the reddish-brown dusting of hair on his legs. "Sleep okay?"

He rubs his eyes and yawns. "I slept great. It's like I'm making up for all those cramped nights on Rigo's couch."

My chest swells a little, as if I've done something good for the world.

"I'm gonna shower," Carter says, shuffling toward the bathroom.

While he's in there, I put some bacon in the oven and stir together another batch of strawberry waffles, because he liked them so much last time.

"Oh wow," he sighs when he sees the plate I've made him. "Unbelievable."

I'm no good at taking compliments, so I don't reply. I set a glass of juice and a mug of coffee in front of him. "Milk?" I offer him the carton.

He doctors his coffee, and after he carries the carton back to the refrigerator, we sit down together at the table. His hair is dark from his shower, and the freckles seem to stand out against his skin.

But I'm staring. I tuck into my breakfast without a word.

"You have practice?"

"Yeah. A short one. Then video. And a flight tonight. Last major road trip before the holidays. Don't forget—we're doing the Christmas tree the night I get back."

"I haven't forgotten," he says, amusement in his voice. "I'll call some tree lots ahead of time to see who has Fraser firs. Then I'll text you a place to meet me."

"Cool," is all I say, even though I can't wait to get that tree up. It was only a few weeks ago when furnishing this house felt like an insurmountable hurdle. And now it's almost done.

"I have a long list of details that still need fixing," Carter says. "Want to see?" He pushes his legal pad across the table toward me. "There's a few questions for you."

"Of course there are." I scan the list, and it is long. It's all stuff that I don't ever think about—welcome mats and soap dishes. A dresser for the guestroom.

"I'm buying wrapping paper and tape for you. Is one roll enough?"

"Yup. And thanks for helping me pick out that gift for my mom."

"Of course." He makes a note on his pad. "Okay, I need to size the table for the back porch. Two-seater or four?"

"Two is plenty."

Another note on the pad. "There's still nothing on your walls. Literally nothing. Do you have any family photos you'd like to hang up?"

I give him a glare. "Maybe one of Gia and the kids, and one of my mom. But that's not going to cover much wall space. Not speaking to the rest of my family, you realize."

He flinches. "Oops. Okay. Art?"

I shrug.

He moves on. "You'll need a TV console. But do you mind if I order it later—when I'm ready to move my bookcase? Or when I find a buyer for it?"

I swivel in my chair and peer into the living room where the sleek wooden piece is holding up my TV. "If that one is for sale, just sell it to me and be done with it. Looks nice there. And I have some books in a box somewhere that I could put on that lower shelf."

"Hmm," he says. "It's midcentury, though. Not exactly the vibe of the living room."

"It's not ruining *my* vibe," I say, mostly because I enjoy arguing with Carter about furniture. "You think replacing a wooden piece with another one about the same height is going to change my life?"

He buries a smile in a bite of waffle. "That's a fair point. Except that shelf is worth at least five grand, and you don't need to spend that much. It's an antique. I'd never sell it if I knew my next place will have a wall for it."

"Won't it?" I press.

He plays with his fork and fails to meet my eyes. "Not if it's in Montana. If I can't find a reasonable apartment in a short amount of time, I might have to move home and regroup."

My stomach drops. "I'm sorry."

"It's okay." He lifts his chin. "Starting over isn't so bad. I've done it before."

"Why don't you just leave that there for now?" I hook a thumb toward the low-slung bookshelf. "Eventually you can take it back or sell it. But it's not causing any trouble."

"Okay," he says quietly. "Thank you."

I shrug. "Furniture is still invisible to me, Carter."

"*Bullshit.*" He pretends to cough into his hand. "I've noticed that you already claimed one end of the couch. There's an empty coffee cup on the coaster, and the pillows have been rearranged."

"My ass loves the couch, and my back likes those fuzzy pillows.

They're comfortable as fuck. But I'd like them just as much if they were ugly," I lie.

"Uh-huh." He gives me smug eyes over the rim of his coffee mug. "If it makes you feel better to say that, sure."

"I'm the customer. Don't you have to just nod and smile?"

He puts the mug down, fashions his perfect face into a deranged smile, and nods like it's hurting him.

I crack up.

TWENTY-EIGHT

Carter

THAT AFTERNOON, after Tommaso leaves for his road trip, I drive over to Rigo's art studio and bring him the signed jersey.

"Sweet baby Jesus," he says, holding up the jersey. "Buck will *love* it."

"You can't show it to anyone yet, though," I remind him.

"No problem!" He folds it carefully. "But why not?"

"It's a brand-new design for an event that's still secret. You'll probably hear about it later."

Rigo looks intrigued. "What kind of event?"

I shrug, helpless. I don't like lying to my friend, but it's not my place to tell what little I know about the Cougars' big reveal after Christmas.

He narrows his eyes. "You look guilty of something."

"I do *not*. You're dreaming."

He tucks the jersey lovingly back into the shopping bag. "Okay. Fine. Be secretive if you want. But are you okay?"

"Me? Of course I am."

"Uh-huh." He picks up a stray paintbrush and examines its bristles. "But would you tell me if you weren't? And have there been any more kisses against the refrigerator?"

"Not a single one." *But I still think about it.* "He's been a gentleman."

Rigo's mouth twists. "I suppose he feels like he has to. The guy has a lot of rules for himself. You can tell just talking to him."

"It's true," I grumble. "So many rules."

"And how are you coping? I know you're kind of hung up on the hockey player. "

"I'm not," I insist. But then I think about it for a moment. "Okay, fine. I'm totally hung up on the hockey player."

Rigo sets down the brush. "I knew it. You're falling for your hot boss."

It's difficult to flop back dramatically when you're sitting on a paint-crusted metal stool, but I manage. "He's so great, though. So kind, under that gruff exterior. So thoughtful and broody. And he makes strawberry waffles, Rigo."

"Oh dear," my friend says heavily. "Ouch."

"I know! And bacon. And he knows how I take my coffee." I heave a sigh. "I'm a sucker for a man who takes care of me. Is that awful? Am I a dope for wanting to wake up with a guy who makes breakfast?"

"No," he says gently. "Of course not. We all deserve a little care. But it also sounds like that man is emotionally unavailable. He basically told you so."

"I know," I say, miserable. "He could at least fool around with me before he casts me aside. It's really only fair. Those abs of glory are just going to waste."

Rigo snickers. "I'm sorry. I think there's a version of reality where that guy gets his shit together and appreciates you for the awesome boyfriend that you would be. I just don't know if he's ready."

My heart sinks. "He isn't. He's scared. And everybody knows you can't get a guy over that hump. He has to want it."

"He has to want to jump the hump," Rigo says. "And then hump the rump."

We both crack up laughing.

When we can breathe again, he shows me his new work. "I've got some abstract stuff, of course, and a few of what my gallery rep calls 'angry landscapes.' He wants more like this because he says he can sell it." He pulls a canvas out of the stack to show me. It's a mountain peak with a moody sky painted above it. The brush-strokes are thick and rough.

"I love it. Show me more?"

There are several in that same series. "You might also like this," he says, revealing a large canvas that's a little more zoomed in than the others. It's a rocky landscape with a cougar staring back at me from left of center. "I watch a lot of hockey. Had cougars on the brain."

"Cool! Can I take a picture of it?"

"Be my guest," Rigo says, propping it up on an easel so I can get a good shot. "Feel free to work your magic."

I'd connected Rigo with a client once before, and he'd sold a painting to her. The cougar painting is very approachable. I'm sure someone will claim it.

"Want to get lunch?" Rigo asks.

"I can't. Gotta shop for the hot, emotionally unavailable boss."

Rigo gives me a sad smile. "Hang in there. He might find his way. You never know."

"You never know," I echo.

But we both know it's a long shot. I learned the hard way not to get involved with confused men. It never ends well.

Shopping improves me. Wandering around buying Christmas decorations for Tommaso is the mood-lifter I didn't know I needed.

I pick out some wool and glass ornaments in a fair-trade boutique. At Target, I fill my cart with colored lights and pick out some mantle hooks for stockings. And a couple of candles. Since everything is returnable, I buy a couple different stockings for his mom, so he can choose one. And a couple of different stars for the top of the tree.

But what is he going to put *in* this stocking? I pull out my phone.

CARTER

I'm at Target. Stocking stuffers for your mom?

TOMMASO

Yes please. But I don't know what.

Paperback books? A Colorado ornament? Scented candle?

Mystery novels! The darker the better. That's all we need—I'll get her favorite candy myself.

On it. Go do the sportsing. Get lots of points or whatever you call them.

Thanks. Could be a highlight reel night. You never know.

I need a highlight reel! Can you picture it? Me, picking the perfect paint color. Testing sofas. Hanging curtains.

I thought we agreed never to talk about curtains again.

Sorry.

Besides I think your highlight reel would be more like a goalie's. Near misses, you know? Painting over the piss yellow. Steering a client away from the scary wallpaper.

God yes! Pulling the client away from the sofa with built-in cupholders. Hiding those rustic signs that say LIVE, LAUGH, LOVE.

That's a thing?

Sadly, it's a thing.

> Maybe that's what people get when their designer
> complains that there's nothing on their walls.
> Maybe I need one of those signs.

> That is not funny.

I buy some gift wrap, because Tommaso will need some to wrap his mom's present. The weighted blanket I helped him pick out has recently arrived.

In the checkout line, I actually find myself humming along to "Silent Night"—the Stevie Nicks version.

This is the most optimistic I've felt all year. I can't wait to pick out a tree and decorate it with my favorite hockey player. I like him so much.

Even if we're only ever friends, I'll take what I can get.

TWENTY-NINE

Tommaso

I CAN'T WAIT to get back to Colorado. The moment the plane pulls up to the gate, I'm on my feet and down the jetway.

Leaving the airport in my SUV, it's a temptation to speed. Carter is waiting for me, and I'm running late because I'd forgotten to account for the jet landing at the Denver airport on this trip.

But there's a light snow falling, and I'm not an idiot. I slow down and make my way safely to the tree lot in Boulder, which is adjacent to a garden center. The moment after I park, I'm scanning for Carter. I hate the idea that he's freezing out in the cold, looking for me.

The garden center is open, and when I don't spot him lingering among the trees, I head for the entrance.

When the double doors slide open, I'm dazzled. The place is practically dripping with greenery and Christmas lights. It smells of greenhouse flowers and potting soil.

But the real reason I'm dazzled is Carter. He's leaning casually against the rustic wooden checkout desk, chatting up an employee. He's wearing tight jeans, and a puffer vest with a soft-looking sweater underneath.

That's it. One glance, and some of the tightness inside my chest eases. I've been looking forward to this for days, and only partly because I like Christmas trees.

I like Carter even more. But I slow my roll so that I can watch him for a moment longer. He's talking to a slender guy wearing a rainbow beanie and a lot of tats. They're both smiling, which means Carter probably said something self-effacing and funny.

Then Carter turns to look over his shoulder, and his smile widens. "Hey! You made it!" He gives the guy at the counter a half wave and sort of bounds in my direction. "Are you ready for this?"

"Totally," I say, my smile inevitable. "Let's pick the best one."

"I scoped out the Fraser firs already," he says as the doors part to expel us into the cold. "There are some beauties. But you want to keep it under eight feet."

"How high is my ceiling?" I ask, although I really should have considered this question sooner.

As always, Carter is ready with the details. "Your living room has a nine-foot ceiling. But the stand takes up some space."

"Got it."

Still, when he shows me an eight-foot tree, I don't like it as much as its nine-foot friend. "Can't we get this one? We'll just trim a few inches off the bottom."

"Don't you want a star on top?" he presses.

"But it's so big and bushy."

"That's what he said," Carter murmurs. Then he bites his lip.

I laugh. "Come on, we can make this one work."

"We could," he agrees. "But the eight-footer would fit better. It's more proportionate to the room. It only *looks* small in comparison to its taller friend. And because we're outside."

"Hmm."

He shrugs. "But, hey, if you want to be a size queen, I can make it work."

I howl. And then I choose the eight-foot tree, because if the taller one doesn't fit, I'll never live it down.

The rainbow beanie guy comes outside to cut two inches off the tree's trunk and take my credit card. He flirts with Carter the whole time.

I don't blame him. But I don't like it.

"You want to bale this up?" he asks after I've tucked my card back into my wallet.

"Yes," Carter says at the same moment that I say "No."

"I got this," I say, waving him off. "We're not going far, and I brought bungee straps."

"Suit yourself." He gives Carter one more hot smile and disappears inside.

When we get home, I unlock the house and then pull the tree off the roof of my SUV.

I hand Carter a pair of work gloves. "You take the top, and I'll take the bottom. It's heavier."

We heft the tree, and he actually rolls his eyes. "Who do you think moved your furniture all over the house?"

I pause on the walk up to my house. "The delivery people, I hope."

"Pfft," he says. "There's no delivery person on Earth with the patience to hang around while I walk slowly around the room and figure out whether the chair needs to be six more inches to the left of the coffee table's edge. Or if the rug should be centered to the windows or the floorboards. I've spent the whole month lifting your furniture. But it builds up my guns, so I'm counting it as a win."

It's a good thing we're busy, or I'd be scrutinizing his biceps right now.

"Hey, Jersey? Let's swing around," he says as I step backwards into the house. "This should go in the other direction."

"Nah, I'm good like this. I skate backwards all day."

"Yeah, but the top of the tree should go first."

"But I'm here already. Is the stand ready?"

"Have you met me? Of course it's ready. But, seriously, stop a sec? We really ought to…"

I take another two steps backward, and it's slow going. I give a good tug, pulling the first couple of branches through, but when I look down, I can tell I've wedged the tree in the open doorway.

Uh-oh.

"Jersey!" Carter tugs on the tree, trying to get it back out. But I'm tugging on my end, too. And if I keep that up, I might rip the branches off.

After an awkward moment of unproductive action on both our parts, Carter drops his end. "I did *try* to tell you."

"Uh-huh. I get it now. This is why people get their trees baled, huh?"

"Yeah, but…" Carter winces. "I'm sure this happens all the time."

I finish the sentence for him. "To idiots."

He laughs. Then he gives the tree one more tug in his direction. "It's pretty stuck."

"You know why I didn't let that dude put this tree through the baler?" I ask.

"Because you're an impatient grump who doesn't listen?"

"Sure. But also because I didn't like that guy."

"Why?" Carter throws his arms out wide. "He was super nice."

"Yeah, he was. He wanted in your tight jeans."

Carter puts his hands on his hips. "You are high. He was just a talker. While I was waiting for you, we discovered that we like the same gay bars."

"Huh." Bars I've never been to, or even thought about before. Meeting Carter has sort of punctured a hole through the bubble I live in. It's like I'm peeking out for the first time, and I don't want to stop. "I was jealous," I admit. "Couldn't wait to get away from him."

"Okay," Carter says with a shrug. "That doesn't seem very relevant since you and I are supposed to be friends. Also, it doesn't help us get the tree unstuck from your front door."

"You're right on both accounts. Just being honest."

He sighs. "What's our play, here? We could remove some branches."

"Fuck no. Back up."

"Why?"

"Out of the way." I wave a hand, motioning him away from the tree. "This is how we fix problems in New Jersey."

Carter steps to the side, a worried look on his face.

I brace my hands against the trunk, give a furious shout, and push with everything I've got.

The tree pops out of the doorway and goes shooting off the porch, right into the snow.

Carter looks up at me in wonder. "That was kind of hot, in an angry sort of way."

I've heard worse words to describe me. "Shall we try again?"

"We'll do it my way this time," he says. "Turn the tree around. Let's go."

His way works great. As I should have guessed.

And he's done a great job sourcing the decorations. We string the tree with colored lights, and then hang the ornaments. There's even a tree skirt for underneath.

He's placed candles between two stocking hooks on the mantle. There's even a centerpiece for the coffee table, made of pine boughs and cranberries. Mom can sit here on the sofa with her teacup, admiring the tree.

"You really are the best," I say from the ladder where I'm putting the star on top of the tree. "I told you I wanted to host Christmas, and you made that happen for me. Mom will love it. And so do I."

Carter collapses on the sofa and gazes up at the tree. "Thank you. I'm pretty proud of the way it's all coming together. And I'm glad I made the deadline. I mean, I still have some details to finish here and there. But it's under control."

"It really is. You want some dinner? I feel like ordering something. My treat."

"I'd love some. But I'll pay my share."

"Whatever makes you comfortable." Although I really just want to feed the man who's done so much for me. Maybe someday he'll let me. "Fried chicken?"

"Hell yes."

After placing the order, I fetch a bottle of wine from my kitchen and two glasses. I pour him one without asking.

Sometimes a guy just likes to drink wine in front of the Christmas tree with his hot interior designer.

This is one of those times.

THIRTY

Carter

I'M DOING IT AGAIN. I'm having cozy fantasies about things that cannot be. Nights in front of the fire. Movies on the sofa. A strong arm around my shoulders.

It's a natural reaction to sprawling out next to a hot hockey player, drinking wine on his sofa, stealing glances at his rugged face.

Tommaso told me he was jealous of the guy at the garden center. I should be annoyed that he'd notice who I talk to, but I can't find it in me to hold it against him. He isn't used to telling people how he feels, and I'm honored that he'll tell me.

Honored, but dying inside. No glass of wine has ever been sipped more slowly than this one. Because I can't get drunk with him. I have the self-control of a pickle, and I don't trust myself.

But I don't want the evening to end, either.

My attraction to Tommaso runs deep. Not because of his muscular shoulders, his glorious abs, or the way his thighs bulge in the sweatpants he changed into after we got the tree set up.

It's not even because of the plate of chicken I ate the minute it arrived, or the way Tommaso offered me the last of the mashed potatoes.

The world is full of hot guys. But the hottest thing about

Tommaso is the way he *listens*. When I'm speaking, he fixes those chocolate eyes on mine. He always makes me feel fascinating.

Like right now, when he's asking about my work. "How'd you choose this job, anyway?"

"Don't you remember? A hot, grumpy guy in a nice suit asked me a question outside the world's worst furniture store."

He rolls his dark eyes. "Not this particular gig. The whole thing."

"I told you. It never occurred to me to do anything else," I admit. "I've been redesigning things since I was a little kid. My mom liked to sew, so she was always dragging me along to JoAnn Fabrics. I used to wander around the store touching everything. But my favorite were the upholstery fabrics. They were garish velvets and weird brocades."

He's listening to every word. And that's almost as sexy as the abs of glory.

"They also had these big pattern books you could look through. I'd flip the pages and find designs for interiors. They were probably tacky as hell—McMansions on a low budget. Still, it dawned on me that a room could feel completely different depending on what you did with it. The colors, the light. Change those, and you completely change the mood. I thought it was powerful. So I kept redesigning my room, once a year, on a very low budget."

He smiles at me over the rim of his wine glass. "And how did that go?"

"Sometimes the results were tragic," I have to admit. "I didn't understand that paint colors reflect and magnify in small spaces. I was aiming for sunny when I tried yellow. My room ended up looking like the inside of a highlighter pen."

He glances around this gorgeous living room. "So you're saying I got lucky with these results?"

"I was *eleven*."

He bumps his knee with mine, and his eyes are smiling at me. "It's just a chirp, Montana. Shake it off."

"Fine. You have your little joke. But I learned that color has power. But with power comes great responsibility."

He snickers.

"Luckily, paint is cheap, and I got better taste."

"Right." I get a serious nod. "Your Harry Styles phase?"

"Hey!" I pick up a very stylish boucle throw pillow and bop him with it.

He laughs. But then his phone rings. "Sorry. One sec. It's family." He scoops it up off the coffee table. "Hey, Gia. What's up?"

It's quiet enough that I can hear a female voice through the speaker of his phone. "Tommy, I need you not to panic."

He goes rigid. "What happened?"

"We're at the hospital, and they're admitting her. But it might be nothing. She fainted during Bingo. They're running some tests."

"*Fainted.*" His breath falters. "What do the tests say?"

"We don't know yet. I only called now because you'd kill me if I didn't."

He sags. "You'll call me when you know more?"

"Yes and no. I don't think I'll hear anything until morning, and I don't want you staying up all night, listening for the phone. I'll call you after six a.m. Your time."

"*Any* hour," he repeats.

"Tommy, you're panicking—"

He hangs up, which seems rude. He slaps the phone down on the coffee table, his knuckles white. And he sucks in a breath like a drowning man.

I hold very still, wondering if there's anything I can do. Pain radiates from his every pore, and I feel so helpless right now.

Suddenly, he grabs a stocking off the table—the cheerful quilted one he'd chosen for his mother, and hurls it at the Christmas tree.

I'd never known a stocking could be aerodynamic. But I guess I'd never seen a professional athlete throw one before, because it catapults into the tree with startling force.

"Tommaso," I gasp. "The tree!"

"So what? It doesn't matter. All this work? A waste." He thrusts his head into his hands. "Big fucking waste. I should have known I wouldn't get the chance to make everything right."

Oh no. My heart seizes. Two minutes ago, he was as happy and relaxed as I'd ever seen him. Now he's practically vibrating with heartbreak.

I put a hand on his back, where the muscles are locked up tight. "Tommaso, is your mom sick?"

"Cancer," he mutters. "She's getting chemo. They say she could beat it, but..." He shakes his head, like it hurts to think about. "They give her a seventy percent chance."

"Oh." So many pieces are falling into place for me. The urgency of his home design. *It has to be perfect.*

This man doesn't just want a perfect Christmas with his mom. He's afraid it will be the *last* Christmas with his mom. If she even reaches Colorado. "I'm so sorry you're going through this," I whisper.

He doesn't move. Touching him is like touching a wall. Maybe he wants me to leave. Sometimes a guy just has to cry, and sometimes he'd rather do that in private.

But I'm torn. Six a.m. is a long time from now. If I walk out the door, he'll just brood for the next seven hours.

Tommaso is a good man, and a strong man. But he's also the loneliest man I know. Someone has to tell him it will be okay.

And I think that someone is me.

I rise slowly. Then I tug one of his oversized hands into mine, forcing him to look up. "Come with me for a second. It's important."

"Where?" he demands.

"Not far."

He lets himself be nudged off the sofa, and I lead him around the furniture to the Christmas tree. I pluck the stocking off the rug where it's landed. "You're catastrophizing," I say quietly. "I understand why. But you're not helping your mother right now." I hand him the stocking, and he looks down at it sheepishly.

"Sorry," he grunts. "Not trying to ruin your tree."

"Your tree," I correct. "Now sit down on the rug. Come on."

"Here?"

To demonstrate, I plunk myself down on the rug. And then I kick my legs out straight and lie down, putting my head under the bottom branches. "Let's go, Jersey. You did this as a kid, right?"

He sinks down beside me. "Yeah. Sure. Whatever."

But he does it. He leans back, resting his head beside mine. He stretches his long legs out on the rug. And now he's staring up at the tree with unseeing eyes.

I take hold of his hand. After a beat, his fingers fold over mine. We just lie there quietly for a while. And after fifteen minutes or so, I hear him sigh as he relaxes against the rug.

"Tell me," I prompt. "What's the first Christmas you remember?"

"Dunno."

I squeeze his hand. "Try harder. I remember getting a Fisher Price farm from Santa Claus when I was four."

A pause. "Did you redecorate it?"

"Well..." I haven't thought about this for years. "Not exactly. But I upgraded the pigsty. It was too small. And I installed a Playmobil TV in the cow's part of the barn."

He laughs, and the sound of it fills my chest with warmth. "What I wouldn't give to see you at four, thinking about an accent wall for your toy barn."

His thumb strokes my palm, and I feel a stir of desire for this big, unpredictable beast of a man. He's obviously in pain, and I hate that. Making him laugh feels like a victory. "Now it's your turn. Earliest Christmas memories."

"Uh... Okay. I remember when I was in kindergarten, my mom told me I couldn't get out of bed until six. But I woke up every hour to check the clock. I wanted a guitar."

"Wait—do you play the guitar?"

"Nope. Not a single chord. But kids think they can do anything, you know? I thought I'd be jamming like the Boss on day one. She gave me the guitar—kid-sized. But I ended up having more fun with my new action figures."

"I can see you as an action-figure kind of guy. Do you lean toward Superman or Batman?"

"Superman all the way," he says immediately. "I especially enjoyed the Henry Cavill movies in my teen years. Possibly because of his bulge."

I cackle. "Hear you. But I'm a Batman guy. Because Batman is a design solution."

"What do you mean?"

"Without his suit and his gear, he's not a superhero at all, right? He's just a lonely dude in a cave. To become Batman, he needed kickass design. The creepy suit. The perfect car and all those tools. He designed the world he needed to survive."

Tommaso rolls onto his side to look at me, and I expect laughter. But when I meet his gaze, I get a little lost in the deep pools of his dark eyes. He's not laughing at all. "You kill me, you know that? I love your brain."

Oh. My heart thuds against my chest as I roll onto my side, too. "This is going to sound weird, but…"

He lifts one hand and strokes the side of my face, his thumb sliding across my cheekbone.

I almost can't breathe. "That's the sexiest thing anyone has said to me in a long time."

"Huh." A flicker of a smile. "I'm not exactly famous for turning people on."

We're so close together that my heart begins to pound. "Maybe you've been hanging out with the wrong people, then."

"Maybe," he says gruffly, his dark gaze sweeping my face and landing on my mouth.

What happens next feels inevitable.

He closes the distance slowly, but without hesitation. His generous mouth meets mine, and that broad hand cups my face.

Bad idea, my brain shouts. *He's just feeling emotional! This will end in tears!*

But my body doesn't listen. At the contact, my body arches toward his, like a reflex. I kiss him back, because I can't help myself. I've spent the last month trying to hold this in.

He makes a soft sound from deep inside his chest as his kiss deepens. He parts my lips with his tongue and invites himself inside.

I love the hot taste of him, and I groan like a fool. He growls in response. "God, the sounds you make."

My heart thumps a little harder. "I thought we weren't doing this," I say, even as I thread my fingers into his thick hair. I don't want to take advantage of him when he's feeling emotional. "You said you couldn't."

He kisses me wetly. "I lied."

Yes, he did. Because now he's hitching his body closer to mine, his chest a warm, supportive wall against the world. I can feel the thump of his heart as he kisses me again.

I'm shameless. One of my hands slides beneath his shirt and onto the ridges of his abs, and the other one cups his muscular ass.

He groans into my mouth, and then his hands go exploring, too. They skim my ass, my face, my neck. Like he can't decide where to touch me first. I'm drowning in his kisses.

Then he's on top of me, pressing me into the rug, and now I understand why weighted blankets are a thing. I could stay here forever, pinned to the floor, his kiss like a benediction.

I don't think anyone has ever kissed me so thoroughly. Like he needs me from every angle. I don't want it to end.

"God," he mumbles against my mouth. "You make me crazy. Always have. And I really want to get you out of these clothes."

This little speech sends shivers through me. "You can have anything you want. But you have to promise me one thing."

He peers down at me, fire burning behind his dark eyes. "What?"

"Don't regret me," I whisper. "Whatever we do here, you can't tell me tomorrow that it's a mistake."

"Yeah, no problem." He furrows his brow and runs a hand down my chest. "My big mistake was not doing this sooner."

It's very hard to argue that point as he pops the button of my jeans. I hiss out a breath. "Right into the deep end, huh?"

"Pretty sure I already know how to swim." He yanks down my zipper. "And here you are right under my tree. Like a wrapped present."

I sit up and shrug off my sweater, taking my T-shirt with it. "Happy to be unwrapped. But kill the lights or close the curtains."

He's on his feet in a flash, and I don't miss the way his sweat-pants are tented in front. There's nothing tentative about that.

He darkens the kitchen and living room. The tree stays lit, and when Tommaso sinks down onto the rug beside me, I'm looking at him in a multicolored glow. With two hands, I push his T-shirt halfway up his chest. And then, impatient, I lean down to press a kiss to his happy trail.

"Fuckkkk," he groans. "More of that, yeah?" He tugs the shirt up and off his body. Tosses it somewhere. Then he uses one broad palm to cup the back of my head, more or less pinning my mouth against the abs of glory.

The roughness of the gesture makes me moan. I lick my way up his chest and use my teeth to tease his nipple.

He makes the deepest, horniest groan I've ever heard.

"What do you want?" I ask him, dropping wet kisses across his chest, then down his abs. The bumps and ridges are even more spectacular up close.

"Jesus Christ. I want everything. I want to kiss you. I want to blow you. I want to be blown by you. Pick something, because I'm like a lit fuse right now." He sprawls onto his back, arms outspread, like a man overwhelmed by his own good fortune.

"Well, if it's up to me..." I lean down and nuzzle the thick column inside his sweats.

"Fuck." He grabs the back of my neck and braces me in place. "I want your mouth so bad. I dream about it sometimes."

Nnngh. My whole body thrums in anticipation. I like the firm grip he has on me, and I love the tension in his muscles as I run my lips over his cotton-covered cock.

He releases his grip on my neck and pushes his pants and underwear down. The most gorgeous, uncut cock I've ever seen springs free, and the salty scent of his arousal is making me high.

"Oh, hell yes," I whisper. I drop my mouth to his shaft and lick a heady stripe across the length of him.

He gasps, and that bossy hand is back at my nape. "Again," he demands.

Like he even needs to ask. I bob my head forward and take the head against my tongue.

A string of curses erupts from his mouth. His fingers tighten in my hair as I work him over. "Aw, yeah," he pants. "Ease up, though. I'm not ready to be done with you."

My own self-control is in short supply. Feeling disobedient, I give him another good suck. Then I raise my eyes to his, as a sort of challenge.

What I find there practically knocks me back on my ass. Dark eyes on fire. His broad chest stained red from exertion, every muscle flexing as he tries to hold himself back.

The brute strength of him is unreal. The sheer *will* of him.

I release him with a gentle pop, as his breath saws in and out. "Come here," he says, crooking his finger. "And lose your clothes on the way."

There's so much heat in my body that shedding my jeans doesn't even cool me off. When I put my thumbs in the waistband of my briefs and ease the elastic past my straining dick, Tommaso makes a noise of appreciation.

"And to think I almost talked myself out of seeing *this*."

THIRTY-ONE

Tommaso
―――――――――

CARTER IS PERFECT.

He has a trim, toned chest and miles of lightly freckled skin. And I can't get enough of the dusting of cinnamon hair on his pecs. I want to skim through it with my fingertips, following it down as it gathers in a line down his flat stomach.

But what really blows my mind is the hard length of his erection, bobbing in front of me like a heat-seeking missile. He wants this as much as I do, and I can hardly believe my luck.

If he has a kink for athletes with messy lives, I should really just be grateful.

"Come here." I sit up, my gruff voice showing just how much I'm dying inside. I pat my bare thigh. "Right here."

He straddles my legs, his knees on the rug, his hands on my shoulders. "How's this?" he asks, like he knows he's killing me, and he's enjoying the torture.

"That'll do," I whisper. I want his mouth on mine, but I don't take it yet. I run my hands over his bare chest and feel the hitch in his breath. "You like that?"

"Fuck yes." He tips his head back, exposing his neck. "I'm trying not to pounce on you. But it's hard."

"Yes it is," I agree. "So hard." I run my hand down his flank and then finally allow myself to take him in hand, the thick column of him hot against my palm.

"More," he gasps, hips rolling. "I like it a little rough."

God. I tighten my grip, and just the sight of my hand on his cock makes my balls feel heavy and tight.

This shouldn't feel so shockingly good. I've handled a dick before—my own—but I'm electric as he leans into my touch. So eager, so in tune with me.

"Give me your mouth," I demand. If I don't kiss him, I'll die.

He complies, and I'm right there, sliding my tongue over his, making him moan. He scoots closer, extinguishing the space between us. The first contact of his cock against my erection makes me hiss.

"Oh yeah," he pants. Then he licks his palm and slides his hand between our bodies, knocking my fingers out of the way. "My turn."

I allow it, because his hand covering both our cocks feels divine. Plus, it frees up my hands for other things. Like pulling his hair as I kiss him senseless. It's almost too much sensation for a guy who never touches anyone. Our mouths are fused together, our bodies like a writhing serpent.

The urge to come is breaking me. I groan deeply into his mouth, almost ready to give up the fight.

"Let go," he says. "I'm ready for it. Make a mess of me."

And that's the image that sends me over the edge. My body ignites like a power surge, and I paint his chest with my release. The sight of my spend on his flushed skin is so perfect that I shudder and gasp.

"Fuck yes," he whispers as I knock his hand away.

I'm clumsy from the high, but he doesn't seem to mind. He leans into my touch as I jack him quickly. It isn't long before he thrusts his face into my neck, then shudders as he comes.

The hot pulse of him against my palm is everything I've always needed. I'm kissing his hair and whispering sloppy words of praise as he sags against me.

He lets out one more huff of satisfaction and then relaxes

against my shoulder. I clamp an arm around his back, hoping he won't go anywhere soon.

I'm a little in awe of everything we just did. And I already know I won't regret it.

We lie there quietly for a few moments, while I try to get my bearings.

"Jersey?" His voice is muffled. "We need a shower."

"I suppose that's true." Although I'd stay here all night if he'd let me.

"One more request?" he asks.

"Hit me."

He lifts his handsome face, and his expression is so serious that I feel a tremor of worry. "Don't get any spooge on the new couch, okay?"

I laugh. "Sure thing. But that's the least of my issues tonight."

He rubs his knuckles against my cheek. "I know. That's why you should let me take care of the little details—so this place will still be perfect when your mom gets here."

The mention of her makes my whole body sag.

"Hey, have some faith, okay? Just a little bit. I'll keep you company until you hear some more news. Unless you'd rather go to sleep."

I wrap my arms around him. "Let's have that shower. I doubt I'm getting any sleep tonight."

He lifts his blue eyes to mine and gives me a cocky smile. "Sure you will. I'll tire you out if I have to. Now come on." He rises to his feet and offers me a hand.

I take it, grab my phone off the coffee table, and then I follow him up the stairs.

Naturally, I admire his bare ass as he walks. He strides into my bathroom with confidence, oblivious to the shock that's still echoing through me. *Carter is naked in my bathroom. And I'm allowed to stare.*

He turns on the spray, testing the temperature with his hand. After a moment, he steps inside.

I check my phone just to make sure my sister didn't text. She did, and the message says: *Go to bed, Tommy. I'll call you after six.*

Figures.

"Aren't you coming?" Carter asks from the shower.

"Uh, yup." Except I don't really know how this part works. Blazing attraction and horny desperation carried me through the last half hour with Carter, as I ticked off a long list of first experiences.

But this—the intimacy of hanging out afterwards—seems more complicated.

"Tommaso? Plenty of room in here. Your bathroom rocks."

"Right. Coming." I open the glass door and step into the steamy space.

His wet hair has darkened to a chestnut color, and his body gleams under the spray. Already, I feel blood rushing southward again.

"Let's get you clean," he says easily. He pumps some body wash into his palm and then runs his hands all over my chest. "Ah, the abs of glory. I can't believe you're even real."

I feel very real, though, as I help myself to some of the body wash.

Strangely, I feel more naked than I did downstairs. Now that lust isn't drowning out all other sensations, I'm clumsy, but not so clumsy that I can't skim my hands over every available inch of Carter's sleek body.

He leans back against the tile wall, his face out of the spray, and blinks up at me. "You good?"

"So good," I promise him. "Just, uh, out of my league, here. I never showered with anyone before."

He blinks. "So Rigo's fantasies about what happens in your locker room are off base, huh? I think there's even fan fiction about that."

I snort. "*Way* off base."

He puts one wet hand on my shoulder muscle and squeezes. "Sorry. I don't mean to make a joke out of your life."

"You're fine. But locker room showers were, like, a place of terror for me when I was young. I got really good at showering fast and exiting quickly."

"Okay, yeah." He flinches. "I was on the track team in high school, and I don't think I ever set foot in the showers. I would stare into the back of my locker while I threw my shorts on, and then hurry out of there."

"That sounds about right." People think the gay kid in the locker room is probably staring at them, but it's just the opposite. The idea of getting turned on in a locker room filled my teen years with abject horror. "In the showers, I used to focus on the tile grout just to keep my mind busy."

"Huh. What color was it?" he asks, lifting his hands to my face.

"Um, gray? Usually. Sometimes white."

"See?" he says, his eyes brightening. "You do notice furnishings. I knew I liked you."

I chuckle, and when he kisses me, it's just so nice. I nudge him back against the tiles and circle his wrists with my fingers. When I raise them overhead—like I'd done that night in front of the fridge —he moans.

Our kisses pick up speed. It isn't long before we're both revved up again. I lose myself in the slickness of heated, wet skin, and a dollop of body wash that Carter applies to us at exactly the right moment.

Sex has always been a fraught concept for me, but tonight I'm easy. Carter's hand—and the sounds of pleasure that he makes— have me cursing and shooting once again.

We sag against the tiles, trading lazy kisses. Carter has to shut off the water as it begins to turn cold. And now I understand where Rigo gets his fan-fiction fantasies.

We're both too spent to talk as we towel off and stagger into my bedroom.

Carter pulls back the covers and gets into bed without discussing it, and I'm grateful, seeing as I can barely keep my eyes open.

Sleeping with a guy will be another first for me. I don't know the etiquette.

As usual, Carter makes it easy. He rolls toward me, throws a knee over mine, and rests his head against my shoulder.

"Mmm," he says, kissing my neck. "You are a good time."

Huh. "You're the first person to ever think so."

"That cannot be true," he mumbles.

But I'm pretty sure it is.

The next thing I know, Carter is putting my phone in my hand. "Wake up, Jersey. Your phone is ringing."

My eyes spring open in the dim light. It's two minutes after seven, and my phone's screen says, *One Missed Call.*

I sit up quickly, and my head spins.

"Hey, take a breath," Carter says. "You want me to go make coffee?"

"Uh, sure," I say, eyeing my phone the way I'd size up a scorpion.

He leaves the room. I scrub the sleep out of my eyes and then poke my sister's number.

"Hey, Tommy," she says, sounding remarkably cheery. "Want the latest?"

"You know I do."

"They suspect anemia, which means..."

"An iron deficiency, right?"

"Right. And her blood-cell count isn't even that terrible. She's getting medication. She slept comfortably, and they'll release her later today."

I let out a giant breath. "Okay. So a manageable problem."

"Very manageable," she says gently. "And not uncommon for chemo patients. You can stop panicking for now. Mom is still coming out there for Christmas."

"Are you *sure*?"

She's quiet for a moment. "Tommy, a meteor could wipe us off the planet by cocktail hour. Nothing is ever for sure."

"I know that," I grumble. "I just wondered if it was safe for her to come here."

"She thinks so," Gia says. "And it's her life. Besides—if anything happened, you have hospitals in Boulder, too."

That's true, but it isn't exactly comforting. "I just wouldn't want her to exhaust herself on my account."

"She's really looking forward to the trip," Gia says softly. "It's all she talks about."

I swallow a big lump in my throat. "So am I. The house is ready. We just did the tree last night."

"*We?*" Gia asks with about as much subtlety as a brick through a window. "Who's we?"

"A friend and I."

"Oh! Is this your designer friend?"

She and my mother have obviously been talking about me. "That's the guy. He's, uh, good at stuff like that." *And other things.*

It's a good thing Gia is a thousand miles away and can't see my ears turn red.

"Here comes the nurse," my sister says. "Mom wants some tea, so I gotta flag her down. Call you after she's discharged?"

"Yeah, let me know what else you learn."

"Will do!"

I sag against the pillow, taking a moment to absorb the news. I panicked last night, my mind traveling from zero to calamity in just a few seconds.

But that's how this year has gone. My mother's illness blind-sided me. I'd been here in Colorado for two seasons, focusing on hockey and feeling grateful that I still had a career. I was so happy to get away from New Jersey and the shame of my failed marriage. I didn't spare a lot of thought for my family.

Maybe it makes me a self-centered jerk, but when my mother got her diagnosis, I took it personally. Like the universe was telling me that I don't deserve to start over or set aside my past mistakes.

I take another deep breath and let it out for a count of four. Then I set my phone down on the nightstand. It's oak—the same wood as the bed—and it appeared here in the last few days. Like magic.

Carter is the magic. He showed up out of nowhere and handled every detail I'd asked of him. And he did it with style and humor.

And then last night...

A slow smile spreads across my face. My life might be ninety percent disastrous right now. But that other ten percent is pretty amazing.

THIRTY-TWO

Carter

TOMMASO'S COFFEE maker is a high-end, pod-style machine, so it only takes me a couple of minutes to make two mugs of coffee.

It's not nearly enough time to get my head together.

I can't believe I woke up under my boss, his hard dick poking me in the hip. And me spreadeagled on his eight-hundred-thread-count, Egyptian-cotton sheets, like the little slut that I've become.

So much for acting like a professional, or even a decent friend. Tommaso had a scary, emotional night, and my big solution was taking him to bed.

I put a splash of milk in his coffee the way he likes and brace myself to go back up there. As I carry the mugs toward the stairs, I can't help noticing how great the living room looks with the tree in the window.

But I should not be admiring it in the boxer shorts that I had to dig out from under the new club chair a few minutes ago.

When I enter the bedroom, Tommaso is leaning back against the headboard, a contemplative look on his face. He doesn't look wrecked, so it can't be terrible news.

"Is she okay?" I ask, handing over his mug.

"Yeah. They say she's anemic. She needs iron and a little monitoring, so it's not the dark omen I took it to be."

"I'm so glad to hear that," I say, walking around to the far side of his giant bed. I shouldn't get back in at all, but it's December, and Tommaso keeps the thermostat turned down. And the rest of my clothes are still cast around his living room.

Tommaso takes a gulp of his coffee. Then he sets it down on the table and turns to examine me. "You okay?"

"Yup," I say briskly.

He frowns. "Remember the promise I made you? About not regretting you?"

I flinch. "Yeah."

"I regret nothing."

Thank God. "That's a relief."

"So why do you look kinda anxious? Doesn't that promise work both ways?"

I blow out a breath. "It ought to. Except I've been trying to work on my professionalism. Last night I failed."

He rolls, eating up the distance that I'd carefully left between us, propping his big body up on his forearms and looking me right in the eyes. "You weren't on duty, soldier. I think you're in the clear."

"Still. You were having a very emotional night. There were better ways to be your friend than stripping off all your clothes. I chose hedonism. It's a theme with me. In my line of work, maybe it's an occupational haz—"

I lose the rest of the word as his hand slides up my thigh. "Do I look like someone who thinks you made the wrong choice?"

"No," I admit, and it comes out sounding breathy.

"When you told me I wasn't allowed to regret you, I understood what you were saying. That you didn't want to feel guilty about it later."

"Exactly." See? He does understand.

"You seem to have a few regrets, though." He gives me a serious frown. "Does that mean *I'm* supposed to feel guilty about the best night ever?"

"No! God no."

He tilts his head to the side, still gazing at me. "Then enough with the regrets, Montana. *Capiche?*"

"I..." At the top edge of the sheet, he strokes a thumb over my hip. "I don't even know what that means."

A flicker of a smile. "It's Italian-American for *got it.*"

"Got it," I repeat, setting my mug down on the side table.

He nods. "Okay, unrelated question. Why do you enjoy it so much when I hold you down?"

I blink, the change of topic startling. "I don't know. I just do?" *And are you going do it again?* I cover my eyes, because maybe it will help me focus.

"But why," he presses. "Serious question. I like how you respond when I pin you down. But I'd still like to understand, so I don't overstep."

"Oh. Um..." The feel of his hand so close to my groin makes it difficult to think. "To be honest, a shrink would probably have a field day with this question. But I've always wanted a man to tell me he loves me and then fuck me like he hates me. Most guys can only do one or the other, which is probably why I'm still single."

"And I thought I was the confusing one."

"Right?" He strokes my skin lightly, and somehow, I'm still talking. "I guess I like the illusion of having to *submit* to whatever you do to me. Like I don't have to second guess my slutty personality because—oops! Not my choice." I pull my hands away from my face and check his reaction. "Okay, that sounds really fucked up when I say it aloud."

He's stoic as always. But his lips twitch in a smile. "I thought maybe it was something like that. I get it."

"You *do?* You seem so toppy to me."

"Yeah, I don't think I'm the same, but there are other things in my life that would just be easier if I didn't have to make all the decisions."

"Like what?" I ask, just to stay in the conversation.

He leans down and kisses my stomach right where the sheet

stops. His beard tickles. The contrast between these questions and the heat of his kiss makes my head swim.

He lifts his chin. "I've been asking myself why I chose the house across the street from Newgate's. That Pride jersey I gave you? It's for his announcement."

"Whoa," I gasp. "No way."

"Yeah. His boyfriend and their daughter live across the street, too. Don't say a word, okay? But the whole world will know soon enough."

"I'm a vault. But *wow*." I run my fingers through his thick hair. "So you think maybe your subconscious wanted to be his neighbor?"

"Maybe." His voice drops. "Like I needed to see what it was like to be Newgate. To go home to a boyfriend every night and not give two shits about what anyone else thinks."

"Oh."

He turns to lay his head across the sheet, but also across my thighs. I like the heavy weight of it. "Yeah. And then I doubled down. I met this hot redhead who wasn't afraid to stand in my kitchen and tell me he was gay."

"Am I the hot redhead in this scenario?" I ask, because I'm a little distracted.

He snorts. "Pay attention, Montana. I'm trying to tell you that you made me nervous, but I hired you anyway. I didn't even consider looking for another designer. I only wanted you."

"Oh."

His finger traces the edge of the sheet that's barely covering my hip. "I've been at war with myself for years, you know? It's just that lately—for the first time—the other side seems to be winning. And I'm kinda digging it." He lifts his head again, tugs down the covers, and kisses my stomach above the waistband of my boxers.

His mouth is so close to my dick that I don't stand a chance. My erection reports for duty, tenting the cotton.

"So how does it work?" he asks, sliding his fingertips across my abs. "Let's say I'm holding you down, and I do something you don't like. How would I know you don't like it?" He punctuates this question by pulling the sheet all the way off my body, and then nosing the erection in my shorts.

"Um…" I let out a hot breath. "If I was unhappy, there's really no way you could miss it. It's easy enough to say *stop that* and mean it. Even with, uh, a gag on."

"A gag," he repeats slowly, his eyes on fire. "I can't decide if that sounds hot, or just awkward."

"It's just, uh, a serving suggestion," I mutter. "Not a requirement."

"I like the visual," he says, tucking his fingertips into my waistband. "But I also like the things you say when you're turned on."

"Nnngh," I say as he drags my underwear down and off my body.

"And as for regrets, I've only got one." He tosses my boxers off the bed, along with the covers.

"A regret?" I ask as goosebumps rise all over me. "Already?"

"Yeah. Kinda wish I'd gone for the four-poster bed." He runs a hand up my bare leg. Slowly. Like he's taking measure of me. "I think I understand the possibilities now."

"Do you?" my voice cracks as he takes my thighs in two hands and parts my legs.

Oh God. He's going to go down on me, and I'm going to let him. We both know it. This man is not the least bit unsure of himself. He knows his own mind. I can tell, because he's practically blowing mine.

"Give me your hands," he orders.

I offer them immediately, palms up.

He wastes no time pinning them to the mattress. "Now don't move. I've never done this before, so need you to hold very still."

"O-okay." My whole body flushes with heat. "Can do."

He drops his lips to my thigh and drags a path of kisses along my skin. I shiver, and his hands tighten against mine. "*Still,*" he repeats.

"Got it."

And then? The jerk spends the next five minutes teasing the hell out of me, dropping kisses on my inner thighs and then brushing his lips, and his beard, against the root of my cock.

"Are you hesitating?" I growl. "Or just mean?"

"Don't rush the new guy," he says maddeningly.

"Oh, for fuck's sake."

He laughs, but he also palms my cock. Then he lowers his chin and takes my tip into his mouth. He's very deliberate about it, his dark eyes thoughtful. The way he does everything.

He's still got my hands pinned to the bed, with a forearm weighing down one of my thighs. I don't have a lot of mobility, so all I can do is watch and breathe through my desire as he opens his mouth wider and slides me onto the heat of his tongue.

Then he *moans*, and the vibration makes my nipples tighten.

"Fuck," I pant, my hips giving an involuntary twitch.

His hands increase their grip in a wordless reminder not to move. Then he tilts his chin, takes me deeper, and experiments with a good, hard suck.

I groan, trying not to thrust. But I'm dying, here.

He releases me with a pop. "You taste good."

"Nnngh," I say again.

"Hands on the sheet. Hold them still yourself, because I need to use mine."

"Okay," I gasp, flipping my palms onto the cotton.

"Good boy."

The praise lights me up, because that's how I'm wired. Later, I'll probably wonder how a self-professed "new guy" so easily got my number.

But right now, I don't care. I tip my head back against the mattress and close my eyes as one of his thumbs begins a tour of my shaft. Then strokes my balls.

Meanwhile, he's using his mouth to slowly drive me insane. Every swipe of his tongue makes me want to thrust into his mouth. But he told me not to move, so I try my best.

Maybe Tommaso doesn't have any experience with this, but he

sure seems to be enjoying it. He's experimenting with the speed and the pressure. And every time I groan, he makes an answering grunt of pleasure.

How is this my life? I open my eyes to make sure he's real, and I find him watching me. "Bend your knees," he says.

"What? Like this?" I drag my heels toward my ass.

"Yeah." He rises up on his knees, props my shins against his bare chest, and bends me in half.

Then he casually slicks up a finger in his mouth before brushing it down my crease.

"Fuuuuuuck." My whole body tightens. I'm so turned on, my muscles tense with the need for release.

Shameless now, he takes me in his mouth again, his hand stroking my taint.

It's too much. "I'm so close."

He pulls off. I expect him to finish me with his hand, like we did last night. But that's not what happens.

With the agility of a professional athlete, he spins his body around until we're positioned sixty-nine style, with him on top. Which means I'm suddenly gazing up at what must be the most perfect specimen of a male erection that ever graced the planet.

Before I've even had a moment to admire it, it comes closer. He's on all fours, poised over my body, taking me into his mouth once again and using one hand to nudge his cock between my lips.

I open on a moan. And then it's like someone fired the starting gun at the start of a race. I sprint toward the finish line, thrusting into his mouth while grabbing his hips to bring his cock more deeply into mine.

There's no finesse. We're both too hyped up to care about technique. All I can do is hold on and take it as he pistons into my mouth.

It's the noise he makes that sends me over the edge. A sudden, soul-deep groan and I'm done for. I slap his hip to warn him, but he doesn't release me. He just takes it.

Bright colors burst against my eyelids, and my body shakes with my release.

He holds on for a moment, then lifts his head, letting out half a laugh. "Fuck, I..." He pulls out suddenly, grabs his cock, and comes with a moan all over my abs.

And all I can do is lie here and try to breathe. My heart is whirring inside my chest. I'm sure I'm red-faced and disheveled, but I've never been so satisfied in my life.

Tommaso gets up while I'm still made of jelly. He trots into the bathroom and returns a minute or two later with a wet cloth, which he uses to wipe up my torso with careful strokes.

Then? He fetches the comforter off the floor and pulls it over both of us, rolling me into his arms once his head hits the pillow.

Now I'm being cuddled by a big, muscular hockey player. And I'm too spent to remember why I felt guilty about it half an hour ago.

THIRTY-THREE

Tommaso

SILENCE DESCENDS ON THE BEDROOM. I'm all wrung out, in the best possible way.

This is a new feeling—a little like the exhaustion that comes after a hard practice, but tinglier.

Sex had always been fraught with my wife. I was always just trying to get through it without embarrassing myself.

This feels totally different. My body is relaxed in a way I don't think I've ever felt before, with Carter tucked against me, skin to skin. I can feel his heartbeat against mine, and my mind is a calm, floaty buzz, courtesy of endorphins.

"You okay?" he asks eventually.

"I'm the best I've ever been."

He laughs, but I'm not really kidding. It's like I've been taken apart and put back together again in a much better way.

What a difference a few hours make. Last night—when Gia called—I was in despair, shaken by the reminder that anyone I love can always be snatched away.

My mother's illness has been terrifying. But also really clarifying. I've fallen in line with her new motto—don't wait to be happy —and I'm naked with a great guy and sexually satisfied for the first time in my life.

So this is how the other half lives.

"Not sure what's more surprising," he mumbles. "The mind-blowing sex or the cuddling."

"Eh," I say, my voice a rasp. "I've never blown anyone's mind before. But I'm a very experienced cuddler."

He laughs into my shoulder. "That's so unexpected."

"Why?"

He gives his head a little shake and then slides a muscular leg over mine, moving us even closer together. "I had the wrong impression of you when we met. I thought you were a rich, cold grouch."

"I'm rich, and I'm a grouch. You were two-thirds right."

"Nah." His thumb traces a pleasing arc across my pec. "You're the strong, silent type. But kind of a teddy bear."

"If you say so. I got nothing against cuddling. It's probably why my marriage lasted two years instead of one."

Carter raises his head and meets my gaze. "You never talk about your marriage."

"Because it's embarrassing. Jessie is a great girl. We spent a lot of time together in college, and I loved her. But not in the way she needed me to."

He puts his head back down. "I'm sorry. That sounds painful."

"It was," I admit. "And also totally avoidable."

"Confession—I googled it. She was your college tutor, right?"

"Yup. She always made me laugh, and she was one of my favorite people at Princeton, where I never really fit in. The guys kept asking me when Jessie and I were going to become a couple. So I invited her out to dinner."

Carter props his head on his hand and just listens. There's no judgment in his eyes.

"We started dating. We took things slow. Jessie knew I was busy with school and spring training. She didn't seem annoyed that I never escalated things physically. Not much, anyway. I told her that I was a traditional guy. That tracked for her because I wasn't much of a partier, either."

"Maybe she appreciated that about you," Carter points out.

"She did," I agree. "When summer rolled around, I was sent to Trenton's training camp, so we didn't see each other. I was playing good hockey, and the franchise asked me if I wanted to go professional the following year.

"And it was becoming increasingly clear that I'm not a scholar. So I told the franchise yes. Jessie cried, and I'm not built to withstand female tears."

"Is anyone?" Carter asks gently.

"Probably not. But most guys probably don't solve the problem with a marriage proposal."

Carter winces.

"Yeah. I know. It was the dumbest thing I've ever done. I realize that now. But it didn't seem like it at the time. Jessie cried again. Happy tears. Swear to God, I'd never made anyone so happy in my life."

He kisses my jaw. Like he knows this story is about to turn sad.

"So that was the high point. We got married in a hurry and made plans to move. My uncle was suddenly less awful. Marco, too —all look who bagged himself a pretty wife."

Carter groans. "I hate that guy, and I've never met him."

And you never will, I silently add. "It wasn't just them. My sister cried, like I'd done something amazing. And my mother was so excited to have a daughter-in-law. I felt like I'd solved a riddle— how to fit in better with the whole world."

Another kiss from Carter. He doesn't comment, which I appreciate. He doesn't need to tell me how awful this story is, because I already know.

"Our honeymoon was a weekend on the Jersey Shore, because hockey waits for no man. The sex was, uh, functional but awkward. I joked that I'd get better at it. Like I'd gotten better at geometry the year before. But then I didn't."

Carter runs a hand through my hair. "I'm sorry."

"Not as sorry as she was. She was nice about it at first. But it made me so *tense*."

"Which only made things worse?" Carter guesses.

"Yeah, of course. So avoidance became my big strategy. I was busy traveling. Or I was too tired. You name it, I used it as an excuse. She took it personally. We started fighting. And eventually she asked me point blank if..."

I swallow hard, because I can still picture her tear-stained face when she asked me if I was gay. She was sobbing. Angry. Hurt.

"You don't have to tell me," Carter whispers. "I don't want to upset you."

"Oh, you aren't." I sigh. "Water under the bridge. I lied to that girl's face, because I was still, uh, lying to myself at that point. I was hanging onto that lie with two hands."

"It happens."

"I know that. But I still feel bad about it. I made that nice girl cry, and then I made her leave me. I couldn't even man up and tell her it wasn't her fault. I'm as bad as that jerk you were with in Montana, Carter."

"Nah. You didn't mock her to your friends, right?"

"Of *course* not."

"You're not blameless, and you probably owe her an apology. But the difference between you and my jerkwad high school boyfriend is whether you've learned anything from the experience."

"I'm trying." I tuck my hands behind my head. "It's hard, though. Talking about it is like pulling off my own skin. And then there's you—willing to tell anyone who you really are. And proud of it."

"I have my moments," he says. "But I knew I was gay from, like, birth."

"Hmm." I stare up at the ceiling. "It took me a little longer. There were clues, but I chose to ignore them. I told myself that I liked looking at men because I admired them."

"You probably did, though," Carter says. "Can't it be both?"

"Sure. But I just didn't want to question why I loved the men's underwear aisle at Target so much. All those models with their biceps and their bulges."

Carter chuckles. "Oh *yaaassss*. Many a queer boy had his sexual awakening staring at a three-pack of briefs."

I don't tell him, though, about what Marco said when he found me there. *What are you doing, you creepy little freak?* The sneer in his voice had been very educational.

I change the subject. "Want some waffles?"

"You know I do."

THIRTY-FOUR

Carter

I'M the kind of man whose conscience is easily bought with good sex and waffles. Tommaso and I sit down to another excellent breakfast, and I let myself enjoy it.

It's easy, because he's in such a good mood. He turns on the Christmas tree lights, and tells me a story about how his nephews pulled the beard off a New Jersey shopping mall Santa.

"My sister has her hands full," he says. "You'd like Gia. She's a charmer. Like you."

I decide to take it as a compliment.

After breakfast, we clean up the kitchen together. It's cozy. His hand on my lower back as he reaches for the dishtowel. His smile as I make him another cup of coffee, since we were too busy jumping each other to drink the first ones.

It's all fun and hot glances until someone suddenly knocks on the front door. "DiCosta! Special delivery!" a voice calls. "Okay, it's not all *that* special. It's a half dozen muffins I just baked."

Just like that, our cozy morning ends as suddenly and painfully as a record-scratch. I check Tommaso's expression, and my heart sags. He looks *spooked*.

"That's my neighbor," he whispers. "Newgate's boyfriend."

His discomfort makes my brain glitch, but only for a second.

Tommaso needs to open the door, and when he does, I can't be shirtless in his kitchen with sex hair.

I put down the bowl I'm drying with a thump. "Go answer it. I'm, uh, stepping into the guestroom for a few minutes." I'm already in motion, carrying my coffee cup with me, and then closing the door behind me.

I sit on the bed in the guestroom, sipping my coffee and feeling like a character in a farce. I'm the secret lover listening to the muffled voices on the other side of the door and wondering if the neighbor will notice the extra shirt draped over the arm of Tommaso's sofa.

All my good vibes deflate like a day-old balloon. My night with Tommaso was impulsive. That's very on brand for me. And look how it's turned out? Hiding out of sight in my lover's back room.

Objectively, I know that Tommaso isn't at fault. He's working through a lot of issues right now. He's an admirable guy.

But right this second, it doesn't matter. I'm still hiding. And I'm still the quasi-homeless fuckup who blew his boss under a Christmas tree.

This is not how an adult behaves.

My face burns as I get up and quietly rummage for another shirt. I do some deep breathing. Then I sit back down on the bed to check the rental listings. Tommaso's mother will soon occupy this room, and I've got to figure out my holiday plans. But there's nothing new to see and no emails from property managers in my inbox, either.

I look up when Tommaso opens the door to the guestroom, his face a storm cloud.

"Everything okay?" I ask.

"Not really." He gives his head a shake. "That sucked. I'm sorry." He clears his throat. "You hid. I didn't stop you. It's not okay, and I feel like a dick."

"You're not a dick," I say quietly. And he isn't. He's just not ready to be the guy who's casually cleaning up the kitchen with his boy toy after breakfast.

"The neighbor is a great guy, too." He leans back against the door frame and stares at the ceiling. "I just don't know how to do this. How to be…"

The sentence dies a quiet death in the space between us.

Gay? Queer? Whatever the word, he can't even say it.

My heart hurts. And then my phone rings suddenly. *Rigo calling.*

I silence it and take a deep breath. "It always sucks. Lying to people. But this stuff takes time."

"What can I do to make it up to you? I don't want to be that guy."

Nothing. "You're on your own schedule, Jersey. You're working on your baggage. But I'm also working on mine. And…"

"I know," he says. "You had an ex who ignored you in front of other people."

"True," I admit. "You're not cruel. But you're also not a guy who's ready to date a guy."

"Fuck." His eyes fall shut. "I want to argue with you. But it's true."

"I know," I whisper. And I wonder—for the hundredth time—how I end up in these situations. "Look… I like you. A lot. You're amazing, but you're not boyfriend material at the moment. And who are we kidding? I'm not either, with my life practically crumbling around me."

He sighs. "You don't have to humor me and pretend it's the same thing. Your issues are just details. Mine are the real obstacle."

I'm not so sure, but I don't want to argue about it. "I need to get my head together. Let me just find my other shirt in your living room, and then I'm out of here for a couple hours."

Tommaso pinches the skin between his eyes. "I kicked it under the couch so that Gavin wouldn't see it."

"Oh." Our eyes meet. His are so conflicted. I believe that he cares about me. But he's got a lot on his plate. A game to win tonight. A sick mom. "I'm going to head out for some last-minute things. You need anything from the outside world?"

He shakes his head. "I'm just sorry about making you feel bad. I really am."

"I'm okay." I take a step toward the door, and I see him hesitate. Like he wants to reach for me.

I don't take the bait. I don't step into his embrace, even though there'd be nothing better than stepping into the strongest arms in Colorado. But I need to stand on my own feet for one goddamn minute, so I slide past him.

"Have a great game tonight," I say quietly.

"I'll try," is his muttered response.

While I'm waiting for my car to heat up, my phone rings. *Rigo Calling.* I'm not really in the mood to talk, but it's odd that he's so desperate to reach me. "Is everything okay?" I ask when I answer.

"Dude! I'm in Boulder, painting your new apartment."

"Wait, what? I wasn't even looking at places in Boulder." It's too expensive. Everybody knows that.

"I'm telling you, this place is perfect for you. Get down here—the owner is in the building. He's got us painting three units. Two of them are pricey, but one is perfect. Get this—it's available on the first of the year! How fast can you get to Fourteenth Street?"

"Pretty damn fast," I say. "Text me the address."

THIRTY-FIVE

Tommaso

AFTER CARTER LEAVES, my house feels really empty. I adjust a few ornaments on the Christmas tree and then sit down on the couch and stare at it.

It's a gorgeous tree. In a gorgeous room. Carter was right about everything, right from the beginning. Even when I made his job difficult, he still built me a refuge. He made me a comfortable, private space to live my life.

If only I had a life.

Last night I had everything I wanted. Tangled up in my bed with the most amazing man I've ever met.

But then I wrecked it this morning.

I pop off the couch and pace around for a few minutes. My gaze lands on the wrapping paper Carter bought. I use some to wrap my mother's present. He's even provided tape and a color-coordinated ribbon.

It takes about fifteen minutes, but once I've finished, there's nothing more to do than wander around my house again, wondering where Carter has gone, and whether he's okay.

When I climb the stairs, I'm confronted by the tousled bed. I almost can't believe what went on in here. Years of wish-fulfillment concentrated into one perfect night.

I make the bed without changing the sheets. Then I pick up the pillow and press my face against it. It smells like him. So at least I didn't dream it.

Except this morning he *hid in the guestroom*. He did that for me when Gavin knocked on the door, probably because he could see the panic in my eyes.

For a moment I'd been relieved. Now I'm just embarrassed.

After another tour of the bedroom, I sit down on the end of the bed and call my mom, and I'm gratified when she picks up.

"Tommaso! You have a game tonight, right? Montreal?"

"Hey, Ma. Yeah, it's game night. But it's always game night. How are you feeling?"

"I'm okay, sweetie. Really. Everyone made a big fuss, and all I needed was some extra vitamins."

"That's underplaying it."

"No, it isn't. I just finished a round of chemo, so I was really drained. But I'm already feeling more lively. My appetite is coming back. I've been keeping myself from going crazy in this hospital bed by thinking about the things I want to cook in your kitchen. You have pots and pans, right?"

Hearing that makes me grin. "The kitchen is fully stocked. I got a Christmas tree last night, too. And there's a wreath on the door. I'm all ready for you."

"I can't wait, Tommy. Seriously. I'm looking forward to it. Is there anything in particular you want for Christmas? Gia wants to send you something, but we're all out of ideas."

"Tell her that's nice, but there's nothing I want." *Nothing you can get at the store, anyway.* I want two things very badly: I want my mother to beat cancer, and I want Carter.

"Thought you'd say that. You need any ideas for your sister?"

"I got her a day at the spa."

"Ooh." My mother sounds impressed. "That's nice. I was going to suggest tickets to the Trenton game for her and Brian."

"The thought had crossed my mind," I admit. My sister let her season tickets go after I got traded. "But, Ma, I don't know if I want you guys at that game."

She's so quiet for a second that I wonder if the call got dropped. "You think there'll be another fight? With Marco?"

My stomach rolls just imagining it. That game is going to be so difficult, and she has no idea. "I think it's a possibility," I say carefully. "All I can promise you is that it won't be me who starts it."

"Well good," she says, and I wince. "You never told me what happened between you two. But I believe in you."

"Thanks, Mom."

"And Tommy—I know I raised you with the idea that family is supposed to try to get along. But maybe that wasn't right. I never accounted for the fact that your cousin is an angry little shithead."

I choke out a laugh, because I've never heard her speak like this before.

"That doesn't mean I want you to punch each other again. There are better ways of dealing with bullies, Tommaso."

Are there, though? I wish I could think of one. "Does it bother you much? That there's a rift between us?"

"No," she says quickly. "Your uncle saved us when I was young and stupid. And I was so grateful, but my gratitude isn't infinite. Not everyone is deserving of our love. And I know you. My boy listens more than he talks. My boy doesn't start fights with his teammates on national TV. So whatever Marco and Vin did, I can only imagine how long it had been brewing. For years, I bet. And I should have known."

I blow out a breath. "It's not on you, Ma. That doesn't make sense."

"Doesn't it?" she grumbles. "I wanted you to play hockey with your uncle and cousins, because I didn't give you a proper father. I thought you needed that. But I grew up in a house with Vin. I know how he can be."

Do you? Then why did you ever subject me to that?

I'm not going to ask, though. It won't help her heal. And Vin's behavior is nobody's fault but his.

"Do you want to see a hockey game while you're here?" I ask her.

"Absolutely," she says immediately. "I don't care if it's a long night. I just want to be near you. And bake Christmas cookies."

"All right, Ma. You're in. And I'm ready for those cookies."

"Now I'd better go. Gia is here to take me home."

"Bye, Ma. Do whatever the doctor wants you to."

She promises she will, and we hang up. I recommence wandering around my house, feeling restless.

Mom wants to meet Carter, but I don't know where things stand with him. And he still isn't here, so I end up shooting him a text.

> Are you all right?

I immediately regret hitting Send. Because of course he's all right. He's a full-grown adult going about his business. I'm just the loser who's on edge about everything that's happened.

He doesn't return by the time I leave for the game, and I drive myself into Denver, almost wishing Newgate's car was still broken. I don't need more time alone, where I'm trapped inside my own head.

Kapski pulls into the parking lot right as I do. "How are you?" he asks me in his team leader's voice as we approach the entrance. "Nice morning off?"

Well, Kapski, I sixty-nined my hot interior designer. And then I made everything awkward. "It was a pretty good morning. You?"

"Can't complain." He holds the door for me, and we head inside.

When I walk into the dressing room, Stoney is wearing nothing but a jock strap and a Santa hat. He's carrying a metal bowl with little strips of paper inside. "Secret Santa time!" he says, shaking the bowl in my direction.

Well, fuck. I'd forgotten about this little ritual. I can never figure out what to buy for my millionaire teammates, but I reach into the bowl, anyway, hoping to pull out my own name. That would make things easy.

No such luck. I get Ivan Cockrell, the backup goalie. I know nothing about him, so I guess I'm buying him a nice bottle of scotch.

"Thanks for playing, DiCosta," Stoney says, turning away, looking ridiculous with his bare ass in the wind. "Don't forget—there's a twenty-five-dollar spending cap."

"Wait, really?" I grumble.

"Yeah, you gotta be creative."

Great. This will go well. The only thing I know about Cockrell is that he's a vegetarian. And he's very bendy, as all goalies are.

I drop my bag in my stall and greet Hessler, who's lacing up his running shoes beside me. "What's a good Secret Santa gift? Twenty-five dollar maximum."

"Fuck if I know." He shrugs, looking unconcerned. "I drew a support-staff guy, so I can give him comp seats. Problem solved."

"Unfair."

"See you on the bikes," he says, jogging off to warm up.

It turns out that some physical activity is just what I'd needed. When the game starts, I'm ready. I'm focused, I'm skating well, and we're beating Montreal.

At the end of the second period, I get an assist, and I hope my mom is watching.

Confession: I hope Carter is watching too.

We all troop back to the locker room to stretch and rehydrate before the third period. "You're killing it tonight," Kapski says to me. "Nice and loose."

"Thanks," I say, allowing myself a private chuckle. I do feel loose, although I'm smart enough to know that a little sexual gratification didn't make me into a whole new person.

For once in my life, I let someone see how I really feel about him, and that's freeing in its own way. There's at least one person alive who knows all my secrets.

And I like it.

We troop out for the third period, and it starts a little rocky. Newgate is having a rough night. He gets stripped of the puck right after the faceoff. It's up to me to chase the guy down and knock him off the puck in front of our own net.

"Open the eyes, Newgate!" our goalie yells. "Thirty-eight is up your ass!"

"Sorry," my teammate mutters at the next line change. "I'm a disaster tonight. I'm all up in my head."

He does seem like a bit of a mess. "Hey—that's me on a good day. You'll muddle through."

He gives me a grateful stick-tap, and we gulp water before we're sent out again.

After our win is final, Newgate thanks me again for saving his ass. "Some of us are going out for beers. You in?"

I feel bad for shaking my head. "Not this time. I gotta get home. By the way, thanks for the muffins."

"That was all Gavin. Catch us next time?"

"Absolutely."

The truth is I'm eager to go home and see if Carter is there. I have a sinking feeling that he won't be.

But when I turn onto my street, my Christmas tree is alight in the window. The knot inside my chest loosens as I park the car and hurry up the walk.

I unlock the door and find the living room empty. In the glow of the tree, I kick off my shoes and drop my suit jacket on a chair. Then I tiptoe toward the back of the house, where I find light bleeding from under the guestroom door. I tap on the door with one finger. "Carter? Could I come in for a second?"

"Yeah," he says. "Of course."

I ease the door open and find him cross-legged on the bed, wearing flannel pants and a tight T-shirt that clings to his trim chest. There's a sketchpad open on his lap and a metal tin of colored pencils on the bed beside him.

My heart tumbles at the sight of him. I know in my gut that we belong together. That there's a world in which I could come home to this man every night. At least I hope so.

But that's not the world I live in tonight, so I remain in the doorway. I'm not going to crowd him unless he asks me to come closer.

"Good game," he says, looking up from his work to give me a shy smile. "Nice assist. Rigo was blowing up my phone to make sure I'd seen it."

"And had you?" I ask, prepared to hear *no*.

"Well, yeah." He clears his throat. "I watched your game. I always do lately. Thanks for making me admit that." He gives me a bratty look from under the lock of hair that's falling into his face.

I give him a cocky smile, even though I don't have much to be cocky about just now. "I like hearing that. If you thought I was the worst guy ever, you might not bother."

He looks up, his face serious. "You're not the worst guy ever, Jersey. I never thought you were."

"Thanks. But *not the worst guy ever* is still a low hurdle to clear."

He gives his head a shake. "I have a big decision to make, and believe it or not, it doesn't have a thing to do with you."

"Yeah? What's that?"

He beckons to me, and my heart leaps. I walk over to the other side of the bed and sit down beside him. I have yet to change out of my suit, and so I loosen my tie and roll up the cuffs of my shirt. "What are you drawing?"

"Rigo called me today from a jobsite. He was painting this place." Carter holds the sketchbook so I can see it.

"Whoa. I had no idea you could draw like that." He's done a 3D rendering of what looks like a colorful office space. There are big windows fronting onto the street. There's a desk along the wall, but most of the space is dominated by furniture arranged for conversation.

And it's so realistic, I feel like I could step right onto the page.

"Drawing is part of the job," he says, staring at the image. "This place is for rent, and it's unusual because it's zoned for mixed use." He flips the page, and I see a floor plan.

In this view, there's a wall behind the office space, and behind that is a bedroom and a tiny kitchen. A small bathroom completes the space.

"So..." I try to make sense of it. "You'd live there, but you could also see clients during the day."

"Right," he says. "The guy who rented this place before was a sales rep for a clothing manufacturer. He kept racks of clothes in the front office and lived in the back. The top half of this wall..." He points at the divider between the bedroom and the front room. "...is made of glass bricks. So it's private, but not a cave."

"That's a pretty cool setup," I have to admit. Even if I'm not in a hurry to send Carter away. And even if I think he deserves twice as much space as that.

He closes the sketchpad and leans back against the headboard. "It's basically perfect for a guy trying to get a small business off the ground. But it costs more than I was hoping to spend. So I shouldn't do it unless I feel sure I can make it work."

"And you don't feel sure?"

He turns to face me, and those blue eyes I like so much are troubled. "I don't feel sure of anything, Jersey."

THIRTY-SIX

Carter

TOMMASO DOESN'T SAY anything for a moment. By now, I know him well enough to recognize his thinking face.

Now that we've spent time together, I've learned to appreciate his silences. I admire the way he doesn't feel a need to fill up a room with the sound of his own voice. He always weighs his opinion before he gives it.

And, fine, the man rocks a suit. Even if he's quiet, his presence is not. He's all furrowed brows and muscular forearms and a chest that rises and falls with each thoughtful breath.

"So..." he finally says. "I have a couple of thoughts."

"Let's hear them. My head is all over the place."

"All right. First of all, I just want to say that you amaze me. That drawing is incredible. You have so much to give, Carter. Even if you're struggling right now, I don't think you should give up."

Warmth blooms behind my breastbone. "Thank you," I say quietly. "I think I needed to hear that tonight."

"The second thing is a question. I once had a coach who always asked us—what's the pinch point? What's standing between you and the thing you want?"

"Money," I say flatly. "A storefront is perfect for me, because it's free advertising. I'd be relaunching my business in a bigger way. If you can't find me, you can't hire me, so the storefront would help. This would be a big step forward. But if it puts me into another financial hole..." I heave a sigh.

"So it's a capital problem. How much capital is standing between you and, say, a year of trying to get your business off the ground?"

"Um..." If I were any good with money, I'd already know this. "Thirty thousand dollars, maybe? There's the rent, of course. But then I'd have to design the office in a stylish way. I'm good at making low-end things look high end, but it wouldn't be free."

"Thirty grand is not a whole lot of capital," he says slowly.

I close the sketchbook and toss it aside. "Maybe not to you. But it sounds like a goddamn fortune to me. And please don't offer to invest. I can't take your money, and it would pain me to say no."

"Wouldn't dream of it." A grin twitches at the corners of his kissable mouth. "But let me show you something. Is your laptop handy?"

"Of course." I grab it off the bedside table and wake it up.

He pulls it onto his lap and types *Kelsey yoga therapy* into the browser. Then he pulls up a Kickstarter page. "Look at this. Kelsey is the girlfriend of one of my teammates. She raised forty grand in fourteen days. And now she has her own yoga-therapy studio."

I take the computer and scroll through the campaign. "But she has so many friends," I point out. "I don't know two hundred people, let alone two hundred who want to chip in to help me launch a business."

"Are you sure?" he asks. "Because look at the tiers. I did that one." He points to the hundred-dollar tier. "I don't really know Kelsey, and I don't need any yoga therapy. But I got a T-shirt that says *Kick Your Own Asana*. I did it to be a good teammate, and I kind of liked the shirt."

I blow out another breath and try to picture it. "That's an expensive shirt."

"That wasn't the point," he insists. "People like good ideas. And they like investing in their friends."

My mind whirls. "I can almost picture it. My thing is home design, so I wouldn't do a shirt. I'd do an overpriced mug instead. Designed by me and made in Colorado. A hundred and fifty bucks."

"See? There you go." He squeezes my knee with one of his oversized hands. "And how about another tier at, say, three hundred dollars that offers a one-hour consultation with you, in person."

"But consultations are free," I argue. "Like when I drove out here to meet you? That's standard."

Tommaso licks his lips. "Best meeting ever. But this wouldn't be the same thing. This would appeal to someone who isn't sure they want to redesign anything. They're on the fence. But they paid for your time, so they don't feel any pressure to commit."

"Oh," I say slowly. Then I lean back and close my eyes. "How are you so in tune with all this business stuff?"

"It's...like a puzzle?" he says with a shrug. "I like problem solving. If I ever go back to school, I'd probably study business."

"I can see that," I realize. "You're practical to a fault."

He shrugs. "I bet you could make this work. You're good at your job, and you have a big personality. Besides—*someone* is going to earn money as a designer in this town. Why not you?"

Well really. Why *not* me? "Thank you, Jersey. That's really nice of you to say."

"I'm not that nice a guy." He picks up my hand and flattens it to his mouth, kissing my palm. I get goosebumps as his beard tickles my skin. "But I believe in you. If you can get *me* to understand what design is for, you could probably convince Attila the Hun to invest in an accent wall."

I let out a startled laugh. And then I give in to the gratuitous desire to wrap my arms around Tommaso's chest. He smells like pressed cotton and heat.

He puts the laptop onto the side table before tugging me closer. "I'm sorry I was a dick this morning. I wish I could have been the guy you deserve."

"Jersey, I know," I say, burying my nose in his neck. "I'm over it already."

He pulls back and gives me an assessing glance. "I'm a work in progress. For example, I used to *dread* sex. And now I have to restrain myself from pushing you down on this bed and humping your leg like a horny Rottweiler."

I laugh. "Sorry. There's nothing funny about dreading sex."

He shrugs. "Apparently I'm over it."

"So then what are you waiting for?" I lift a hand and brush my knuckles through his beard.

Our gazes lock, and his is hungry. But he doesn't kiss me, and my heart drops when he climbs off the bed.

"Where are you going?" I ask.

He stops in the doorway and turns around. "Come here."

Um, okay? I slide off the bed and join him in the doorway.

He hooks a finger into my waistband and tows me into the kitchen. Now we're getting somewhere. "Listen, Montana, I can't strip you down in that room."

I glance back at the perfectly good bed behind me. "Why not? Is it because you bought that bed for your mom?"

"Nah." He runs a thick finger down my nose. "But when I invited you to stay here, it wasn't an exchange for sexual favors. You taught me what it means to have a refuge, and I wanted to give you a refuge from your troubles. So that room is off limits."

I blink. "Wow. That's really considerate. But not for one second did I imagine you were taking advantage of me."

"Fine. But that's still my rule. Besides, I have other plans for you." His dark gaze sweeps my body from head to toe.

"You do?"

He does. A moment later my back hits the refrigerator, and my wrists are pinned above my head again. I blink up at him, my body warming.

"I still dream about you right here," he says quietly.

"Oh," is my witty response. But it doesn't matter, because he's kissing me.

And wow. It's just as good this time. Urgent kisses, and the tickle of his beard. Just when I'm sure it can't get any better, he slides one of his oak-like thighs between my legs. I'm pinned in place and loving every minute of it.

He kisses me again, and his free hand strokes my chest. Time starts to lose all meaning. I ride this wave of lust wherever it's going to take me.

But then he groans and breaks the kiss. This time he doesn't jump back like he's been electrocuted. He presses his forehead against mine and asks a crucial question. "Carter, do you think we should take this upstairs?"

"You know I want to."

"I can't promise you I won't screw up again," he says. "Still kind of a mess, here."

"You're not so bad. Let go of my wrists, though."

He drops them immediately.

I take hold of his face, stroking my fingers down his beard. "The thing is, I understand your issues, just like you seem to understand mine. My eyes are wide open."

His gaze dips down my body, and then he sighs. "Mine are wide open, too, which is why I need to get you naked."

"So go upstairs already."

He gives me a dark look. Then he steps back, turns on his heel, and heads for the living room.

For a second, I'm distracted by the sight of his muscular ass in those suit pants. *Athletes, wow*, my brain offers up. *I bet he has to have those trousers specially made.* But then I realize time is wasting, so I hurry after him.

In the living room, Tommaso picks up his suit jacket and his gym bag. He gives me a hungry, glare as I pass him.

I like the weight of his gaze as I climb the stairs. So I stop halfway up and peel off my shirt.

"Christ," he mutters. And now I feel him following me up the stairs, his footfalls slow and heavy.

My pulse kicks into a higher gear, and I loosen the drawstring on my flannel pants as I reach the second floor.

"Go on," he says in a low voice. "Take it all off. Then pull down the comforter and get on the bed."

The timbre of his voice brings goosebumps to my skin. I do exactly as I've been told, except that when he disappears into the bathroom to brush his teeth, I light a blocky candle on the dresser. It's something I'd picked up in a Denver boutique, and now it will serve its true purpose. Everyone knows that a candle in the bedroom is a sex candle.

I guess maybe there's some guy *somewhere* who lights a bedroom candle for some other purpose. Meditation maybe.

But fuck that guy. This candle is for sex.

Tommaso isn't done yet, so I lie naked in the center of the sheet, cock one leg to the side, and begin to stroke myself.

"Hot damn," he rumbles, reentering the room. "I guess you understood the assignment. A-plus."

"Thank you, Coach."

He chuckles as he unbuttons his shirt. "I wondered what that candle was for. Now I know."

His hungry eyes are fixed on my cock, so I slow down my strokes and luxuriate in the attention. "Flattering lighting is everything," I mumble. "Are you getting onto this bed, or what?"

"In a second. I have to hang up my suit."

I roll onto my side to watch him. "Okay—I have a question. How do you have such beautifully designed clothes, but home furnishings are invisible to you?"

He snorts. "That's an easy one. My sister picks out the suits." He shrugs his big shoulders and then takes care of his clothes. He's like an advertisement for the perfect male physique. The rippling back muscles. The trim waist. "I don't have to even walk into the store. Gia ships them to me, and then I take them to the tailor."

I chuckle, because I should have expected that.

But when he turns around, I stop laughing. There's an unusual intensity to Tommaso. I've always thought so. But now it's focused entirely on me. He stalks toward the bed with the grace of someone who moves his body for a living.

"Lie back," he says. "I've been thinking about this all evening."

"*Yessir.*" I roll onto my back. "What are you going to...*oh.*"

He's already climbing on top of me, bracing his bulk onto his forearms. He dips down to kiss my jaw, just once. "I missed you today."

Oh oh oh. Hearing it feels as good as his hunky body on mine.

"Been thinking about you a lot."

"S-same," I stammer, reaching up to run my fingers through his thick hair. His gaze is so intense. Like a tiger's. But his touch is sweet. "So... what's on your to-do list tonight?"

"How much time you got? It's a pretty long list."

I groan.

He kisses me again. And again. And my heart nearly breaks from trying to contain so much joy.

THIRTY-SEVEN

Carter

WHEN I OPEN MY EYES, I'm naked and pressed against Tommaso's body. This morning it's not a shock, because I haven't slept in the guestroom for days.

Kisses up against the refrigerator are a nightly occurrence now.

Tommaso wasn't kidding when he said he was an experienced cuddler. Usually, he tucks me against his side, like a favorite stuffed animal. But sometimes—like now—I wake up pancaked against his back, with one arm tucked over his muscular body and his hand pressing my palm to his chest.

But if his cuddling has serious game, his sex drive has even more.

I indulge in a memory of the previous evening. He'd had the night off, and it had been snowing. I'd lit a fire in the fireplace, and we'd tucked up onto the sofa together, our stocking feet propped on the coffee table.

At first, we'd pretended to watch a hockey game on TV. It was Dallas versus...

Okay, I don't remember who. But it's not my fault, because Tommaso began sucking on my neck during the first period. And he put his hand down my sweatpants in the second period.

By the third period, we were on the rug in front of the fireplace, kissing like the world was ending, and stripping each other's clothes off.

The evening ended with another round of fun in the shower before we tumbled into bed. I'm getting hard just thinking about it. But the sun is trying to blast its way through the new curtains, and his alarm will go off any minute, so I put our morning routine into action.

I slip out of bed and head downstairs to make coffee. The kitchen is warm and tidy, and I lean against the counter while our coffee brews.

For just a moment, I let myself imagine that this isn't just a temporary arrangement. That the man upstairs is asleep in *our* bed. That we're a real couple, the kind who plans date nights and vacations together.

I want that life. And it isn't because Tommaso has a fancy kitchen and makes seven figures a year. If belonging to him meant living in a crappy little apartment with seven-foot ceilings, I would still feel this way.

Even if there was fluorescent lighting, and even if the walls were piss yellow.

Okay, I'd probably repaint and get better lightbulbs. I wouldn't be able to help myself. But I'd still give up a lot for the love of the man upstairs. Because I want what Rigo and Buck have. Even if that means some sacrifices.

After the coffee finishes brewing, I carry our mugs upstairs. After I place them on the nightstand, I sit on Tommaso's side of the bed and pass my fingertips through his shiny, dark hair.

This is the best part of my morning, because when he wakes, he gives me a completely unguarded smile. It's the smile I get before he remembers that he's a professional athlete trying to make it to the playoffs. Before he remembers that he's the world's most intense human. Before he gets up to make us a healthy breakfast and checks his phone for team messages and meetings and touches base with his family.

For a split second, there's only me and that smile. And I cherish it.

—————

Tommaso's days are still chaotic, but mine are winding down. The house is finished. And after he leaves for the rink, it's very quiet here.

I spend the afternoon sending out feelers, but there's no new design work to be had until January. That's just the way it is.

So after a couple hours of spinning my wheels, I start to think about dinner. That means a trip to the grocery store. I prompted Tommaso to pause his grocery delivery service, because it's expensive. And with all my free time, I can cook for him. It makes me feel useful.

Not that it's a hardship. Cooking in his kitchen is a pleasure, and Tommaso is always grateful to come home to a hot meal. A *large* hot meal. The man can put away the food. It's very gratifying.

When he walks in the door after practice, I'm plating up tonight's offering.

"Hot diggity," he says, stripping off his coat and tossing it onto the club chair. "Dinner smells great. What did you make?"

"Roast salmon with couscous and carrots. Hungry?"

"You know it."

Moments later, we're sitting at the table together. I've served the meal with a glass of wine and candlelight. I've got a reggae Christmas playlist on in the background.

But I'm a little self-conscious. I'm trying to be a good house guest, not act like a contestant for Husband of the Year. Does it seem like I'm trying too hard?

If it does, it's probably because I'm trying too hard.

"You know," he says, scooping couscous onto his fork. "I like pulling into Red Rock and seeing the house lit up."

"Yeah?" Well, this is a problem I can solve. "You know, they have timers for that. I could put your lights on a system that you control with your phone."

He eyes me over his fork, and the candlelight flickers on his handsome face. "That's not what I meant, Carter. I don't need to turn the lights on with an app. I like seeing the house lit up, because I know that you're inside it."

"Oh." I snap my mouth shut before I say anything else stupid.

"Thank you for cooking. This is great."

"It's my pleasure," I stammer. "Really the least I could do."

He gives me a slight frown, like maybe I've said something wrong. Or not, though. Tommaso has a serious face, which I now find sexy. Along with every single other thing about him.

The problem is that I like him too much, and we're running out of time together. "Have you given any thought to, uh, your mother's arrival?" I ask. "Of course, I'll leave the guestroom in pristine condition."

He frowns again and gives his head a quick shake. "Place looks great already. I'm not worried."

"Yeah, but..." I clear my throat. The truth is that I'm waiting for him to say that he wants to introduce me to his mother. But we haven't discussed it yet. "My plan is to ask Rigo and Buck if I can spend a few nights with them over the holidays. So I'm out of your hair."

His frown deepens. "You're *never* in my hair. Except in all the fun ways."

"Okay, but..." I've run out of ways to skirt this topic. "Your mom is going to be here in just a few days. And you've been planning this family holiday for months. Just the two of you." *And I clearly don't fit into that plan.*

He shrugs, like it doesn't matter. "Want some more wine? I'm going to grab the bottle."

"Sure," I say slowly.

He gives me a little smile, and then rises from the table. On his way into the kitchen, he actually drags his knuckles lightly over my cheekbone. It's a very macho expression of affection, and so very Tommaso.

I admire his backside as he heads for the kitchen.

I'm so confused. I don't know what happens next between us. I can't really picture him introducing me to his mom as his boyfriend. Not that I wouldn't like to meet her.

He doesn't want to discuss it, though. That much is clear. So for now, I'm just living in the moment.

And the moment is pretty damn great.

Tommaso's deck furniture arrives the next morning while he's at practice. I arrange it on the screened-in porch.

Come summer, this will be a great spot to hang out. The porch faces south, so there'll be morning light. I could install a hook in the corner for a hanging planter.

A guy could sit out here with his coffee in the morning and watch the sun rise. Or, in the evening, sit with a beer and watch the fireflies.

I realize that I'm picturing myself in this tableau, and it's incredibly presumptuous. Like, wildly presumptuous.

I change the scene in my mind. It's Christmas Eve, and there's a small fire pit on the porch. Ooh! That's a great idea. I know they make smaller models that are safe for screened-in spaces.

And now I know what to get Tommaso as a Christmas gift.

After the furniture is arranged and the packing material vanquished into the Red Rock dumpster, I get into my car and head for the nearest Home Warehouse.

You know you're falling for somebody when you're willing to go into a big box store for them. I hate fluorescent lighting, and giant corporations. But if I can't relaunch my design business, I'll probably end up donning an orange apron and working someplace like this.

In the garden center, I scope out the fire pits. Most of them are wrong for Tommaso's space, but there's one that works. It's pricey, and I'll also need a flame-proof mat for underneath it.

But Tommaso is worth it. I'll pick up some marshmallows and graham crackers on the way home, too, so we can make s'mores.

This all seems like a great idea until I get to the checkout counter. And then I get a shock.

It's Macklin. My ex. The man who ruined everything. "What are you *doing* here?" I yelp. "You said you went to Phoenix!"

"I did." He points a hand-held barcode scanner at my purchases. "Then I came back and got a job."

"You still owe me rent money," I hiss. "I got *evicted* after you left!"

He drops his voice and looms a little closer. "You think you're the only one with trashed credit? Think again."

"Whose fault is *that?*" I demand, not caring who hears. "It was *your* brilliant idea to put Mrs. Clotterfeld's furniture on our personal credit cards."

"Look." He sets down his scanner and gives me a glare. "Get *off* your high horse already, cowboy. You left me all alone to handle the most high-maintenance client I've *ever* met. While you were off dealing with the sane clients."

"So you could *focus,*" I snap. "She was a lot of work."

"She was hellish," he seethes. "And when I got stressed out and upset, and I didn't know what to do, you didn't even want to *hear* the details."

"That's not true," I hiss as I tap my credit card.

Except maybe it is a teeny bit true. I was afraid for our business. I'm better at design than conflict resolution. And the numbers she was racking up on her bill were big and scary.

"Are you sure about that, Carter?" he asks quietly. "Because I don't think I hallucinated your unwillingness to deal with her."

"But you're better at conflict," I point out. Besides, I'm not the one who skipped town when shit went wrong.

"I'm better at conflict, because you *made* me be," he thunders. "You like the fun parts of the job, and you ignore the tough ones.

You just want a guy to take care of you, so you don't have to do anything difficult."

Well, ouch.

He grabs my receipt off the register and thrusts it at me. "I see your credit card still works. So you're doing fine."

"Yeah, super fine," I growl. "Trying to dig myself out from the hole you made. I had to sell our furniture. And now I'm functionally homeless."

He rolls his eyes. "You don't *look* homeless. And you're too pretty to end up sleeping in your car. I'll bet you're warming some guy's bed, right? A fun little arrangement between friends. Or acquaintances. Why be picky?"

I stiffen.

Macklin snorts. "You should see your face. I called that one, huh? Knowing you, though, you probably think you're in love with him, just like you told yourself you were in love with me. Who's the new Prince Charming? The one who's going to sweep you off your feet and make all your troubles go away? Do I know him?"

"Now that's just cruel," I whisper.

He shrugs. "But is it wrong? You probably tell yourself that I'm a horrible person, and that our losses are all my fault. Because it's so much easier than acknowledging that running a business is really fucking hard, and nobody is coming to save you."

"Fuck you, Macklin," I say. Because it's impossible to come up with the right zinger for your ex when you're choking on your own anger.

And it's even harder when you're afraid that he could be right.

THIRTY-EIGHT

Tommaso

WHEN I ARRIVE HOME from practice, I head to the kitchen for a glass of water. When I look out the window, I do a double take. Furniture has appeared on my screened-in porch.

I open the sliding door and step out in my socks. You'd think I'd be used to these sudden upgrades to my life. A porch that was just an empty square at breakfast time now looks inviting in spite of the cold.

But each time Carter works his magic, it still feels like a miracle. The place looks *great*. As usual, he's found furnishings that are simple, yet appealing. The chairs are made of some kind of metal that's coated to be weatherproof, plus a simple seat cushion in an evergreen color.

There's a table between the chairs. When the weather gets warm, we can carry out a couple of plates and eat here.

It's going to be awesome.

I shoot him a text, thanking him for the surprise. But he doesn't text back, and he doesn't return to the house, either—not until I'm putting on my suit for tonight's game.

"Up here!" I call after I hear the front door open.

Carter doesn't appear. He doesn't say a word until I walk down the stairs and find him sitting on one of the leather chairs, looking both thoughtful and distracted. "Hey," he says, not quite meeting my eyes. "You're leaving early for your game?"

"Yeah. I gotta buy a Secret Santa gift on my way to the stadium. It's almost Christmas."

"I could have done that for you," he says. "I like to help."

"Yeah, but I'd feel like a dick tacking extra stuff onto your job."

"Oh." He takes a deep breath. "Look, you're right. My work here is done. And your mother arrives in, what, forty-eight hours?"

I nod, even though I can't quite process how soon that is.

Carter looks really tense. "Look, I've mentioned before that I plan to make myself scarce before she arrives. But you always change the subject."

"Well..." I rub the back of my neck. "I don't really want you to go. I don't like thinking of you staying somewhere unsafe over Christmas, or somewhere you feel unwanted."

He lifts his gaze to mine, but it's guarded. "You definitely don't have to worry about my safety. I'll be just fine."

"Okay, but..." I take a deep breath, and then I make a suggestion. My feelings are so messy, but I'm just not ready for Carter to walk out of my life. "What if you just stayed here?"

His lips part, and I get momentarily distracted by how kissable he looks right now, with his cheeks still red from the December chill. He flushes when we're in bed, too. His face. His chest. It's my new favorite thing.

"How would that work?" he asks, jolting me back to the present.

"Uh..." This is the part I can't quite figure out. "You'd stay upstairs, with me."

His eyes widen. "Which I would definitely enjoy. But what are you telling your mom?"

"Um..." This is where I always get stuck. "That you're in between apartments, so you're staying with me. The rest is nobody's business, right?"

His expression deflates. "Yeah, okay. But passing me off as a friend or a roommate—that's a lie of omission. For me, anyway. I have feelings for you. So if I'm staying with you over Christmas, I can't play a *role* like an actor on a stage."

"Fuck," I say under my breath. "I'm not good at this. I'm sorry."

"I'm sorry too," he says, rising to his feet. "And I know you have a big heart and good intentions. But I can't do this, okay? I need to go."

"Right now?" He can't mean that.

"Why not now?" he asks. "Why delay the inevitable?"

"Because..." *Because I need you here.* I can't say that though, can I? You can't ask someone to lie, and then tell them you need them in the same breath.

This is all happening too fast. And I'm supposed to be walking out the door right now. "Look, this conversation isn't finished, okay? You and I aren't done."

"All right," he says quietly, but his sad blue eyes don't seem to believe me.

"Come here," I say, and it comes out sounding way too bossy. Oops.

But Carter moves to stand in front of me. I put my hands on his shoulders and squeeze gently. He's warm and solid in my grip, and I feel a little zing of amazement that I'm lucky enough to touch him.

Carter studies me with a guarded expression, waiting to hear what I have to say.

But I'm not good with words. Never have been. So I tell him what needs telling in the best way I know how. I lower my mouth to his.

It's nothing like our first crazy kiss against the refrigerator. It's not impulsive. It's deliberate. A slow, heady press, and the quiet *snick* of our lips in the silence of this room that Carter made for me.

It's just a kiss, but it feels bigger. Like dropping a penny into a well. It only takes a second, but it's irreversible. My heart is a lot like that penny, dropping slowly and quietly into the deep.

He pulls away first, his eyes still sad. "Have a good game tonight," he whispers. "I'll be watching."

All I can think to say is, "Thank you." And then I take my bag and go.

––––––

I'm in a melancholy mood when I reach the stadium. But at least I'm clutching a Christmas-themed soccer ball—because I remembered at the last minute that our backup goalie is a fan of elimination soccer—and a bag of jalapeño cheese puffs that I think should be regulated as a controlled substance. They're that addictive.

In the dressing room, Stoney is wearing his Santa hat again. "Let's do this, guys! Secret Santa time. Who's gonna kick us off?"

"I'll go," Kapski says with the same dad energy that makes him a good captain.

"Awesome!" Stoney says, practically bouncing with anticipation. "Who'd you get?"

"You." Kapski draws two gifts out of his duffel bag. "Here you go, Stoney."

"Sweeeeet!" My teammate darts across the floor to take his prizes. "Let's see, I got..." He rips the wrapping paper off a gift. "What the hell is a boot banana? I love it already." He holds up a product that looks like two bananas.

"They go in your shoes to reduce odor," Kapski says with a smug smile. "Thought you could use them."

The whole room laughs.

Stoney beams, as if this were a compliment. Then he rips the paper off the second gift. "Ooh, beer. Always the right size and color, amirite?"

"Thought you could use that, too. And now it's your turn."

Stoney announces another player's name, and the giving goes on. Meanwhile, I change out of my suit and into some warmup gear.

Eventually, Hessler calls my name. He gives me a case of my favorite sparkling water, which is nice, and... "Okay, I don't know what this is?" I hold up some kind of plant cutting, with a ribbon around it.

More laughter. "That's mistletoe," Hessler says. "For your new house at Christmas. I thought about getting you some sage, yeah? To drive away the ghosts. But then I thought *nah*. What a man really needs is to get laid."

"Good thought," I say, and there's another chuckle from the room. "Thanks, Hessler."

"Not sure he needs the help," Stoney says, pulling on his socks. "There's a beat-up old Subaru parked all the time in his guest spot at Red Rock. And when's the last time DiCosta came out with us for drinks after the game?"

Various comments of "oooh" and "busted" ripple through the room, and I can feel my ears turning red.

"Who's the lucky girl?" someone calls out.

Shit. My pulse pounds in my ears, and I realize I could just open my mouth and explain exactly who I've been spending all my time with. *Since you asked...*

My heart glugs again. The moment stretches wide. I could do it.

Then I hear a competing voice in my head. Dutka jeering at me. *They say you were eye-fucking guys in the shower.*

And I flush with a lifetime of shame, and the certainty that nobody really wants to know me all that well.

"Whose name did you get, DiCosta?" Stoney prompts. "Let's finish this up."

"Um..." I swallow hard and drop back into my body. "I got something for Cockrell."

"Where is that guy?" Kapski asks, looking around. "Dude is never late."

"About that," our coach says, striding into the room. His hands are jammed in his pockets, and his forehead is creased in troubled waves. "Management has decided to participate in a three-way trade involving Cockrell and a forward on our AHL team. Cockrell is getting on a plane tonight for Florida."

The energy in the room changes as quickly as flipping a switch.

Trades will do that. Most of the guys are probably saying a silent prayer of thanks that it wasn't their turn to get traded.

"Who'd we get?" Kapski asks quietly. "It better be another goalie."

"Yeah. He's, uh, on his way in," Coach says, eyeing the door.

We all turn at the same time to watch a guy stalk into the room. And mine is surely not the only jaw to drop at the sight of Jethro Hale, a goalie with three championship rings. He's been making other teams cry for more than a decade. Today he's wearing an expensive suit and a very grumpy frown.

We all stare.

He glowers back at us. "Well? I'm here already. Where do you want me?"

Coach glances around the room until his eye lands on Cockrell's half-empty stall. "Banks!" he shouts.

Our equipment guy comes scurrying in from the skate room. "Coach?"

"Set up Mr. Hale in Cockrell's old spot, please."

"Will do, sir." The young man heads over and begins grabbing the practice garb he'd probably laid out for our goalie an hour ago.

We're still quiet, all of us waiting for Coach to give some kind of welcoming speech. But that's not what happens. Coach Powers turns and exits the room without another word.

Okay. That's weird.

There's an awkward beat of silence, and then Kapski shakes off his surprise and approaches Hale with an outstretched hand. "Hi. Welcome to the team. I'm sure you're as surprised to be here as we are to see you. But it's an honor, man."

Hale shakes his hand, but he doesn't look all that honored. "Thanks," he says gruffly. "Merry Christmas to me."

"This really fucks up the Secret Santa chain," Stoney mutters.

Kapski gives him an elbow to the ribs. "Dude, seriously?"

"I love my rituals," Stoney says sourly. "But I'll prolly love not having to shoot past Hale next time we play Detroit. So welcome, man."

"Thanks," Hale says stiffly.

"Where are you staying?" Kapski asks. "The holidays are a rough time for a trade."

"You're telling me," he says, rubbing his temples. "My family is taking it hard. I'm in a hotel in Denver for a few nights. The team found us a condo. It's empty, though. I gotta get some beds and stuff before my dad brings my kid out to Colorado."

I rise and cross the room. "Hey, I got a furniture guy for you. He did my whole place in a few weeks. Looks great, too. You want the name?"

"Absofuckinglutely," Hale says. "Give me all the names. Or—better yet—wake me up from this nightmare."

Kapski and I exchange glances. Stoney rolls his eyes. Trades are hard, but our new goalie is bringing the drama.

"You know you've got to suit up, right?" Kapski says. "They didn't call up a third stringer to back up Volkov tonight."

"Yeah. Sure. I'll get on that. Right after my breakdown."

My teammates look uneasy, but for once, the drama doesn't have a thing to do with me.

So I consciously relax my shoulders and turn my attention to tonight's game.

THIRTY-NINE

Tommaso

WITH VOLKOV IN THE NET, and a glowering Hale on the bench, we defeat Calgary 3-2.

Afterward, my mother and my sister both send me congratulatory texts. From Carter I hear nothing.

"We're taking Hale out to get 'im drunk," Stoney says in the locker room. "Who's with me?"

I give a noncommittal answer and drive home. When I turn into Red Rock Circle, I instinctively look for the light of the Christmas tree in my front windows.

Tonight, the house is dark. My stomach sinks with the sudden certainty that Carter isn't there.

My mood doesn't improve when I let myself into the house. Everything is immaculate. Every throw pillow fluffed into place. Every chair tucked into the table. There are vacuum stripes on the rug.

In the rear of the house, the air is lemon scented. Carter has cleaned the downstairs bath and the guestroom. The bed is freshly remade.

In the center of the guestroom quilt is another needlepoint pillow with a ribbon around it, and a gift tag: *For Mrs. DiCosta*. The pillow reads: *I'm not a regular mom. I'm a cool mom.*

It's beautiful, of course. But I don't even care. Because Carter is gone, and once again my house is quiet. Before I met Carter, I never used to notice the silence, but now it's deafening.

I turn the tree on to cheer myself up. Then I make my way upstairs to take off my suit.

There's a note on the bed. And the house key I gave him as well. Oh no.

Jersey—

You needed your house furnished for Christmas with your mom. I told you I could make that happen. Honestly, it made me so happy to do this for you. I needed this job. But I got so much more from the experience than I ever expected.

When I met you, I'd had a bad run. People kept letting me down.

But not you. I mean that.

I had to leave tonight, but not because you did anything wrong. It's because we're both at a crossroads, with lots of issues to settle. You probably can't settle yours while I'm in your house. And I can't settle mine while I'm freeloading off you.

I'm thinking I might need to go home to Montana and reboot my life. I'm sorry it has to be like this. I'll miss you more than you know, and I wish life was easier right now for both of us.

Please take care of yourself. I'll be thinking about you.

— C.

P.S. There is a gift for you on the porch.

I curse into the silence of my bedroom. He's going to *Montana?*

I reread the letter and notice it doesn't say for sure that he's leaving Colorado. Just that he's considering it.

Am I grasping at straws?

Depressed, I pad downstairs and find my present. It's a little gas fireplace and a bag of marshmallows. He's even provided me with a sharpened stick for roasting them.

With nothing better to do than brood, I figure out how to operate the fireplace. It makes a warm glow on the porch. I sit down and put a marshmallow on the stick.

Alone in the firelight, I miss Carter terribly. He should be here, eating the first marshmallow.

Okay—the second one. I burned the first one.

I set down the stick, and drop my head into my hands. My chest aches.

Letting him go is a terrible mistake. It's just that I don't know how to quit making it.

It's hard to get out of bed the next morning. Practice is a gloomy blur. And then we're down to one more game before the holidays, an out-and-back in St. Louis.

It's a brutal one, as if St. Louis is so desperate to get to their holiday break that they don't mind crosschecking us all to hell to get there.

I watch their rookie center take Stoney down in a blatantly illegal hit. The penalty is called, but only for two minutes, when by rights it should be a game disqualification.

Anger roars through me. I'm suddenly so damn frustrated that my hands are coiled into fists.

A hand clamps down on my shoulder. It belongs to Coach Powers. "Not your problem," he hisses. "Let Dougherty take the fight."

I want to argue. I *hate* that cowardly bullshit. The sport is supposed to be about what you can *do*, not what you can get away with.

"Not your problem," Coach repeats, his voice a warning.

But my coach lies. This is *exactly* my problem. I've chosen hockey over every other thing in my life. I've chosen it over my family and over my private life.

I've chosen it over Carter.

It's all I've got, so I want it done right. Besides—this hot, burning anger in my veins is the only proof that I'm alive.

Dougherty—we call him Doughey—is already throwing down his gloves. "You stupid little punk," he says, circling the guy. "This better not bust up my hand, 'cause I gotta put together a tricycle for my nephew tomorrow."

Then he punches the kid, who goes down like a sack of bowling balls. Shortest fight I've ever seen.

It doesn't soothe the anger in my veins. Only exhaustion will. So I skate like a man on fire. St. Louis doesn't get near the net again, and we win the damn game.

When our jet touches down a few hours later in Colorado, I'm as tired as I've ever been. The holiday break is finally upon us. I've been leaning into this moment for months.

But all I want to do is sleep for a week.

Instead, I get five hours of shut-eye before I pour myself into my SUV and drive to the Denver airport to pick up my mom.

I'm a little early, but that's okay. You don't let your sick mom wait in the baggage-claim area. I buy a cup of coffee, find a seat, and give in to my temptation to text Carter.

> You doing okay? Are you with Rigo?

He doesn't answer.

When Mom's flight lands, I scan the throng of passengers for her face, but I almost miss it.

In the first place, her hair isn't quite the right color. It's a jolt to realize that I'm looking at a wig. Worse—she's so thin that I want to cry when I spot her. I take a deep breath through my nose and smile as best I can.

Because she made it. She's actually here.

"Tommy boy!" she hollers. So I guess her lungs are still at top capacity. "Happy Christmas, baby!"

I hug her carefully, and my voice is close to breaking. "I'm so glad to see you." This is it. I got exactly what I set out to do.

So why do I feel so broken inside?

"Tommaso," she whispers. "Have faith."

Faith. In what, though? My faith in myself has sure taken a hit.

I stand up tall, take a deep breath, and shove all my fear back into the tiny box where I keep it. "Okay, Mom. All right. Let's find your suitcase."

My mother oohs and ahhs over my new house, as if I've shown her the holy grail. "It's so beautiful! So comfortable!"

As predicted, she loves the guestroom. "That wallpaper! So inventive. And what's this?" She fingers the needlepoint pillow.

"That's, uh, a gift," I say haltingly. "From my friend Carter. I told him right up front that my deadline for furnishing this place was Christmas, because you were coming to visit. So he made that for you."

She looks up at me. And I swear to God that her dark, DiCosta eyes see right through me. She sees my struggle, and probably a whole lot of pain. "That was lovely of him."

"It was." I suddenly have no idea what to do with my hands. I try crossing my arms, but that feels wrong. So I jam them in my pockets.

She sets the pillow down on the bed. Then she steps close and hugs me.

I close my eyes and let her hold me, as if I were a little boy again. My eyes feel hot.

"Oh, sweetheart," she says gently. "I've been telling myself that Colorado has been good for you."

"It has," I croak. "Really."

She steps back and puts her hands on my shoulders. "Let's make your friend Carter some cookies. Does he like cookies?"

"Probably." If his love for waffles is any indication, I'm pretty sure it's a safe bet.

"Will I be meeting him?"

My mouth opens and then closes again. Like a fish. Twice. "No, I don't think you will."

She frowns. "Honey, is he important to you?"

My heart practically detonates, and there is suddenly not enough oxygen in this room. This is it, right? The river I swore never to cross. I've always been sure that if I tried, the current would instantly drown me.

But what if I could drag my sorry ass to the other side? There will never be a better time. Besides, there's probably a special place in hell for men who lie to their ailing mothers.

I don't meet her eyes, though, as I swallow past the dry spot in my throat. "He could be," I manage to say. "But it's complicated."

"I can only imagine," she says softly. "Still—do you think he'd like my raspberry thumbprint cookies? Or is he more of a chocolate man? I need to know."

Another deep breath, and I picture Carter's smile. Would he be proud of me right now? Would it make a difference? Or have I already fucked things up too badly? "Strawberry thumbprints, I think. But they'll go stale before I see him again."

"You never know." She claps her hands together. "Let's make a shopping list. We're going to need some strawberry jam."

She sends me to the store, which is crammed full of last-minute shoppers like myself. Yet I survive it.

And then we cook for hours and hours, with breaks for watching Christmas movies and lounging on the sofa that will always make me think of Carter.

It's exactly the holiday I'd been planning. Except for the heartache, of course. I can't stop wondering where Carter is, and if he's okay.

On Christmas Eve, my mother gives me a jigsaw puzzle. A thousand pieces. And the picture is an artistic map of Colorado. "Your new home," she says.

"Thanks, Mom." I give her another careful hug. She's still too thin, but I have to admit that she seems perky. And she's eating. It's something.

I text Newgate.

> My mom is visiting, and we made a dozen cookies for you guys. I know you're not big on carbs so yours are peanut butter. Can I bring them by?

> I'll come over instead! My house is covered in wrapping paper and I've been up since six. Christmas with a kid is like surviving a hurricane.

> Come over whenever.

Newgate knocks on the door a little later, and I wave him in. "Happy Christmas. Want coffee?"

"Sure," he says. "This is for you." He hands me a bottle of wine. "One of Gavin's favorites."

"Thanks, man."

"And these are for you!" my mother announces, carrying a tin of cookies out of the kitchen. "I'm the pushy mother. How do you take your coffee?"

I introduce Newgate to my mom. My teammate doctors his coffee and then follows me into the living room to sit on the sofa.

"Wow, DiCosta. Your place rocks." His eyes take a tour of the fire-place wall and all the new furniture. "Your designer guy has it goin' on."

"Isn't it beautiful?" my mother pipes up. "He's so talented."

I hold back a sigh.

Newgate sets his coffee down on a coaster. "I brought you something else," he says, fishing an envelope out of his shirt pocket. "These are my comp seats for tomorrow night's game. They're for your friends—the ones who wanted the Pride jersey?"

"Oh, right," I say, taking them in hand. "I'd forgotten all about this."

"Can you still get the tickets to them? My, uh, article went live today," he says, rubbing his forehead. "Making some dude's day would take my mind off it."

"Oh shit. *Sports Illustrated*, right?" I lean forward in my seat. "How'd it come out?"

"Fine, fine," he says, worrying the rim of his coffee mug. "No surprises. The journalist did a nice job. Now we'll see what the reaction is."

"To what?" my mother asks, helping herself to a cookie.

Newgate chuckles awkwardly. "I gave an interview, letting the whole world know that my partner is a man. We're actually getting married in the new year."

My mother does a slow blink. And then she sets the cookie down on her saucer and smiles at my teammate. "Congratulations! That's fantastic."

"Thank you, ma'am. Maybe I should have gotten the team bottles of antacids instead of wine, though. There's going to be some media attention."

My mother flings her skinny arms out wide. "So what! You can't live your life for other people."

"That's the idea," Newgate says with a tense smile. Then he nudges me with his knee. "You probably haven't been in your email, but Tate sent it around with some thoughts for all of us."

"Oh, yeah?" I pull out my phone and check.

PLEASE READ is the subject line.

Boys,

Here's Newgate's interview. It's very well done. Feel free to read it or not. Share it or not. If you're on social media, messages of support are always welcome. But that's not my big request. There's something else I need from you instead.

Here goes: don't read the comments.

No really. Don't. That's my job, and I'll read every stinking one of them.

You shouldn't, though, because they won't capture this moment in the way it deserves to be captured. There are millions of people who will see themselves in Newgate's act of bravery. You won't be able to hear all their joy, but it will be real.

Conversely, the interwebs are populated by a lesser breed—the warrior trolls. They are few in number but have an overblown sense of the value of their voice. They live to say cowardly things from the safety of their hand-held device.

But if you close Twitter on your phone, do those trolls even exist?

Reading their shitposts is not your job.

Letting them take up space in your head is not your job.

It doesn't matter what they say about us. We're a strong organization, and we became an even stronger one today.

Go enjoy your holiday. Be well. Be happy. And I'll see you tomorrow with your skates on.

—Tate

"Now look at that," my mother says, reading over my shoulder. "This Tate person seems like a smart man."

Not always. "He has his moments. Here—you can read the interview." I hand her the phone.

My mother taps on the link. "Well, Mr. Newgate, you look very handsome in your photograph."

"Thank you, ma'am." He glances at me with amused eyes.

"No family photo?" she asks, scrolling.

"Afraid not. We don't want our daughter's face in the media."

"Ah," she says with a sigh. "That makes sense. I hope she likes peanutbutter cookies."

"She likes everything that resembles a cookie. Thank you for these." He rises from the sofa, taking his tin with him. "I'd better get back."

"So nice to meet you," my mother says, rising. "Congratulations on your engagement."

"Thank you. It means a lot." He carries his empty mug to the kitchen and then shows himself out.

My mother pounces practically the moment the door closes. "Tommaso! You didn't tell me your teammate was a gay man."

"Bisexual," I clarify.

She just stares at me. "That's *quite* a development."

"Uh-huh," I say.

She waits for me to say more.

I don't.

She sighs. "I'm going to this game, yes? Tomorrow?"

"Of course. You're in row C."

"And who's sitting next to me?" She puts her hands on her hips.

"That's a good question." I pick up the tickets that Newgate brought over and open them up. They're also in Row C, across the aisle. "I need to make a call or two. These are for a couple of friends of Carter's. But I don't have their number."

"*Carter*," she repeats with a gleam in her eye. "Now wouldn't it make sense to offer *him* your extra ticket? Why should he stay home when he could watch a hockey game with his friends. And with me?"

Well, fuck. My mind spins as I try to think of a way out of this pickle. I quail at the thought of my mother bending Carter's ear for three hours tomorrow night.

On the other hand, I'll take any excuse to see Carter. If he's not already in Montana. "Let me track these guys down," I say reluctantly. "We don't even know if they're all free."

"They might be," she says smugly. "Why don't you find out?"

FORTY

Carter

THE DRIVE from Denver to Briarton, Montana takes eleven hours. My big plan had been to do it all on Christmas Day and surprise my mom.

I'd downloaded a long audio book. I'd packed the car. I'd hugged Rigo and Buck goodbye.

But I'd only made it as far as Cheyenne, Wyoming, before my car ground to a halt. Literally ground, I'm afraid. The noise it made as the engine died will haunt my dreams.

So I'm spending Christmas at the Motel 6, a short walk from the Subaru dealership parking lot, where the tow truck driver has left me. I'd had to pay him the Christmas rate, too, for dragging him out of his house on a holiday.

Then I spend the evening mentally redecorating my motel room. The industrial carpeting has to go. Along with the popcorn ceiling. And don't even get me started on these lampshades.

As it happens, I'm naked and mentally redesigning the shower when Tommaso calls me. So I can't answer.

It's just as well. I'm not a strong man, so I would have answered that call. And if he'd asked me where I was, I'd be obligated to tell him the truth. Then he'd feel sorry for me.

And I'd hate that.

It's a blessing that I've missed him, but I'm not strong enough to leave his follow-up texts unread.

> Look, I know you're keeping your distance from me, and you have your reasons. But there will be three excellent tickets for tomorrow's game at the Will Call window. (Photo attached.)Two for Rigo and his dude. And one for you.

> Warning, the one for you is beside my mother's.

> Another warning—she seems to have some fabulous intuition about me and you. Not that I've said a word. Maybe it's the hangdog face I've been wearing since you left.

> I know that's my fault, too. I'm working on it. You were right to leave, because right away it made me realize how much I'd miss you. I'm sick of being alone, and lately I can't remember why I thought I had to be.

> Please come to my game, okay? And later I will introduce you to my mom, and not just as a friend. If that's okay with you.

> But if you can't, I understand. And I won't hold it against you. Please do me the favor, though, of telling Rigo about the tickets. I hope they have a great time.

I don't respond. Instead, I curl up on the bed and stare at the popcorn ceiling.

The next day finds me on a hideous plastic chair at the Subaru dealership, while a guy with a lot of motor oil under his fingernails works on the broken thing in my car.

He said it might be the fuel filter. Or the fuel injector? Something that manly, competent dudes would understand.

Stuck here, I have a lot of time on my hands. I spend it contemplating all my life choices.

When I'd run into Macklin at the store, he'd had a lot to say. And much of it had been true. He was right that I had more dreams than plans. I don't know how to run a business.

Leaving had felt like the right thing to do—at least until my car sputtered to a halt.

As I sit thinking on my plastic chair, I'm trying to be honest with myself about where my life stands. Thanks to Tommaso, I'm not in debt anymore. My credit will soon bounce back. Things could really be worse.

And I miss Tommaso. Desperately. What if I sold our relationship short? I care about him. Running away feels like cowardice now—not like strength.

Besides, I can't stop thinking about the storefront apartment on Fourteenth Street. I can't stop picturing myself there, starting over, and taking another run at my dream.

What does fate want from me, anyway? Does a busted fuel-thinger mean that I'm supposed to stay in Colorado? Or does it mean the opposite? Maybe fate is telling me to man up and work an hourly job until I can afford a car that won't die on the highway exit.

And what about that ticket to the hockey game? I've already given Rigo and Buck the good news. They'd be cheering from Row C.

But there might be an empty seat across the aisle. I still haven't figured out what to do.

Tommaso offered me the ticket, though. Right beside his mother. That has to mean something. Doesn't it?

I open the banking app on my phone and check the balance. Most of my apartment rental fund is still there. But hotel rooms and car repairs will kill that off pretty quickly.

So what to do? After a few minutes of contemplation, I strike a bargain with myself.

If the repair can't be completed today, or if it costs more than five hundred dollars, I'll go home to Montana and rebuild my savings.

But if I'm out of here by five o'clock, and if it costs less than five hundred, I'll turn around and see tonight's game.

With that decision made, I sit back and mentally redecorate the waiting room. The place is ugly enough that it will take hours. Wood floors would warm the space up. The cinder block wall could be hidden behind some paneling.

The feng shui is all wrong, so I'll have to move all the furniture after I have it reupholstered. And this lighting? It's tragic. We're going to need some track lighting with a warmer color temperature...

"You're all set."

I look up to see Mr. Oily Nails, and he's offering me my key. "Oh wow. Thank you." I glance at the clock. It's 4:57. I could almost make it to Tommaso's game.

He'd be there. Live. In person. I haven't set eyes on him in a few days, and the idea of seeing his face again fills me with a dozen emotions at once.

And the loudest one is hope.

"Yeah, so... Kinda pricey, but at least we had the part in stock."

My eyes snap back to Mr. Oily, who's handing me a folded bill. "Pricey. Right." My heart drops.

"You can pay at the desk," he says. "Good luck on your trip to Montana."

"Thank you," I whisper. Then I open the bill.

FORTY-ONE

Tommaso

"HOLY HELL," Newgate says as we tromp down the tunnel toward the ice. "I had no idea."

"Crazy, right?" Stoney chirps. "It looks like a rainbow threw up out there. Whaddaya think, Hot Tommaso? I kinda dig it."

I don't even register the question, because I'm too busy staring. The seats are heaving with fans. And a shocking number of them are garbed in Pride gear. Jerseys and headbands and rainbow face paint. Hoodies and banners and signs. WE LOVE YOU NEWGATE.

Like my teammates, I'm wearing a warmup jersey in rainbow tie-die with a cougar on the front and my name on the back. There's so much color in this room, it's hard to focus my eyes.

"Let's go, boys. Clock's tickin'," Coach barks.

He isn't wrong. I push my blades against the ice and start a slow warmup lap. But it's hard not to stare at the rambunctious crowd. They let out a shriek of encouragement as Newgate takes his first lap.

My teammate's face is bright red. I don't think he knows what to do with all that attention.

"NEW-GATE. NEW-GATE." Now they're actually chanting.

"Huh," Stoney says, skating up to me and a couple other guys.

"If I kiss a dude, will they chant my name? Anybody wanna test that out with me?"

"You score a goal in the first five minutes, I'll kiss you myself," Kapski says. "Get a hat trick tonight, and I'll even give you tongue."

"NEW-GATE, NEW-GATE!" says the crowd.

"We are gonna razz you so hard about this later," Doughey calls as Newgate skates past.

Newgate ignores him and skates toward center ice, where a couple of his ex-teammates from Brooklyn are waiting for him.

The crowd erupts as he fist-bumps Castro and Crikey.

"Jesus Christ," one of them says. "All you gotta do is burp, and they'll cheer."

"Is this gonna go to your head?" the other one chuckles. "Might make you easier to beat."

I tuck my chin and skate past them, trying to get my head into the game. But none of this feels real.

Could it be this easy? Is anything ever?

I skate past the penalty box, and then I lift my eyes to find Row C. It's easy to spot Rigo and his husband, who is wearing the same jersey as me.

But then I skate a little farther, and I spot my mom. She's wearing a blue jersey with my number on it. She's bought herself a little Pride flag, which she's waving madly, and she's smiling at me.

The seat beside hers, though, is empty.

A split second later, I've skated past that empty seat. I pump my legs and increase my speed. I know how to win hockey games. I've got that figured out.

My personal highlight reel is a work in progress, though.

Maybe it's not too late.

FORTY-TWO

Carter

"PARDON ME." I slide between a giant man in a rainbow jersey and a woman with a rainbow-dyed buzz cut. "Excuse me."

It's a sea of humanity here in the stadium. I'm dodging every size and shape of human as I trot toward Tunnel F with a ticket in my hand. The game is starting right now.

I still don't know if I made the right choice. Driving back to Colorado feels like another frantic leap of faith. I can only imagine what Macklin would say. *You let your car repair bill decide your future? Who does that?*

Me, I guess. Because here I am taking another chance—not on Tommaso, exactly, but on me. I'm not ready to give up on my business and my fledgling connection with Tommaso.

Not yet anyway. Not quite.

I shove my ticket toward an usher with a scanner, and the electronic gate swings open for me. Here goes nothing.

The tunnel leads me toward the roar of the crowd. I've never been to a hockey game, so I'm unprepared for how bright and how loud the place is when I emerge into my seating section.

And, wow, that's a lot of rainbow garb.

On the ice below me, a chorus of men dressed in rainbow ties is finishing up the national anthem. On either side of them, hockey players are lined up, sticks in hand, facing the center of the rink.

And the home of the braaave!

The crowd stamps its feet in appreciation. I hurry down the rows of seats, counting down toward C. I almost stumble when I realize that Tommaso is one of the players on the ice, holding his helmet under his arm like a gladiator.

"Oh wow," I mutter to myself as I arrive at Row C, which is even closer to the action than I would have guessed. In fact, I turn around and gape up at the dizzying number of seats behind me. "Holy shit."

"It's something, isn't it? You must be Carter."

I whip around and spot a small woman with big brown eyes watching me from the second seat from the end. "Uh, yup. Hi," is my brilliant greeting.

She gives me a tentative smile. "We weren't sure you were going to make it. I saved you the aisle seat. Just in case."

"I wasn't sure I was going to make it either." I sit down and hold out a hand. "You must be Ms. DiCosta."

We shake. "Call me Emilia. And I think those two are trying to get your attention."

I spot Rigo and Buck across the aisle and a few seats in. They're both holding beers and waving madly. "This is amazing!" Buck yells. "You're my hero, Carter! Hudson Newgate's seats!"

"Third row!" Rigo whoops. "I'm getting *epically* laid tonight."

"Uh, have fun guys!" I give them a wave, my face on fire. Then I sort of slump down into my seat and take a deep breath.

"They seem exuberant," Emilia says brightly. "Do you and your friends make it to Tommaso's games very often? At least you're in time for the faceoff."

Faceoff. That's what you call it. "This is my first game. In person," I add quickly. "I usually watch on TV."

"Your *first* game?" she asks, brown eyes warming. They're just like Tommaso's. Dark and calm. "So you're a new hockey fan?"

"Well, sure." I wrestle off my coat and wonder what to say. "I never followed sportsball until I met your son."

"*Interesting*," she says, her eyes glittering with something like wonder. "Then I'm a little sorry you missed the announcement of the starting lineup. When they introduced Hudson Newgate, the rafters shook, it was so loud."

A smile spreads across my face. "That's really incredible. What a moment."

"It was!" She reaches over and pats my hand. "But let's talk about you, Carter. It's lovely to meet someone who means so much to Tommaso."

Oh boy. I honestly don't know how important I am to her son. "It's a pleasure to meet you, too. I hope you're having a great trip. He wanted the house to be perfect for you."

"It is! And that pillow you made me is just wonderful." She claps her hands together. "Thank you so much."

"My pleasure. I made my mother a similar one, but it's a little less polite."

"Really?" She leans toward me. "What does it say?"

"It says—*Woke up sexy as hell again.*" And then I tell her about the one I made for Tommaso, too.

She cackles. "If you don't mind me asking, how did you meet my Tommy?"

"At a furniture shop. It's a horrible furniture store, where the staff is a nightmare. As I recall, he couldn't get them to help him, so he followed me outside and asked me where he should shop instead."

"Oh, he must have been such a grouch!" she says gleefully. "He hates shopping."

"I've gathered that."

She grins. But then she grabs my wrist. "Here we go! It's gametime!"

Tommaso is on the ice, his body tensed for the drop of the puck. His teammate wins it and flips it to Tommaso. And he takes off like a streak of lightning, his powerful legs carrying him off.

Somehow the game seems faster in person than it does on TV. I can see the whole rink at once, and every time Tommaso takes the ice, his mom and I both lean forward in our seats.

"Get 'im, Tommy!" she shrieks when he's trying to get the puck away from Brooklyn. "That's it, baby! Win it!"

I adore her.

"Dude! This is for you guys!"

I look up to see Buck standing over me with a tray. "Thanks for scoring us these incredible seats."

"Wow, thanks?"

He passes me the tray, and I gaze down at a platter of mini tacos, a basket of fries, bottles of beer, Coke, and two cups. "Well, Emilia, I hope you like tacos." I pick up the beer and a cup. "Care for some lager? We can split it."

Her smile is delighted. "I'd *love* some! It's been ages since anyone offered me a beer."

"Oh." And now I wonder if I shouldn't have.

"It's no fun playing the part of the fragile old lady," she says, taking the cup out of my hands. "Let's enjoy our night out. I don't have enough of those."

"Me neither." I pour some beer into my cup, too. "Cheers."

"Cheers!"

———

Emilia and I do a respectable job finishing the tacos. Indecision and car repair can make a guy really hungry. But when Tommaso is sent to the penalty box for tripping somebody, and Brooklyn gets a power play, I start stress-eating the fries.

"That was a bullshit call, ref!" Emilia shouts. "Does your wife know that you're fucking us?"

I choke on a French fry.

"Sorry," Tommaso's mom says, patting me on the back. "I'm from New Jersey."

When I can breathe again, I laugh.

It's a tense couple of minutes as Colorado fights to survive without one of their guys. Tommaso sits in the penalty box, no more than ten feet away. I watch the back of his neck, willing him to turn around.

Maybe I should stop looking for signs everywhere, but I want him to notice that I came tonight. And I want him to feel the pull that I feel whenever I see his face.

He doesn't turn around, though. He keeps his head in the game. It works, too, because Colorado gets a goal right before the end of the first period.

"Goal by David Stoneman, assisted by Hudson Newgate!" the announcer shouts.

The stadium *flips right out*. Wild applause. Stomping feet. And a Nirvana tune over the sound system.

My heart soars. I'm so happy right now. *So this is what sports is for!* I glance toward Rigo and Buck and note that they're making out.

Huh. I guess hockey really is for everyone.

"That's it, boys!" Emilia yells. "Way to get some momentum!"

She's not wrong. I don't know much about hockey, but when the Cougars skate out for the second period, they look fired up.

I spend twenty minutes staring at Tommaso whenever he's on the ice. It's miraculous how focused he is. I can't imagine doing my job in front of thirty thousand screaming critics.

"This is really intense," I say, sitting back as Tommaso leaves the ice after one of his shifts.

"Let's have a cookie," Emilia suggests, pulling a metal tin out of her shoulder bag. "Tommaso made these for you. He said that strawberry was your favorite."

She whips the lid off the tin, and I'm staring down at a bunch of golden-brown cookies, each one with a little well of strawberry jam in the center.

I take one and then take a bite. It's nutty and delicious, with a burst of fruit against my tongue. "Oh wow," I say with a mouthful of cookie. "That's spectacular."

She munches on one, too. "Mmm. I taught that boy well. These are pretty good."

But biting into a cookie that Tommaso made for me is not just *pretty good*. It's a fricking miracle. Maybe Macklin was right about me. I just want someone to take care of me sometimes.

But is that really so awful? It doesn't have to mean I'm a failure. So what if I want to be cared for? I want to take care of Tommaso, too.

If he'll let me.

FORTY-THREE

Tommaso

IT'S STILL A TIED game when we troop into the dressing room after the second period.

"Let's go, boys," Coach Powers shouts. "I know Tate told you not to read the comments. That's nice and everything, but let me try on a headline for tomorrow…"

He raises his hands as if holding up a banner. "*The Colorado Cougars are awesome people… who couldn't close the deal against Brooklyn last night.* Is that what you want to be reading? No? Then you're gonna have to dig deep."

"We can do this," Kapski says.

"Yeah, we got this," Doughey says.

"Damn straight," Coach agrees. Then he gives his head a shake. "Or not straight. What the fuck ever."

The team snickers.

"You know what I mean." Powers waves us toward the tunnel. "Go out there and kick Brooklyn's ass in a very progressive and uplifting way. And don't come back until you've won it."

My teammates are down with this plan, and I see a lot of determination on their faces. But Brooklyn wants it too, and the third period is a battle, with both sides getting chippy as the clock winds down on regulation play.

"Three minutes," Kapski growls at the bench. "There's still time. Tommaso. Hessler. Shut down their sniper. He's got a fire lit under his ass."

He's not wrong. Their guy—a winger named Drake—has found some extra gas somewhere, and he's using it to keep the puck away from Stoney. I vault over the wall and go to work.

My mom is here. I need this win. So I do the thing I do best, which is to become a real pain in the ass. I'm up in his face, trying to push him off the puck, and trying not to foul him.

The world shrinks down to the puck, the glare of the surface, and the sound of our skates tearing up the ice.

"Get a hobby," Drake growls.

"Got one. You're it." I'm skating backward, keeping my stick angled toward the puck, turning any potential shot he might have into garbage.

He's looking for a pass, but I've spoiled those, too.

And then I see it—the moment when his aggravation overtakes his concentration. In a blink, I find the poke check and steal the puck.

Before he even reacts, I've sent it to Stoney, who ships it to Kapski.

Who scores.

"Fuck you," Drake snarls as our goal song begins to play.

But I'm not even paying attention. I'm turning around to spot my seats in Row C. And when I do, I see the best thing ever—my mom and Carter jumping up and down and smiling at me.

For once in my life, I don't hold back what I'm feeling. I wave like a peewee player at his very first game.

Carter waves back, a shy smile on his face.

And now I need this game to be officially over, so I can get the hell out of here and tell him how I feel.

Except it doesn't quite work that way.

The minute we hit the locker rooms, approximately one million journalists descend. It's mayhem.

Newgate is the man of the hour, of course. The poor guy. He and Kapski can't even get their gear off before a bouquet of cameras is pointed in their faces.

The rest of us try to maneuver in and out of the showers and back into our suits amid the chaos.

I've almost got my shirt buttoned when a reporter thrusts a microphone in my face. "Tommaso DiCosta—how does it feel to have so much attention focused on your team tonight?"

"It feels great," I say, forcing a smile in spite of the cameraman's too-bright light. "Teamwork makes the dream work." It's unoriginal, but so what.

"Are you supportive of your teammate who came out this week?"

"Of course I am. Newgate's a great guy, a great player, and I wish him all the best."

"You've had friction with your teammates in the past. Any bad blood in the room in Colorado?" His grin turns feral.

My anger flares, because he's just looking for trouble. And he assumes I can provide it. "No way," I say even as my pulse pounds in my ears.

"Yeah? Not even a little?" The guy shoves the microphone back into my face.

For fuck's sake. I look away, wondering how I'm supposed to get rid of this jerk. But all I see around me are happy teammates, flushed from a win. Nobody else is getting asked this question.

Yeah, but nobody else is a stupid little punk like you, Vin's voice says inside my head.

Taking a deep breath, I shove that voice aside and picture my mother and Carter in the stands, practically glowing with joy.

Then I turn back to the reporter. "Man, I don't know why you'd ask me that question on a night as sweet as this one. If you're looking for trouble, you better go find it in some other locker room."

He blinks. "Great game tonight, DiCosta. Thanks for your time."

When he walks away, I sit on the bench in front of my stall and shove my feet into my shoes.

Tate threads his way through the crowd, and I brace myself for a question about that interview. But that's not why he's here.

"DiCosta, Hessler—I got a bus outside. It's leaving in five minutes for the afterparty," Tate says. "I need as many guys on it as possible."

"Where's the party?" Hessler asks.

"A gay bar called Sportsballs," Tate says. "They had a huge crowd tonight for the game. I called over there and said we'd swing by for an hour of beer and autographs."

"*Sportsballs?*" Hessler laughs. "Okay, I gotta see this place."

"DiCosta?" Tate says, flashing his teeth at me. "I think you should come with us. It'll be good for your image."

Well, crap. "Yeah, maybe..." What if Carter is waiting for me outside? I want to see him so bad.

"Maybe nothing," Tate says. "Get your ass on that bus. And I hope you realize that the Trenton game is only two days from now. We never officially said no to the photo op. I still think you should do it."

This again. "I'll get on the bus to the bar. But the Trenton game could be a goddamn disaster."

"You let me worry about that," Tate says firmly. "Focus on tonight. I need hockey players signing autographs at a gay bar, and I need it now."

"File that under things I never expected to hear a publicist say," Coach Powers says, buttoning his jacket. "Where's this bus? There'll be beer, right?"

"You know it," Tate says. "Right this way."

I reach for my phone and text Carter. *You'll never guess where I'm going...*

FORTY-FOUR

Carter

MRS. DICOSTA MOVES SLOWLY, so it takes us a long time to get to the car that's waiting outside for her. After I help her find the sedan in the taxi line, I open one of the back doors for her, like a valet. "It was great meeting you. I had a great time tonight. And thank you for explaining the icing rule."

She laughs. Then she lunges, pulling me into a hug. "It was amazing to meet you! Maybe you should come by for breakfast tomorrow. Do you like waffles? The DiCostas make really good waffles."

I stop myself from blurting that I'm familiar with those waffles. "That's a really nice offer, but I'm not sure where I'll be tomorrow."

She stands back, patting my arm. "Well, I'll get Tommy to text you about it, anyway. I have a feeling I'll see you again sometime soon."

"Absolutely," I say, hoping she's right. "I'm so glad you made it out to Denver. I can tell how close you two are."

"Are we, though?" she asks, her face turning sad. "I used to think so. But my boy has been suffering, and I couldn't see it."

I don't know what to say, because I think that's true. But I also think Mrs. DiCosta is a hall-of-fame kind of mom.

Before I can answer, the driver rolls down his window and glares at us. "We going any time soon?"

Tommaso's mother rolls her eyes and then climbs into the car. "Good night, Carter. It's been a pleasure."

"Good night and be well." I close the door and watch the car slide off into the night. Then I turn around and head back to find Rigo and Buck. I'd promised to have a drink with the two of them, and they'd promised to help me figure out my next move.

I find them leaning against the door, their blue face-paint smeared. Buck is a little drunk, and Rigo—the designated driver—is merely high on life.

"You're staying with us tonight," Buck says sloppily.

"We'll figure out your life tomorrow," Rigo says. "Over lunch."

"Thank you. I appreciate that." My phone pings in my pocket, and I pull it out. I read the text and then laugh. "You guys—can I choose our destination? You're not going to want to miss this."

By the time we maneuver through the post-game carmaggedon, a half hour has passed. And when we arrive at Sportsballs, the place is packed, with the whole crowd facing toward the back corner, where a lineup of hockey players has arranged themselves at high-top tables.

Every queer sports fan in the Denver metro area has formed a line waiting to meet them.

"Wow," Buck says as we take in the queue of fans snaking around the bar, waiting to talk to the hockey players. "This is epic! I'm gonna get more signatures on my jersey."

"Do we get a beer first? Or do we get in line?" Rigo wonders aloud.

I raise my hand. "One vote for beer. My treat. We can drink while we wait."

"Oh no, he didn't," Buck says, pulling his credit card out of his pocket. "Best night of my life. Your money is no good here."

"Hey!" Rigo yelps. "I thought our wedding night was at the top of your list."

"Second best!" Buck calls over his shoulder.

Rigo shakes his head. "The Cougars' publicist should get a raise for this."

"Why?"

Rigo waves a hand. "Look how happy these fans are? The guys on the team need to see this. It's an antidote to all those nasty comments on Twitter."

I stiffen. "What comments? Is it bad?"

"Same old crap. Lots of the f-word. Lots of complaints that sports teams shouldn't be—" He makes finger quotes. "—'political.' The world is full of trolls, and they're willing to say anything. The more vile, the better. But you already knew that."

My heart sags anyway. "A guy came out, and then he won a fucking game. What more could they want?"

Rigo shrugs. "They want to make their tiny penises look bigger, Carter. And putting us down is sure to do the trick."

I've been alive long enough to know that he's right, but I wonder if Tommaso saw all those comments, and I wonder how much that hurt.

Buck comes back with three beers and a big grin. "Drink up, boys! Let's get me some autographs."

We join the line, and I sip my beer. Sportsballs is loud and joyful. They're already replaying tonight's game on all the TVs. If I had to bet, that game will play on a continuous loop in this bar for the foreseeable future.

When the crowd shifts, I spot Tommaso's dark head bent over something he's signing. Then he lifts his handsome face and shakes the hand of the hockey fan in front of him.

That's my guy. I can't help thinking it, even if it's not quite true.

But I want it to be.

Just as I'm forming this thought, Tommaso raises his eyes. I see the moment he finds me in the crowd, his gaze locking onto mine.

And then he smiles—and it's that same unguarded smile I used to get first thing in the morning. The one that's just for me.

Come here, he mouths, and I hear it in a sex voice inside my head.

Yes sir. Coming sir.

Tommaso beckons to me, as if I haven't understood. But I have. I'm just too busy experiencing an honest-to-god sexual reaction right here in the middle of a sports bar.

"Ooh! Carter has been *summoned*." Rigo cackles. "Go get it, boy. I'll hold your beer."

I glance around the crowded room, wondering if it's even possible to cut the line without being shanked. Word must have gotten out about tonight's famous visitors, because the doors keep opening to admit more fans to join the line.

"Go on," Buck orders. He puts his hands on my shoulders and steers me toward the bar. "Go around the line. You got this."

So I try. "Excuse me. Pardon me." I slip between eager sports fans, working my way toward the row of hockey players. When I'm almost there, a tan guy in a suit with very white teeth gives me a cautious frown, as if to discourage me from approaching the players' side of the tables.

Tommaso rises from his barstool and uses one of his strong forearms to sort of bulldoze that guy out of the way. Then he grabs me by the jacket and pulls me toward him.

Later, I'll replay this in my mind. Can you blame me? It's a scorching-hot move. But in the moment, all I can do is collide with the starched perfection of his shirt collar as he folds me into the hug that I've needed for days.

"God, I've missed you," he huffs into my ear. "Were you really going to leave town?"

"I tried," I admit, distantly aware of Rigo's hoot of approval from several yards away. "But here I am anyway. Good game, by the way."

He chuckles and holds me tighter.

I inhale the scent of his shower soap and let myself enjoy it.

Only one thing bothers me, though. "Jersey? Are we causing a spectacle?"

"Nah," he says, rubbing my back. "Look."

Reluctantly, I peel myself out of his embrace. And when I turn my head, I see that the crowd is facing the other way. Hudson Newgate has arrived. He and a cute blond guy are being escorted through the throngs toward the signing station. But it's slow going, because every person in this bar wants to give them a back-pat or a high five.

"The man of the hour," one of the other hockey players says. "Make room, boys."

"He can have my spot," Tommaso says. "I got things to do."

I'm hoping one of those things is me. His teammates turn to look at us, and Tommaso's big hand is still clutching my jacket possessively.

Their gazes drop to his hand. They totally notice.

But Tommaso doesn't. He tows me out of the players' zone, around a giant potted plant, and toward the far end of the bar. It's the only quiet place in this whole establishment, because it's hidden from the action.

Then he pulls out a barstool for me and waits.

My mind is a sluggish, romantic mess, but I take a seat.

He yanks out another stool and puts his hot self onto it. Then he turns to me with a serious frown. "Look, I know why you left. But it was a real wakeup call for me. I can't even begin to guess what you and my mother talked about all night, but I let her know how much I care about you. I'm not incapable of being honest. I'm just slow."

I swallow hard.

He notices and waves a hand at the bartender. "Could we have two Cosmos, please?"

Omigod. I press my hands to my mouth and laugh as the bartender—a total bear with a Cougars jersey on—blinks. "Uh, yup. No problem, pal. Great game tonight."

"Thanks, man. I do my best."

When he moves down the bar, I lean closer to Tommaso. "You're killing me right now. I'm not sure what you're trying to prove, but I'm convinced."

He shrugs. "You made me a Cosmo the first night I fucked everything up, and you never got to finish yours. And I'm trying to undo all the stupid shit I did before. Is it working?"

"You're basically killing it," I tell him, and he gives me a faint smile. "Look, I know you're trying. And I'm rooting for you one hundred percent. But even if you're making big strides, I've still got all my own issues. I'm not sure I can afford to stay in Colorado."

"I get that," he says. "But I'd wait for you. As long as it takes."

"*Jersey.*" I swallow a gulp of air. "You shouldn't say things like that. We just met, like, two months ago. And if you're really doing this—if you're going to accept yourself and live your truth—there are a lot of great guys in the world who'd form a line as long as that one..." I wave a hand toward the throngs of people queued up to meet Newgate. "...to try to date you."

His rolls his big brown eyes. "You aren't listening, Carter. You're not some free sample that I tasted in order to decide whether I like dudes. You are *the* dude. The one who made me realize I want to change my life. So that I can have *you.*"

I just gape at him. The bartender picks that moment to slide two glasses across the bar to us. I pick mine up and take a gulp, wondering if this is a fever dream.

"Are you listening now?" Tommaso asks me. He picks up his drink, tastes it, and makes a face.

"Um..." I'm still trying to process what he just said. "You have my full attention. But—"

"But nothing," he says. "Carter, I love you. I want to be with you. And even if you go back to Montana, it will still be true."

FORTY-FIVE

Tommaso

I DIDN'T THINK this was possible, but I've shocked Carter into silence. His eyes are wide, and he's gone completely still.

It's not a good sign. He's probably trying to figure out how to let me down gently. And that's going to hurt. But I had to shoot my shot.

"Breathe," I remind him. Because even if I'm about to get dumped, my guy still needs oxygen. "You don't have to say it back. You just have to know that it's true."

He lets out a whoosh of breath, and his blue eyes are as serious as I've ever seen them. "Say it again," he whispers.

"Which part?"

He grabs his drink and takes another gulp. "The important part. No guy has ever said that to me before, and I'm worried that I just hallucinated it."

I replay my speech in my head. It had all been important. "You mean that I love you? That's the easy part. Think about it—I chased you out of a furniture store the first time I ever saw you. Then I bribed a cop so you wouldn't run away from me. Seems pretty obvious looking back on it, doesn't it?"

He smiles, but it's shy. "When you put it that way."

"That's the first clip of our highlight reel."

He props an elbow on the bar. "What's the second clip? Me forcing you to go shopping?"

"Yeah. And me accidentally calling you in the middle of the night when I'm mostly naked."

His smile spreads across his kissable mouth. "That *was* a highlight. Not as exciting as the refrigerator incident. But close."

I scowl. "That one's for the blooper reel."

"Not true. My entire year has been a blooper reel, and I know a highlight when I see it." He sips his drink. "Look, I have big feelings for you, but they still don't take my problems away. And I don't want to lean on you. I need to sort some things out for myself. Business things."

And now I'm smiling like I just won the lottery. Because "business things" don't sound so bad. I reach over to squeeze his arm. "You don't have to figure out your whole life tonight. I just want to make sure I'm a part of it when you do."

He shakes his head and smiles back at me. "I can't believe we're sitting here drinking pink vodka at Sportsballs and having this conversation."

"Can you think of a better place to have it?"

"Not really."

I cover his hand briefly, and his gaze shoots down to our hands. As if he's witnessing a miracle. "This place doesn't take itself too seriously. I need more of that in my life. See?" I point at the walls. "Check out the tags on all the pictures."

Carter looks. The walls are covered with framed, signed photographs of athletes from every sport. Each one is accompanied by a yellow circle labeled *hotness factor*. For example, there's a photo of a baseball player hanging behind the bar, and his hotness-factor label reads: *Hottest Rockies player with a batting average over 300.*

And so on.

Coach Powers suddenly looms over me, a frown on his face. "DiCosta! Why are you hiding in the damn corner? You're supposed to be signing autographs right now. Get back out there and support your teammate."

Fuck me. I open my mouth to argue, but someone else beats me to it.

"Coach Powers," the bartender thunders. "I gotta blow the whistle here. You get paid millions more than me, but we both need the same skills, you know? So *read the damn room.* If you'd been paying attention, you woulda noticed these two are havin' some kind of come-to-Jesus conversation about the whole future of their relationship."

As I watch, my coach's eyes widen. And Carter suddenly looks freaked.

"I mean," the bartender continues. "If you were watching the body language, you'd see it. Your boy is drinkin' a drink he don't even like, just to make a point. I think maybe he screwed up pretty good somehow, because his guy looks kinda skittish. But he was holding his own until you came over here and interrupted."

Coach stares.

I sigh. Then I push my Cosmo glass across the bar. "You are very good at your job. Can I have a light beer? I have to go sign some coasters now." Then I turn to Carter. "Don't leave. We're not done yet."

"Good man," the bartender says, grabbing me a bottle of Tecate and uncapping it. "Maybe Coach Powers feels like covering your tab, since he interrupted y'all."

"Um…" Powers says. "Sure."

The bartender puts his beefy arms on the bar and stares at Coach. "In lieu of a tip, I really wanna get some assurances that this midseason goalie trade isn't gonna go down as the great disaster of all time. I notice you haven't played Hale in the net yet. Kinda wondering why."

"We're working on it," Coach says through gritted teeth. Then he slaps his credit card down on the bar.

I slide off my stool. "Carter, I don't have my car here. You feel like carpooling to my place in an hour? I'll drive if you want to drink."

"I think that sounds great," he says, giving me a tiny smile.

"Hallelujah. Now excuse me, boys. But feel free to work out that whole goalie thing while I'm gone. We're all wondering what's up with that."

When I walk away, Coach Powers is staring after me.

Whatever. I don't care. So long as Carter is nearby, I can handle anything.

For the next hour, I sign so many autographs that my hand cramps. The fans are mostly men, but there are some women, too. And they come in all sizes and colors. Literally *all* the colors, if we're counting hair.

The one thing they have in common is joy. The bar is loud and happy and drunk, and I've never met such effusive fans before. They want us to know how much it means to them to have Hudson go public.

"The world is ready, guys," one young fan in a Cougars hoodie says. "You're the proof. It's *happening*."

His optimism is contagious. I don't know if I'll ever be ready to give an interview to a major sports outlet and talk about my personal life. There's some darkness in here, and I don't feel like sharing.

But can I be open to my friends about what Carter means to me? Yeah, I can see how that works now. Hell, after tonight, I'm halfway there.

Maybe more than halfway. When I'm finally done with the fans, I find Carter sitting with Gavin at the bar. He's introduced himself to Hudson's fiancé, and they're discussing...

Okay, I have no idea. None of the words are familiar. "What the hell is a fairy light canopy?"

"Gavin's daughter wants a glow-up in her bedroom," Carter explains. "And I have big ideas."

"*Cheap* ideas," Gavin says, "because Jordyn changes her mind a lot."

They clink glasses. Carter looks a little drunk, which makes me happy. He deserves to have fun.

I wrap an arm around his shoulder. "Drink up. Let's go home before I'm too tired to drive. Can we leave my car in Denver and fetch it tomorrow?"

"Sure," he says. "Anything you want."

Gavin looks from me to Carter and back again. "Huh. Interesting."

"Isn't it?" Newgate says from over my shoulder. "I feel kind of stupid right now."

"Never," I assure him. "We'll talk later. Night guys."

"Night!" Gavin says. "Nice meeting you, Carter."

Carter sets his empty glass down and gives a slightly drunken wave. "Text me about the canopy, Gavin. I'll help you find the fabric."

Then I march him out of there.

FORTY-SIX

Carter

"I'M KIND OF TIPSY," I admit from the passenger seat of my car.

"Is that a good thing or a bad thing?"

I think it over. "Well, both. It's a good thing you offered to be the driver, because I don't think you could have fit in this seat."

"Hmm," he says mildly.

I'm right about this, though. My legs are draped awkwardly over the sewing machine. Everything I own is in this car. It's ridiculous.

"On the other hand, I'm ridiculous," I confess, because he might as well know. "You just told a ridiculous person that you love him. And now you can't take it back."

He chuckles. "I've never seen you drunk before. It's cute."

"It's not cute. I have no tolerance anymore, because I have no money to drink. I have no money to drink because I'm broke. And broke ain't very cute."

"Yeah, you're in a rough patch," he says. "We've covered this."

"Last week I ran into my ex at Home Warehouse. Macklin. He's kind of a jerk. But he said I'm always looking for a man to rescue me."

"Abrupt segue," Tommaso says. "But I'll roll with it. Why did your ex feel like bringing that up in a big box store?"

"Um..." I try to think. "He was working there to get his life back on track. I said he'd abandoned me. He said I'd abandoned *him* to our horrible client. And that I don't solve my own problems and always look for a man to do it for me."

"Huh," he says. Then he reaches over and places a firm hand on my knee. "On the other hand, you've solved a *lot* of problems for me. Some of them I didn't even know I had. So doesn't that make it fair?"

"But you paid me for that. Paid me well, too."

"Yes and no." He shrugs. "No other designer would have taken such good care of me. I was so apathetic. But you made me care. You *insisted*, Carter. You showed me another way to think about my life."

Wow. That seems like an exaggerated version of events. "We had *really good sex*," I point out. "I think that's why you're saying this."

He laughs. "Don't cheapen my heartfelt speech, Montana. The sex was important. But it wasn't everything. Not by a mile."

"But you haven't even banged me yet."

"Am I going to?" Stepping on the brake for a stop sign, he turns his chin and gives me a searing look.

"Of course," I say. "Obviously. Every time I see you in a suit, I just want you to bend me over the nearest piece of designer furniture."

He gives me a wolfish grin, looks both ways, and accelerates onto the highway ramp.

"We're going pretty fast," I say, as we leave Denver behind.

"I'm very motivated to get home now," he says.

———

"Carter."

I press my eyes shut. It's been a long day of uncertainty.

"Carter, I could carry you into the house, but it would be more fun for both of us if you walked."

Tommaso.

291

I shake myself awake. "Whoa. Are we there? Is it time for the sex?"

He smiles fondly at me from the driver's seat. "Maybe you should sober up a little first."

"I already am." As proof, I slide out of the car without getting tangled up in the sewing machine cord. And I follow on his heels from the carport to the front door.

"We have to be quiet," I hiss. "Your mom is sleeping."

"It's fine, Carter." He takes my hand as he unlocks the door. "I don't think she'd be too surprised to know that you've been here overnight before."

"She'll think I'm a slut."

He snorts. "You're drunk."

"Nope. Not anymore. But I've never slept with a client before you. It was a hard line."

"I'll show you a hard line." He pushes open the door, closes and locks it carefully behind us, and we tiptoe across the living room.

Even in the dark, the house looks amazing. "Damn, I'm good."

"Told you," he whispers back. Then he nudges me up the stairs.

"I need a shower," I say when we reach the bedroom. "And I left all my stuff in the car."

"Get it in the morning," he says as he hangs up his suit coat. "I have a toothbrush for you. Come here. Follow me."

Dutifully, I shed my coat and shoes, and follow him into the bathroom. I expect to be pushed up against the nearest surface and mauled. I'm so ready for it.

But that's not what happens.

He pulls a new toothbrush out of his medicine cabinet and sets a clean towel on the counter. Then he turns to me and catches my face in both hands. Aw, yeah. I love it when he does that.

He doesn't kiss me, though. He strokes a thumb through my stubble and then kisses my jaw. Gently. "Make yourself comfortable, sweetheart. Take your time."

"What? Aren't you joining me?"

I get another kiss on the jaw. "You seem a little fragile tonight.

Take a shower and relax, okay? I'm not going anywhere." Then he leaves me alone.

Fragile. That's exactly what I'm trying not to be. Maybe when he's got me on my hands and knees, I won't seem so fragile.

I strip down and slide into the marble shower, where a fixture the size of a dinner plate that rains hot water down on my tired body.

As I'm finishing up, I have a troubling thought. I shut off the water, wrap a towel around my waist, and pad into the bedroom. "Tommaso?"

"Hmm?" He's lying on his back in bed, his strong arms tucked under the pillow. The lights are low, casting shadows on his muscles. It's quite a sight.

"You didn't buy a fixer-upper," I say, chasing drops of water off my skin. "You bought a house that was perfect. It didn't need any work."

"Yeah, so? I was in a hurry." He rolls to watch me work, and his gaze dances all over my naked body. I'd enjoy that if I weren't a little worked up about something.

I hang the towel up in the bathroom and then come around to the other side of the bed. "Look, I'm a fixer-upper. Lots of issues. And that's not your style."

"Oh, please." He reaches across the mattress and pulls me into his body. "There's nothing wrong with being a fixer-upper. I've been one all my life. And—unlike when I was buying a house—I'm not in a hurry. I'll wait for you to fix all your leaks and repaint. I'm willing to hold a paintbrush, too, if you let me."

For a long beat, I stare into his serious brown eyes. I love that gaze so much. And I wish I had as much confidence in me as he seems to.

But I'm all talked out, so I kiss his neck, because he likes that. And he runs his hands down my back.

My eyelids feel droopy. It was such a long day, that I'm fighting to stay awake. And Tommaso's caress feels more soothing than sexual.

"Shh," he says.

The next thing I know, I'm adjusting my head on the pillow. Except the pillow is a very muscular shoulder. And when I realize I've nodded off on Tommaso, I jerk awake in the pitch dark.

"Easy." A firm hand presses down between my shoulder blades. "I got you."

I lift my head. Tommaso's clock says two a.m. "Weren't you sleeping?"

"I was at first. You're awfully cuddly, and I drifted right off. But then I had a dream about the Trenton game."

"Oh." I find his hand under the covers and squeeze it. "Was it bad?"

"The worst." He chuckles. "I dread that game. And I made it worse by waffling about the whole photo-op thing. I dragged it out, which was a stupid move. I kept wondering if it would help my family to heal the rift. But if my mom knew why we fought, I don't think she'd want me to apologize."

"Jersey," I whisper. "What did he *do?*"

He blows out a breath. "I haven't told a soul. It's deeply embarrassing to me."

"Okay, sorry. Forget I asked."

"No, I want to tell you." He clears his throat. "We were in the middle of a game, and it wasn't going well. I was playing okay that night. But it was only a couple of weeks after my wife left me. I'd told a few of the guys on the team. Most of them were like, 'Sorry, man.' And that was it. We weren't a very close-knit team. But my cousin..." He sighs.

"What did he do?"

"He was just a dick about it. Cracking jokes about how my marriage was shorter than my NHL contract."

"God, I'm sorry."

"He mixed it up with his usual bullshit. The night of that game,

I was trying to shrug it off. I thought—I'll focus only on hockey until the day I die. And we needed that win, so I was trying to coach Marco on how to shut down a winger that was giving us trouble."

"But he didn't want to hear it?" I guess.

He shakes his head. "Not from me, anyway. Marco said, 'Why should I listen to you? You couldn't even get it up for your own wife.'"

I suck in a breath.

"And I just snapped."

"Of course you did! That's impossibly cruel."

"And also true," he whispers. "I had a lot of guilt about it."

"Fuck that guy! It's none of his damn business. And you *cannot* apologize, or smile for a photo with him. I'll punch him myself."

Tommaso looks up at me and smiles, which is how I realize that I'm so lathered up with indignation that I'm sitting up and clenching my fists. "Calm down. I'm not going to do it. I just wish I could think of a good excuse. Because I'm never telling that story again. To anyone."

"Okay." I unclench my fists. Then I punch my pillow and lie down on it. I mingle my feet with Tommaso's and try to relax again. When I close my eyes, I picture all the smiling fans at Sportsballs and the rainbow jerseys at the game tonight. That's my happy thought.

And why not make more fans happy? "You know..."

"Hmm?"

"I have an idea, but it's probably stupid."

"Let's hear it anyway," he says.

"Okay. What if you tell your cousin that you're willing to do a family photo, but it has to be a charity thing. You know—one of those photos with an oversized check? Only the check is made out to the Trevor Project. Or to a New Jersey charity serving LGBTQ youth."

He barks out a laugh. "God, can you just picture it?"

"I can, actually." This idea might be better than I'd first thought. "The cool thing is that you're not making it about you. It's a cause that your team is focused on right now. So you tell your publicist that you've decided to donate... whatever amount a rich athlete gives to charity. But you want to make it a family affair."

Tommaso goes quiet for a long moment. And then he suddenly rolls on top of me, braces his forearms on the bed, and looks down into my startled face. "You are a fucking *genius*."

"It's just an idea..."

"No, it's *perfect*. My team publicist would eat that up with a spoon. Tate would get off my back. And when Marco and Vin say no, then he'll understand how they really are."

"You sure they'll say no?"

"*Very* sure. They think standing next to a check for queer charities would singe their dicks right off."

I laugh at the image. But then I stop laughing, because Tommaso leans down, all muscular shoulders and dark-eyed attitude, and he kisses the living daylights out of me.

FORTY-SEVEN

Tommaso

OUR KISSES QUICKLY GET HEATED, and I could swear there are actual flames licking my body.

That's how it always is with Carter. I touch him, and my brain starts to melt. Everything is magic. Sifting his soft hair through my fingers, I tilt my head just right to taste him more deeply.

He has no idea. Really no idea how much I care about him. His laughing eyes. His big ideas. And the bone-deep certainty that I could wake up next to him for the rest of my life and still find him fascinating every single day.

Maybe he's not there yet. Maybe he needs time. I'm not going to talk him to death about it. Not when I have a better weapon: sex. Carter loves sex. When I kiss his neck, he stops worrying. And when I fuck his mouth with my tongue, he stops telling me all the ways he's screwed up his life.

When he grabs my shoulders, that's how I know he's really turned on. As if he thinks I'll sneak away if he doesn't hang on tightly enough to my body. And just to make sure, he also pins my hips between two muscular knees. So I can't run away.

Not that I ever would.

"Lube?" he asks between kisses. "Got any?"

"Sure." Like I haven't been storing condoms and lube in the bedside table, just in case we needed them.

I haven't pushed for this, though. I wanted him to say he wanted it.

I wanted him to say he wanted *me*.

And here we go. I'm handing him the bottle, and he's slicking up his fingers.

My voice is a hoarse whisper. "Show me."

He does. He's all long limbs and tensed muscles as he penetrates himself with a glistening finger. "Like this."

My whole body tightens with lust as I watch him.

"My turn." I'm so keyed up I almost spill the lube. But then I'm stroking and stretching him. He hisses and curses as I slowly open him up.

The anticipation is killing me. When I roll on the condom, I'm so hard I'm leaking.

So is he. I lower my mouth and tease his body with kisses. Everywhere. Until he's squirming against me. Riding my fingers.

"God God God," he babbles. "Do it. Now."

"You sure you're ready?"

His response is a moan.

I've dreamed about this moment, but my fantasies didn't do it justice. As I brace myself against him, the sight of his kiss-bitten lips and flushed face is so erotic that I have to take a deep breath.

And when I press inside, the heat and pressure is so mind-bending that I have to stop midway.

"You're not hurting me," he says, by way of encouragement.

"I know," I rasp. "I just need a second."

He's not the one who's likely to get hurt in this scenario. That person is me.

"Don't regret me," I whisper, all my muscles shaking.

He rolls his hips in a way that almost short-circuits my brain. "I could never," he pants. "Promise."

Afterward, we lay in a satisfied heap. I can't stop touching him.

"We didn't even light the sex candle," Carter says sleepily.

"Next time," I slur, running my fingertips down his spine.

He sighs happily and relaxes against my body. I can feel his heartbeat against mine. And I'm as happy as I've ever been.

I'm still worried about Trenton. That game is going to be a trial, and I'm still not totally comfortable exposing my raw, needy heart to the world.

But the things I want are bigger than the things I fear. So I'm finally ready.

I only hope Carter is, too.

FORTY-EIGHT

Tommaso

"YOU WANT TO DO WHAT, NOW?" the publicist asks me from across his desk.

Having decided to put Carter's big idea into practice, I'd gotten up early and asked Tate for a morning meeting. Now I just have to convince him I'm sincere about this plan.

"My donation will be a charitable contribution to the New Jersey branch of an LGBT organization. You can help me pick it out today. I'll give all the money myself, but I'll make it a DiCosta family gift. And Marco and Vin can pose for the picture with me."

Tate taps an expensive-looking silver pen against his desk blotter. "That's a terrific gesture," he says. "I like it. And I can probably get one of those giant checks printed out at, like, Staples by tomorrow morning. So you ran this by your family members?"

"Nope. That's where you come in. Just let their publicist know that this is how we're doing it. These are my conditions. And see what they say."

He frowns. "You're worried they won't go for it? Is that it?"

"I am," I admit. "But this decision is firm. We do it this way, or our photo op won't happen. And I'll make the donation either way."

"Okay, dude." He shrugs. "I like this idea a lot. Thanks for making my job easier. Wasn't sure if you'd come through for me."

I hold back my sigh.

He grabs his phone, scrolls for the right contact information, and then taps out a text. "Photo op is a go...one condition...contribution of..." He glances up at me. "I'm gonna ask them to contribute ten percent of the total, just to make this a legit family effort, okay?"

"Be my guest."

He keeps tapping for a minute. Then he sends the text and sets down his phone. "What are you wearing for this photo op?" he asks. "We could do game-day suits. You'd all look great, but maybe the vibe is a little stuffy. Competing jerseys might be a fun alternative. We'd need a shot from the back, too, so we could see the names on the jerseys—DiCosta, DiCosta, DiCosta..."

"Cool. Let's pick a charity."

He's deep in the Google search results when his phone dings. I wait for him to pick it up.

"Excuse me a sec. Let's see if this is the Trenton publicist." He grabs the phone and reads the message. Then his mouth flops open.

Yup. Called it.

I get up and walk around the desk so I can see the reply.

TRENTON P.R.

Not funny. Tell Tommaso to go fuck himself.

Tate blinks rapidly. Then he scrubs a hand across his forehead. "This can't really be their response."

My chuckle is dry. "Looks pretty real to me."

He picks up the phone and squints at it again, as if he can't quite believe it. "Jesus. That's..." He doesn't even finish the sentence. I've never seen a publicist at a loss for words, but I guess there's a first time for everything.

I return to my seat. "Sorry, dude. I guess the photo shoot is off. I'll still make the donation, though."

He waves a hand, as if pushing that detail aside. The he puts his elbows on the desk and sinks his head into his hands. "You just played me."

"A little," I admit. "But you needed convincing."

He groans. "Brilliant idea, though. You really proved your point."

"It *was* a brilliant idea," I agree. "Can't take credit, though. My boyfriend thought of it."

"Your...?" He looks up at me, his mouth hanging open again.

Yeah, plot twist. Deal with it. "We're done here, right? I got a busy day ahead."

Without waiting for his answer, I get up and leave his office to change into some workout clothes. The gym is quiet at this hour, and I'm just finishing my warmup set when Coach Powers pushes open the door to the gym and strides purposefully over to me. "DiCosta? Got a second?"

"Sure. But can we talk here?"

He glances around. There are only a few other players in the room. "If you don't mind, I guess I don't mind. It'll only take a second. First of all, how's your mom doing? Is she having a good visit?"

"Yeah, great." I load another plate onto the hex bar. "It'll be a while before we know her long-term prognosis. But she's doing okay for now."

"Glad to hear it." He rubs his hands together. "So... Tate just flagged me down and told me what happened. The man is scandalized."

"The man is naïve." I step into the center of the hex bar.

Coach lets out a snort. "You just schooled him up, didn't you?"

"Sure. But now I have to worry about the consequences. I probably just made things worse for the game." I take a moment to settle my form, and I lift the bar.

When I finish the set, Coach is frowning thoughtfully at me. "You think Marco is going to come after you in Trenton?"

"Maybe." I shrug. "I can handle him. But I'm more worried that he'll do something worse. Like trying to punish me by hurting a teammate."

Coach takes a step closer and drops his voice. "Like maybe Newgate?"

"Yeah," I whisper.

Then we both glance over to where Newgate is spotting Hessler on the bench press. When our eyes meet again, Coach's are worried.

"Look," Coach says with a sigh. "I might owe you an apology. I completely misread your discomfort with the whole Newgate situation."

"Eh." I chalk up my hands for my next set. "My life has been complicated, and I don't like explaining it."

"Thanksgiving must be really awkward."

I laugh. "It would be if I were still in Jersey. So thanks for that."

Powers rubs his forehead. "Is this Trenton game gonna be a brawl?"

"Maybe? I can't guarantee you that I won't fight him. If he's a danger to others, I'll have to shut that shit down."

"*Don't* challenge him. And don't throw—"

"—the first punch. Yeah, I understand. And I will deescalate the situation if I can, because I don't want *another* picture of me punching my cousin on the internet. But I will not let that team go after one of our own."

"But here's the thing—Marco has to realize that attacking Newgate would draw a lot of extra attention at this moment in time," Coach says, thinking out loud. "He'd get a lot of scrutiny from the league."

"Yeah, but subtlety is not a DiCosta family value. And he's not prone to thinking things through."

"Hear you." He taps a foot nervously. "I'll be vigilant. If I don't like what I see, I'll have the trainer pull Newgate."

"He won't like it," I say.

"What won't I like?" Newgate appears at Coach's shoulder. "I heard my name."

Coach's mouth forms a grim line. "We're strategizing for the

Trenton game. DiCosta says to treat his cousin like a bomb with a wire loose."

Newgate scowls. "I know how bullies work. I won't give him an opening."

"Would be nice if we could focus on the actual game," I grumble. "Although I'm used to this. I've been watching my back since childhood."

Newgate blanches. "Jesus Christ. No wonder you're such a capable defenseman."

I snort. "Never thought of it that way before. Thanks, man. Happy to be of service."

Newgate steps closer and drops his voice. "Look, I got a weird question. Hope I'm not putting my foot in my mouth." He glances at Coach Powers. "When I joined this team, Coach said there might be other players with secrets." He clears his throat, and glances at me. "Coach, did you mean DiCosta?"

Wait, what?

Powers lets out a startled laugh, and slaps both our backs quickly. "Nope. No way. I remember that conversation, though. I wanted you to know that you could have a positive impact on the sport and on this organization. And obviously you have."

"So it was someone else?" Newgate asks, his expression skeptical.

Coach suddenly looks sheepish. "Yeah, well. It's hard to admit this, but the only struggling Cougar I could name at the time was me." He gives an embarrassed shrug.

Then he turns and walks out of the gym, leaving Newgate and me standing there with twin expressions of shock on our faces.

"And here I thought I was special," I say.

Newgate laughs.

FORTY-NINE

Carter

I WAKE up in an empty bed, daylight leaking in around the Belgian Linen curtains.

Sitting up, I look at the alarm clock on the bedside table. It's already past nine, and I didn't even hear Tommaso leave. His gym bag is missing from the corner of the room.

A radio weather report is playing from somewhere in the house. And I smell bacon. That ought to be an enticement to go downstairs, but I've never really done this before—the whole "meet the parents" thing. I don't relish the idea of trotting down the stairs with bedhead and wearing yesterday's clothes.

I'm not proud of it, but for a moment, I actually consider whether I could just hide up here until Tommaso takes his mom to the airport.

Okay, I'm not that big a coward. Am I?

I stall a few more minutes, reading my email. There's a message from some guy named Hale, asking if I can call him about furnishing a condo.

When I google his name—because I'm wiser now—I learn that he's a goalie who's just been traded to the Colorado Cougars.

Holy heck. Another hockey-player client?

That's exciting enough to get me out of bed. I spend a few minutes making myself presentable. Not that it's easy.

I open Tommaso's dresser drawers and scan the contents until I find a waffle-knit T-shirt that looks like it's probably a little too snug on him. Which means it won't completely drown me.

I put it on, push my shoulders back, and walk downstairs like I belong here.

I'm probably not very convincing, though, because redheads blush very easily. It's a curse. It really is.

"Carter! Good morning," Mrs. DiCosta says when I enter the kitchen. "I knew you could make it here for breakfast! But it's the weirdest thing—I didn't hear the door open."

If there were a mirror in here (and there isn't, because what self-respecting designer puts a mirror in the kitchen?) I'm sure I'd see a bright red face looking back at me. "I guess I'm stealthy like that."

"Hmm," she says. "Maybe my hearing is going. You look nice in that color," she says, indicating my stolen shirt.

"Thanks."

"So does Tommaso. I bought that for him a few birthdays ago."

"Oh," I say, my shoulders sagging. "Figures."

She laughs so hard she has to grip the countertop. "Sorry," she says, gasping. "I couldn't resist. An old lady has to get her kicks somehow. I kept the bacon warm for you." She opens the oven door. "And I'll pour you a waffle."

"Thank you. I think."

She grins.

"Coffee? Tea?" I offer.

She waves me off, and I put a coffee pod into the coffee maker for myself.

"Are you familiar with the DiCosta family strawberry waffle recipe?" she asks.

"I might have a passing familiarity," I grumble.

She laughs again. "You are the cutest thing," she says, taking a breath. "So easily embarrassed."

I sink down at the table when my coffee's done brewing. "This is new for me. I never meet the parents."

"How come?" She slides waffles and bacon onto a plate for me. "Want eggs? I could scramble a couple."

I shake my head. "This is already perfect. And, well, guys never introduce me, I guess. They've usually ended things before we get to that stage."

"Then they're missing out," she says, placing the plate and a fork in front of me. "Are you close to your own parents?"

"To my mom, yes. She's great. My father passed."

"Oh, I'm sorry, honey."

"It happens."

I hear the sound of the front door opening. "I'm back!" Tommaso calls out. "You all packed, Mom?"

"I am," she replies. "Want a protein shake? We've got a half hour until we have to go."

"Hell yes." Tommaso comes into the room and stops beside my chair. "That shirt fits you better than me." He ruffles the hair at the nape of my neck.

"Doesn't it?" his mother agrees.

"Yup." He heads over to the coffee machine and puts a pod in for himself.

We all end up sitting at the table together—Emilia with her tea, me with my breakfast, and Tommaso with his shake.

"The house is so beautiful, boys," she says. "I've really enjoyed seeing it."

"So come back," Tommaso says. "Anytime."

"I want to." She pats the table. "The furniture is all just perfect. Except there's no art on the walls. Is that a work in progress?"

"Yes," I say. "Because art should have a deeper, personal connection. And that's hard to pull off when your son won't set foot in a gallery or give his designer any direction."

"Ah." She smiles.

But this conversation reminds me of something I'd forgotten. "Actually, there's a painting I meant to show you." I pull my phone out of my pocket and open the photo app. "I saw this in the studio. It hasn't gone to the gallery yet."

Tommaso takes the phone and looks at the picture. "A cougar?" He laughs. "I like it. Local artist?"

"You've met him. This is Rigo's painting."

Tommaso blinks. "Really? I thought he painted walls."

"He does—to pay the bills. But I met him in art school, remember? This is his art."

"Oh shit." He looks more closely at the painting. "I love it. Let's buy that."

"How about we go to his studio, and you can have a real look around."

"Nope. I like cougars, and it's my team mascot. This painting speaks to my most inner...soul, or whatever I have to say to convince you that it's a good fit."

I sigh.

Emilia laughs. "I think he's got you there. I'm going to put the last few things in my suitcase. Can you arrange for a car to the airport?"

"Of course." He reaches for his phone as she leaves the table.

"Wait." I put my hand on his wrist. "I said I'd drive you into Denver to pick up your car. If you want to drop her off, we could go to your car after."

"Oh." He puts down his phone. "Are you sure you want to drive all the way out to the airport?"

"I don't mind," I whisper. "The only problem is that we'd have to stash some of my stuff in your basement for a couple hours. My whole life is in that car."

"Let's move it upstairs instead. Stay a while."

"But I'm going to rent that place I talked about. The one with the storefront. I've decided."

His expression eases, and he reaches out to rub the back of my neck. "I like this plan. I know you need to be your own man. I'm glad you're doing that here in Boulder, where I can keep an eye on you and feed you waffles."

"I'm not too proud to eat the waffles," I admit as he rubs a knot in my neck. "And did you give my name to a goalie? I have a message to call him about furnishing a condo."

"Yes!" Tommaso pumps his fist. "I'm glad he called you. Word of warning, though? That dude is seriously unhappy to be in Colorado. Seems like a big grump, too."

"Grumpier than you?" Emilia asks, rolling her bag into the kitchen.

"Definitely," he says.

"Maybe that's Carter's new market niche—designer to the grumpiest hockey players in Colorado. He'll need new business cards."

If that's all it took, I'd have them printed out by dinner time.

It takes about fifteen minutes to move my stuff into Tommaso's basement. Then we all get in my car and head for the Denver airport.

"Are you sure I shouldn't come to the Trenton game?" Emilia asks as we exit the highway.

"I'm sure," he says. "But Gia is messaging me, saying she wants to see me at the hotel. She's bringing me an Italian sub from Sal's and disco fries."

"That's generous of her," Emilia says. "Driving a sub all the way to Trenton."

"It is," he agrees. "Kinda makes me think she has an ulterior motive."

"Gia? Never," his mother says, and then they both laugh.

After we pull up to the departures area, Tommaso gets out of the car. He hefts his mother's bag out of my trunk and says goodbye to her at the curb.

I watch as he wraps his big arms around her frail body and hugs her goodbye. Then he stands there, forlorn, as she rolls her bag toward the automatic sliding doors.

Before she goes, she turns to give her son one more wave and a smile. I can't hear them through the window, but I can tell she's said, "See you soon!"

Please, Lord, let that be true. I watch her disappear into the airport.

Tommaso stands there another moment. Then he turns and slowly climbs back into my car.

I pull away from the curb and pretend not to see his red eyes. And I pretend not to notice that he's staring silently out the window so that I won't see his anguished face.

Eventually, though, he reaches for my hand. And we have a quiet but peaceful ride downtown to collect his car.

After we separate, I call Hale while I'm driving back alone to Red Rock Circle.

"Hi there!" I say when the goalie answers. "My name is Carter Flynn, and I believe one of your new teammates gave me your name..."

"You're the decorator," says a gruff voice. "Tommaso's guy."

"Yeah." *Tommaso's guy.* I like the sound of it so much that I don't even argue with the fact that he called me *the decorator.*

"Looks like I'm stuck in Colorado," the goalie grumbles. "Gotta make the best of it. I'm renting a condo in Boulder. Starting from scratch. Need some furniture."

What is it with hockey players and a lack of furniture? "I understand," I tell him. "If you could show me the space, we could go over your options."

He sighs. "I don't have a lot of free time."

"I'm familiar with your time constraints." I try to sound soothing. "And I can do a lot of work remotely. But I can't furnish a space that I've never seen. And you don't want to hire anyone who thinks they can."

Another broody sigh. "I'm leaving on a trip tonight."

"For Trenton," I say. "That's fine. Why don't I text you after the team is back, and we'll find a moment that works for you."

"All right," he grumbles. "Uh, thanks."

"You're welcome. Now go beat Trenton to a bloody pulp and we'll talk after you get back."

I think I hear him snickering as we end the call.

Tommaso and I arrive back at Red Rock Circle at around the same time. He gives me a smile as he unlocks the door, and I'm glad to see that he's not too sad.

"You probably have to pack, right?" I ask as I take off my coat and hang it in the closet. "Your flight is tonight?"

"Yeah. I guess," he says, tossing his own coat onto a chair. "There's something else I need to do first."

"What's that?"

"I'll show you. Come on." He turns on his heel, crosses to the stairs, and begins to climb.

I hurry after him. By the time I get into the bedroom, he's already stripping off his clothes.

"Oh, I see how it is."

He pushes me down on the bed, and his kiss is molten.

My body responds the way a cheerleader responds to a touchdown. "You sure you've got time for this?"

He shuts me up with a kiss and reaches for my fly.

FIFTY

Tommaso

I'M PRACTICALLY MANHANDLING HIM, but Carter is into it. Not five minutes later I've got both of us naked. I'm kneeling over his chest and grabbing the headboard. Feeding him my dick.

The heat of his mouth makes me close my eyes and groan. And when I back off to let him breathe, he says, "Force me a little. I like it."

I groan again. He has no idea what he does to me. I tease him instead, tracing his lips with my cockhead.

"You tease."

I have my reasons. If I go full-throttle, I won't last longer than a minute. But this is a good problem to have. The *best* problem.

After torturing him a little longer, I flip my body around like a wrestler so I can go down on him. I slide his hard length along my tongue as he moans his approval. Then I nudge my own cock between his lips and sink into the wet heaven of his mouth.

I close my eyes and let the moment overtake me. I'll need to carry this memory with me while I'm gone. To remember how good it feels to let myself go for once in my life. To let myself fly, without judgement.

My own, or anyone else's.

As we catch our breath, we're on the wrong end of the bed, our feet on the pillows. Panting and spent.

He flops a hand onto my hip. "You nervous about the trip?"

"Is it obvious?"

He chuckles. "I'd be nervous too. If it were my relatives who wanted to pound me into the ground."

"I'm not afraid of their fists. But I don't know how to stop dreading their toxic bullshit."

He takes my hand and holds it. "There's no excuse for the way they act. But try to remember that toxic people aren't happy people."

"I believe that," I say grudgingly.

"Tell me this," he says. "Of all the crap that might go down tomorrow night, what would make them the *most* unhappy? What's the worst outcome for Marco?"

"Humiliation," I say immediately.

"And what does that look like?"

I try to think. "Losing a fight to me, I guess. But I can't let him make me look like a goon."

Carter strokes my hand. "He wants to bang 30s so he can feel like a big man. But remember—he has no real power over you. You're flying out of Jersey after the game, no matter what."

I roll on top of him and gaze into his blue eyes.

"What?" he asks.

The real answer to that question would probably scare him— that I'm so overwhelmed by love for him that it hurts.

I've really missed this—being half of a team. "You said I was confusing great sex with something more. But I know what I'm doing. You're a fucking guru with great taste and pretty eyes."

"Nah, I'm just being selfish." His lips twitch with a smile. "I don't want your cousin to break your jaw. Not when your blowjob game is getting so good."

I shout with laughter. "Good point. You'll still be here when I get back from my trip, right? I might need more practice."

"Tell you what." He reaches up and runs a finger down my nose. "If you can get through that game without a fight, I'll let you tie me to this bed when you come home."

"Hot diggity." I kiss him. "But how? I should've gotten the four-poster bed."

He rolls his eyes. "You really think the best, most professional designer in Boulder, Colorado can't sort this out while you're away?"

I kiss his neck. "My apologies. You have a deal."

The next afternoon, I'm pacing my hotel room, waiting for my sister to show up with my sub and fries. My phone dings with a text.

CARTER

Just ordered this for next-day shipping. King sized, of course.

There's a link to an Amazon listing for a set of... What the heck are "bed restraints"? I zoom in on the photo and see that they're basically handcuffs that loop *under* the mattress, holding one wrist or ankle on each side.

TOMMASO

You are a damn genius.

I know. And I got kinda horny after I one-clicked. Sorry. Had to spread out on your bed and get myself off. Should have taken a picture for you, but I didn't think of it in time.

You might be a genius, but you are also kind of mean.

And now I have a boner while waiting for my sister to show up. Not cool.

I pace the room some more, and finally my phone rings. *Gia Calling.*

"Hi!" she says when I answer. "Brace yourself, but I'm not coming out there."

"What? Why?" I demand. "I'm supposed to be eating disco fries right now."

"Don't panic, Tommy, you're still getting your order from Sal's."

"How?" I demand. "What's going on?"

"I can't be there today, but I'm sending it over anyway."

"*Gia.* Is there a problem you're not telling me? Is it Mom?"

"It's *not* Mom," she says firmly. "Billy stayed home from school today with a fever, and I don't want to drive to Trenton with his little cranky ass whining at me from the backseat. So I found a willing volunteer to bring you a sub."

"Forget the sub." I rub my forehead, where a headache is suddenly blooming. "They have food in the hotel."

"Too late. She'll be there any minute."

"Who's *she*? You mean Mom?"

"Nope. Gotta go give the sick kid some Tylenol. Bye, Tommy! Have a good game tonight!"

The call disconnects, and I stare at my phone for a second, trying to figure out what just happened. My sister just played the sick-kid card, but she sounded a little dodgy about it. Like she didn't want to explain.

There's a knock on my door. I get a bad feeling as I cross the room to answer it.

And, yup, it's bad. When I open the door, I see Jessie, my ex. Sure, she's holding a bag from Sal's, but that doesn't make me feel much better.

Thanks, Gia. Thanks a lot.

"Tommaso," Jessie says, and her eyes are nervous. "Hi."

"Hi." I gesture for her to come into the room, because you don't leave a lady standing in the hallway. Still, I wonder if I can fake a missed appointment and run out of here.

Too obvious?

315

"You should see your face right now," she says. "Gia didn't warn you?"

I just shake my head.

"Sorry. I'd asked her if she knew when you were coming to town. And she said she had an idea..." She puts the sandwich bag down on the TV console and turns to face me. "Can we talk for a second? I promise not to take up much of your time."

"Uh, sure." Thank God my hotel room has a desk with chairs on either side of it. Neither of us glances at the bed as we sit down across from each other.

It's funny what you remember about a person. As she folds her hands on the surface of the desk, the gesture is so familiar that I feel a stab of pain behind my breastbone.

God, it's stupid to grieve a marriage that was so fundamentally wrong. But it hurts me to realize all over again that I loved Jessie, and that losing her still hurts in a complicated way.

I failed both of us, and ruined a pretty great friendship, too.

"So I wanted to apologize to you," she says softly.

To me? "God, why? You didn't do anything wrong."

She tips her head to the side, as if considering this idea. "Look, I've been to therapy, and I've had to admit a few things to myself. Our bad marriage wasn't *only* your fault."

"Yeah, it kinda was." I stop short of saying why, because I don't need to. We both already know.

She shakes her head. "See, I used to see it that way. I liked thinking of myself as the injured party. It's a good story—I'm the girl you married, but you really should not have married a..." She clears her throat. "Me."

I shrug. "Accurate."

She squirms in her chair. "That's actually too simple. The truth is that I wasn't very satisfied in our relationship before we got married. And when you proposed, I shouldn't have expected things to suddenly change. That's not how people work."

Well, ouch.

"So maybe you omitted a few crucial details. But so did I, Tom."

She actually sounds anguished. "I *knew* we didn't have the right kind of spark, and I could have let you go off to the new team alone. But that's not what I did. I cried, and you proposed to me out of guilt, I think." She clears her throat. "I knew it was a bad idea, but I went along with it anyway. And when it didn't magically work, I made it all your fault. I'm sorry."

"But..." This conversation has taken an unexpected turn. "I couldn't even admit the truth when you asked me point blank. I lied. Hell—I've *never* spoken the truth out loud. And that's not what a real man does."

She startles me with an eye roll. "Not what a real man does," she repeats with a snort. "Can we just cut out this 'real man' bullshit and be honest for a moment?"

"Um..."

"I miss you, Tom. I fucked up our friendship by always pushing it to be more than it was."

A slightly hysterical laugh erupts from my chest. "I'm sorry, too, okay? You want honesty? Here's some—I have a boyfriend."

Her eyes widen, and she actually laughs. "You *do?* Omigod, that's *great*. I have one too, by the way."

I relax for the first time since I opened the door. "Really? That makes me happy. I hate to think about how I derailed your life just to lie to myself."

"*Really?*" she mimics me again. "Don't sound so shocked." Her smile grows wider. "Where'd you meet your guy? Can I see a pic?"

"Uh, sure..." I pick up my phone. "The only photos I have of him are with furniture he was showing me. We met when I hired him to furnish my new house."

"Oh!" She covers her mouth with delight. "That's the cutest thing I've ever heard. Come on. Show me."

I hand her the phone. It's a photo of Carter sitting on the edge of a bed at Bob's Denver Bedrooms. He's holding out his hand like a game show host and smiling.

"What a cutie." She grins. "Here's mine."

She hands me her phone, and I see a selfie of Jessie under the arm of a blondish man with a wide smile. "You look really happy in this," I say, and the pain comes back to my chest.

Except this time the pain feels necessary—like a bruise after a game I've won. It feels like the spoils of war.

"I am happy," she says softly. "And I hope you are, too."

We glance up at each other at the same time. Our gazes lock and get stuck for a second, until Jessie smiles. "Are you going to eat that sandwich?"

"Want half?" I say immediately.

She pats the purse on her lap. "I have my own. I wasn't going to swing by Sal's without getting something for myself."

"Well, whip it out, then." I get up and grab the bag she left for me by the TV. "Let me pour us some water and find some napkins. Disco fries are messy."

"Will you share those fries?" she asks.

"You know I will."

Then I sit down for lunch with my ex-wife. And it's a strangely good time.

FIFTY-ONE

Tommaso

IT'S weird warming up on this familiar ice while wearing a different jersey.

A good kind of weird.

"Head in the game," Kapski says as we circle the ice together. "These punks don't fucking matter."

"I know," I agree. "I'm solid."

It's true, too. I've blocked Marco's and Vin's numbers, so I have no idea whether either of them tried to harass me about the photo shoot. They don't matter. All I have to do is play a hockey game and go home tomorrow.

I got this.

After warmups, I skate back to the visitors' bench. That's a little strange, too. But it's not like I'm going to accidentally take a seat with my old teammates. This place isn't home anymore.

I regret nothing.

The announcer calls the starting lineup, beginning with the visiting team. One by one, my teammates are quietly booed, a Trenton tradition.

When it's my turn, though, the boos are really damn loud. As they die down, I hear a particular piercing voice from the crowd. I'd forgotten about the guy we called Loudmouth Lou. "Welcome back, fucker!" he screams.

I snort with laughter, and then wave to the crowd, as if they'd given me a hero's welcome. Because fuck it.

Then it's time for Trenton's starting lineup. It's probably no accident that Marco lines up right in front of me. This time the crowd roars its approval. He grins like he's just won an Oscar.

Then he settles into position and stares at me with so much aggression in his posture that it's comical. Like he can't wait to rush across the neutral zone and maul me.

So this is going to be a long night, then. Fine. Whatever.

The national anthem starts, and I stare over my cousin's head and center myself. I think of Carter watching the game on the sofa he picked out for me. He's probably sitting there this very minute. The Christmas tree we decorated is by the window, lighting the room with a colorful glow.

He gave me a reason to get through this game without a fight. We're about to find out if that's possible. But he'll still be waiting for me at home either way.

That's huge for me. So I'll try not to let him down.

We win the first faceoff, and Kapski gets a shot on goal within the first two minutes of play. It's deflected, but the rebound creates an opportunity for Newgate. He shoots.

Denied. The goalie falls on the puck in the crease.

Still, it's a good start. They're already scrambling. We like that.

I settle in and try to work the natural advantage of knowing more about this team's play than most of our other opponents'. There's Mayhew's hesitation behind the net. And my cousin's inability to track a lefthanded sniper's deke.

The pace of play is fast and furious. We all want this win, and nothing seems off during the scoreless first period. But then both teams score in the second.

We dig in and look for that next goal. I'm blocking their center when I happen to get a look at David Stoneman's face. He's *furious*. And it takes a lot to make Stoney mad.

Whatever happened, I missed it.

"What's the issue?" I ask at the next stoppage of play.

"Nothing." He gives his head a shake. "Forget it."

But I get a look at Newgate a few minutes later, and his face is red with anger, too.

"What's the deal?" I ask a winger on the bench.

"These assholes," he says, squirting water into his mouth. "They're harassing our guys. Newgate's getting the worst of it."

"Harassing him how?" I demand.

"Uh, nasty chirps whenever the ref can't hear it. But also they're handsy."

"Handsy?" It's a contact sport, so I don't really get it.

He makes a face and looks away.

When I'm back on the ice, I pay closer attention. That's when I see Newgate field the puck and take a hit. As one does.

It's not an illegal hit, and not particularly brutal. But right after the hit, I see Orloff's hand briefly disappear...between Newgate's legs.

I blink, and the moment is over. Orloff is skating off to defend his zone. Newgate does the same, but his face is the color of a beet.

That's when I understand what handsy means. It means a *violation*. No matter that there's a lot of padding between the other player and my teammate's junk. No matter that nobody is injured.

It's just gross to be grabbed. And sometimes humiliation is worse than a punch to the face.

I've had both, so I would know.

Within seconds, my sweat cools into beads of ice. Now I understand their strategy. It's fucking twisted and so fucking personal. Cold shame washes down my spine.

"Pay attention, DiCosta!" Hale chirps from the goal. It's his first start for Colorado.

I look up just in time to receive the pass but get stripped a second later, because I'm distracted.

Hale curses and braces for trouble.

Kapski saves the day, getting his stick on the puck and slipping it to Stoney. We're back in the hunt, for a minute anyway. Our forwards try to make some magic, sneaking the puck back to Newgate, who sets up a shot.

I flick my gaze from the puck to see Newgate taking another hit. This time he ends up underneath two Trenton players.

The whistle blows, because Trenton's goalie has the puck in his glove. The fallen players pick themselves up off the ice.

But it takes a minute. And Newgate rises slowly. Very slowly.

Shit.

We both head for the bench as Hessler and Doughey skate out to replace us. "What happened?" I demand as Newgate eases himself down on the bench.

"Nothing," he growls. Then he blows out a heavy breath.

"Christ, are you hurt?" Powers asks. "One of 'em shielded the other one, and I couldn't see what went down."

My teammate gives his head a quick shake. "It's just...middle school bullshit." His eyes are pained.

From behind the bench, the trainer makes a noise of surprise. "There's a scratch on your back. What the hell?" He lifts the back of his jersey for a better look.

Newgate reaches around and slaps his hand away. "Leave it. It's nothing."

"Whoa." Coach puts a hand on Newgate's shoulder pad. "What did they *do?*"

I hear myself answer, because suddenly I know. "They put a stick down his shorts. Asked him if he liked it that way."

Newgate's face whips toward mine, his expression full of cold fury. "I said *leave it.*"

"Jesus fucking Christ," Coach Powers mutters. "Are you good to play?"

"Of *course* I fucking am!"

And maybe he is, but now I'm bubbling with rage. Because this is how they try to break you. There's no penalty in the rulebook for humiliation. You're just supposed to "man up" and pretend that shit didn't happen. Pretend you're not dying inside.

I'm seeing red when we retake the ice. Newgate seems to shake it off, skating fast, getting the job done. So I try to do the same. But every time I get near Marco, I want to choke him.

He knows it. Hell, he's planned this. And now he's chirping me in the corners. "You want some of what he's getting? Bet you'd love it."

I'm about to lunge when Stoney skates between us in a swish of ice chips. "You Trenton boys got some stupid hobbies." Then he runs off with the puck.

I'm trying to shut down my rage. It helps when Stoney scores, and we're up by a goal. It helps a lot. And in the third period, I finally believe this game might someday end.

Until Marco slides in and trips Newgate. Again. They go down hard, with Marco on top.

I'm over them in a flash, kneeling down and shoving Marco off.

"Whoa, cuz," he says. "You okay? Gotta check in on your little friend?"

Newgate has bounced to his feet without incident, and now he's giving me an angry stare. "Move it, Tommaso."

"Is this the pussy club?" Marco asks, circling us. "Figures you'd find the gayest team in the league. Good for you, bro."

"I'm not your bro," I growl.

The crowd is paying attention now. They start up the familiar chant. *Fight fight fight!*

"You heard 'em," Marco says with a laugh. "Gotta give the crowd what they want. You're too good to take a fucking picture with me. And too chicken to fight, too?"

Some of our teammates are closing in, sensing trouble. Lurking at the edges of my vision.

"Don't fall for it," Kapski mutters.

"Ooh, your captain has you on a leash?" Marco calls. "Whole team of pussies."

"Fuck off." I turn to skate away.

But Marco does it—he drops his gloves on the ice, one after another.

Fuck.

"Fight me, dumbass." He beckons. "You skate away right now, and *that's* what's going up on YouTube. You know I'm right. The comments will be brutal. 'Tommaso DiCosta is a chickenshit little faggot, with his pussy and his little rainbow friends.'"

It's the lamest chirp in the history of chirps. Newgate actually rolls his eyes, like, *Can you believe this shit?*

But I've had a lifetime of this, and I can't take it anymore. My vision tunnels, until all I can see is Marco's ugly face. His soulless eyes, and that smirk that just begs to be obliterated.

Somewhere in the back of my consciousness I know I should walk away. And that Coach will lose his mind. But I don't care right now. I just want revenge.

I flick my fingers to loosen my gloves. Fuck Trenton. Fuck them all. Marco won't even be able to *pronounce* a slur when I'm finished, because he won't have any teeth left.

Just as I'm making this decision, an angry red blur shoots through my vision, and Marco's head snaps back unpredictably.

For a split second I'm so confused. But then the blur resolves, and I see another Trenton player—a younger dude I don't know—rearing back to cock his fist again. "Fuck you and your homophobic bullshit! Shut your fucking mouth!"

This time, my cousin ducks the punch. Then he grabs his teammate by the jersey and responds with his own right cross. "Make me, punk!"

They grapple like wrestlers, and I'm deafened by whistles from every officiant.

"What is *happening?*" Stoney asks, his tone awed.

"Team chaos," Kapski says. "It's a look. Back away, DiCosta." He tugs on my arm. "Let Trenton star in their own shitshow. It's gonna be all over social media in a hot second."

He isn't wrong. As we back off to stand in front of our own bench, the officiants are struggling to hold my cousin and his teammate back. And now the rest of the Trenton bench is shouting at each other. Looks like a few more of them want in on the action.

"Big yikes," I say, as Carter would. Then I take a deep breath and try to find my calm. "We're still winning this game, right?"

"We're winning this damn game," Stoney says. "Then we're getting drunk at the hotel after."

"I'm down with this plan," Newgate says.

"Hey, DiCosta," Coach Powers calls from behind the bench. "That was close. You were going to fight him, against my *express* wishes."

"Ooh!" Stoney says. "Somebody almost got in trouble."

"I *was* going to fight him," I admit. "And I was probably going to throw the first punch. But I woulda won—just saying. Me and my pussy and my little rainbow friends."

Coach puts his clipboard in front of his face, so the cameras won't catch him laughing.

FIFTY-TWO

Carter

I'M MAKING A SPECTACULAR DINNER. It's my big accomplishment for the day. Well, aside from renting that apartment with the storefront on Fourteenth Street.

But the dinner is going to be a highlight reel kind of meal. I've got bacon-wrapped marinated pork chops, whipped garlic potatoes, and sautéed broccolini.

The table is set, the candles are burning. The wine is uncorked. And I just saw Newgate's car pull into his parking spot across the street, so I know that Tommaso won't be far behind.

Last night we video-chatted. On purpose this time. But it was late, and not our best conversation.

"I'm suuuuuper drunk," he'd said when he'd called from the bed in his hotel room, his dress shirt half unbuttoned.

It had been a struggle not to laugh. "I see that. Any particular reason?"

He'd shaken his head in an exaggerated manner. "I never get super drunk! Gonna have a bad headache prolly. But we were in a super good mood."

"Excellent," I'd said. "But you made it back to your hotel room okay?"

"Kapski helped," he'd said with a shrug. "I gotta favor to ask."

"Shoot."

"Can you wait for me?"

"Um...sure? Where?"

"At home. Tomorrow." He'd burped. "Like, with the lights on? I really like it when you're there. And I'm there. At the same time. When I come home."

"Okay?" I'd tried to piece this together. "Why don't you text me tomorrow, so I know when you're coming home, and I'll wait for you. With the lights on."

"Cool," he'd said, nodding drunkenly. "I know you gotta be your own man and stuff. But tonight went good, and I like to see you when I come home from trips. I also like to see you naked. But not at the same time? I mean..." He'd broken off and sighed, and then his eyes closed halfway.

"Time for bed," I'd said brightly. "We'll talk tomorrow."

"'Kay." He'd closed his eyes all the way. "Love you."

"I love you too," I'd said. But then I'd slapped my hand across my mouth, because I shouldn't have just blurted it out like that when he was drunk and half asleep.

"I heard that. You can say it again tomorrow. Can you maybe end the call now? I might forget."

"Sure, honey. See you tomorrow."

"Tomorrow," he'd mumbled, and I'd hit the red button.

Today they'd had some kind of skating clinic with a guru in New York. I'd spent the day trying to plan my uncertain future and hoping that signing a new lease wasn't irresponsible.

And wondering if Tommaso would remember me telling him that I loved him. Which I do. It just slipped out, because I couldn't hold it in any longer.

On paper, we're a risky bet. New couple. Very little in common. And he's a rookie at dating a man. And yet the pull I feel toward him is so strong it takes my breath away.

Trusting him is easier than it should be, given my history. But

Tommaso is the most serious person I've ever met. If he tells me his feelings are real, then I have to believe him.

There are no guarantees, and I still don't know what I did to deserve him. But maybe I don't need to keep torturing myself with that question. Maybe I can just relax for a minute and enjoy the fact that another set of headlights is illuminating Red Rock Circle.

My pulse kicks into a higher gear, and I pour the wine. It's a long two-minute wait until the front door opens, and Tommaso steps into view. "Carter?"

"Right here!" I carry his glass into the living room. "I cooked. Welcome home."

For a moment, he just watches me approach. Then he seems to collect himself all at once, tossing his coat into the closet, then taking both glasses of wine and setting them on the coffee table. "Sit with me," he says. "On the cloud couch."

"Okay."

"I'm not sure you know what sitting means," I say a minute later, after he's pushed me down on the sofa and climbed on top of me. Now he's kissing my neck.

He laughs. "Couldn't help myself. You're too good to be true, and I thought maybe I'd come home, and you'd be gone again."

"I said I'd be here. When you called me last night."

He drags his teeth lightly through the whiskers at my jaw. "Well, that conversation is a little hazy. I can't believe I called you that late and demanded that you wait at home for me."

"You asked nicely," I say, tugging his dress shirt out of his trousers. "And I missed you."

He makes a happy noise as his hungry mouth finds mine. It's a luxurious, full-hearted kiss, and I wonder how I ever doubted this man. I taste him shamelessly and let my hands wander all over his exquisite body. I'm really getting into it when he suddenly lifts his head and breaks our kiss.

"Did you say you cooked dinner?"

"Yup." I help myself to the top button of his dress shirt. "It's in the warmer drawer."

"Then let's eat it."

I groan. "You're a tease."

"Absolutely. And it's only getting started." He sits up and offers me a hand. "What's the smell?"

"My sexual desperation," I grumble. "And garlic mashed potatoes and bacon pork chops..."

"I'm so there." He picks up our wine glasses and carries them toward the table.

After dinner, he insists on doing the dishes.

"The dishes could wait," I point out.

"It'll only take ten minutes." He begins unbuttoning his shirt.

"What are you doing?"

"I don't want to get any grease on this. You know I hate shopping." He unbuttons it all the way and tosses it over a dining chair.

The abs of glory are *right* there. My mouth waters. And when he picks up the scrub pad and faces the sink, I'm confronted with the buns of glory, too. Hockey butts are awesome. His particularly.

"Are you fucking with me right now?" I ask his backside.

"Huh? I'm washing up, Carter. You did all the cooking."

"Right. Well." I sigh. "Maybe I'll wait upstairs."

"Cool."

"Naked."

"Yup," he says. "That'll save me the trouble of stripping you down. With my teeth."

I hold back a horny groan. "Okay. Cool. Here goes." I lift my sweater over my head and drop it on the floor.

He looks over his shoulder, his eyes heating. So I take off my T-shirt, too, and unzip my fly.

"Okay, bluff called." He shuts the water off with a slap of his hand. "You win."

With a laugh, I turn and jog out of the kitchen. He's close on my heels, so I keep going, pounding up the stairs.

He chases me into the bedroom, where I'm flinging myself onto the mattress. But he stops short when he sees how I've prepped the place.

The comforter is folded up and stashed on the chair.

The sex candle is already lit.

And the restraints I bought have been fitted under the mattress, their loops poised on top, waiting.

"Holy fuck," he says in a low voice. "You weren't kidding."

"Oh, I wouldn't joke about something like this." I shed my jeans and toss them aside. "You were a very good boy in Trenton. Now it's time for your reward."

"Boxers off. Then lie down," he says gruffly.

"Yessir." His eyes flare as I drop my underwear and toe off my socks. I'm totally naked, my cock pointing right at him like an arrow.

"On the bed," he says. "On your back."

I hurry to comply, spreadeagling my arms and legs.

He sits on the edge of the bed and studies one of the loops. He tests its elasticity in his hand and then picks up my wrist and kisses the pulse point, his beard tickling my skin. "You think these will be comfortable enough?"

"Yeah, but I'll let you know if they're not."

He hums his approval, and then slips the loop over my wrist, tightening it gently until my hand is flush against the sheet.

Three more tightened loops, and I'm largely immobile, trussed into place like a Thanksgiving turkey.

For all the sex I've had, I've never actually done this before. I guess I never trusted anyone enough to offer myself like this.

The only discomfort I'm feeling right now is desperation. Tommaso's dark gaze is like a flame across my overheated skin, and when he slides one roughened palm up my thigh, I shiver with anticipation.

Then he backs away to unzip his trousers and undress.

"I never knew you were so mean," I complain from the bed.

Although I'm enjoying the view of his thighs flexing in the candlelight.

"It's called anticipation. I've been thinking about this for two days, and I just want to pounce. So I'm making myself wait."

He finally stalks toward me and my cock tightens with need. "God, you're hot." I sigh. "Thank you for not blindfolding me."

"Huh," he says. "Maybe next time." He kneels on the floor, parking his elbows onto the end of the bed and gazing up my body. I feel so exposed, my legs spread for him, and I fucking *love* it.

He rises, slowly crawling onto the bed. He drops his head and kisses my inner thigh. A zing of electricity shoots up my body, and I twitch with need. "Yeah, baby. I know." He continues on, kissing his way up my leg, his beard grazing my sensitive skin.

I forget myself for a moment and strain against the wrist loops, trying to reach for him. And when I realize I can't, I let out a sound of frustration.

"Easy." He chuckles. "Going somewhere?"

I lie back against the pillows and let out a hot breath. "So hard for you."

"Mmm. Let's end every road trip like this, 'kay?" He noses past my cock, his breath a tickle, and desire pings through my veins once again. But then he kisses his way down the other leg, heading in the wrong direction.

I growl.

"Isn't this fun?" He cruises upwards again, placing a kiss at my hip bone, and then nosing into the fine hair at my belly. "I love your body so much. You're lean and mean, like a jungle cat."

His gaze is like a laser, and my wrists strain against the restraints. I want to reach down and run my fingers through his thick hair. And, fine, I want to shove his face closer to my cock.

"Fuuuuuck," I breathe. "Get over here, will you?"

"All right." He does an army crawl up my body and at last we're skin on skin. I sigh with relief as he settles his hips onto mine, the tip of my cock dampening his belly.

"Now let's talk," he says.

"Wait, what?" I roll my hips. "Depends what you mean by *talk*."

His big brown eyes smile down at me. "I've been thinking."

"Does that sentence end with—*about blowing you*? Because I'm in."

He laughs. "Oh, I've been thinking about that. But I've also been thinking about that storefront you sketched out and your big plans."

I groan. "Really? We could be having sex right now, and you want to talk about a lease?"

"Yeah," he says, pausing to nibble on my neck. "I want you to rent that place. And when it comes time to investing, I want you to let me help you. I'll introduce you to that friend who did the Kickstarter. And you can't get mad if I invest in the highest tier and share the campaign with the team."

I blow out a breath. "Okay. You win. Now let's have all the sex."

He blinks. "That's it? I thought I'd have to tease you for hours."

"I signed the lease today, and I opened a Kickstarter account. Happy?"

He pushes his face into my neck and laughs. "Seriously?"

"I'll show you something serious." I roll my hips, looking for friction. "You didn't need to tie me up to convince me to stay in Colorado. I love you. I told you last night when you drunk dialed me. And I'll tell you again whenever you want to hear it. But for the love of God..."

"You do?" he asks, suddenly serious.

"I do. I love you and I trust you and I understand why you want to see my face when you come home from a trip. Because I spent the day wishing I could see yours."

He blinks again. "Why didn't you just lead with that?"

"Fine. Sure. I lo—"

Athletes. They move fast. Before I can even get the word out, he's moved down the bed and taken me into the heat of his mouth.

"—ve youuuuu," I moan. "Oh yeah. Love you lots. Big love. Just like that..."

He groans. I buck against the bed. And I realize I'm living out the stuff of my dreams. A hot athlete has me tied to the bed. It's a fine piece of hand-made furniture, with high-thread-count sheets. There's even good lighting.

But the way he looks at me in the candlelight—the love shining in his eyes? That's the dreamiest thing of all.

Epilogue

TOMMASO

Three Months Later

The minute I get Carter's text, I'm plunking my beer down on a waiter's tray and hustling for the hotel ballroom's doors. I've been on another road trip, and it's been four days since I've seen his face.

I'd rather greet him naked in my bedroom, and not overdressed at this boondoggle. But we can't always get everything we want.

"Whoa, whoa," Tate says, stepping in front of me. "Not so fast. They're going to serve the first course in five minutes."

Was he *guarding* the door? *Jesus.* "I know that. But my date just arrived, and I need to find him."

"Well, okay," he says in the barely tolerant voice of a middle-school hall monitor. "But hurry back."

By the time I make it to the top of the carpeted staircase, Carter —dressed to the nines—is climbing toward me, a smile on his face. "Sorry I'm late!"

"It's fine." I pull him into a hug, swiping a kiss across his smooth jaw. "Good meeting?"

"Very good. She's going to be a fun client. Eighty-six years old, and more energetic than a poodle on caffeine." He takes a step back and holds out his arms, inviting me to examine his outfit. "Is this okay? Not too much?"

He's wearing a tux, like I am. But his is a deep-plum color that sets off his hair.

"Oh, damn." I drop my voice. "You look *very* fuckable. It's going to be a long night."

He grins. "Haven't worn a tux since art school. I figure if there are enough of these events, I'll save up and get a black one."

"This one works for me." I take him by the elbow. "Now come with me. They're serving the first course in a minute. If the appetizers they passed around are anything to go by, I think the food will be terrific."

"It should be," he says as I escort him into the ballroom. "How much did you say people were paying to eat dinner with the team?"

"Two grand a head."

He whistles. "I guess that's good. More money for heart-disease research."

"Yeah. But see how lucky you are?" I point at my chest. "You're getting my company for *free* most nights. And you don't have to wear a tux."

"Hashtag *blessed*. Now where's my table? I know you're supposed to move around the room."

"We get to eat the first course together," I tell him, steering him toward Table 3, where I've saved him a seat. "Here." I pull out his chair.

He's greeted by some of my teammates, including Newgate and Gavin, who we see a lot of these days.

"Nice tux, Carter," Stoney says. "You look great tonight."

"Thanks." Carter shakes out his napkin and drops it into his lap. "Likewise."

"Do you really think so?" Stoney asks, straightening his tie. "Do you think I look good enough to vote for?" He actually bats his eyelashes at Carter. "I'm in third place, and I could really use your support."

Carter gives me a confused glance.

"There's an online competition going on at Sportsballs," I explain. "Hottest local athlete. Stoney wants the title bad."

"It's the *sexiest* local athlete," Stoney corrects me. "Don't you think I deserve to win?"

"Sure, man." I point at the bottle of red wine a waiter is offering and wait as he pours some into my glass. "As long as you realize you're volunteering yourself for the spank bank of every queer dude in Colorado."

"Work it, Stoney," Newgate says. "Work it hard. Someone's going to win. Why not you?"

"That's right," Stoney says. "Why not me?"

"I have to see this contest," Carter says, pulling out his phone.

"Just click the banner at the top of their website," Stoney says.

"Hey, nice pics," Carter says. "Love the Speedo." But then my boyfriend gasps. "Tommaso! You're in *twenty-first* place. That's just wrong. I'm voting for you. And I have two email addresses, so I can vote twice..."

"Dude, no!" Stoney complains. "It's too late for him. Don't throw your vote away when you could be helping me get to the top of the pile."

"Hmm." Carter is still tapping on his phone. "I don't know if I see you as a top."

Everyone howls, but Stoney just shrugs. "When a man is *this* sexy, no label can hold him down."

A small salad plate lands on the table in front of me, and my stomach growls.

"Butter lettuce. Local strawberries, and candied pecans," the server says.

"Ooh, strawberries," Carter hums after he thanks the server. "I like this party already."

"But where's the rest of it?" Kapski complains after the first few bites. "I'm gonna starve if all the courses are this size."

"At least there are five of them, not counting dessert," Stoney says. "One every ten minutes. I counted. But I'm still not sure how this round-robin thing works. Am I supposed to carry my silverware around from table to table?"

"Nah," Newgate says. "They'll bring it for you. Just carry your drink. You're going to need it."

That's good advice, so when Tate rings a little silver bell to start the rotation, I grab my wineglass as I get up from the table.

"Have fun, baby," Gavin says as Newgate stands up, too. "Come back before dessert, or I'm eating yours."

"You can have mine anyway," his fiancé says. "It's not a cheat day."

Carter picks up his wine glass and gives me a relaxed smile, and I almost can't walk away from the table.

But duty calls. I find Table 10—per the list in my pocket—and take a seat. The player who sits down opposite me is Hale, the grumpy goalie. He hasn't warmed up to us much yet, but he backed us in a shutout last night, so I can't complain.

"Hi, folks," he says, wearing the expression of a man who'd rather be anywhere else. "I'm Jethro Hale, a goalie."

"And I'm Tommaso DiCosta. I play defense. So professionally, I'm a pain in the ass. Anyone have questions?"

"I've got one!" A young dude raises his hand. He's maybe twenty years old, with slicked back hair and a giant gold watch. "Who's your date tonight? Is she hot?"

I open my mouth to say, *his name is Carter*. But I don't get the chance. Because Hale gives the guy a death glare. "Kid, literally the only rule here is no personal questions. Try again."

He laughs nervously. "Fine. This one is for DiCosta. Why did you hit your cousin?"

Hale rolls his eyes so hard that I think he might strain something. But I have an answer prepared, nonetheless. "I'll only say that it was not my finest hour."

"Does anybody have a question that is *not* personal?" Hale asks.

And his tone is so irritated that I'm worried a fight will break out right here at Table 10.

"What do you think about a rule change to get rid of the trapezoid?" an older man asks. "Could that ever go through?"

"Now *that's* a question," Hale says. "I love this idea. Obviously, the game would be more fun for me if we abolished the trapezoid. I want that extra space to play the puck..."

A dish lands in front of me. It's a cup of soup. Some kind of bisque. I pick up the spoon that came with it and taste the broth. There's a zing to it, probably from tomatoes. Carter will like it. He likes tangy flavors.

As my teammate chatters on about hockey rules, I sneak a look at Table 3. I see Carter in profile, chatting with Gavin. I wish I could just get up and walk back over there.

When we're on the road, I miss him. But things are good between us. With a little help from our friends and my teammates, his Kickstarter campaign brought in tens of thousands of dollars. His storefront is finished, and business is thriving. He seems so happy lately, and I like knowing I had something to do with it.

On the nights when I'm in town, he usually stays with me. Sometimes we go out for dinner. Sometimes we cook dinner together and watch a movie. A few times we've hung out at Stoney's place or Newgate's.

I never really had to come out to my team the way Newgate did. They've all met Carter by now, and they know we're a couple.

Tate asked me if I wanted to make a public announcement, and I said no. That's not really my style. I don't want Carter and me to end up on any news sites. We're still a relatively new thing.

I don't hide, though. When anyone asks, I tell the truth. But it hasn't shown up as a news headline yet.

Newgate's story, on the other hand, was big news...for about ten days. Then a hockey player in another city got a six-game suspension for stalking his ex-girlfriend, and suddenly nobody cared about Newgate, except for his game stats, and that's as it should be.

He was brave to be the guy who broke the ice, and I'll always be grateful. But I hope to live in a world where being queer doesn't make the headlines.

For the first time in my life, I truly believe it's possible. And even if it isn't, being Carter's partner is more important to me than other people's opinions.

The bell dings, and I carry my wine glass to another table listed on the scrap of paper in my pocket. I choose the seat that gives me a view of Carter.

This time it's Kapski who sits down opposite me. As the captain, he's a fan favorite. So after introducing myself, I enjoy a lovely (if small) shrimp kabob while listening to my table mates asking Kapski questions.

My eyes drift to Carter once again. This time I catch him watching me. He gives me a sly smile, like maybe he's thinking about our plans for later tonight.

I wink. He smiles. But then he does a double take, his mouth falling open as he fixes his gaze on the woman sitting next to me.

With a subtle glance, I take her in. She's in her seventies, maybe. She's wearing a fussy purple gown with sparkly beads on it. It's kinda ugly but not exactly shocking.

Then I spy her event ticket on the table. It reads *Agnes Clotterfeld, Table 21*. But I don't know where I've heard that name.

My phone chimes in my breast pocket, and Mrs. Clotterfeld gives me a look of irritation. "You could silence that phone," she says.

Not likely. I pull it out and glance at the screen. I've got two texts. One is from my mother, but I don't have to jump on it like I used to, because my mom is doing great. She's done with chemo, and she's back to her old tricks.

The other text is more crucial.

CARTER

OMG that woman beside you is the one who almost sent me to the poorhouse last year! Can't imagine she'd give money to charity without trying to steal it back again.

HER??? How much does she still owe you?

$19,400. But who's counting?

I slip my phone back into my pocket and turn to her. "Mrs. Clotterfeld, are you very involved with the foundation?"

"Of course," she says with a sniff. "I'm on the board of this and *several* other charities."

"Wow. That's very generous. Did you bring your checkbook? I heard the silent auction is coming next."

She gives me a sly grin and taps her pocketbook. "I certainly did. But I won't tell you which item I'm bidding on. I don't like competition."

"Cool, cool. See that gentleman over there?" I move back a few inches to improve her sightline to Carter. "A notable interior designer. I think you might remember him?"

She looks. She squints. Then she turns away quickly. "I don't believe I do."

"That's interesting." I lower my voice. "Because he showed me a contract between the two of you, one you violated for nineteen thousand and four hundred dollars. The furniture you failed to buy almost sent him into bankruptcy."

She stiffens. "That's ridiculous. And keep your voice down."

"I don't think so," I say. "The president of this charity might like to know which of his board members don't keep their promises. Don't you think?"

Her eyes bulge, and her face begins to turn more red than white. I must be getting through. Although, I'm bluffing my ass off right now. Do charities even have presidents?

"Listen," I say quietly. "You could write Carter a check right now and hand it to him. Then there'd be no story, would there?"

She draws in a deep breath, and for a second, I think she might start screaming or something. That's gonna be awkward.

But there's nothing I wouldn't do for Carter. So I had to try.

She lunges, and I fear for my balls, but it's her pocketbook she pounces on, not me. She yanks a checkbook—also purple—out of her bag and flips it open. Then she grabs a gold pen.

"Carter Flynn," I say, just in case she's forgotten. "The memo line should say *I'm sorry*. And the amount is nineteen—"

"Hush," she says, scribbling furiously. "Don't speak to me. Ever again."

I clamp my mouth shut. With my luck, she'll tell a journalist that I'm a tormentor of women as well as a cousin-puncher. Won't that be fun to explain?

Then I hear two sounds, both of them beautiful. One is the dry tear of a check being pulled from a checkbook. And the other is Tate's silver bell.

She drops the check into my lap. I grab it, push back my chair, and pick up my empty wine glass.

Without another word, I thread my way back to Table 3 and place the check into Carter's palm.

He gasps, looking up at me in wonder. "My God. How did you *do* this?"

"What can I say?" I shrug. "I have a certain reputation. People are scared of me. Little kids don't wear my jersey. And little old ladies don't cross me. Just roll with it."

He's stares at the check. "Is this even real? It says, *I'm sorry*."

"She'd *better* be sorry. Deposit it tomorrow, though, before she can change her mind."

With a strangled laugh, and after one more long glance at the check, he tucks it into his jacket pocket. "You will be *hugely* rewarded for this later. Just know that."

I lean over and whisper into his ear. "I'll hold you to it. While I hold you down."

He lets out a little growl, and when I straighten up, I make sure to drag a finger across the nape of his neck in a suggestive way.

Before I can walk away, he turns and catches my hand. "You're a miracle worker," he says. "And I don't really understand it. But thank you. I feel *outrageously* lucky right now."

He moves to drop my hand, but I hold on tightly. "Nah, I'm the lucky one. And you can bet I'll never forget it."

THE END

Printed in Great Britain
by Amazon

31142291R00196